ML

3'

A CHATTO & WINDUS PAPERBACK
CWP 2

SWANN'S WAY
PART TWO

Marcel Proust's continuous novel *À la Recherche du Temps Perdu* (REMEMBRANCE OF THINGS PAST) was originally published in eight parts, the titles and dates of which were: I. *Du Côté de Chez Swann* (1913); II. *À l'Ombre des Jeunes Filles en Fleurs* (1918), awarded the Prix Goncourt in 1919; III. *Le Côté de Guermantes* I (1920); IV. *Le Côté de Guermantes* II, *Sodome et Gomorrhe* I (1921); V. *Sodome et Gomorrhe* II (1922); VI. *La Prisonnière* (1923); VII. *Albertine Disparue* (1925); VIII. *Le Temps Retrouvé* (1927).

Du Côté de Chez Swann has been published in English as SWANN'S WAY: *À l'Ombre des Jeunes Filles en Fleurs* as WITHIN A BUDDING GROVE: *Le Côté de Guermantes* as THE GUERMANTES WAY: *Sodome et Gomorrhe* as CITIES OF THE PLAIN: *La Prisonnière* as THE CAPTIVE: *Albertine Disparue* as THE SWEET CHEAT GONE: and *Le Temps Retrouvé* as TIME REGAINED. The first seven parts were translated by C. K. Scott Moncrieff; the eighth was first translated by Stephen Hudson, but is now reissued in a new translation by Andreas Mayor.

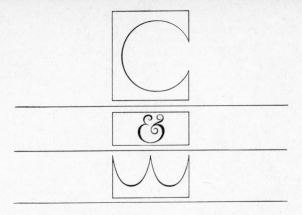

SWANN'S WAY

PART TWO

MARCEL PROUST

Translated by
C. K. Scott Moncrieff

CHATTO & WINDUS
LONDON

First published in English 1922
Reprinted 1923, 1924, 1925, 1928, 1929, 1934
1941, 1943, 1949, 1951, 1955, 1957
1960 and 1965
This Edition first published in 1966
Reprinted 1970

ISBN 0 7011 1051 1

Printed photo litho in Great Britain
by Ebenezer Baylis and Son, Ltd.
The Trinity Press, Worcester, and London

CONTENTS

*

Part 2

SWANN'S WAY

SWANN IN LOVE

AND so, night after night, she would be taken home in
Swann's carriage ; and one night, after she had got
down, and while he stood at the gate and murmured
" Till to-morrow, then ! " she turned impulsively from him,
plucked a last lingering chrysanthemum in the tiny garden
which flanked the pathway from the street to her house, and
as he went back to his carriage thrust it into his hand. He
held it pressed to his lips during the drive home, and when, in
due course, the flower withered, locked it away, like something very precious, in a secret drawer of his desk.

He would escort her to her gate, but no farther. Twice
only had he gone inside to take part in the ceremony—of such
vital importance in her life—of ' afternoon tea.' The loneliness and emptiness of those short streets (consisting, almost
entirely, of low-roofed houses, self-contained but not detached, their monotony interrupted here and there by the
dark intrusion of some sinister little shop, at once an historical
document and a sordid survival from the days when the district was still one of ill repute), the snow which had lain
on the garden-beds or clung to the branches of the trees, the
careless disarray of the season, the assertion, in this man-made
city, of a state of nature, had all combined to add an element
of mystery to the warmth, the flowers, the luxury which he
had found inside.

Passing by (on his left-hand side, and on what, although
raised some way above the street, was the ground floor of
the house) Odette's bedroom, which looked out to the back

over another little street running parallel with her own, he had climbed a staircase that went straight up between dark painted walls, from which hung Oriental draperies, strings of Turkish beads, and a huge Japanese lantern, suspended by a silken cord from the ceiling (which last, however, so that her visitors should not have to complain of the want of any of the latest comforts of Western civilisation, was lighted by a gas-jet inside), to the two drawing-rooms, large and small. These were entered through a narrow lobby, the wall of which, chequered with the lozenges of a wooden trellis such as you see on garden walls, only gilded, was lined from end to end by a long rectangular box in which bloomed, as though in a hothouse, a row of large chrysanthemums, at that time still uncommon, though by no means so large as the mammoth blossoms which horticulturists have since succeeded in making grow. Swann was irritated, as a rule, by the sight of these flowers, which had then been 'the rage' in Paris for about a year, but it had pleased him, on this occasion, to see the gloom of the little lobby shot with rays of pink and gold and white by the fragrant petals of these ephemeral stars, which kindle their cold fires in the murky atmosphere of winter afternoons. Odette had received him in a tea-gown of pink silk, which left her neck and arms bare. She had made him sit down beside her in one of the many mysterious little retreats which had been contrived in the various recesses of the room, sheltered by enormous palm-trees growing out of pots of Chinese porcelain, or by screens upon which were fastened photographs and fans and bows of ribbon. She had said at once, " You're not comfortable there ; wait a minute, I'll arrange things for you," and with a titter of laughter, the complacency of which implied that some little invention of her own was being brought into play, she had installed behind

2

his head and beneath his feet great cushions of Japanese silk, which she pummelled and buffeted as though determined to lavish on him all her riches, and regardless of their value. But when her footman began to come into the room, bringing, one after another, the innumerable lamps which (contained, mostly, in porcelain vases) burned singly or in pairs upon the different pieces of furniture as upon so many altars, rekindling in the twilight, already almost nocturnal, of this winter afternoon, the glow of a sunset more lasting, more roseate, more human—filling, perhaps, with romantic wonder the thoughts of some solitary lover, wandering in the street below and brought to a standstill before the mystery of the human presence which those lighted windows at once revealed and screened from sight—she had kept an eye sharply fixed on the servant, to see whether he set each of the lamps down in the place appointed it. She felt that, if he were to put even one of them where it ought not to be, the general effect of her drawing-room would be destroyed, and that her portrait, which rested upon a sloping easel draped with plush, would not catch the light. And so, with feverish impatience, she followed the man's clumsy movements, scolding him severely when he passed too close to a pair of beaupots, which she made a point of always tidying herself, in case the plants should be knocked over—and went across to them now to make sure that he had not broken off any of the flowers. She found something 'quaint' in the shape of each of her Chinese ornaments, and also in her orchids, the cattleyas especially (these being, with chrysanthemums, her favourite flowers), because they had the supreme merit of not looking in the least like other flowers, but of being made, apparently, out of scraps of silk or satin. " It looks just as though it had been cut out of the lining of my cloak," she said to Swann,

3

pointing to an orchid, with a shade of respect in her voice for so 'smart' a flower, for this distinguished, unexpected sister whom nature had suddenly bestowed upon her, so far removed from her in the scale of existence, and yet so delicate, so refined, so much more worthy than many real women of admission to her drawing-room. As she drew his attention, now to the fiery-tongued dragons painted upon a bowl or stitched upon a fire-screen, now to a fleshy cluster of orchids, now to a dromedary of inlaid silver-work with ruby eyes, which kept company, upon her mantelpiece, with a toad carved in jade, she would pretend now to be shrinking from the ferocity of the monsters or laughing at their absurdity, now blushing at the indecency of the flowers, now carried away by an irresistible desire to run across and kiss the toad and dromedary, calling them 'darlings.' And these affectations were in sharp contrast to the sincerity of some of her attitudes, notably her devotion to Our Lady of the Laghetto, who had once, when Odette was living at Nice, cured her of a mortal illness, and whose medal, in gold, she always carried on her person, attributing to it unlimited powers. She poured out Swann's tea, inquired " Lemon or cream ? " and, on his answering " Cream, please," went on, smiling, " A cloud ! " And as he pronounced it excellent, " You see, I know just how you like it." This tea had indeed seemed to Swann, just as it seemed to her, something precious, and love is so far obliged to find some justification for itself, some guarantee of its duration in pleasures which, on the contrary, would have no existence apart from love and must cease with its passing, that when he left her, at seven o'clock, to go and dress for the evening, all the way home, sitting bolt upright in his brougham, unable to repress the happiness with which the afternoon's adventure had filled him, he kept on repeating to himself : " What fun it would be to have a little woman like that in a place where one could always be certain of finding, what one never can be certain of finding, a really good cup of tea." An hour or so later he received a note from Odette, and at once recognised that florid handwriting, in which an affectation of British stiffness imposed an apparent discipline upon its shapeless characters, significant, perhaps, to less intimate eyes than his, of an untidiness of mind, a fragmentary education, a want of sincerity and decision. Swann had left his cigarette-case at her house. " Why," she wrote, " did you not forget your heart also ? I should never have let you have that back."

More important, perhaps, was a second visit which he paid her, a little later. On his way to the house, as always when he knew that they were to meet, he formed a picture of her in his mind ; and the necessity, if he was to find any beauty in her face, of fixing his eyes on the fresh and rosy protuberance of her cheekbones, and of shutting out all the rest of those cheeks which were so often languorous and sallow, except when they were punctuated with little fiery spots, plunged him in acute depression, as proving that one's ideal is always unattainable, and one's actual happiness mediocre. He was taking her an engraving which she had asked to see. She was not very well ; she received him, wearing a wrapper of mauve *crêpe de Chine*, which draped her bosom, like a mantle, with a richly embroidered web. As she stood there beside him, brushing his cheek with the loosened tresses of her hair, bending one knee in what was almost a dancer's pose, so that she could lean without tiring herself over the picture, at which she was gazing, with bended head, out of those great eyes, which seemed so weary and so sullen when there was nothing to animate her, Swann was struck by her resemblance to the

5

figure of Zipporah, Jethro's Daughter, which is to be seen in one of the Sixtine frescoes. He had always found a peculiar fascination in tracing in the paintings of the Old Masters, not merely the general characteristics of the people whom he encountered in his daily life, but rather what seems least susceptible of generalisation, the individual features of men and women whom he knew, as, for instance, in a bust of the Doge Loredan by Antonio Rizzo, the prominent cheekbones, the slanting eyebrows, in short, a speaking likeness to his own coachman Rémi ; in the colouring of a Ghirlandaio, the nose of M. de Palancy ; in a portrait by Tintoretto, the invasion of the plumpness of the cheek by an outcrop of whisker, the broken nose, the penetrating stare, the swollen eyelids of Dr. du Boulbon. Perhaps because he had always regretted, in his heart, that he had confined his attention to the social side of life, had talked, always, rather than acted, he felt that he might find a sort of indulgence bestowed upon him by those great artists, in his perception of the fact that they also had regarded with pleasure and had admitted into the canon of their works such types of physiognomy as give those works the strongest possible certificate of reality and trueness to life ; a modern, almost a topical savour ; perhaps, also, he had so far succumbed to the prevailing frivolity of the world of fashion that he felt the necessity of finding in an old master-piece some such obvious and refreshing allusion to a person about whom jokes could be made and repeated and enjoyed to-day. Perhaps, on the other hand, he had retained enough of the artistic temperament to be able to find a genuine satisfaction in watching these individual features take on a more general significance when he saw them, uprooted and disembodied, in the abstract idea of similarity between an historic portrait and a modern original, whom it was not in-

6

tended to represent. However that might be, and perhaps because the abundance of impressions which he, for some time past, had been receiving—though, indeed, they had come to him rather through the channel of his appreciation of music—had enriched his appetite for painting as well, it was with an unusual intensity of pleasure, a pleasure destined to have a lasting effect upon his character and conduct, that Swann remarked Odette's resemblance to the Zipporah of that Alessandro de Mariano, to whom one shrinks from giving his more popular surname, now that ' Botticelli ' suggests not so much the actual work of the Master as that false and banal conception of it which has of late obtained common currency. He no longer based his estimate of the merit of Odette's face on the more or less good quality of her cheeks, and the softness and sweetness—as of carnation-petals—which, he supposed, would greet his lips there, should he ever hazard an embrace, but regarded it rather as a skein of subtle and lovely silken threads, which his gazing eyes collected and wound together, following the curving line from the skein to the ball, where he mingled the cadence of her neck with the spring of her hair and the droop of her eyelids, as though from a portrait of herself, in which her type was made clearly intelligible.

He stood gazing at her ; traces of the old fresco were apparent in her face and limbs, and these he tried incessantly, afterwards, to recapture, both when he was with Odette, and when he was only thinking of her in her absence ; and, albeit his admiration for the Florentine masterpiece was probably based upon his discovery that it had been reproduced in her, the similarity enhanced her beauty also, and rendered her more precious in his sight. Swann reproached himself with his failure, hitherto, to estimate at her true worth a creature whom the great Sandro would have adored, and counted himself fortunate that his pleasure in the contemplation of Odette found a justification in his own system of aesthetic. He told himself that, in choosing the thought of Odette as the inspiration of his dreams of ideal happiness, he was not, as he had until then supposed, falling back, merely, upon an expedient of doubtful and certainly inadequate value, since she contained in herself what satisfied the utmost refinement of his taste in art. He failed to observe that this quality would not naturally avail to bring Odette into the category of women whom he found desirable, simply because his desires had always run counter to his aesthetic taste. The words 'Florentine painting' were invaluable to Swann. They enabled him (gave him, as it were, a legal title) to introduce the image of Odette into a world of dreams and fancies which, until then, she had been debarred from entering, and where she assumed a new and nobler form. And whereas the mere sight of her in the flesh, by perpetually reviving his misgivings as to the quality of her face, her figure, the whole of her beauty, used to cool the ardour of his love, those misgivings were swept away and that love confirmed now that he could re-erect his estimate of her on the sure foundations of his aesthetic principles ; while the kiss, the bodily surrender which would have seemed natural and but moderately attractive, had they been granted him by a creature of somewhat withered flesh and sluggish blood, coming, as now they came, to crown his adoration of a masterpiece in a gallery, must, it seemed, prove as exquisite as they would be supernatural.

And when he was tempted to regret that, for months past, he had done nothing but visit Odette, he would assure himself that he was not unreasonable in giving up much of his time to the study of an inestimably precious work of art, cast

8

for once in a new, a different, an especially charming metal, in an unmatched exemplar which he would contemplate at one moment with the humble, spiritual, disinterested mind of an artist, at another with the pride, the selfishness, the sensual thrill of a collector.

On his study table, at which he worked, he had placed, as it were a photograph of Odette, a reproduction of Jethro's Daughter. He would gaze in admiration at the large eyes, the delicate features in which the imperfection of her skin might be surmised, the marvellous locks of hair that fell along her tired cheeks ; and, adapting what he had already felt to be beautiful, on aesthetic grounds, to the idea of a living woman, he converted it into a series of physical merits which he congratulated himself on finding assembled in the person of one whom he might, ultimately, possess. The vague feeling of sympathy which attracts a spectator to a work of art, now that he knew the type, in warm flesh and blood, of Jethro's Daughter, became a desire which more than compensated, thenceforward, for that with which Odette's physical charms had at first failed to inspire him. When he had sat for a long time gazing at the Botticelli, he would think of his own living Botticelli, who seemed all the lovelier in contrast, and as he drew towards him the photograph of Zipporah he would imagine that he was holding Odette against his heart.

It was not only Odette's indifference, however, that he must take pains to circumvent ; it was also, not infrequently, his own ; feeling that, since Odette had had every facility for seeing him, she seemed no longer to have very much to say to him when they did meet, he was afraid lest the manner— at once trivial, monotonous, and seemingly unalterable— which she now adopted when they were together should ultimately destroy in him that romantic hope, that a day

A*   9

might come when she would make avowal of her passion, by
which hope alone he had become and would remain her lover.
And so to alter, to give a fresh moral aspect to that Odette,
of whose unchanging mood he was afraid of growing weary,
he wrote, suddenly, a letter full of hinted discoveries and
feigned indignation, which he sent off so that it should reach
her before dinner-time. He knew that she would be
frightened, and that she would reply, and he hoped that, when
the fear of losing him clutched at her heart, it would force
from her words such as he had never yet heard her utter :
and he was right—by repeating this device he had won from
her the most affectionate letters that she had, so far, written
him, one of them (which she had sent to him at midday by a
special messenger from the Maison Dorée—it was the day
of the Paris-Murcie Fête given for the victims of the recent
floods in Murcia) beginning " My dear, my hand trembles so
that I can scarcely write——" ; and these letters he had
kept in the same drawer as the withered chrysanthemum.
Or else, if she had not had time to write, when he arrived at
the Verdurins' she would come running up to him with an
" I've something to say to you ! " and he would gaze
curiously at the revelation in her face and speech of what she
had hitherto kept concealed from him of her heart.

Even as he drew near to the Verdurins' door, and caught
sight of the great lamp-lit spaces of the drawing-room
windows, whose shutters were never closed, he would begin
to melt at the thought of the charming creature whom he
would see, as he entered the room, basking in that golden
light. Here and there the figures of the guests stood out,
sharp and black, between lamp and window, shutting off the
light, like those little pictures which one sees sometimes
pasted here and there upon a glass screen, whose other panes

are mere transparencies. He would try to make out Odette. And then, when he was once inside, without thinking, his eyes sparkled suddenly with such radiant happiness that M. Verdurin said to the painter : " Hm. Seems to be getting warm." Indeed, her presence gave the house what none other of the houses that he visited seemed to possess ; a sort of tactual sense, a nervous system which ramified into each of its rooms and sent a constant stimulus to his heart.

And so the simple and regular manifestations of a social organism, namely the ' little clan,' were transformed for Swann into a series of daily encounters with Odette, and enabled him to feign indifference to the prospect of seeing her, or even a desire not to see her ; in doing which he incurred no very great risk since, even although he had written to her during the day, he would of necessity see her in the evening and accompany her home.

But one evening, when, irritated by the thought of that inevitable dark drive together, he had taken his other ' little girl ' all the way to the Bois, so as to delay as long as possible the moment of his appearance at the Verdurins', he was so late in reaching them that Odette, supposing that he did not intend to come, had already left. Seeing the room bare of her, Swann felt his heart wrung by sudden anguish ; he shook with the sense that he was being deprived of a pleasure whose intensity he began then for the first time to estimate, having always, hitherto, had that certainty of finding it whenever he would, which (as in the case of all our pleasures) reduced, if it did not altogether blind him to its dimensions.

" Did you notice the face he pulled when he saw that she wasn't here ? " M. Verdurin asked his wife. " I think we may say that he's hooked."

" The face he pulled ? " exploded Dr. Cottard who, having

left the house for a moment to visit a patient, had just returned to fetch his wife and did not know whom they were discussing.

" D'you mean to say you didn't meet him on the doorstep —the loveliest of Swanns ? "

" No. M. Swann has been here ? "

" Just for a moment. We had a glimpse of a Swann tremendously agitated. In a state of nerves. You see, Odette had left."

" You mean to say that she has gone the ' whole hog ' with him ; that she has ' burned her boats ' ? " inquired the Doctor cautiously, testing the meaning of his phrases.

" Why, of course not ; there's absolutely nothing in it ; in fact, between you and me, I think she's making a great mistake, and behaving like a silly little fool, which she is, incidentally."

" Come, come, come ! " said M. Verdurin, " How on earth do you know that there's ' nothing in it ' ? We haven't been there to see, have we now ? "

" She would have told me," answered Mme. Verdurin with dignity. " I may say that she tells me everything. As she has no one else at present, I told her that she ought to live with him. She makes out that she can't ; she admits, she was immensely attracted by him, at first ; but he's always shy with her, and that makes her shy with him. Besides, she doesn't care for him in that way, she says ; it's an ideal love, ' Platonic,' you know ; she's afraid of rubbing the bloom off —oh, I don't know half the things she says, how should I ? And yet he's exactly the sort of man she wants."

" I beg to differ from you," M. Verdurin courteously interrupted. " I am only half satisfied with the gentleman. I feel that he ' poses.' "

12

Mme. Verdurin's whole body stiffened, her eyes stared blankly as though she had suddenly been turned into a statue ; a device by means of which she might be supposed not to have caught the sound of that unutterable word which seemed to imply that it was possible for people to ' pose ' in her house, and, therefore, that there were people in the world who ' mattered more ' than herself.

" Anyhow, if there is nothing in it, I don't suppose it's because our friend believes in her virtue. And yet, you never know ; he seems to believe in her intelligence. I don't know whether you heard the way he lectured her the other evening about Vinteuil's sonata. I am devoted to Odette, but really —to expound theories of aesthetic to her—the man must be a prize idiot."

" Look here, I won't have you saying nasty things about Odette," broke in Mme. Verdurin in her ' spoiled child ' manner. " She is charming."

" There's no reason why she shouldn't be charming ; we are not saying anything nasty about her, only that she is not the embodiment of either virtue or intellect. After all," he turned to the painter, " does it matter so very much whether she is virtuous or not ? You can't tell ; she might be a great deal less charming if she were."

On the landing Swann had run into the Verdurins' butler, who had been somewhere else a moment earlier, when he arrived, and who had been asked by Odette to tell Swann (but that was at least an hour ago) that she would probably stop to drink a cup of chocolate at Prévost's on her way home. Swann set off at once for Prévost's, but every few yards his carriage was held up by others, or by people crossing the street, loathsome obstacles each of which he would gladly have crushed beneath his wheels, were it not that a policeman

fumbling with a note-book would delay him even longer than
the actual passage of the pedestrian. He counted the minutes
feverishly, adding a few seconds to each so as to be quite
certain that he had not given himself short measure, and so,
possibly, exaggerated whatever chance there might actually
be of his arriving at Prévost's in time, and of finding her still
there. And then, in a moment of illumination, like a man in
a fever who awakes from sleep and is conscious of the absurdity of the dream-shapes among which his mind has been
wandering without any clear distinction between himself and
them, Swann suddenly perceived how foreign to his nature
were the thoughts which he had been revolving in his mind
ever since he had heard at the Verdurins' that Odette had
left, how novel the heartache from which he was suffering,
but of which he was only now conscious, as though he had
just woken up. What ! all this disturbance simply because
he would not see Odette, now, till to-morrow, exactly what
he had been hoping, not an hour before, as he drove towards
Mme. Verdurin's. He was obliged to admit also that now,
as he sat in the same carriage and drove to Prévost's, he was
no longer the same man, was no longer alone even—but that
a new personality was there beside him, adhering to him,
amalgamated with him, a creature from whom he might,
perhaps, be unable to liberate himself, towards whom he
might have to adopt some such stratagem as one uses to outwit a master or a malady. And yet, during this last moment
in which he had felt that another, a fresh personality was thus
conjoined with his own, life had seemed, somehow, more
interesting.

It was in vain that he assured himself that this possible
meeting at Prévost's (the tension of waiting for which so
ravished, stripped so bare the intervening moments that he

could find nothing, not one idea, not one memory in his mind
beneath which his troubled spirit might take shelter and repose) would probably, after all, should it take place, be much
the same as all their meetings, of no great importance. As on
every other evening, once he was in Odette's company, once
he had begun to cast furtive glances at her changing countenance, and instantly to withdraw his eyes lest she should read
in them the first symbols of desire and believe no more in his
indifference, he would cease to be able even to think of her,
so busy would he be in the search for pretexts which would
enable him not to leave her immediately, and to assure himself, without betraying his concern, that he would find her
again, next evening, at the Verdurins' ; pretexts, that is to say,
which would enable him to prolong for the time being,
and to renew for one day more the disappointment, the torturing deception that must always come to him with the vain
presence of this woman, whom he might approach, yet never
dared embrace.

She was not at Prévost's ; he must search for her, then,
in every restaurant upon the boulevards. To save time, while
he went in one direction, he sent in the other his coachman
Rémi (Rizzo's Doge Loredan) for whom he presently—
after a fruitless search—found himself waiting at the spot
where the carriage was to meet him. It did not appear, and
Swann tantalised himself with alternate pictures of the approaching moment, as one in which Rémi would say to him :
" Sir, the lady is there," or as one in which Rémi would say
to him : " Sir, the lady was not in any of the cafés." And so
he saw himself faced by the close of his evening—a thing
uniform, and yet bifurcated by the intervening accident which
would either put an end to his agony by discovering Odette,
or would oblige him to abandon any hope of finding her that

night, to accept the necessity of returning home without having seen her.

The coachman returned ; but, as he drew up opposite him, Swann asked, not " Did you find the lady ? " but " Remind me, to-morrow, to order in some more firewood. I am sure we must be running short." Perhaps he had persuaded himself that, if Rémi had at last found Odette in some café, where she was waiting for him still, then his night of misery was already obliterated by the realisation, begun already in his mind, of a night of joy, and that there was no need for him to hasten towards the attainment of a happiness already captured and held in a safe place, which would not escape his grasp again. But it was also by the force of inertia ; there was in his soul that want of adaptability which can be seen in the bodies of certain people who, when the moment comes to avoid a collision, to snatch their clothes out of reach of a flame, or to perform any other such necessary movement, take their time (as the saying is), begin by remaining for a moment in their original position, as though seeking to find in it a starting-point, a source of strength and motion. And probably, if the coachman had interrupted him with, " I have found the lady," he would have answered, " Oh, yes, of course ; that's what I told you to do. I had quite forgotten." and would have continued to discuss his supply of firewood, so as to hide from his servant the emotion that he had felt, and to give himself time to break away from the thraldom of his anxieties and abandon himself to pleasure.

The coachman came back, however, with the report that he could not find her anywhere, and added the advice, as an old and privileged servant, " I think, sir, that all we can do now is to go home."

But the air of indifference which Swann could so lightly

assume when Rémi uttered his final, unalterable response, fell from him like a cast-off cloak when he saw Rémi attempt to make him abandon hope and retire from the quest.

"Certainly not!" he exclaimed. "We must find the lady. It is most important. She would be extremely put out —it's a business matter—and vexed with me if she didn't see me."

"But I do not see how the lady can be vexed, sir," answered Rémi, "since it was she that went away without waiting for you, sir, and said she was going to Prévost's, and then wasn't there."

Meanwhile the restaurants were closing, and their lights began to go out. Under the trees of the boulevards there were still a few people strolling to and fro, barely distinguishable in the gathering darkness. Now and then the ghost of a woman glided up to Swann, murmured a few words in his ear, asked him to take her home, and left him shuddering. Anxiously he explored every one of these vaguely seen shapes, as though among the phantoms of the dead, in the realms of darkness, he had been searching for a lost Eurydice.

Among all the methods by which love is brought into being, among all the agents which disseminate that blessed bane, there are few so efficacious as the great gust of agitation which, now and then, sweeps over the human spirit. For then the creature in whose company we are seeking amusement at the moment, her lot is cast, her fate and ours decided, that is the creature whom we shall henceforward love. It is not necessary that she should have pleased us, up till then, any more, or even as much as others. All that is necessary is that our taste for her should become exclusive. And that condition is fulfilled so soon as—in the moment when she has failed to meet us—for the pleasure which we were on the point of enjoying in her charming company is abruptly substituted an anxious torturing desire, whose object is the creature herself, an irrational, absurd desire, which the laws of civilised society make it impossible to satisfy and difficult to assuage—the insensate, agonising desire to possess her.

Swann made Rémi drive him to such restaurants as were still open ; it was the sole hypothesis, now, of that happiness which he had contemplated so calmly ; he no longer concealed his agitation, the price he set upon their meeting, and promised, in case of success, to reward his coachman, as though, by inspiring in him a will to triumph which would reinforce his own, he could bring it to pass, by a miracle, that Odette—assuming that she had long since gone home to bed, —might yet be found seated in some restaurant on the boulevards. He pursued the quest as far as the Maison Dorée, burst twice into Tortoni's and, still without catching sight of her, was emerging from the Café Anglais, striding with haggard gaze towards his carriage, which was waiting for him at the corner of the Boulevard des Italiens, when he collided with a person coming in the opposite direction ; it was Odette ; she explained, later, that there had been no room at Prévost's, that she had gone, instead, to sup at the Maison Dorée, and had been sitting there in an alcove where he must have overlooked her, and that she was now looking for her carriage.

She had so little expected to see him that she started back in alarm. As for him, he had ransacked the streets of Paris, not that he supposed it possible that he should find her, but because he would have suffered even more cruelly by abandoning the attempt. But now the joy (which, his reason had never ceased to assure him, was not, that evening at least, to be realised) was suddenly apparent, and more real than ever before; for he himself had contributed nothing to it by anticipating probabilities,—it remained integral and external to himself; there was no need for him to draw on his own resources to endow it with truth—'twas from itself that there emanated, 'twas itself that projected towards him that truth whose glorious rays melted and scattered like the cloud of a dream the sense of loneliness which had lowered over him, that truth upon which he had supported, nay founded, albeit unconsciously, his vision of bliss. So will a traveller, who has come down, on a day of glorious weather, to the Mediterranean shore, and is doubtful whether they still exist, those lands which he has left, let his eyes be dazzled, rather than cast a backward glance, by the radiance streaming towards him from the luminous and unfading azure at his feet.

He climbed after her into the carriage which she had kept waiting, and ordered his own to follow.

She had in her hand a bunch of cattleyas, and Swann could see, beneath the film of lace that covered her head, more of the same flowers fastened to a swansdown plume. She was wearing, under her cloak, a flowing gown of black velvet, caught up on one side so as to reveal a large triangular patch of her white silk skirt, with an 'insertion,' also of white silk, in the cleft of her low-necked bodice, in which were fastened a few more cattleyas. She had scarcely recovered from the shock which the sight of Swann had given her, when some obstacle made the horse start to one side. They were thrown forward from their seats; she uttered a cry, and fell back quivering and breathless.

" It's all right," he assured her, " don't be frightened." And he slipped his arm round her shoulder, supporting her body against his own; then went on : " Whatever you do, don't utter a word; just make a sign, yes or no, or you'll be out of breath again. You won't mind if I put the flowers straight on your bodice ; the jolt has loosened them. I'm afraid of their dropping out ; I'm just going to fasten them a little more securely."

She was not used to being treated with so much formality by men, and smiled as she answered : " No, not at all ; I don't mind in the least."

But he, chilled a little by her answer, perhaps, also, to bear out the pretence that he had been sincere in adopting the stratagem, or even because he was already beginning to believe that he had been, exclaimed : " No, no ; you mustn't speak. You will be out of breath again You can easily answer in signs ; I shall understand. Really and truly now, you don't mind my doing this ? Look, there is a little—I think it must be pollen, spilt over your dress,—may I brush it off with my hand ? That's not too hard ; I'm not hurting you, am I ? I'm tickling you, perhaps, a little ; but I don't want to touch the velvet in case I rub it the wrong way. But, don't you see, I really had to fasten the flowers ; they would have fallen out if I hadn't. Like that, now ; if I just push them a little farther down. . . . Seriously, I'm not annoying you, am I ? And if I just sniff them to see whether they've really lost all their scent ? I don't believe I ever smelt any before ; may I ? Tell the truth, now."

Still smiling, she shrugged her shoulders ever so slightly, as who should say, " You're quite mad ; you know very well that I like it."

He slipped his other hand upwards along Odette's cheek ; she fixed her eyes on him with that languishing and solemn air which marks the women of the old Florentine's paintings, in whose faces he had found the type of hers ; swimming at the brink of her fringed lids, her brilliant eyes, large and finely drawn as theirs, seemed on the verge of breaking from her face and rolling down her cheeks like two great tears. She bent her neck, as all their necks may be seen to bend, in the pagan scenes as well as in the scriptural. And although her attitude was, doubtless, habitual and instinctive, one which she knew to be appropriate to such moments, and was careful not to forget to assume, she seemed to need all her strength to hold her face back, as though some invisible force were drawing it down towards Swann's. And Swann it was who, before she allowed her face, as though despite her efforts, to fall upon his lips, held it back for a moment longer, at a little distance, between his hands. He had intended to leave time for her mind to overtake her body's movements, to recognise the dream which she had so long cherished and to assist at its realisation, like a mother invited as a spectator when a prize is given to the child whom she has reared and loves. Perhaps, moreover, Swann himself was fixing upon these features of an Odette not yet possessed, not even kissed by him, on whom he was looking now for the last time, that comprehensive gaze with which, on the day of his departure, a traveller strives to bear away with him in memory the view of a country to which he may never return.

But he was so shy in approaching her that, after this evening which had begun by his arranging her cattleyas and had ended in her complete surrender, whether from fear of chilling her, or from reluctance to appear, even retrospectively, to have lied, or perhaps because he lacked the audacity to formulate a more urgent requirement than this (which could always be repeated, since it had not annoyed her on the first occasion), he resorted to the same pretext on the following days. If she had any cattleyas pinned to her bodice, he would say : " It is most unfortunate ; the cattleyas don't need tucking in this evening ; they've not been disturbed as they were the other night ; I think, though, that this one isn't quite straight. May I see if they have more scent than the others ? " Or else, if she had none : " Oh ! no cattleyas this evening ; then there's nothing for me to arrange." So that for some time there was no change from the procedure which he had followed on that first evening, when he had started by touching her throat, with his fingers first and then with his lips, but their caresses began invariably with this modest exploration. And long afterwards, when the arrangement (or, rather, the ritual pretence of an arrangement) of her cattleyas had quite fallen into desuetude, the metaphor " Do a cattleya," transmuted into a simple verb which they would employ without a thought of its original meaning when they wished to refer to the act of physical possession (in which, paradoxically, the possessor possesses nothing), survived to commemorate in their vocabulary the long forgotten custom from which it sprang. And yet possibly this particular manner of saying " to make love " had not the precise significance of its synonyms. However disillusioned we may be about women, however we may regard the possession of even the most divergent types as an invariable and monotonous experience, every detail of which is known and can be described in advance, it still becomes a fresh and stimulating pleasure if the women concerned be—or be thought to be—so difficult as to oblige us to base our attack upon some unrehearsed incident in our relations with them, as was originally for Swann the arrangement of the cattleyas. He trembled as he hoped, that evening, (but Odette, he told himself, if she were deceived by his stratagem, could not guess his intention) that it was the possession of this woman that would emerge for him from their large and richly coloured petals ; and the pleasure which he already felt, and which Odette tolerated, he thought, perhaps only because she was not yet aware of it herself, seemed to him for that reason—as it might have seemed to the first man when he enjoyed it amid the flowers of the earthly paradise—a pleasure which had never before existed, which he was striving now to create, a pleasure—and the special name which he was to give to it preserved its identity—entirely individual and new.

The ice once broken, every evening, when he had taken her home, he must follow her into the house ; and often she would come out again in her dressing-gown, and escort him to his carriage, and would kiss him before the eyes of his coachman, saying : " What on earth does it matter what people see ? " And on evenings when he did not go to the Verdurins' (which happened occasionally, now that he had opportunities of meeting Odette elsewhere), when—more and more rarely—he went into society, she would beg him to come to her on his way home, however late he might be. The season was spring, the nights clear and frosty. He would come away from an evening party, jump into his victoria, spread a rug over his knees, tell the friends who were leaving at the same time, and who insisted on his going home with them, that he could not, that he was not going in their direction ; then the coachman would start off at a fast trot without further orders, knowing quite well where he had to go. His friends would be left marvelling, and, as a matter of fact, Swann was no longer the same man. No one ever received a letter from him now demanding an introduction to a woman. He had ceased to pay any attention to women, and kept away from the places in which they were ordinarily to be met. In a restaurant, or in the country, his manner was deliberately and directly the opposite of that by which, only

a few days earlier, his friends would have recognised him,
that manner which had seemed permanently and unalterably
his own. To such an extent does passion manifest itself in us
as a temporary and distinct character, which not only takes
the place of our normal character but actually obliterates the
signs by which that character has hitherto been discernible.
On the other hand, there was one thing that was, now, invariable, namely that wherever Swann might be spending the
evening, he never failed to go on afterwards to Odette. The
interval of space separating her from him was one which he
must as inevitably traverse as he must descend, by an irresistible gravitation, the steep slope of life itself. To be frank,
as often as not, when he had stayed late at a party, he would
have preferred to return home at once, without going so far
out of his way, and to postpone their meeting until the
morrow ; but the very fact of his putting himself to such inconvenience at an abnormal hour in order to visit her, while
he guessed that his friends, as he left them, were saying to
one another : " He is tied hand and foot ; there must
certainly be a woman somewhere who insists on his going to
her at all hours," made him feel that he was leading the life
of the class of men whose existence is coloured by a love-
affair, and in whom the perpetual sacrifice which they are
making of their comfort and of their practical interests has
engendered a spiritual charm. Then, though he may not
consciously have taken this into consideration, the certainty
that she was waiting for him, that she was not anywhere or
with anyone else, that he would see her before he went home,
drew the sting from that anguish, forgotten, it is true, but
latent and ever ready to be reawakened, which he had felt
on the evening when Odette had left the Verdurins' before
his arrival, an anguish the actual cessation of which was so

24

agreeable that it might even be called a state of happiness. Perhaps it was to that hour of anguish that there must be attributed the importance which Odette had since assumed in his life. Other people are, as a rule, so immaterial to us that, when we have entrusted to any one of them the power to cause so much suffering or happiness to ourselves, that person seems at once to belong to a different universe, is surrounded with poetry, makes of our lives a vast expanse, quick with sensation, on which that person and ourselves are ever more or less in contact. Swann could not without anxiety ask himself what Odette would mean to him in the years that were to come. Sometimes, as he looked up from his victoria on those fine and frosty nights of early spring, and saw the dazzling moonbeams fall between his eyes and the deserted streets, he would think of that other face, gleaming and faintly roseate like the moon's, which had, one day, risen on the horizon of his mind, and since then had shed upon the world that mysterious light in which he saw it bathed. If he arrived after the hour at which Odette sent her servants to bed, before ringing the bell at the gate of her little garden, he would go round first into the other street, over which, at the ground-level, among the windows (all exactly alike, but darkened) of the adjoining houses, shone the solitary lighted window of her room. He would rap upon the pane, and she would hear the signal, and answer, before running to meet him at the gate. He would find, lying open on the piano, some of her favourite music, the *Valse des Roses*, the *Pauvre Fou* of Tagliafico (which, according to the instructions embodied in her will, was to be played at her funeral) ; but he would ask her, instead, to give him the little phrase from Vinteuil's sonata. It was true that Odette played vilely, but often the fairest impression that remains in our minds of a favourite air

25

is one which has arisen out of a jumble of wrong notes struck
by unskilful fingers upon a tuneless piano. The little phrase
was associated still, in Swann's mind, with his love for
Odette. He felt clearly that this love was something to which
there were no corresponding external signs, whose meaning
could not be proved by any but himself ; he realised, too,
that Odette's qualities were not such as to justify his setting
so high a value on the hours he spent in her company. And
often, when the cold government of reason stood unchallenged, he would readily have ceased to sacrifice so many of
his intellectual and social interests to this imaginary pleasure.
But the little phrase, as soon as it struck his ear, had the power
to liberate in him the room that was needed to contain it ;
the proportions of Swann's soul were altered ; a margin was
left for a form of enjoyment which corresponded no more
than his love for Odette to any external object, and yet was
not, like his enjoyment of that love, purely individual, but
assumed for him an objective reality superior to that of other
concrete things. This thirst for an untasted charm, the little
phrase would stimulate it anew in him, but without bringing
him any definite gratification to assuage it. With the result
that those parts of Swann's soul in which the little phrase had
obliterated all care for material interests, those human con-
siderations which affect all men alike, were left bare by it,
blank pages on which he was at liberty to inscribe the name
of Odette. Moreover, where Odette's affection might seem
ever so little abrupt and disappointing, the little phrase would
come to supplement it, to amalgamate with it its own mysterious essence. Watching Swann's face while he listened to the
phrase, one would have said that he was inhaling an an-
aesthetic which allowed him to breathe more deeply. And the
pleasure which the music gave him, which was shortly to

create in him a real longing, was in fact closely akin, at such
moments, to the pleasure which he would have derived from
experimenting with perfumes, from entering into contact with
a world for which we men were not created, which appears
to lack form because our eyes cannot perceive it, to lack
significance because it escapes our intelligence, to which we
may attain by way of one sense only. Deep repose, mysterious
refreshment for Swann,—for him whose eyes, although delicate interpreters of painting, whose mind, although an acute
observer of manners, must bear for ever the indelible imprint
of the barrenness of his life,—to feel himself transformed into
a creature foreign to humanity, blinded, deprived of his logical
faculty, almost a fantastic unicorn, a chimaera-like creature
conscious of the world through his two ears alone. And as,
notwithstanding, he sought in the little phrase for a meaning
to which his intelligence could not descend, with what a
strange frenzy of intoxication must he strip bare his inner-
most soul of the whole armour of reason, and make it pass,
unattended, through the straining vessel, down into the dark
filter of sound. He began to reckon up how much that was
painful, perhaps even how much secret and unappeased
sorrow underlay the sweetness of the phrase ; and yet to him
it brought no suffering. What matter though the phrase repeated that love is frail and fleeting, when his love was
so strong ! He played with the melancholy which the phrase
diffused, he felt it stealing over him, but like a caress which
only deepened and sweetened his sense of his own happiness.
He would make Odette play him the phrase again, ten,
twenty times on end, insisting that, while she played, she must
never cease to kiss him. Every kiss provokes another. Ah,
in those earliest days of love how naturally the kisses spring
into life. How closely, in their abundance, are they pressed

one against another ; until lovers would find it as hard to count the kisses exchanged in an hour, as to count the flowers in a meadow in May. Then she would pretend to stop, saying : " How do you expect me to play when you keep on holding me ? I can't do everything at once. Make up your mind what you want ; am I to play the phrase or do you want to play with me ? " Then he would become annoyed, and she would burst out with a laugh which was transformed, as it left her lips, and descended upon him in a shower of kisses. Or else she would look at him sulkily, and he would see once again a face worthy to figure in Botticelli's ' Life of Moses,' he would place it there, giving to Odette's neck the necessary inclination ; and when he had finished her portrait in distemper, in the fifteenth century, on the wall of the Sixtine, the idea that she was, none the less, in the room with him still, by the piano, at that very moment, ready to be kissed and won, the idea of her material existence, of her being alive, would sweep over him with so violent an intoxication that, with eyes starting from his head and jaws that parted as though to devour her, he would fling himself upon this Botticelli maiden and kiss and bite her cheeks. And then, as soon as he had left the house, not without returning to kiss her once again, because he had forgotten to take away with him, in memory, some detail of her fragrance or of her features, while he drove home in his victoria, blessing the name of Odette who allowed him to pay her these daily visits, which, although they could not, he felt, bring any great happiness to her, still, by keeping him immune from the fever of jealousy —by removing from him every possibility of a fresh outbreak of the heart-sickness which had manifested itself in him that evening, when he had failed to find her at the Verdurins'— might help him to arrive, without any recurrence of those

28

crises, of which the first had been so distressing that it must
also be the last, at the termination of this strange series of
hours in his life, hours almost enchanted, in the same manner
as these other, following hours, in which he drove through a
deserted Paris by the light of the moon : noticing as he drove
home that the satellite had now changed its position, relatively
to his own, and was almost touching the horizon ; feeling
that his love, also, was obedient to these immutable laws of
nature, he asked himself whether this period, upon which
he had entered, was to last much longer, whether presently
his mind's eye would cease to behold that dear countenance,
save as occupying a distant and diminished position, and on
the verge of ceasing to shed on him the radiance of its charm.
For Swann was finding in things once more, since he had
fallen in love, the charm that he had found when, in his
adolescence, he had fancied himself an artist ; with this
difference, that what charm lay in them now was conferred
by Odette alone. He could feel reawakening in himself the
inspirations of his boyhood, which had been dissipated among
the frivolities of his later life, but they all bore, now, the reflection, the stamp of a particular being ; and during the long
hours which he now found a subtle pleasure in spending at
home, alone with his convalescent spirit, he became gradually himself again, but himself in thraldom to another.

He went to her only in the evenings, and knew nothing of
how she spent her time during the day, any more than he
knew of her past ; so little, indeed, that he had not even the
tiny, initial clue which, by allowing us to imagine what we
do not know, stimulates a desire for knowledge. And so he
never asked himself what she might be doing, or what her
life had been. Only he smiled sometimes at the thought of
how, some years earlier, when he still did not know her,

some one had spoken to him of a woman who, if he remembered rightly, must certainly have been Odette, as of a
'tart,' a 'kept' woman, one of those women to whom he
still attributed (having lived but little in their company)
the entire set of characteristics, fundamentally perverse, with
which they had been, for many years, endowed by the imagination of certain novelists. He would say to himself that one has,
as often as not, only to take the exact counterpart of the reputation created by the world in order to judge a person
fairly, when with such a character he contrasted that of
Odette, so good, so simple, so enthusiastic in the pursuit of
ideals, so nearly incapable of not telling the truth that, when
he had once begged her, so that they might dine together
alone, to write to Mme. Verdurin, saying that she was unwell, the next day he had seen her, face to face with Mme.
Verdurin, who asked whether she had recovered, blushing,
stammering, and, in spite of herself, revealing in every feature
how painful, what a torture it was to her to act a lie ; and,
while in her answer she multiplied the fictitious details of an
imaginary illness, seeming to ask pardon, by her suppliant
look and her stricken accents, for the obvious falsehood of her
words.

On certain days, however, though these came seldom, she
would call upon him in the afternoon, to interrupt his musings
or the essay on Vermeer to which he had latterly returned.
His servant would come in to say that Mme. de Crécy was
in the small drawing-room. He would go in search of her,
and, when he opened the door, on Odette's blushing countenance, as soon as she caught sight of Swann, would appear—
changing the curve of her lips, the look in her eyes, the moulding of her cheeks—an all-absorbing smile. Once he was left
alone he would see again that smile, and her smile of the day

before, another with which she had greeted him sometime else, the smile which had been her answer, in the carriage that night, when he had asked her whether she objected to his rearranging her cattleyas ; and the life of Odette at all other times, since he knew nothing of it, appeared to him upon a neutral and colourless background, like those sheets of sketches by Watteau upon which one sees, here and there, in every corner and in all directions, traced in three colours upon the buff paper, innumerable smiles. But, once in a while, illuminating a chink of that existence which Swann still saw as a complete blank, even if his mind assured him that it was not so, because he was unable to imagine anything that might occupy it, some friend who knew them both, and, suspecting that they were in love, had not dared to tell him anything about her that was of the least importance, would describe Odette's figure, as he had seen her, that very morning, going on foot up the Rue Abbattucci, in a cape trimmed with skunks, wearing a Rembrandt hat, and a bunch of violets in her bosom. This simple outline reduced Swann to utter confusion by enabling him suddenly to perceive that Odette had an existence which was not wholly subordinated to his own ; he burned to know whom she had been seeking to fascinate by this costume in which he had never seen her ; he registered a vow to insist upon her telling him where she had been going at that intercepted moment, as though, in all the colourless life—a life almost non-existent, since she was then invisible to him—of his mistress, there had been but a single incident apart from all those smiles directed towards himself ; namely, her walking abroad beneath a Rembrandt hat, with a bunch of violets in her bosom.

Except when he asked her for Vinteuil's little phrase instead of the *Valse des Roses*, Swann made no effort to induce

her to play the things that he himself preferred, nor, in
literature any more than in music, to correct the manifold
errors of her taste. He fully realised that she was not intelligent. When she said how much she would like him to
tell her about the great poets, she had imagined that she would
suddenly get to know whole pages of romantic and heroic
verse, in the style of the Vicomte de Borelli, only even more
moving. As for Vermeer of Delft, she asked whether he had
been made to suffer by a woman, if it was a woman that had
inspired him, and once Swann had told her that no one knew,
she had lost all interest in that painter. She would often say :
" I'm sure, poetry ; well, of course, there'ld be nothing like
it if it was all true, if the poets really believed the things they
said. But as often as not you'll find there's no one so mean
and calculating as those fellows. I know something about
poetry. I had a friend, once, who was in love with a poet of
sorts. In his verses he never spoke of anything but love, and
heaven, and the stars. Oh! she was properly taken in! He
had more than three hundred thousand francs out of her
before he'd finished." If, then, Swann tried to shew her in
what artistic beauty consisted, how one ought to appreciate
poetry or painting, after a minute or two she would cease to
listen, saying : " Yes . . . I never thought it would be like
that." And he felt that her disappointment was so great that
he preferred to lie to her, assuring her that what he had said
was nothing, that he had only touched the surface, that he
had not time to go into it all properly, that there was more
in it than that. Then she would interrupt with a brisk,
" More in it ? What ? . . . Do tell me !", but he did not
tell her, for he realised how petty it would appear to her, and
how different from what she had expected, less sensational and
less touching ; he was afraid, too, lest, disillusioned in the

matter of art, she might at the same time be disillusioned in
the greater matter of love.

With the result that she found Swann inferior, intellectu-
ally, to what she had supposed. " You're always so reserved ;
I can't make you out." She marvelled increasingly at his indifference to money, at his courtesy to everyone alike, at the
delicacy of his mind. And indeed it happens, often enough,
to a greater man than Swann ever was, to a scientist or artist,
when he is not wholly misunderstood by the people among
whom he lives, that the feeling in them which proves that
they have been convinced of the superiority of his intellect is
created not by any admiration for his ideas—for those are
entirely beyond them—but by their respect for what they
term his good qualities. There was also the respect with
which Odette was inspired by the thought of Swann's social
position, although she had no desire that he should attempt to
secure invitations for herself. Perhaps she felt that such
attempts would be bound to fail ; perhaps, indeed, she feared
lest, merely by speaking of her to his friends, he should provoke disclosures of an unwelcome kind. The fact remains
that she had consistently held him to his promise never to
mention her name. Her reason for not wishing to go into
society was, she had told him, a quarrel which she had had,
long ago, with another girl, who had avenged herself by
saying nasty things about her. " But," Swann objected,
"surely, people don't all know your friend." "Yes, don't you
see, it's like a spot of oil ; people are so horrid." Swann was
unable, frankly, to appreciate this point ; on the other hand,
he knew that such generalisations as " People are so horrid,"
and " A word of scandal spreads like a spot of oil," were
generally accepted as true ; there must, therefore, be cases
to which they were literally applicable. Could Odette's case

be one of these ? He teased himself with the question, though
not for long, for he too was subject to that mental oppression
which had so weighed upon his father, whenever he was faced
by a difficult problem. In any event, that world of society
which concealed such terrors for Odette inspired her, probably, with no very great longing to enter it, since it was too
far removed from the world which she already knew for her
to be able to form any clear conception of it. At the same
time, while in certain respects she had retained a genuine
simplicity (she had, for instance, kept up a friendship with a
little dressmaker, now retired from business, up whose steep
and dark and fetid staircase she clambered almost every day),
she still thirsted to be in the fashion, though her idea of it was
not altogether that held by fashionable people. For the latter,
fashion is a thing that emanates from a comparatively small
number of leaders, who project it to a considerable distance
—with more or less strength according as one is nearer to or
farther from their intimate centre—over the widening circle
of their friends and the friends of their friends, whose names
form a sort of tabulated index. People ' in society ' know this
index by heart, they are gifted in such matters with an erudi-
tion from which they have extracted a sort of taste, of tact,
so automatic in its operation that Swann, for example, without needing to draw upon his knowledge of the world, if he
read in a newspaper the names of the people who had been
guests at a dinner, could tell at once how fashionable the
dinner had been, just as a man of letters, merely by reading a
phrase, can estimate exactly the literary merit of its author.
But Odette was one of those persons (an extremely numerous
class, whatever the fashionable world may think, and to be
found in every section of society) who do not share this knowledge, but imagine fashion to be something of quite another

kind, which assumes different aspects according to the circle
to which they themselves belong, but has the special characteristic—common alike to the fashion of which Odette used
to dream and to that before which Mme. Cottard bowed—
of being directly accessible to all. The other kind, the
fashion of 'fashionable people,' is, it must be admitted,
accessible also ; but there are inevitable delays. Odette would
say of some one : "He never goes to any place that isn't
really smart."

And if Swann were to ask her what she meant by that, she
would answer, with a touch of contempt, "Smart places !
Why, good heavens, just fancy, at your age, having to be told
what the smart places are in Paris ! What do you expect me
to say ? Well, on Sunday mornings there's the Avenue de
l'Impératrice, and round the lake at five o'clock, and on
Thursdays the Eden-Théâtre, and the Hippodrome on
Fridays ; then there are the balls . . ."

"What balls ? "

"Why, silly, the balls people give in Paris ; the smart ones,
I mean. Wait now, Herbinger, you know who' I mean, the
fellow who's in one of the jobbers' offices ; yes, of course,
you must know him, he's one of the best-known men in
Paris, that great big fair-haired boy who wears such swagger
clothes ; he always has a flower in his buttonhole and a light-
coloured overcoat with a fold down the back ; he goes about
with that old image, takes her to all the first-nights. Very
well ! He gave a ball the other night, and all the smart people
in Paris were there. I should have loved to go ! but you had
to shew your invitation at the door, and I couldn't get one
anywhere. After all, I'm just as glad, now, that I didn't go ;
I should have been killed in the crush, and seen nothing.
Still, just to be able to say one had been to Herbinger's ball.

You know how vain I am ! However, you may be quite
certain that half the people who tell you they were there are
telling stories. . . . But I am surprised that you weren't
there, a regular ' tip-topper ' like you."

Swann made no attempt, however, to modify this conception of fashion ; feeling that his own came no nearer to the
truth, was just as fatuous, devoid of all importance, he saw
no advantage to be gained by imparting it to his mistress, with
the result that, after a few months, she ceased to take any
interest in the people to whose houses he went, except when
they were the means of his obtaining tickets for the paddock
at race-meetings or first-nights at the theatre. She hoped that
he would continue to cultivate such profitable acquaintances,
but she had come to regard them as less smart since the day
when she had passed the Marquise de Villeparisis in the
street, wearing a black serge dress and a bonnet with strings.

" But she looks like a pew-opener, like an old charwoman,
darling ! That a marquise ! Goodness knows I'm not a
marquise, but you'd have to pay me a lot of money before
you'd get me to go about Paris rigged out like that ! "

Nor could she understand Swann's continuing to live in
his house on the Quai d'Orléans, which, though she dared
not tell him so, she considered unworthy of him.

It was true that she claimed to be fond of ' antiques,' and
used to assume a rapturous and knowing air when she confessed how she loved to spend the whole day ' rummaging '
in second-hand shops, hunting for ' bric-à-brac,' and things
of the ' right date.' Although it was a point of honour, to
which she obstinately clung, as though obeying some old
family custom, that she should never answer any questions,
never give any account of what she did during the daytime,
she spoke to Swann once about a friend to whose house she

had been invited, and had found that everything in it was
' of the period.' Swann could not get her to tell him what
' period ' it was. Only after thinking the matter over she
replied that it was ' mediaeval ' ; by which she meant that
the walls were panelled. Some time later she spoke to him
again of her friend, and added, in the hesitating but confident
tone in which one refers to a person whom one has met
somewhere, at dinner, the night before, of whom one had
never heard until then, but whom one's hosts seemed to regard as some one so celebrated and important that one hopes
that one's listener will know quite well who is meant, and
will be duly impressed : " Her dining-room . . . is . . .
eighteenth century ! " Incidentally, she had thought it
hideous, all bare, as though the house were still unfinished ;
women looked frightful in it, and it would never become the
fashion. She mentioned it again, a third time, when she
shewed Swann a card with the name and address of the man
who had designed the dining-room, and whom she wanted to
send for, when she had enough money, to see whether he
could not do one for her too ; not one like that, of course, but
one of the sort she used to dream of, one which, unfortunately,
her little house would not be large enough to contain, with
tall sideboards, Renaissance furniture and fireplaces like the
Château at Blois. It was on this occasion that she let out to
Swann what she really thought of his abode on the Quai
d'Orléans ; he having ventured the criticism that her friend
had indulged, not in the Louis XVI style, for, he went on,
although that was not, of course, done, still it might be
made charming, but in the ' Sham-Antique.'

" You wouldn't have her live, like you, among a lot of
broken-down chairs and threadbare carpets ! " she exclaimed,
the innate respectability of the middle-class housewife rising

impulsively to the surface through the acquired dilettantism of the ' light woman.'

People who enjoyed 'picking-up' things, who admired poetry, despised sordid calculations of profit and loss, and nourished ideals of honour and love, she placed in a class by themselves, superior to the rest of humanity. There was no need actually to have those tastes, provided one talked enough about them ; when a man had told her at dinner that he loved to wander about and get his hands all covered with dust in the old furniture shops, that he would never be really appreciated in this commercial age, since he was not concerned about the things that interested it, and that he belonged to another generation altogether, she would come home saying : " Why, he's an adorable creature ; so sensitive ! I had no idea," and she would conceive for him a strong and sudden friendship. But, on the other hand, men who, like Swann, had these tastes but did not speak of them, left her cold. She was obliged, of course, to admit that Swann was most generous with his money, but she would add, pouting : " It's not the same thing, you see, with him," and, as a matter of fact, what appealed to her imagination was not the practice of disinterestedness, but its vocabulary.

Feeling that, often, he could not give her in reality the pleasures of which she dreamed, he tried at least to ensure that she should be happy in his company, tried not to contradict those vulgar ideas, that bad taste which she displayed on every possible occasion, which all the same he loved, as he could not help loving everything that came from her, which even fascinated him, for were they not so many more of those characteristic features, by virtue of which the essential qualities of the woman emerged, and were made visible ? And so, when she was in a happy mood because she was going to see

38

the *Reine Topaze*, or when her eyes grew serious, troubled, petulant, if she was afraid of missing the flower-show, or merely of not being in time for tea, with muffins and toast, at the Rue Royale tea-rooms, where she believed that regular attendance was indispensable, and set the seal upon a woman's certificate of 'smartness,' Swann, enraptured, as all of us are, at times, by the natural behaviour of a child, or by the likeness of a portrait, which appears to be on the point of speaking, would feel so distinctly the soul of his mistress rising to fill the outlines of her face that he could not refrain from going across and welcoming it with his lips. "Oh, then, so little Odette wants us to take her to the flower-show, does she? she wants to be admired, does she? very well, we will take her there, we can but obey her wishes." As Swann's sight was beginning to fail, he had to resign himself to a pair of spectacles, which he wore at home, when working, while to face the world he adopted a single eyeglass, as being less disfiguring. The first time that she saw it in his eye, she could not contain herself for joy : " I really do think—for a man, that is to say—it is tremendously smart ! How nice you look with it ! Every inch a gentleman. All you want now is a title !" she concluded, with a tinge of regret in her voice. He liked Odette to say these things, just as, if he had been in love with a Breton girl, he would have enjoyed seeing her in her coif and hearing her say that she believed in ghosts. Always until then, as is common among men whose taste for the fine arts develops independently of their sensuality, a grotesque disparity had existed between the satisfactions which he would accord to either taste simultaneously ; yielding to the seduction of works of art which grew more and more subtle as the women in whose company he enjoyed them grew more illiterate and common, he would take a little servant-

39

girl to a screened box in a theatre where there was some de-
cadent piece which he had wished to see performed, or to an
exhibition of impressionist painting, with the conviction,
moreover, that an educated, 'society' woman would have
understood them no better, but would not have managed to
keep quiet about them so prettily. But, now that he was in
love with Odette, all this was changed ; to share her sym-
pathies, to strive to be one with her in spirit was a task so
attractive that he tried to find satisfaction in the things that
she liked, and did find a pleasure, not only in copying her
habits but in adopting her opinions, which was all the deeper
because, as those habits and opinions sprang from no roots in
her intelligence, they suggested to him nothing except that
love, for the sake of which he had preferred them to his own.
If he went again to *Serge Panine*, if he looked out for opportunities of going to watch Olivier Métra conducting, it
was for the pleasure of being initiated into every one of the
ideas in Odette's mind, of feeling that he had an equal share
in all her tastes. This charm of drawing him closer to her,
which her favourite plays and pictures and places possessed,
struck him as being more mysterious than the intrinsic charm
of more beautiful things and places, which appealed to him
by their beauty, but without recalling her. Besides, having
allowed the intellectual beliefs of his youth to grow faint,
until his scepticism, as a finished 'man of the world,' had
gradually penetrated them unawares, he held (or at least he
had held for so long that he had fallen into the habit of saying)
that the objects which we admire have no absolute value in
themselves, that the whole thing is a matter of dates and
castes, and consists in a series of fashions, the most vulgar of
which are worth just as much as those which are regarded
as the most refined. And as he had decided that the import-

ance which Odette attached to receiving cards for a private
view was not in itself any more ridiculous than the pleasure
which he himself had at one time felt in going to luncheon
with the Prince of Wales, so he did not think that the admiration which she professed for Monte-Carlo or for the
Righi was any more unreasonable than his own liking for
Holland (which she imagined as ugly) and for Versailles
(which bored her to tears). And so he denied himself the
pleasure of visiting those places, consoling himself with the
reflection that it was for her sake that he wished to feel, to
like nothing that was not equally felt and liked by her.

Like everything else that formed part of Odette's environment, and was no more, in a sense, than the means whereby
he might see and talk to her more often, he enjoyed the society
of the Verdurins. With them, since, at the heart of all their
entertainments, dinners, musical evenings, games, suppers in
fancy dress, excursions to the country, theatre parties, even
the infrequent 'big evenings' when they entertained
'bores,' there were the presence of Odette, the sight of
Odette, conversation with Odette, an inestimable boon which
the Verdurins, by inviting him to their house, bestowed on
Swann, he was happier in the little 'nucleus' than anywhere
else, and tried to find some genuine merit in each of its
members, imagining that his tastes would lead him to
frequent their society for the rest of his life. Never daring to
whisper to himself, lest he should doubt the truth of the suggestion, that he would always be in love with Odette, at least
when he tried to suppose that he would always go to the
Verdurins' (a proposition which, *a priori*, raised fewer
fundamental objections on the part of his intelligence), he
saw himself for the future continuing to meet Odette every
evening ; that did not, perhaps, come quite to the same thing

as his being permanently in love with her, but for the moment, while he was in love with her, to feel that he would not, one day, cease to see her was all that he could ask. " What a charming atmosphere ! " he said to himself. " How entirely genuine life is to these people ! They are far more intelligent, far more artistic, surely, than the people one knows. Mme. Verdurin, in spite of a few trifling exaggerations which are rather absurd, has a sincere love of painting and music ! What a passion for works of art, what anxiety to give pleasure to artists ! Her ideas about some of the people one knows are not quite right, but then their ideas about artistic circles are altogether wrong ! Possibly I make no great intellectual de-mands upon conversation, but I am perfectly happy talking to Cottard, although he does trot out those idiotic puns. And as for the painter, if he is rather unpleasantly affected when he tries to be paradoxical, still he has one of the finest brains that I have ever come across. Besides, what is most important, one feels quite free there, one does what one likes without constraint or fuss. What a flow of humour there is every day in that drawing-room ! Certainly, with a few rare exceptions, I never want to go anywhere else again. It will become more and more of a habit, and I shall spend the rest of my life among them."

And as the qualities which he supposed to be an intrinsic part of the Verdurin character were no more, really, than their superficial reflection of the pleasure which had been enjoyed in their society by his love for Odette, those qualities became more serious, more profound, more vital, as that pleasure increased. Since Mme. Verdurin gave Swann, now and then, what alone could constitute his happiness ; since, on an evening when he felt anxious because Odette had talked rather more to one of the party than to another, and, in a spasm of irritation, would not take the initiative by asking her whether she was coming home, Mme. Verdurin brought peace and joy to his troubled spirit by the spontaneous exclamation : " Odette ! You'll see M. Swann home, won't you ? "; since, when the summer holidays came, and after he had asked himself uneasily whether Odette might not leave Paris without him, whether he would still be able to see her every day, Mme. Verdurin was going to invite them both to spend the summer with her in the country ; Swann, unconsciously allowing gratitude and self-interest to filter into his intelligence and to influence his ideas, went so far as to proclaim that Mme. Verdurin was " a great and noble soul." Should any of his old fellow-pupils in the Louvre school of painting speak to him of some rare or eminent artist, " I'ld a hundred times rather," he would reply, " have the Verdurins." And, with a solemnity of diction which was new in him : " They are magnanimous creatures, and magnanimity is, after all, the one thing that matters, the one thing that gives us distinction here on earth. Look you, there are only two classes of men, the magnanimous, and the rest ; and I have reached an age when one has to take sides, to decide once and for all whom one is going to like and dislike, to stick to the people one likes, and, to make up for the time one has wasted with the others, never to leave them again as long as one lives. Very well ! " he went on, with the slight emotion which a man feels when, even without being fully aware of what he is doing, he says something, not because it is true but because he enjoys saying it, and listens to his own voice uttering the words as though they came from some one else, " The die is now cast ; I have elected to love none but magnanimous souls, and to live only in an atmosphere of magnanimity. You ask me whether Mme. Verdurin is really intelligent. I can assure you that she has given me proofs of a nobility of heart, of a loftiness of soul, to which no one could possibly attain—how could they ?—without a corresponding loftiness of mind. Without question, she has a profound understanding of art. But it is not, perhaps, in that that she is most admirable ; every little action, ingeniously, exquisitely kind, which she has performed for my sake, every friendly attention, simple little things, quite domestic and yet quite sublime, reveal a more profound comprehension of existence than all your text-books of philosophy."

He might have reminded himself, all the same, that there were various old friends of his family who were just as simple as the Verdurins, companions of his early days who were just as fond of art, that he knew other ' great-hearted creatures,' and that, nevertheless, since he had cast his vote in favour of simplicity, the arts, and magnanimity, he had entirely ceased to see them. But these people did not know Odette, and, if they had known her, would never have thought of introducing her to him.

And so there was probably not, in the whole of the Verdurin circle, a single one of the ' faithful ' who loved them, or believed that he loved them as dearly as did Swann. And yet, when M. Verdurin said that he was not satisfied with Swann, he had not only expressed his own sentiments, he had unwittingly discovered his wife's. Doubtless Swann had too particular an affection for Odette, as to which he had failed to take Mme. Verdurin daily into his confidence ; doubtless the very discretion with which he availed himself of the Verdurins' hospitality, refraining, often, from coming to dine with them for a reason which they never suspected, and in

place of which they saw only an anxiety on his part not to have
to decline an invitation to the house of some 'bore' or
other ; doubtless, also, and despite all the precautions which
he had taken to keep it from them, the gradual discovery
which they were making of his brilliant position in society—
doubtless all these things contributed to their general annoy-
ance with Swann. But the real, the fundamental reason was
quite different. What had happened was that they had at once
discovered in him a locked door, a reserved, impenetrable
chamber in which he still professed silently to himself that the
Princesse de Sagan was not grotesque, and that Cottard's
jokes were not amusing; in a word (and ˙ for all that he
never once abandoned his friendly attitude towards them all,
or revolted from their dogmas), they had discovered an impossibility of imposing those dogmas upon him, of entirely
converting him to their faith, the like of which they had
never come across in anyone before. They would have forgiven his going to the houses of 'bores' (to whom, as it
happened, in his heart of hearts he infinitely preferred the
Verdurins and all their little 'nucleus') had he consented
to set a good example by openly renouncing those 'bores'
in the presence of the 'faithful.' But that was an abjuration
which, as they well knew, they were powerless to extort.

What a difference was there in a 'newcomer' whom
Odette had asked them to invite, although she herself had
met him only a few times, and on whom they were building
great hopes—the Comte de Forcheville ! (It turned out that
he was nothing more nor less than the brother-in-law of
Saniette, a discovery which filled all the 'faithful' with
amazement: the manners of the old palaeographer were so
humble that they had always supposed him to be of a class
inferior, socially, to their own, and had never expected to

learn that he came of a rich and relatively aristocratic family.)
Of course, Forcheville was enormously the 'swell,' which
Swann was not or had quite ceased to be ; of course he would
never dream of placing, as Swann now placed, the Verdurin
circle above any other. But he lacked that natural refinement
which prevented Swann from associating himself with the
criticisms (too obviously false to be worth his notice) that
Mme. Verdurin levelled at people whom he knew. As for
the vulgar and affected tirades in which the painter sometimes indulged, the bagman's pleasantries which Cottard used
to hazard,—whereas Swann, who liked both men sincerely,
could easily find excuses for these without having either the
courage or the hypocrisy to applaud them, Forcheville, on
the other hand, was on an intellectual level which permitted
him to be stupefied, amazed by the invective (without in the
least understanding what it all was about), and to be frankly
delighted by the wit. And the very first dinner at the
Verdurins' at which Forcheville was present threw a glaring
light upon all the differences between them, made his qualities
start into prominence and precipitated the disgrace of Swann.

There was, at this dinner, besides the usual party, a professor from the Sorbonne, one Brichot, who had met M. and
Mme. Verdurin at a watering-place somewhere, and, if his
duties at the university and his other works of scholarship
had not left him with very little time to spare, would gladly
have come to them more often. For he had that curiosity,
that superstitious outlook on life, which, combined with a
certain amount of scepticism with regard to the object of their
studies, earn for men of intelligence, whatever their profes-
sion, for doctors who do not believe in medicine, for school-
masters who do not believe in Latin exercises, the reputation
of having broad, brilliant, and indeed superior minds. He

46

affected, when at Mme. Verdurin's, to choose his illustrations
from among the most topical subjects of the day, when he
spoke of philosophy or history, principally because he regarded those sciences as no more, really, than a preparation
for life itself, and imagined that he was seeing put into practice by the ' little clan ' what hitherto he had known only
from books ; and also, perhaps, because, having had drilled
into him as a boy, and having unconsciously preserved a
feeling of reverence for certain subjects, he thought that he
was casting aside the scholar's gown when he ventured to
treat those subjects with a conversational licence, which
seemed so to him only because the folds of the gown still
clung.

Early in the course of the dinner, when M. de Forcheville,
seated on the right of Mme. Verdurin, who, in the ' newcomer's ' honour, had taken great pains with her toilet, observed to her : " Quite original, that white dress," the
Doctor, who had never taken his eyes off him, so curious
was he to learn the nature and attributes of what he called a
" de," and was on the look-out for an opportunity of attract-
ing his attention, so as to come into closer contact with him,
caught in its flight the adjective *blanche* and, his eyes still
glued to his plate, snapped out, " *Blanche ?* Blanche of Castile ? " then, without moving his head, shot a furtive glance
to right and left of him, doubtful, but happy on the whole.
While Swann, by the painful and futile effort which he made
to smile, testified that he thought the pun absurd, Forcheville
had shewn at once that he could appreciate its subtlety, and
that he was a man of the world, by keeping within its proper
limits a mirth the spontaneity of which had charmed Mme.
Verdurin.

" What are you to say of a scientist like that ? " she asked

Forcheville. " You can't talk seriously to him for two minutes on end. Is that the sort of thing you tell them at your hospital?" she went on, turning to the Doctor. " They must have some pretty lively times there, if that's the case. I can see that I shall have to get taken in as a patient ! "

" I think I heard the Doctor speak of that wicked old humbug, Blanche of Castile, if I may so express myself. Am I not right, Madame ? " Brichot appealed to Mme. Verdurin, who, swooning with merriment, her eyes tightly closed, had buried her face in her two hands, from between which, now and then, escaped a muffled scream.

" Good gracious, Madame, I would not dream of shocking the reverent-minded, if there are any such around this table, *sub rosa* . . . I recognise, moreover, that our ineffable and Athenian—oh, how infinitely Athenian—Republic is capable of honouring, in the person of that obscurantist old she-Capet, the first of our chiefs of police. Yes, indeed, my dear host, yes, indeed ! " he repeated in his ringing voice, which sounded a separate note for each syllable, in reply to a protest by M. Verdurin. " The Chronicle of Saint Denis, and the authenticity of its information is beyond question, leaves us no room for doubt on that point. No one could be more fitly chosen as Patron by a secularising proletariat than that mother of a Saint, who let him see some pretty fishy saints besides, as Suger says, and other great St. Bernards of the sort ; for with her it was a case of taking just what you pleased."

" Who is that gentleman ? " Forcheville asked Mme. Verdurin. " He seems to speak with great authority."

" What ! Do you mean to say you don't know the famous Brichot ? Why, he's celebrated all over Europe."

" Oh, that's Bréchot, is it ? " exclaimed Forcheville, who had not quite caught the name. " You must tell me all about him " ; he went on, fastening a pair of goggle eyes on the celebrity. "It's always interesting to meet well-known people at dinner. But, I say, you ask us to very select parties here. No dull evenings in this house, I'm sure."

"Well, you know what it is really," said Mme. Verdurin modestly. "They feel safe here. They can talk about whatever they like, and the conversation goes off like fireworks. Now Brichot, this evening, is nothing. I've seen him, don't you know, when he's been with me, simply dazzling ; you'd want to go on your knees to him. Well, with anyone else he's not the same man, he's not in the least witty, you have to drag the words out of him, he's even boring."

"That's strange," remarked Forcheville with fitting astonishment.

A sort of wit like Brichot's would have been regarded as out-and-out stupidity by the people among whom Swann had spent his early life, for all that it is quite compatible with real intelligence. And the intelligence of the Professor's vigorous and well-nourished brain might easily have been envied by many of the people in society who seemed witty enough to Swann. But these last had so thoroughly inculcated into him their likes and dislikes, at least in everything that pertained to their ordinary social existence, including that annex to social existence which belongs, strictly speaking, to the domain of intelligence, namely, conversation, that Swann could not see anything in Brichot's pleasantries ; to him they were merely pedantic, vulgar, and disgustingly coarse. He was shocked, too, being accustomed to good manners, by the rude, almost barrack-room tone which this student-in-arms adopted, no matter to whom he was speaking. Finally, perhaps, he had lost all patience that evening as he watched Mme. Verdurin welcoming, with such unnecessary warmth, this

49

Forcheville fellow, whom it had been Odette's unaccountable idea to bring to the house. Feeling a little awkward, with Swann there also, she had asked him on her arrival : " What do you think of my guest ? "

And he, suddenly realising for the first time that Forcheville, whom he had known for years, could actually attract a woman, and was quite a good specimen of a man, had retorted : " Beastly ! " He had, certainly, no idea of being jealous of Odette, but did not feel quite so happy as usual, and when Brichot, having begun to tell them the story of Blanche of Castile's mother, who, according to him, " had been with Henry Plantagenet for years before they were married," tried to prompt Swann to beg him to continue the story, by interjecting " Isn't that so, M. Swann ? " in the martial accents which one uses in order to get down to the level of an unintelligent rustic or to put the 'fear of God' into a trooper, Swann cut his story short, to the intense fury of their hostess, by begging to be excused for taking so little interest in Blanche of Castile, as he had something that he wished to ask the painter. He, it appeared, had been that afternoon to an exhibition of the work of another artist, also a friend of Mme. Verdurin, who had recently died, and Swann wished to find out from him (for he valued his discrimination) whether there had really been anything more in this later work than the virtuosity which had struck people so forcibly in his earlier exhibitions.

" From that point of view it was extraordinary, but it did not seem to me to be a form of art which you could call 'elevated,' " said Swann with a smile.

" Elevated . . . to the height of an Institute ! " interrupted Cottard, raising his arms with mock solemnity. The whole table burst out laughing.

" What did I tell you ? " said Mme. Verdurin to Forcheville. "It's simply impossible to be serious with him. When
you least expect it, out he comes with a joke."

But she observed that Swann, and Swann alone, had not
unbent. For one thing he was none too well pleased with
Cottard for having secured a laugh at his expense in front of
Forcheville. But the painter, instead of replying in a way
that might have interested Swann, as he would probably have
done had they been alone together, preferred to win the easy
admiration of the rest by exercising his wit upon the talent
of their dead friend.

" I went up to one of them," he began, " just to see how it
was done ; I stuck my nose into it. Yes, I don't think !
Impossible to say whether it was done with glue, with soap,
with sealing-wax, with sunshine, with leaven, with ex-
crem . . ."

" And one make twelve ! " shouted the Doctor, wittily,
but just too late, for no one saw the point of his interruption.

" It looks as though it were done with nothing at all," resumed the painter. " No more chance of discovering the
trick than there is in the ' Night Watch,' or the ' Regents,'
and it's even bigger work than either Rembrandt or Hals ever
did. It's all there,—and yet, no, I'll take my oath it isn't."

Then, just as singers who have reached the highest note in
their compass, proceed to hum the rest of the air in falsetto, he
had to be satisfied with murmuring, smiling the while, as if,
after all, there had been something irresistibly amusing in the
sheer beauty of the painting : " It smells all right ; it makes
your head go round ; it catches your breath ; you feel
ticklish all over—and not the faintest clue to how it's done.
The man's a sorcerer ; the thing's a conjuring-trick, it's a
miracle," bursting outright into laughter, " it's dishonest ! "

Then stopping, solemnly raising his head, pitching his voice on a double-bass note which he struggled to bring into harmony, he concluded, " And it's so loyal ! "

Except at the moment when he had called it " bigger than the ' Night Watch,' " a blasphemy which had called forth an instant protest from Mme. Verdurin, who regarded the ' Night Watch ' as the supreme masterpiece of the universe (conjointly with the 'Ninth' and the 'Samothrace'), and at the word " excrement," which had made Forcheville throw a sweeping glance round the table to see whether it was ' all right,' before he allowed his lips to curve in a prudish and conciliatory smile, all the party (save Swann) had kept their fascinated and adoring eyes fixed upon the painter.

" I do so love him when he goes up in the air like that ! " cried Mme. Verdurin, the moment that he had finished, enraptured that the table-talk should have proved so entertaining on the very night that Forcheville was dining with them for the first time. " Hallo, you ! " she turned to her husband, " What's the matter with you, sitting there gaping like a great animal ? You know, though, don't you," she apologised for him to the painter, " that he can talk quite well when he chooses ; anybody would think it was the first time he had ever listened to you. If you had only seen him while you were speaking ; he was just drinking it all in. And to-morrow he will tell us everything you said, without missing a word."

" No, really, I'm not joking ! " protested the painter, enchanted by the success of his speech. " You all look as if you thought I was pulling your legs, that it was just a trick. I'll take you to see the show, and then you can say whether I've been exaggerating ; I'll bet you anything you like, you'll come away more ' up in the air ' than I am ! "

" But we don't suppose for a moment that you're exaggerating ; we only want you to go on with your dinner, and my husband too. Give M. Biche some more sole, can't you see his has got cold? We're not in any hurry; you're dashing round as if the house was on fire. Wait a little ; don't serve the salad just yet."

Mme. Cottard, who was a shy woman and spoke but seldom, was not lacking, for all that, in self-assurance when a happy inspiration put the right word in her mouth. She felt that it would be well received ; the thought gave her confidence, and what she was doing was done with the object not so much of shining herself, as of helping her husband on in his career. And so she did not allow the word 'salad,' which Mme. Verdurin had just uttered, to pass unchallenged.

" It's not a Japanese salad, is it ? " she whispered, turning towards Odette.

And then, in her joy and confusion at the combination of neatness and daring which there had been in making so discreet and yet so unmistakable an allusion to the new and brilliantly successful play by Dumas, she broke down in a charming, girlish laugh, not very loud, but so irresistible that it was some time before she could control it.

" Who is that lady ? She seems devilish clever," said Forcheville.

" No, it is not. But we will have one for you if you will all come to dinner on Friday."

" You will think me dreadfully provincial, sir," said Mme. Cottard to Swann, " but, do you know, I haven't been yet to this famous *Francillon* that everybody's talking about. The Doctor has been (I remember now, he told me what a very great pleasure it had been to him to spend the evening with you there) and I must confess, I don't see much sense in spending money on seats for him to take me, when he's seen the play already. Of course an evening at the Théâtre-Français is never wasted, really ; the acting's so good there always; but we have some very nice friends," (Mme. Cottard would hardly ever utter a proper name, but restricted herself to "some friends of ours" or " one of my friends," as being more ' distinguished,' speaking in an affected tone and with all the importance of a person who need give names only when she chooses) " who often have a box, and are kind enough to take us to all the new pieces that are worth going to, and so I'm certain to see this *Francillon* sooner or later, and then I shall know what to think. But I do feel such a fool about it, I must confess, for, whenever I pay a call anywhere, I find everybody talking—it's only natural—about that wretched Japanese salad. Really and truly, one's beginning to get just a little tired of hearing about it," she went on, seeing that Swann seemed less interested than she had hoped in so burning a topic. " I must admit, though, that it's sometimes quite amusing, the way they joke about it : I've got a friend, now, who is most original, though she's really a beautiful woman, most popular in society, goes everywhere, and she tells me that she got her cook to make one of these Japanese salads, putting in everything that young M. Dumas says you're to put in, in the play. Then she asked just a few friends to come and taste it. I was not among the favoured few, I'm sorry to say. But she told us all about it on her next ' day '; it seems it was quite horrible, she made us all laugh till we cried. I don't know; perhaps it was the way she told it," Mme. Cottard added doubtfully, seeing that Swann still looked grave.

And, imagining that it was, perhaps, because he had not been amused by *Francillon* ; " Well, I daresay I shall be disappointed with it, after all. I don't suppose it's as good as the piece Mme. de Crécy worships, *Serge Panine.* There's a play, if you like ; so deep, makes you think ! But just fancy giving a receipt for a salad on the stage of the Théâtre-Français ! Now, *Serge Panine*——! But then, it's like everything that comes from the pen of M. Georges Ohnet, it's so well written. I wonder if you know the *Maître des Forges,* which I like even better than *Serge Panine.*"

" Pardon me," said Swann with polite irony, " but I can assure you that my want of admiration is almost equally divided between those masterpieces."

" Really, now ; that's very interesting. And what don't you like about them ? Won't you ever change your mind ? Perhaps you think he's a little too sad. Well, well, what I always say is, one should never argue about plays or novels. Everyone has his own way of looking at things, and what may be horrible to you is, perhaps, just what I like best."

She was interrupted by Forcheville's addressing Swann. What had happened was that, while Mme. Cottard was discussing *Francillon,* Forcheville had been expressing to Mme. Verdurin his admiration for what he called the "little speech " of the painter. " Your friend has such a flow of language, such a memory ! " he had said to her when the painter had come to a standstill, " I've seldom seen anything like it. He'ld make a first-rate preacher. By Jove, I wish I was like that. What with him and M. Bréchot you've drawn two lucky numbers to-night ; though I'm not so sure that, simply as a speaker, this one doesn't knock spots off the Professor. It comes more naturally with him, less like reading from a book. Of course, the way he goes on, he does use some words that are a bit realistic, and all that ; but that's quite the thing nowadays ; anyhow, it's not often I've seen a

55

man hold the floor as cleverly as that, 'hold the spittoon,' as we used to say in the regiment, where, by the way, we had a man he rather reminds me of. You could take anything you liked—I don't know what—this glass, say ; and he'ld talk away about it for hours ; no, not this glass ; that's a silly thing to say, I'm sorry ; but something a little bigger, like the battle of Waterloo, or anything of that sort, he'ld tell you things you simply wouldn't believe. Why, Swann was in the regiment then ; he must have known him."

" Do you see much of M. Swann ? " asked Mme. Verdurin.

" Oh dear, no ! " he answered, and then, thinking that if he made himself pleasant to Swann he might find favour with Odette, he decided to take this opportunity of flattering him by speaking of his fashionable friends, but speaking as a man of the world himself, in a tone of good-natured criticism, and not as though he were congratulating Swann upon some undeserved good fortune : " Isn't that so, Swann ? I never see anything of you, do I ?— But then, where on earth is one to see him ? The creature spends all his time shut up with the La Trémoïlles, with the Laumes and all that lot ! " The imputation would have been false at any time, and was all the more so, now that for at least a year Swann had given up going to almost any house but the Verdurins'. But the mere names of families whom the Verdurins did not know were received by them in a reproachful silence. M. Verdurin, dreading the painful impression which the mention of these 'bores,' especially when flung at her in this tactless fashion, and in front of all the 'faithful,' was bound to make on his wife, cast a covert glance at her, instinct with anxious solicitude, He saw then that in her fixed resolution to take no notice. to have escaped contact, altogether, with the news which had

just been addressed to her, not merely to remain dumb but
to have been deaf as well, as we pretend to be when a friend
who has been in the wrong attempts to slip into his conversation some excuse which we should appear to be accept-
ing, should we appear to have heard it without protesting, or
when some one utters the name of an enemy, the very mention of whom in our presence is forbidden ; Mme. Verdurin,
so that her silence should have the appearance, not of consent
but of the unconscious silence which inanimate objects preserve, had suddenly emptied her face of all life, of all mobility ;
her rounded forehead was nothing, now, but an exquisite
study in high relief, which the name of those La Trémoïlles,
with whom Swann was always 'shut up,' had failed to
penetrate ; her nose, just perceptibly wrinkled in a frown,
exposed to view two dark cavities that were, surely, modelled
from life. You would have said that her half-opened lips
were just about to speak. It was all no more, however, than a
wax cast, a mask in plaster, the sculptor's design for a monu-
ment, a bust to be exhibited in the Palace of Industry, where
the public would most certainly gather in front of it and
marvel to see how the sculptor, in expressing the unchal-
lengeable dignity of the Verdurins, as opposed to that of the
La Trémoïlles or Laumes, whose equals (if not, indeed, their
betters) they were, and the equals and betters of all other
'bores' upon the face of the earth, had managed to invest
with a majesty that was almost Papal the whiteness and
rigidity of his stone. But the marble at last grew animated
and let it be understood that it didn't do to be at all squeamish
if one went to that house, since the woman was always tipsy
and the husband so uneducated that he called a corridor a
'collidor' !

"You'ld need to pay me a lot of money before I'ld let any

of that lot set foot inside my house," Mme. Verdurin concluded, gazing imperially down on Swann.

She could scarcely have expected him to capitulate so
completely as to echo the holy simplicity of the pianist's
aunt, who at once exclaimed : " To think of that, now !
What surprises me is that they can get anybody to go
near them ; I'm sure I should be afraid ; one can't be too
careful. How can people be so common as to go running
after them ? "

But he might, at least, have replied, like Forcheville :
" Gad, she's a duchess ; there are still plenty of people who
are impressed by that sort of thing," which would at least
have permitted Mme. Verdurin the final retort, " And a lot
of good may it do them ! " Instead of which, Swann merely
smiled, in a manner which shewed, quite clearly, that he could
not, of course, take such an absurd suggestion seriously.
M. Verdurin, who was still casting furtive and intermittent
glances at his wife, could see with regret, and could understand only too well that she was now inflamed with the passion of a Grand Inquisitor who cannot succeed in stamping
out a heresy ; and so, in the hope of bringing Swann round to
a retractation (for the courage of one's opinions is always a
form of calculating cowardice in the eyes of the ' other side '),
he broke in :

" Tell us frankly, now, what you think of them yourself.
We shan't repeat it to them, you may be sure."

To which Swann answered : " Why, I'm not in the least
afraid of the Duchess (if it is of the La Trémoïlles that you're
speaking). I can assure you that everyone likes going to see
her. I don't go so far as to say that she's at all ' deep ' —"
he pronounced the word as if it meant something ridiculous,
for his speech kept the traces of certain mental habits which

the recent change in his life, a rejuvenation illustrated by his passion for music, had inclined him temporarily to discard, so that at times he would actually state his views with considerable warmth—" but I am quite sincere when I say that she is intelligent, while her husband is positively a bookworm. They are charming people."

His explanation was terribly effective ; Mme. Verdurin now realised that this one state of unbelief would prevent her ' little nucleus ' from ever attaining to complete unanimity, and was unable to restrain herself, in her fury at the obstinacy of this wretch who could not see what anguish his words were causing her, but cried aloud, from the depths of her tortured heart, "You may think so if you wish, but at least you need not say so to us."

"It all depends upon what you call intelligence." Forcheville felt that it was his turn to be brilliant. " Come now, Swann, tell us what you mean by intelligence "

"There," cried Odette, " that's one of the big things I beg him to tell me about, and he never will."

" Oh, but . . ." protested Swann.

" Oh, but nonsense ! " said Odette.

" A water-butt ? " asked the Doctor.

" To you," pursued Forcheville, " does intelligence mean what they call clever talk ; you know, the sort of people who worm their way into society ? "

" Finish your sweet, so that they can take your plate away ! " said Mme. Verdurin sourly to Saniette, who was lost in thought and had stopped eating. And then, perhaps a little ashamed of her rudeness, " It doesn't matter ; take your time about it ; there's no hurry ; I only reminded you because of the others, you know ; it keeps the servants back."

" There is," began Brichot, with a resonant smack upon
every syllable, " a rather curious definition of intelligence by
that pleasing old anarchist Fénelon . . ."

" Just listen to this ! " Mme. Verdurin rallied Forcheville and the Doctor. " He's going to give us Fénelon's
definition of intelligence. That's interesting. It's not often
you get a chance of hearing that ! "

But Brichot was keeping Fénelon's definition until Swann
should have given his own. Swann remained silent, and, by
this fresh act of recreancy, spoiled the brilliant tournament of
dialectic which Mme. Verdurin was rejoicing at being able
to offer to Forcheville.

" You see, it's just the same as with me ! " Odette was
peevish. " I'm not at all sorry to see that I'm not the only
one he doesn't find quite up to his level."

" These de La Trémouailles whom Mme. Verdurin has
exhibited to us as so little to be desired," inquired Brichot,
articulating vigorously, " are they, by any chance, descended
from the couple whom that worthy old snob, Sévigné, said she
was delighted to know, because it was so good for her pea-
sants ? True, the Marquise had another reason, which in her
case probably came first, for she was a thorough journalist at
heart, and always on the look-out for ' copy.' And, in the
journal which she used to send regularly to her daughter,
it was Mme. de La Trémouaille, kept well-informed through
all her grand connections, who supplied the foreign
politics."

" Oh dear, no. I'm quite sure they aren't the same
family," said Mme. Verdurin desperately.

Saniette who, ever since he had surrendered his untouched
plate to the butler, had been plunged once more in silent
meditation, emerged finally to tell them, with a nervous

laugh, a story of how he had once dined with the Duc de La Trémoïlle, the point of which was that the Duke did not know that George Sand was the pseudonym of a woman. Swann, who really liked Saniette, felt bound to supply him with a few facts illustrative of the Duke's culture, which would prove that such ignorance on his part was literally impossible ; but suddenly he stopped short ; he had realised, as he was speaking, that Saniette needed no proof, but knew already that the story was untrue for the simple reason that he had at that moment invented it. The worthy man suffered acutely from the Verdurins' always finding him so dull ; and as he was conscious of having been more than ordinarily morose this evening, he had made up his mind that he would succeed in being amusing, at least once, before the end of dinner. He surrendered so quickly, looked so wretched at the sight of his castle in ruins, and replied in so craven a tone to Swann, appealing to him not to persist in a refutation which was already superfluous, " All right ; all right ; anyhow, even if I have made a mistake that's not a crime, I hope," that Swann longed to be able to console him by insisting that the story was indubitably true and exquisitely funny. The Doctor, who had been listening, had an idea that it was the right moment to interject " *Se non è vero,*" but he was not quite certain of the words, and was afraid of being caught out.

After dinner, Forcheville went up to the Doctor. " She can't have been at all bad looking, Mme. Verdurin ; anyhow, she's a woman you can really talk to ; that's all I want. Of course she's getting a bit broad in the beam. But Mme. de Crécy ! There's a little woman who knows what's what, all right. Upon my word and soul, you can see at a glance she's got the American eye, that girl has. We are speaking of

Mme. de Crécy," he explained, as M. Verdurin joined them, his pipe in his mouth. "I should say that, as a specimen of the female form——"

"I'ld rather have it in my bed than a clap of thunder!" the words came tumbling from Cottard, who had for some time been waiting in vain until Forcheville should pause for breath, so that he might get in this hoary old joke, a chance for which might not, he feared, come again, if the conversation should take a different turn ; and he produced it now with that excessive spontaneity and confidence which may often be noticed attempting to cover up the coldness, and the slight flutter of emotion, inseparable from a prepared recitation. Forcheville knew and saw the joke, and was thoroughly amused. As for M. Verdurin, he was unsparing of his merriment, having recently discovered a way of expressing it by a symbol, different from his wife's, but equally simple and obvious. Scarcely had he begun the movement of head and shoulders of a man who was 'shaking with laughter' than he would begin also to cough, as though, in laughing too violently, he had swallowed a mouthful of smoke from his pipe. And by keeping the pipe firmly in his mouth he could prolong indefinitely the dumb-show of suffocation and hilarity. So he and Mme. Verdurin (who, at the other side of the room, where the painter was telling her a story, was shutting her eyes preparatory to flinging her face into her hands) resembled two masks in a theatre, each representing Comedy, but in a different way.

M. Verdurin had been wiser than he knew in not taking his pipe out of his mouth, for Cottard, having occasion to leave the room for a moment, murmured a witty euphemism which he had recently acquired and repeated now whenever he had to go to the place in question : " I must just go and

see the Duc d'Aumale for a minute," so drolly, that M.
Verdurin's cough began all over again.

" Now, then, take your pipe out of your mouth ; can't
you see, you'll choke if you try to bottle up your laughter
like that," counselled Mme. Verdurin, as she came round
with a tray of liqueurs.

" What a delightful man your husband is ; he has the
wit of a dozen !" declared Forcheville to Mme. Cottard.
" Thank you, thank you, an old soldier like me can never say
' No ' to a drink."

" M. de Forcheville thinks Odette charming," M. Verdurin told his wife.

" Why, do you know, she wants so much to meet you
again some day at luncheon. We must arrange it, but don't
on any account let Swann hear about it. He spoils everything,
don't you know. I don't mean to say that you're not to come
to dinner too, of course ; we hope to see you very often.
Now that the warm weather's coming, we're going to have
dinner out of doors whenever we can. That won't bore you,
will it, a quiet little dinner, now and then, in the Bois ?
Splendid, splendid, that will be quite delightful. . . .

" Aren't you going to do any work this evening, I say ? "
she screamed suddenly to the little pianist, seeing an opportunity for displaying, before a ' newcomer ' of Forcheville's
importance, at once her unfailing wit and her despotic power
over the ' faithful.'

" M. de Forcheville was just going to say something
dreadful about you," Mme. Cottard warned her husband as
he reappeared in the room. And he, still following up the
idea of Forcheville's noble birth, which had obsessed him all
through dinner, began again with : "I am treating a Baroness
just now, Baroness Putbus ; wern't there some Putbuses in the

63

Crusades ? Anyhow they've got a lake in Pomerania that's ten times the size of the Place de la Concorde. I am treating her for dry arthritis ; she's a charming woman. Mme. Verdurin knows her too, I believe."

Which enabled Forcheville, a moment later, finding himself alone with Mme. Cottard, to complete his favourable verdict on her husband with : " He's an interesting man, too ; you can see that he knows some good people. Gad ! but they get to know a lot of things, those doctors."

" D'you want me to play the phrase from the sonata for M. Swann ? " asked the pianist.

" What the devil's that ? Not the sonata-snake, I hope ! " shouted M. de Forcheville, hoping to create an effect. But Dr. Cottard, who had never heard this pun, missed the point of it, and imagined that M. de Forcheville had made a mistake. He dashed in boldly to correct it : " No, no. The word isn't *serpent-à-sonates*, it's *serpent-à-sonnettes* ! " he explained in a tone at once zealous, impatient, and triumphant.

Forcheville explained the joke to him. The Doctor blushed.

" You'll admit it's not bad, eh, Doctor ? "

" Oh ! I've known it for ages."

Then they were silenced ; heralded by the waving *tremolo* of the violin-part, which formed a bristling bodyguard of sound two octaves above it—and as in a mountainous country, against the seeming immobility of a vertically falling torrent, one may distinguish, two hundred feet below, the tiny form of a woman walking in the valley—the little phrase had just appeared, distant but graceful, protected by the long, gradual unfurling of its transparent, incessant and sonorous curtain. And Swann, in his heart of hearts, turned to it, spoke to it as to a confidant in the secret of his love, as to a friend of Odette who would assure him that he need pay no attention to this Forcheville.

" Ah ! you've come too late ! " Mme. Verdurin greeted one of the ' faithful,' whose invitation had been only ' to look in after dinner,' " we've been having a simply incomparable Brichot ! You never heard such eloquence ! But he's gone. Isn't that so, M. Swann ? I believe it's the first time you've met him," she went on, to emphasise the fact that it was to her that Swann owed the introduction. " Isn't that so ; wasn't he delicious, our Brichot ? "

Swann bowed politely.

" No ? You weren't interested ? " she asked dryly.

" Oh, but I assure you, I was quite enthralled. He is perhaps a little too peremptory, a little too jovial for my taste. I should like to see him a little less confident at times, a little more tolerant, but one feels that he knows a great deal, and on the whole he seems a very sound fellow."

The party broke up very late. Cottard's first words to his wife were : " I have rarely seen Mme. Verdurin in such form as she was to-night."

" What exactly is your Mme. Verdurin ? A bit of a bad hat, eh ? " said Forcheville to the painter, to whom he had offered a ' lift.' Odette watched his departure with regret ; she dared not refuse to let Swann take her home, but she was moody and irritable in the carriage, and, when he asked whether he might come in, replied, " I suppose so," with an impatient shrug of her shoulders. When they had all gone, Mme. Verdurin said to her husband : " Did you notice the way Swann laughed, such an idiotic laugh, when we spoke about Mme. La Trémoïlle ? "

She had remarked, more than once, how Swann and Forcheville suppressed the particle ' de ' before that lady's name. Never doubting that it was done on purpose, to shew that they were not afraid of a title, she had made up her mind to imitate their arrogance, but had not quite grasped what grammatical form it ought to take. Moreover, the natural corruptness of her speech overcoming her implacable republicanism, she still said instinctively "the de La Trémoïlles," or, rather (by an abbreviation sanctified by the usage of music-hall singers and the writers of the 'captions' beneath caricatures, who elide the 'de'), "the d'La Trémoïlles," but she corrected herself at once to "Madame La Trémoïlle.— The *Duchess*, as Swann calls her," she added ironically, with a smile which proved that she was merely quoting, and would not, herself, accept the least responsibility for a classification so puerile and absurd.

"I don't mind saying that I thought him extremely stupid."

M. Verdurin took it up. "He's not sincere. He's a crafty customer, always hovering between one side and the other. He's always trying to run with the hare and hunt with the hounds. What a difference between him and Forcheville. There, at least, you have a man who tells you straight out what he thinks. Either you agree with him or you don't. Not like the other fellow, who's never definitely fish or fowl. Did you notice, by the way, that Odette seemed all out for Forcheville, and I don't blame her, either. And then, after all, if Swann tries to come the man of fashion over us, the champion of distressed Duchesses, at any rate the other man has got a title; he's always Comte de Forcheville!" he let the words slip delicately from his lips, as though, familiar with every page of the history of that dignity, he were making a scrupulously exact estimate of its value, in relation to others of the sort.

" I don't mind saying," Mme. Verdurin went on, " that he saw fit to utter some most venomous, and quite absurd insinuations against Brichot. Naturally, once he saw that Brichot was popular in this house, it was a way of hitting back at us, of spoiling our party. I know his sort, the dear, good friend of the family, who pulls you all to pieces on the stairs as he's going away."

" Didn't I say so ? " retorted her husband. " He's simply a failure ; a poor little wretch who goes through life mad with jealousy of anything that's at all big."

Had the truth been known, there was not one of the 'faithful' who was not infinitely more malicious than Swann ; but the others would all take the precaution of tempering their malice with obvious pleasantries, with little sparks of emotion and cordiality ; while the least indication of reserve on Swann's part, undraped in any such conventional formula as " Of course, I don't want to say anything—" to which he would have scorned to descend, appeared to them a deliberate act of treachery. There are certain original and distinguished authors in whom the least ' freedom of speech ' is thought revolting because they have not begun by flattering the public taste, and serving up to it the commonplace expressions to which it is used ; it was by the same process that Swann infuriated M. Verdurin. In his case as in theirs it was the novelty of his language which led his audience to suspect the blackness of his designs.

Swann was still unconscious of the disgrace that threatened him at the Verdurins', and continued to regard all their absurdities in the most rosy light, through the admiring eyes of love.

As a rule he made no appointments with Odette except for the evenings ; he was afraid of her growing tired of him if he visited her during the day as well ; at the same time he was reluctant to forfeit, even for an hour, the place that he held in her thoughts, and so was constantly looking out for an opportunity of claiming her attention, in any way that would not be displeasing to her. If, in a florist's or a jeweller's window, a plant or an ornament caught his eye, he would at once think of sending them to Odette, imagining that the pleasure which the casual sight of them had given him would instinctively be felt, also, by her, and would increase her affection for himself ; and he would order them to be taken at once to the Rue La Pérouse, so as to accelerate the moment in which, as she received an offering from him, he might feel himself, in a sense, transported into her presence. He was particularly anxious, always, that she should receive these presents before she went out for the evening, so that her sense of gratitude towards him might give additional tenderness to her welcome when he arrived at the Verdurins', might even—for all he knew—if the shopkeeper made haste, bring him a letter from her before dinner, or herself, in person, upon his doorstep, come on a little extraordinary visit of thanks. As in an earlier phase, when he had experimented with the reflex action of anger and contempt upon her character, he sought now by that of gratification to elicit from her fresh particles of her intimate feelings, which she had never yet revealed.

Often she was embarrassed by lack of money, and under pressure from a creditor would come to him for assistance. He enjoyed this, as he enjoyed everything which could impress Odette with his love for herself, or merely with his influence, with the extent of the use that she might make of him. Probably if anyone had said to him, at the beginning, " It's your position that attracts her," or at this stage, " It's your money that she's really in love with," he would not have

believed the suggestion, nor would he have been greatly distressed by the thought that people supposed her to be attached
to him, that people felt them to be united by any ties so bind-
ing as those of snobbishness or wealth. But even if he had
accepted the possibility, it might not have caused him any
suffering to discover that Odette's love for him was based on a
foundation more lasting than mere affection, or any attractive
qualities which she might have found in him ; on a sound,
commercial interest ; an interest which would postpone for
ever the fatal day on which she might be tempted to bring
their relations to an end. For the moment, while he lavished
presents upon her, and performed all manner of services, he
could rely on advantages not contained in his person, or in his
intellect, could forego the endless, killing effort to make himself attractive. And this delight in being a lover, in living by
love alone, of the reality of which he was inclined to be doubtful, the price which, in the long run, he must pay for it, as a
dilettante in immaterial sensations, enhanced its value in his
eyes—as one sees people who are doubtful whether the sight
of the sea and the sound of its waves are really enjoyable,
become convinced that they are, as also of the rare quality and
absolute detachment of their own taste, when they have
agreed to pay several pounds a day for a room in an hotel,
from which that sight and that sound may be enjoyed.

One day, when reflections of this order had brought him
once again to the memory of the time when some one had
spoken to him of Odette as of a 'kept' woman, and when,
once again, he had amused himself with contrasting that
strange personification, the 'kept' woman—an iridescent
mixture of unknown and demoniacal qualities, embroidered,
as in some fantasy of Gustave Moreau, with poison-dripping
flowers, interwoven with precious jewels—with that Odette

upon whose face he had watched the passage of the same expressions of pity for a sufferer, resentment of an act of
injustice, gratitude for an act of kindness, which he had
seen, in earlier days, on his own mother's face, and on the
faces of friends ; that Odette, whose conversation had so
frequently turned on the things that he himself knew better
than anyone, his collections, his room, his old servant, his
banker, who kept all his title-deeds and bonds ;—the thought
of the banker reminded him that he must call on him shortly,
to draw some money. And indeed, if, during the current
month, he were to come less liberally to the aid of Odette in
her financial difficulties than in the month before, when he
had given her five thousand francs, if he refrained from offering her a diamond necklace for which she longed, he would be
allowing her admiration for his generosity to decline, that
gratitude which had made him so happy, and would even be
running the risk of her imagining that his love for her (as
she saw its visible manifestations grow fewer) had itself
diminished. And then, suddenly, he asked himself whether
that was not precisely what was implied by ' keeping ' a
woman (as if, in fact, that idea of ' keeping ' could be derived
from elements not at all mysterious nor perverse, but belong-
ing to the intimate routine of his daily life, such as that
thousand-franc note, a familiar and domestic object, torn in
places and mended with gummed paper, which his valet, after
paying the household accounts and the rent, had locked up in
a drawer in the old writing-desk whence he had extracted it
to send it, with four others, to Odette) and whether it was not
possible to apply to Odette, since he had known her (for he
never imagined for a moment that she could ever have taken
a penny from anyone else, before), that title, which he had
believed so wholly inapplicable to her, of ' kept ' woman.

He could not explore the idea further, for a sudden access of that mental lethargy which was, with him, congenital, intermittent and providential, happened, at that moment, to extinguish every particle of light in his brain, as instantaneously as, at a later period, when electric lighting had been everywhere installed, it became possible, merely by fingering a switch, to cut off all the supply of light from a house. His mind fumbled, for a moment, in the darkness, he took off his spectacles, wiped the glasses, passed his hands over his eyes, but saw no light until he found himself face to face with a wholly different idea, the realisation that he must endeavour, in the coming month, to send Odette six or seven thousand-franc notes instead of five, simply as a surprise for her and to give her pleasure.

In the evening, when he did not stay at home until it was time to meet Odette at the Verdurins', or rather at one of the open-air restaurants which they liked to frequent in the Bois and especially at Saint-Cloud, he would go to dine in one of those fashionable houses in which, at one time, he had been a constant guest. He did not wish to lose touch with people who, for all that he knew, might be of use, some day, to Odette, and thanks to whom he was often, in the meantime, able to procure for her some privilege or pleasure. Besides, he had been used for so long to the refinement and comfort of good society that, side by side with his contempt, there had grown up also a desperate need for it, with the result that, when he had reached the point after which the humblest lodgings appeared to him as precisely on a par with the most princely mansions, his senses were so thoroughly accustomed to the latter that he could not enter the former without a feeling of acute discomfort. He had the same regard—to a degree of identity which they would never have suspected—for the

little families with small incomes who asked him to dances
in their flats ("straight upstairs to the fifth floor, and the door
on the left") as for the Princesse de Parme, who gave the
most splendid parties in Paris ; but he had not the feeling of
being actually 'at the ball' when he found himself herded
with the fathers of families in the bedroom of the lady of the
house, while the spectacle of wash-hand-stands covered over
with towels, and of beds converted into cloak-rooms, with a
mass of hats and greatcoats sprawling over their counterpanes,
gave him the same stifling sensation that, nowadays, people
who have been used for half a lifetime to electric light derive
from a smoking lamp or a candle that needs to be snuffed.
If he were dining out, he would order his carriage for half-
past seven ; while he changed his clothes, he would be
wondering, all the time, about Odette, and in this way was
never alone, for the constant thought of Odette gave to the
moments in which he was separated from her the same
peculiar charm as to those in which she was at his side
He would get into his carriage and drive off, but he knew that
this thought had jumped in after him and had settled down
upon his knee, like a pet animal which he might take everywhere, and would keep with him at the dinner-table, unobserved by his fellow-guests. He would stroke and fondle
it, warm himself with it, and, as a feeling of languor swept
over him, would give way to a slight shuddering movement
which contracted his throat and nostrils—a new experience,
this,—as he fastened the bunch of columbines in his buttonhole. He had for some time been feeling neither well nor
happy, especially since Odette had brought Forcheville to the
Verdurins', and he would have liked to go away for a while
to rest in the country. But he could never summon up
courage to leave Paris, even for a day, while Odette was there.

The weather was warm ; it was the finest part of the spring. And for all that he was driving through a city of stone to immure himself in a house without grass or garden, what was incessantly before his eyes was a park which he owned, near Combray, where, at four in the afternoon, before coming to the asparagus-bed, thanks to the breeze that was wafted across the fields from Méséglise, he could enjoy the fragrant coolness of the air as well beneath an arbour of hornbeams in the garden as by the bank of the pond, fringed with forget-me-not and iris ; and where, when he sat down to dinner, trained and twined by the gardener's skilful hand, there ran all about his table currant-bush and rose.

After dinner, if he had an early appointment in the Bois or at Saint-Cloud, he would rise from table and leave the house so abruptly—especially if it threatened to rain, and so to scatter the 'faithful' before their normal time—that on one occasion the Princesse des Laumes (at whose house dinner had been so late that Swann had left before the coffee came in, to join the Verdurins on the Island in the Bois) observed :

"Really, if Swann were thirty years older, and had diabetes, there might be some excuse for his running away like that. He seems to look upon us all as a joke."

He persuaded himself that the spring-time charm, which he could not go down to Combray to enjoy, he would find at least on the Ile des Cygnes or at Saint-Cloud. But as he could think only of Odette, he would return home not knowing even if he had tasted the fragrance of the young leaves, or if the moon had been shining. He would be welcomed by the little phrase from the sonata, played in the garden on the restaurant piano. If there was none in the garden, the Verdurins would have taken immense pains to have a piano brought out either from a private room or from the restaurant itself ; not because Swann was now restored to favour ; far from it. But the idea of arranging an ingenious form of entertainment for some one, even for some one whom they disliked, would stimulate them, during the time spent in its preparation, to a momentary sense of cordiality and affection. Now and then he would remind himself that another fine spring evening was drawing to a close, and would force himself to notice the trees and the sky. But the state of excitement into which Odette's presence never failed to throw him, added to a feverish ailment which, for some time now, had scarcely left him, robbed him of that sense of quiet and comfort which is an indispensable background to the impressions that we derive from nature.

One evening, when Swann had consented to dine with the Verdurins, and had mentioned during dinner that he had to attend, next day, the annual banquet of an old comrades' association, Odette had at once exclaimed across the table, in front of everyone, in front of Forcheville, who was now one of the ' faithful,' in front of the painter, in front of Cottard :

" Yes, I know, you have your banquet to-morrow ; I shan't see you, then, till I get home ; don't be too late."

And although Swann had never yet taken offence, at all seriously, at Odette's demonstrations of friendship for one or other of the ' faithful,' he felt an exquisite pleasure on hearing her thus avow, before them all, with that calm immodesty, the fact that they saw each other regularly every evening, his privileged position in her house, and her own preference for him which it implied. It was true that Swann had often reflected that Odette was in no way a remarkable woman ; and in the supremacy which he wielded over a creature so distinctly inferior to himself there was nothing that especially flattered him when he heard it proclaimed to all the ' faithful ' ; but since he had observed that, to several other men than himself, Odette seemed a fascinating and desirable woman, the attraction which her body held for him had aroused a painful longing to secure the absolute mastery of even the tiniest particles of her heart. And he had begun to attach an incalculable value to those moments passed in her house in the evenings, when he held her upon his knee, made her tell him what she thought about this or that, and counted over that treasure to which, alone of all his earthly possessions, he still clung. And so, after this dinner, drawing her aside, he took care to thank her effusively, seeking to indicate to her by the extent of his gratitude the corresponding intensity of the pleasures which it was in her power to bestow on him, the supreme pleasure being to guarantee him immunity, for so long as his love should last and he remain vulnerable, from the assaults of jealousy.

When he came away from his banquet, the next evening, it was pouring with rain, and he had nothing but his victoria. A friend offered to take him home in a closed carriage, and as Odette, by the fact of her having invited him to come, had given him an assurance that she was expecting no one else, he could, with a quiet mind and an untroubled heart, rather than set off thus in the rain, have gone home and to bed. But perhaps, if she saw that he seemed not to adhere to his resolution to end every evening, without exception, in her company, she might grow careless, and fail to keep free for him just the one evening on which he particularly desired it.

It was after eleven when he reached her door, and as he made his apology for having been unable to come away earlier, she complained that it was indeed very late ; the storm had made her unwell, her head ached, and she warned him that she would not let him stay longer than half an hour, that at midnight she would send him away ; a little while later she felt tired and wished to sleep.

" No cattleya, then, to-night ? " he asked, " and I've been looking forward so to a nice little cattleya."

But she was irresponsive ; saying nervously : " No, dear, no cattleya to-night. Can't you see, I'm not well ? "

" It might have done you good, but I won't bother you."

She begged him to put out the light before he went ; he drew the curtains close round her bed and left her. But, when he was in his own house again, the idea suddenly struck him that, perhaps, Odette was expecting some one else that evening, that she had merely pretended to be tired, that she had asked him to put the light out only so that he should suppose that she was going to sleep, that the moment he had left the house she had lighted it again, and had reopened her door to the stranger who was to be her guest for the night. He looked at his watch. It was about an hour and a half since he had left her ; he went out, took a cab, and stopped it close to her house, in a little street running at right angles to that other street, which lay at the back of her house, and along which he used to go, sometimes, to tap upon her bedroom window, for her to let him in. He left his cab ; the streets were all deserted and dark ; he walked a few yards and came out almost opposite her house. Amid the glimmering blackness of all the row of windows, the lights in which had long since been put out, he saw one, and only one, from which overflowed, between the slats of its shutters, closed like a wine-press over its mysterious golden juice, the light that filled the room within, a light which on so many evenings, as soon as he saw it, far off, as he turned into the street, had rejoiced his heart with its message : " She is there—expecting you," and now tortured him with : " She is there with the man she was expecting." He must know who ; he tiptoed along by the wall until he reached the window, but between the slanting bars of the shutters he could see nothing ; he could hear, only, in the silence of the night, the murmur of conversation. What agony he suffered as he watched that light, in whose golden atmosphere were moving, behind the closed sash, the unseen and detested pair, as he listened to that murmur which revealed the presence of the man who had crept in after his own departure, the perfidy of Odette, and the pleasures which she was at that moment tasting with the stranger.

And yet he was not sorry that he had come ; the torment which had forced him to leave his own house had lost its sharpness when it lost its uncertainty, now that Odette's other life, of which he had had, at that first moment, a sudden helpless suspicion, was definitely there, almost within his grasp, before his eyes, in the full glare of the lamp-light, caught and kept there, an unwitting prisoner, in that room into which, when he would, he might force his way to surprise and seize it ; or rather he would tap upon the shutters, as he had often done when he had come there very late, and by that signal Odette would at least learn that he knew, that he had seen the light and had heard the voices ; while he himself, who a moment ago had been picturing her as laughing at him, as sharing with that other the knowledge of how effectively he had been tricked, now it was he that saw them, confident and persistent in their error, tricked and trapped by none other than himself, whom they believed to be a mile away, but who was there, in person, there with a plan, there with the knowledge that he was going, in another minute, to tap upon the shutter. And, perhaps, what he felt (almost an agreeable feeling) at that moment was something more than relief at

the solution of a doubt, at the soothing of a pain ; was an
intellectual pleasure. If, since he had fallen in love, things
had recovered a little of the delicate attraction that they had
had for him long ago—though only when a light was shed
upon them by a thought, a memory of Odette—now it was
another of the faculties, prominent in the studious days of his
youth, that Odette had quickened with new life, the passion
for truth, but for a truth which, too, was interposed between
himself and his mistress, receiving its light from her alone, a
private and personal truth the sole object of which (an
infinitely precious object, and one almost impersonal in its
absolute beauty) was Odette—Odette in her activities, her
environment, her projects, and her past. At every other
period in his life, the little everyday words and actions of
another person had always seemed wholly valueless to Swann ;
if gossip about such things were repeated to him, he would
dismiss it as insignificant, and while he listened it was only the
lowest, the most commonplace part of his mind that was interested ; at such moments he felt utterly dull and unin-
spired. But in this strange phase of love the personality
of another person becomes so enlarged, so deepened, that the
curiosity which he could now feel aroused in himself, to know
the least details of a woman's daily occupation, was the same
thirst for knowledge with which he had once studied history.
And all manner of actions, from which, until now, he would
have recoiled in shame, such as spying, to-night, outside a
window, to-morrow, for all he knew, putting adroitly
provocative questions to casual witnesses, bribing servants,
listening at doors, seemed to him, now, to be precisely on a
level with the deciphering of manuscripts, the weighing of
evidence, the interpretation of old monuments, that was to
say, so many different methods of scientific investigation,

each one having a definite intellectual value and being legiti-
mately employable in the search for truth.

As his hand stole out towards the shutters he felt a pang
of shame at the thought that Odette would now know that
he had suspected her, that he had returned, that he had posted
himself outside her window. She had often told him what a
horror she had of jealous men, of lovers who spied. What
he was going to do would be extremely awkward, and she
would detest him for ever after, whereas now, for the moment,
for so long as he refrained from knocking, perhaps even in the
act of infidelity, she loved him still. How often is not the
prospect of future happiness thus sacrificed to one's impatient
insistence upon an immediate gratification. But his desire to
know the truth was stronger, and seemed to him nobler than
his desire for her. He knew that the true story of certain
events, which he would have given his life to be able to reconstruct accurately and in full, was to be read within that
window, streaked with bars of light, as within the illuminated,
golden boards of one of those precious manuscripts, by whose
wealth of artistic treasures the scholar who consults them
cannot remain unmoved. He yearned for the satisfaction of
knowing the truth which so impassioned him in that brief,
fleeting, precious transcript, on that translucent page, so
warm, so beautiful. And besides, the advantage which he felt
—which he so desperately wanted to feel—that he had over
them, lay perhaps not so much in knowing as in being able
to shew them that he knew. He drew himself up on tiptoe.
He knocked. They had not heard ; he knocked again ;
louder ; their conversation ceased. A man's voice—he
strained his ears to distinguish whose, among such of Odette's
friends as he knew, the voice could be—asked :

" Who's that ? "

He could not be certain of the voice. He knocked once again. The window first, then the shutters were thrown open. It was too late, now, to retire, and since she must know all, so as not to seem too contemptible, too jealous and inquisitive, he called out in a careless, hearty, welcoming tone :

" Please don't bother ; I just happened to be passing, and saw the light. I wanted to know if you were feeling better."

He looked up. Two old gentlemen stood facing him, in the window, one of them with a lamp in his hand ; and beyond them he could see into the room, a room that he had never seen before. Having fallen into the habit, when he came late to Odette, of identifying her window by the fact that it was the only one still lighted in a row of windows otherwise all alike, he had been misled, this time, by the light, and had knocked at the window beyond hers, in the adjoining house. He made what apology he could and hurried home, overjoyed that the satisfaction of his curiosity had preserved their love intact, and that, having feigned for so long, when in Odette's company, a sort of indifference, he had not now, by a demonstration of jealousy, given her that proof of the excess of his own passion which, in a pair of lovers, fully and finally dispenses the recipient from the obligation to love the other enough. He never spoke to her of this misadventure, he ceased even to think of it himself. But now and then his thoughts in their wandering course would come upon this memory where it lay unobserved, would startle it into life, thrust it more deeply down into his consciousness, and leave him aching with a sharp, far-rooted pain. As though this had been a bodily pain, Swann's mind was powerless to alleviate it ; in the case of bodily pain, however, since it is independent of the mind, the mind can dwell upon it, can note that it has diminished, that it has momentarily ceased. But with this mental pain, the mind, merely by recalling it, created it afresh. To determine not to think of it was but to think of it still, to suffer from it still. And when, in conversation with his friends, he forgot his sufferings, suddenly a word casually uttered would make him change countenance as a wounded man does when a clumsy hand has touched his aching limb. When he came away from Odette, he was happy, he felt calm, he recalled the smile with which, in gentle mockery, she had spoken to him of this man or of that, a smile which was all tenderness for himself ; he recalled the gravity of her head which she seemed to have lifted from its axis to let it droop and fall, as though against her will, upon his lips, as she had done on that first evening in the carriage ; her languishing gaze at him while she lay nestling in his arms, her bended head seeming to recede between her shoulders, as though shrinking from the cold.

But then, at once, his jealousy, as it had been the shadow of his love, presented him with the complement, with the converse of that new smile with which she had greeted him that very evening,—with which, now, perversely, she was mocking Swann while she tendered her love to another—of that lowering of her head, but lowered now to fall on other lips, and (but bestowed upon a stranger) of all the marks of affection that she had shewn to him. And all these voluptuous memories which he bore away from her house were, as one might say, but so many sketches, rough plans, like the schemes of decoration which a designer submits to one in outline, enabling Swann to form an idea of the various attitudes, aflame or faint with passion, which she was capable of adopting for others. With the result that he came to regret every pleasure that he tasted in her company, every new caress that he invented (and had been so imprudent as to point out to her how delightful it was) every fresh charm that he found in her, for he knew that, a moment later, they would go to enrich the collection of instruments in his secret torture-chamber.

A fresh turn was given to the screw when Swann recalled a sudden expression which he had intercepted, a few days earlier, and for the first time, in Odette's eyes. It was after dinner at the Verdurins'. Whether it was because Forcheville, aware that Saniette, his brother-in-law, was not in favour with them, had decided to make a butt of him, and to shine at his expense, or because he had been annoyed by some awkward remark which Saniette had made to him, although it had passed unnoticed by the rest of the party who knew nothing of whatever tactless allusion it might conceal, or possibly because he had been for some time looking out for an opportunity of securing the expulsion from the house of a fellow-guest who knew rather too much about him, and whom he knew to be so nice-minded that he himself could not help feeling embarrassed at times merely by his presence in the room, Forcheville replied to Saniette's tactless utterance with such a volley of abuse, going out of his way to insult him, emboldened, the louder he shouted, by the fear, the pain, the entreaties of his victim, that the poor creature, after asking Mme. Verdurin whether he should stay and receiving no answer, had left the house in stammering confusion and with tears in his eyes. Odette had looked on, impassive, at this scene ; but when the door had closed behind Saniette, she had forced the normal expression of her face down, as the saying is, by several pegs, so as to bring herself on to the same level of vulgarity as Forcheville ; her eyes had sparkled with a malicious smile of congratulation upon his audacity, of ironical pity for the poor wretch who had been its victim ; she had darted at him a look of complicity in the crime, which so clearly implied : " That's finished him off, or I'm very much mistaken. Did you see what a fool he looked? He was actually crying!" that Forcheville, when his eyes met hers, sobered in a moment from the anger, or pretended anger with which he was still flushed, smiled as he explained : " He need only have made himself pleasant and he'ld have been here still ; a good scolding does a man no harm, at any time."

One day when Swann had gone out early in the afternoon to pay a call, and had failed to find the person at home whom he wished to see, it occurred to him to go, instead, to Odette, at an hour when, although he never went to her house then as a rule, he knew that she was always at home, resting or writing letters until tea-time, and would enjoy seeing her for a moment, if it did not disturb her. The porter told him that he believed Odette to be in ; Swann rang the bell, thought that he heard a sound, that he heard footsteps, but no one came to the door. Anxious and annoyed, he went round to the other little street, at the back of her house, and' stood beneath her bedroom window ; the curtains were drawn and he could see nothing ; he knocked loudly upon the pane, he shouted ; still no one came. He could see that the neighbours were staring at him. He turned away, thinking that, after all, he had perhaps been mistaken in believing that he heard footsteps ; but he remained so preoccupied with the suspicion that he could turn his mind to nothing else. After waiting for an hour, he returned. He found her at home ; she told him that she had been in the house when he rang, but had been asleep ; the bell had awakened her ; she had guessed that it must be Swann, and had run out to meet him, but he had already gone. She had, of course, heard him knocking at the window. Swann could at once detect in this story one of those fragments of literal truth which liars, when taken by surprise, console themselves by introducing into the composition of the falsehood which they have to invent, thinking that it can be safely incorporated, and will lend the whole story an air of verisimilitude. It was true that, when Odette had just done something which she did not wish to disclose, she would take pains to conceal it in a secret place in her heart. But as soon as she found herself face to face with the man to whom she was obliged to lie, she became uneasy, all her ideas melted like wax before a flame, her inventive and her reasoning faculties were paralysed, she might ransack her brain but would find only a void ; still, she must say something, and there lay within her reach precisely the fact which she had wished to conceal, which, being the truth, was the one thing that had remained. She broke off from it a tiny fragment, of no importance in itself, assuring herself that, after all, it was the best thing to do, since it was a detail of the truth, and less dangerous, therefore, than a falsehood. " At any rate, this is true ; " she said to herself ; " that's always something to the good ; he may make inquiries ; he will see that this is true ; it won't be this, anyhow, that will give me away." But she was wrong ; it was what gave her away ; she had not taken into account that this fragmentary detail of the truth had sharp edges which could not be made to fit in, except to those contiguous fragments of the truth from which she had arbitrarily detached it, edges which, whatever the fictitious details in which she might embed it, would continue to shew, by their overlapping angles and by the gaps which she had forgotten to fill, that its proper place was elsewhere.

" She admits that she heard me ring, and then knock, that she knew it was myself, that she wanted to see me," Swann thought to himself. " But that doesn't correspond with the fact that she did not let me in."

He did not, however, draw her attention to this inconsistency, for he thought that, if left to herself, Odette might perhaps produce some falsehood which would give him a faint indication of the truth ; she spoke ; he did not interrupt her, he gathered up, with an eager and sorrowful piety, the words that fell from her lips, feeling (and rightly feeling, since she was hiding the truth behind them as she spoke) that, like the veil of a sanctuary, they kept a vague imprint, traced a faint outline of that infinitely precious and, alas, undiscoverable truth ;—what she had been doing, that afternoon, at three o'clock, when he had called,—a truth of which he would never possess any more than these falsifications, illegible and divine traces, a truth which would exist henceforward only in the secretive memory of this creature, who could contemplate it in utter ignorance of its value, but would never yield it up to him. It was true that he had, now and then, a strong suspicion that Odette's daily activities were not in themselves passionately interesting, and that such relations as she might have with other men did not exhale, naturally, in a universal sense, or for every rational being, a spirit of morbid gloom capable of infecting with fever or of inciting to suicide. He realised, at such moments, that that interest, that gloom, existed in him only as a malady might exist, and that, once he was cured of the malady, the actions of Odette, the kisses that she might have bestowed, would become once again as innocuous as those of countless other women. But the consciousness that the painful curiosity with which Swann now studied them had its origin only in himself was not enough to make him decide that it was unreasonable to regard that curiosity as important, and to take every possible step to satisfy it. Swann had, in fact, reached an age the philosophy of which—supported, in his case, by the current philosophy of the day, as well as by that of the circle in which he had spent most of his life, the group that surrounded the Princesse des Laumes, in which one's intelligence was understood to increase with the strength of one's disbelief in everything, and nothing real and incontestable was to be discovered, except the individual tastes of each of its members—is no longer that of youth, but a positive, almost a medical philosophy, the philosophy of men who, instead of fixing their aspirations upon external objects, endeavour to separate from the accumulation of the years already spent a definite residue of habits and passions which they can regard as characteristic and permanent, and with which they will deliberately arrange, before anything else, that the kind of existence which they choose to adopt shall not prove inharmonious. Swann deemed it wise to make allowance in his life for the suffering which he derived from not knowing what Odette had done, just as he made allowance for the impetus which a damp climate always gave to his eczema ; to anticipate in his budget the expenditure of a considerable sum on procuring, with regard to the daily occupations of Odette, information the lack of which would make him unhappy, just as he reserved a margin for the gratification of other tastes from which he knew that pleasure was to be expected (at·least, before he had fallen in love) such as his taste for collecting things, or for good cooking.

When he proposed to take leave of Odette, and to return home, she begged him to stay a little longer, and even detained him forcibly, seizing him by the arm as he was opening

the door to go. But he gave no thought to that, for, among
the crowd of gestures and speeches and other little incidents
which go to make up a conversation, it is inevitable that we
should pass (without noticing anything that arouses our
interest) by those that hide a truth for which our suspicions
are blindly searching, whereas we stop to examine others beneath which nothing lies concealed. She kept on saying :
" What a dreadful pity ; you never by any chance come in
the afternoon, and the one time you do come then I miss you."
He knew very well that she was not sufficiently in love with
him to be so keenly distressed merely at having missed his
visit, but as she was a good-natured woman, anxious to give
him pleasure, and often sorry when she had done anything
that annoyed him, he found it quite natural that she should be
sorry, on this occasion, that she had deprived him of that
pleasure of spending an hour in her company, which was so
very great a pleasure, if not to herself, at any rate to him.
All the same, it was a matter of so little importance that her
air of unrelieved sorrow began at length to bewilder him.
She reminded him, even more than was usual, of the faces of
some of the women created by the painter of the ' Primavera.'
She had, at that moment, their downcast, heartbroken expression, which seems ready to succumb beneath the burden
of a grief too heavy to be borne, when they are merely allowing the Infant Jesus to play with a pomegranate, or watching
Moses pour water into a trough. He had seen the same
sorrow once before on her face, but when, he could no longer
say. Then, suddenly, he remembered ; it was when Odette
had lied, in apologising to Mme. Verdurin on the evening
after the dinner from which she had stayed away on a pretext
of illness, but really so that she might be alone with Swann.
Surely, even had she been the most scrupulous of women, she

could hardly have felt remorse for so innocent a lie. But the lies which Odette ordinarily told were less innocent, and served to prevent discoveries which might have involved her in the most terrible difficulties with one or another of her friends. And so, when she lied, smitten with fear, feeling herself to be but feebly armed for her defence, unconfident of success, she was inclined to weep from sheer exhaustion, as children weep sometimes when they have not slept. She knew, also, that her lie, as a rule, was doing a serious injury to the man to whom she was telling it, and that she might find herself at his mercy if she told it badly. Therefore she felt at once humble and culpable in his presence. And when she had to tell an insignificant, social lie its hazardous associations, and the memories which it recalled, would leave her weak with a sense of exhaustion and penitent with a consciousness of wrongdoing.

What depressing lie was she now concocting for Swann's benefit, to give her that pained expression, that plaintive voice, which seemed to falter beneath the effort that she was forcing herself to make, and to plead for pardon ? He had an idea that it was not merely the truth about what had occurred that afternoon that she was endeavouring to hide from him, but something more immediate, something, possibly, which had not yet happened, but might happen now at any time, and, when it did, would throw a light upon that earlier event. At that moment, he heard the front-door bell ring. Odette never stopped speaking, but her words dwindled into an inarticulate moan. Her regret at not having seen Swann that afternoon, at not having opened the door to him, had melted into a universal despair.

He could hear the gate being closed, and the sound of a carriage, as though some one were going away—probably the person whom Swann must on no account meet—after being told that Odette was not at home. And then, when he reflected that, merely by coming at an hour when he was not in the habit of coming, he had managed to disturb so many arrangements of which she did not wish him to know, he had a feeling of discouragement that amounted, almost, to distress. But since he was in love with Odette, since he was in the habit of turning all his thoughts towards her, the pity with which he might have been inspired for himself he felt for her only, and murmured : " Poor darling ! " When finally he left her, she took up several letters which were lying on the table, and asked him if he would be so good as to post them for her. He walked along to the post-office, took the letters from his pocket, and, before dropping each of them into the box, scanned its address. They were all to tradesmen, except the last, which was to Forcheville. He kept it in his hand. " If I saw what was in this," he argued, " I should know what she calls him, what she says to him, whether there really is any-thing between them. Perhaps, if I don't look inside, I shall be lacking in delicacy towards Odette, since in this way alone I can rid myself of a suspicion which is, perhaps, a calumny on her, which must, in any case, cause her suffering, and which can never possibly be set at rest, once the letter is posted."

He left the post-office and went home, but he had kept the last letter in his pocket. He lighted a candle, and held up close to its flame the envelope which he had not dared to open. At first he could distinguish nothing, but the envelope was thin, and by pressing it down on to the stiff card which it en-closed he was able, through the transparent paper, to read the concluding words. They were a coldly formal signature. If, instead of its being himself who was looking at a letter addressed to Forcheville, it had been Forcheville who had read a letter addressed to Swann, he might have found words in it of another, a far more tender kind ! He took a firm hold of the card, which was sliding to and fro, the envelope being too large for it, and then, by moving it with his finger and thumb, brought one line after another beneath the part of the envelope where the paper was not doubled, through which alone it was possible to read.

In spite of all these manœuvres he could not make it out clearly. Not that it mattered, for he had seen enough to assure himself that the letter was about some trifling incident of no importance, and had nothing at all to do with love ; it was something to do with Odette's uncle. Swann had read quite plainly at the beginning of the line " I was right," but did not understand what Odette had been right in doing, until suddenly a word which he had not been able, at first, to decipher, came to light and made the whole sentence intelligible : " I was right to open the door ; it was my uncle." To open the door ! Then Forcheville had been there when Swann rang the bell, and she had sent him away, hence the sound that Swann had heard.

After that he read the whole letter ; at the end she apologised for having treated Forcheville with so little ceremony, and reminded him that he had left his cigarette-case at her house, precisely what she had written to Swann after one of his first visits. But to Swann she had added : " Why did you not forget your heart also ? I should never have let you have that back." To Forcheville nothing of that sort ; no allusion that could suggest any intrigue between them. And, really, he was obliged to admit that in all this business Forcheville had been worse treated than himself, since Odette was writing to him to make him believe that her visitor had been an uncle. From which it followed that he, Swann, was the man to whom she attached importance, and for whose sake she had sent the other away. And yet, if there had been nothing between Odette and Forcheville, why not have opened the door at once, why have said, " I was right to open the door ; it was my uncle." Right ? if she was doing nothing wrong at that moment how could Forcheville possibly have accounted for her not opening the door ? For a time Swann stood still there, heartbroken, bewildered, and yet happy ; gazing at this envelope which Odette had handed to him without a scruple, so absolute was her trust in his honour ; through its transparent window there had been disclosed to him, with the secret history of an incident which he had despaired of ever being able to learn, a fragment of the life of Odette, seen as through a narrow, luminous incision, cut into its surface without her knowledge. Then his jealousy rejoiced at the discovery, as though that jealousy had had an independent existence, fiercely egotistical, gluttonous of everything that would feed its vitality, even at the expense of Swann himself. Now it had food in store, and Swann could begin to grow uneasy afresh every evening, over the visits that Odette had received about five o'clock, and could seek to discover where Forcheville had been at that hour. For Swann's affection for Odette still preserved the form which had been imposed on it, from the beginning, by his ignorance of the occupations in which she passed her days, as well as by the mental lethargy which prevented him from supplementing that ignorance by imagination. He was not jealous, at first, of the whole of Odette's life, but of those moments only in which an incident, which he had perhaps misinterpreted, had led him to suppose that Odette might have played him false. His jealousy, like an octopus which throws out a first,

then a second, and finally a third tentacle, fastened itself
irremovably first to that moment, five o'clock in the afternoon, then to another, then to another again. But Swann was
incapable of inventing his sufferings. They were only the
memory, the perpetuation of a suffering that had come to
him from without.

From without, however, everything brought him fresh
suffering. He decided to separate Odette from Forcheville,
by taking her away for a few days to the south. But he
imagined that she was coveted by every male person in the
hotel, and that she coveted them in return. And so he, who,
in old days, when he travelled, used always to seek out new
people and crowded places, might now be seen fleeing savagely
from human society as if it had cruelly injured him. And how
could he not have turned misanthrope, when in every man he
saw a potential lover for Odette ? Thus his jealousy did even
more than the happy, passionate desire which he had originally
felt for Odette had done to alter Swann's character, completely changing, in the eyes of the world, even the outward
signs by which that character had been intelligible.

A month after the evening on which he had intercepted
and read Odette's letter to Forcheville, Swann went to a
dinner which the Verdurins were giving in the Bois. As the
party was breaking up he noticed a series of whispered dis-
cussions between Mme. Verdurin and several of her guests,
and thought that he heard the pianist being reminded to come
next day to a party at Chatou ; now he, Swann, had not been
invited to any party.

The Verdurins had spoken only in whispers, and in vague
terms, but the painter, perhaps without thinking, shouted
out : " There must be no lights of any sort, and he must play
the Moonlight Sonata in the dark, for us to see by.'

Mme. Verdurin, seeing that Swann was within earshot, assumed that expression in which the two-fold desire to make the speaker be quiet and to preserve, oneself, an appearance of guilelessness in the eyes of the listener, is neutralised in an intense vacuity ; in which the unflinching signs of intelligent complicity are overlaid by the smiles of innocence, an expression invariably adopted by anyone who has noticed a blunder, the enormity of which is thereby at once revealed if not to those who have made it, at any rate to him in whose hearing it ought not to have been made. Odette seemed suddenly to be in despair, as though she had decided not to struggle any longer against the crushing difficulties of life, and Swann was anxiously counting the minutes that still separated him from the point at which, after leaving the restaurant, while he drove her home, he would be able to ask for an explanation, to make her promise, either that she would not go to Chatou next day, or that she would procure an invitation for him also, and to lull to rest in her arms the anguish that still tormented him. At last the carriages were ordered. Mme. Verdurin said to Swann :

" Good-bye, then. We shall see you soon, I hope," trying, by the friendliness of her manner and the constraint of her smile, to prevent him from noticing that she was not saying, as she would always have until then :

" To-morrow, then, at Chatou, and at my house the day after."

M. and Mme. Verdurin made Forcheville get into their carriage ; Swann's was drawn up behind it, and he waited for theirs to start before helping Odette into his own.

" Odette, we'll take you," said Mme. Verdurin, " we've kept a little corner specially for you, beside M. de Forcheville."

" Yes, Mme. Verdurin," said Odette meekly.

" What ! I thought, I was to take you home," cried Swann, flinging discretion to the winds, for the carriage-door hung open, time was precious, and he could not, in his present state, go home without her.

" But Mme. Verdurin has asked me . . ."

" That's all right, you can quite well go home alone ; we've left you like this dozens of times," said Mme. Verdurin.

" But I had something important to tell Mme. de Crécy."

" Very well, you can write it to her instead."

" Good-bye," said Odette, holding out her hand.

He tried hard to smile, but could only succeed in looking utterly dejected.

" What do you think of the airs that Swann is pleased to put on with us ? " Mme. Verdurin asked her husband when they had reached home. " I was afraid he was going to eat me, simply because we offered to take Odette back. It really is too bad, that sort of thing. Why doesn't he say, straight out, that we keep a disorderly house ? I can't conceive how Odette can stand such manners. He positively seems to be saying, all the time, ' You belong to me ! ' I shall tell Odette exactly what I think about it all, and I hope she will have the sense to understand me." A moment later she added, inarticulate with rage : " No, but, don't you see, the filthy creature . . ." using unconsciously, and perhaps in satisfaction of the same obscure need to justify herself—like Françoise at Combray when the chicken refused to die—the very words which the last convulsions of an inoffensive animal in its death agony wring from the peasant who is engaged in taking its life. And when Mme. Verdurin's carriage had moved on, and Swann's took its place, his coachman, catching sight of his face, asked whether he was unwell, or had heard bad news.

Swann sent him away ; he preferred to walk, and it was on foot, through the Bois, that he came home. He talked to himself, aloud, and in the same slightly affected tone which he had been used to adopt when describing the charms of the ' little nucleus ' and extolling the magnanimity of the Verdurins. But just as the conversation, the smiles, the kisses of Odette became as odious to him as he had once found them charming, if they were diverted to others than himself, so the Verdurins' drawing-room, which, not an hour before, had still seemed to him amusing, inspired with a genuine feeling for art and even with a sort of moral aristocracy, now that it was another than himself whom Odette was going to meet there, to love there without restraint, laid bare to him all its absurdities, its stupidity, its shame.

He drew a fanciful picture, at which he shuddered in disgust, of the party next evening at Chatou. " Imagine going to Chatou, of all places ! Like a lot of drapers after closing time ! Upon my word, these people are sublime in their smugness ; they can't really exist ; they must all have come out of one of Labiche's plays ! "

The Cottards would be there ; possibly Brichot. " Could anything be more grotesque than the lives of these little creatures, hanging on to one another like that. They'ld imagine they were utterly lost, upon my soul they would, if they didn't all meet again to-morrow at *Chatou* ! " Alas ! there would be the painter there also, the painter who enjoyed match-making, who would invite Forcheville to come with Odette to his studio. He could see Odette, in a dress far too smart for the country, " for she is so vulgar in that way, and, poor little thing, she is such a fool ! "

He could hear the jokes that Mme. Verdurin would make after dinner, jokes which, whoever the ' bore ' might be at whom they were aimed, had always amused him because he could watch Odette laughing at them, laughing with him, her laughter almost a part of his. Now he felt that it was possibly at him that they would make Odette laugh. "What a fetid form of humour!" he exclaimed, twisting his mouth into an expression of disgust so violent that he could feel the muscles of his throat stiffen against his collar. "How, in God's name, can a creature made in His image find anything to laugh at in those nauseating witticisms? The least sensitive nose must be driven away in horror from such stale exhalations. It is really impossible to believe that any human being is incapable of understanding that, in allowing herself merely to smile at the expense of a fellow-creature who has loyally held out his hand to her, she is casting herself into a mire from which it will be impossible, with the best will in the world, ever to rescue her. I dwell so many miles above the puddles in which these filthy little vermin sprawl and crawl and bawl their cheap obscenities, that I cannot possibly be spattered by the witticisms of a Verdurin!" he cried, tossing up his head and arrogantly straightening his body. "God knows that I have honestly attempted to pull Odette out of that sewer, and to teach her to breathe a nobler and a purer air. But human patience has its limits, and mine is at an end," he concluded, as though this sacred mission to tear Odette away from an atmosphere of sarcasms dated from longer than a few minutes ago, as though he had not undertaken it only since it had occurred to him that those sarcasms might, perchance, be directed at himself, and might have the effect of detaching Odette from him.

He could see the pianist sitting down to play the Moonlight Sonata, and the grimaces of Mme. Verdurin, in terrified anticipation of the wrecking of her nerves by Beethoven's music. " Idiot, liar ! " he shouted, " and a creature like that imagines that she's fond of *Art* ! " She would say to Odette, after deftly insinuating a few words of praise for Forcheville, as she had so often done for himself : " You can make room for M. de Forcheville there, can't you, Odette?" . . . " ' In the dark !' Codfish ! Pander ! " . . . ' Pander ' was the name he applied also to the music which would invite them to sit in silence, to dream together, to gaze in each other's eyes, to feel for each other's hands. He felt that there was much to be said, after all, for a sternly censorious attitude towards the arts, such as Plato adopted, and Bossuet, and the old school of education in France.

In a word, the life which they led at the Verdurins', which he had so often described as ' genuine,' seemed to him now the worst possible form of life, and their ' little nucleus ' the most degraded class of society. " It really is," he repeated, "beneath the lowest rung of the social ladder, the nethermost circle of Dante. Beyond a doubt, the august words of the Florentine refer to the Verdurins ! When one comes to think of it, surely people ' in society ' (and, though one may find fault with them now and then, still, after all they are a very different matter from that gang of blackmailers) shew a profound sagacity in refusing to know them, or even to dirty the tips of their fingers with them. What a sound intuition there is in that ' *Noli me tangere*' motto of the Faubourg Saint-Germain."

He had long since emerged from the paths and avenues of the Bois, he had almost reached his own house, and still, for he had not yet thrown off the intoxication of grief, or his whim of insincerity, but was ever more and more exhilarated by the false intonation, the artificial sonority of his own voice, he continued to perorate aloud in the silence of the night :

" People ' in society ' have their failings, as no one knows better than I ; but, after all, they are people to whom some things, at least, are impossible. So-and-so " (a fashionable woman whom he had known) " was far from being perfect, but, after all, one did find in her a fundamental delicacy, a loyalty in her conduct which made her, whatever happened, incapable of a felony, which fixes a vast gulf between her and an old hag like Verdurin. Verdurin ! What a name ! Oh, there's something complete about them, something almost fine in their trueness to type ; they're the most perfect specimens of their disgusting class ! Thank God, it was high time that I stopped condescending to promiscuous intercourse with such infamy, such dung."

But, just as the virtues which he had still attributed, an hour or so earlier, to the Verdurins, would not have sufficed, even although the Verdurins had actually possessed them, if they had not also favoured and protected his love, to excite Swann to that state of intoxication in which he waxed tender over their magnanimity, an intoxication which, even when disseminated through the medium of other persons, could have come to him from Odette alone ;—so the immorality (had it really existed) which he now found in the Verdurins would have been powerless, if they had not invited Odette with Forcheville and without him, to unstop the vials of his wrath and to make him scarify their ' infamy.' Doubtless Swann's voice shewed a finer perspicacity than his own when it refused to utter those words full of disgust at the Verdurins and their circle, and of joy at his having shaken himself free of it, save in an artificial and rhetorical tone, and as though his words had been chosen rather to appease his anger than to express his thoughts. The latter, in fact, while he abandoned himself to invective, were probably, though he did not know it, occupied with a wholly different matter, for once he had reached his house, no sooner had he closed the front-door behind him than he suddenly struck his forehead, and, making his servant open the door again, dashed out into the street shouting, in a voice which, this time, was quite natural : " I believe I have found a way of getting invited to the dinner at Chatou to-morrow ! " But it must have been a bad way, for M. Swann was not invited ; Dr. Cottard, who, having been summoned to attend a serious case in the country, had not seen the Verdurins for some days, and had been prevented from appearing at Chatou, said, on the evening after this dinner, as he sat down to table at their house :

" Why, aren't we going to see M. Swann this evening ? He is quite what you might call a personal friend of . . ."

" I sincerely trust that we shan't ! " cried Mme. Verdurin. " Heaven preserve us from him ; he's too deadly for words, a stupid, ill-bred boor."

On hearing these words Cottard exhibited an intense astonishment blended with entire submission, as though in the face of a scientific truth which contradicted everything that he had previously believed, but was supported by an irresistible weight of evidence ; with timorous emotion he bowed his head over his plate, and merely replied : " Oh—oh—oh—oh—oh ! " traversing, in an orderly retirement of his forces, into the depths of his being, along a descending scale, the whole compass of his voice. After which there was no more talk of Swann at the Verdurins'.

And so that drawing-room which had brought Swann and Odette together became an obstacle in the way of their meeting. She no longer said to him, as she had said in the early days of their love : " We shall meet, anyhow, to-morrow evening ; there's a supper-party at the Verdurins," but " We shan't be able to meet to-morrow evening ; there's a supper-party at the Verdurins." Or else the Verdurins were taking her to the Opéra-Comique, to see *Une Nuit de Cléopâtre*, and Swann could read in her eyes that terror lest he should ask her not to go, which, but a little time before, he could not have refrained from greeting with a kiss as it flitted across the face of his mistress, but which now exasperated him. " Yet I'm not really angry," he assured himself, " when I see how she longs to run away and scratch for maggots in that dunghill of cacophony. I'm disappointed ; not for myself, but for her ; disappointed to find that, after living for more than six months in daily contact with myself, she has not been capable of improving her mind even to the point of spontaneously eradicating from it a taste for Victor Massé ! More than that, to find that she has not arrived at the stage of understanding that there are evenings on which anyone with the least shade of refinement of feeling should be willing to forego an amusement when she is asked to do so. She ought to have the sense to say : ' I shall not go,' if it were only from policy, since it is by what she answers now that the quality of her soul will be determined once and for all." And having persuaded himself that it was solely, after all, in order that he might arrive at a favourable estimate of Odette's spiritual worth that he wished her to stay at home with him that evening instead of going to the Opéra-Comique, he adopted the same line of reasoning with her, with the same degree of insincerity as he had used with himself, or even with a degree more, for in her case he was yielding also to the desire to capture her by her own self-esteem.

" I swear to you," he told her, shortly before she was to leave for the theatre, " that, in asking you not to go, I should hope, were I a selfish man, for nothing so much as that you should refuse, for I have a thousand other things to do this evening, and I shall feel that I have been tricked and trapped myself, and shall be thoroughly annoyed, if, after all, you tell me that you are not going. But my occupations, my pleasures are not everything ; I must think of you also A day may come when, seeing me irrevocably sundered from you, you will be entitled to reproach me with not having warned you at the decisive hour in which I felt that I was going to pass judgment on you, one of those stern judgments which love cannot long resist. You see, your *Nuit de Cléopâtre* (what a title !) has no bearing on the point. What I must know is whether you are indeed one of those creatures in the lowest grade of mentality and even of charm, one of those contemptible creatures who are incapable of foregoing a pleasure. For if you are such, how could anyone love you, for you are not even a person, a definite, imperfect, but at least perceptible entity. You are a formless water that will trickle down any slope that it may come upon, a fish devoid of memory, incapable of thought, which all its life long in its aquarium will continue to dash itself, a hundred times a day, against a wall of glass, always mistaking it for water. Do you realise that your answer will have the effect—I do not say of making me cease from that moment to love you, that goes without saying, but of making you less attractive to my eyes when I realise that you are not a person, that you are beneath everything in the world and have not the intelligence to raise yourself one inch higher. Obviously, I should have preferred to ask you, as though it had been a matter of little or no importance, to give up your *Nuit de Cléopâtre* (since you compel me to sully my lips with so abject a name), in the hope that you would go to it none the less. But, since I had resolved to weigh you in the balance, to make so grave an issue depend upon your answer, I considered it more honourable to give you due warning."

Meanwhile, Odette had shewn signs of increasing emotion and uncertainty. Although the meaning of his tirade was beyond her, she grasped that it was to be included among the scenes of reproach or supplication, scenes which her familiarity with the ways of men enabled her, without paying any heed to the words that were uttered, to conclude that men would not make unless they were in love ; that, from the moment when they were in love, it was superfluous to obey them, since they would only be more in love later on. And so, she would have heard Swann out with the utmost tranquillity had she not noticed that it was growing late, and that if he went on speaking for any length of time she would " never " as she told him with a fond smile, obstinate but slightly abashed, " get there in time for the Overture."

On other occasions he had assured himself that the one thing which, more than anything else, would make him cease to love her, would be her refusal to abandon the habit of lying. " Even from the point of view of coquetry, pure and simple," he had told her, " can't you see how much of your attraction you throw away when you stoop to lying ? By a frank admission—how many faults you might redeem ! Really, you are far less intelligent than I supposed ! " In vain, however, did Swann expound to her thus all the reasons that she had for not lying ; they might have succeeded in overthrowing any universal system of mendacity, but Odette had no such system ; she contented herself, merely, whenever she wished Swann to remain in ignorance of anything that she had done, with not telling him of it. So that a lie was, to her, something to be used only as a special expedient ; and the one thing that could make her decide whether she should avail herself of a lie or not was a reason which, too, was of a special and contingent order, namely the risk of Swann's discovering that she had not told him the truth.

Physically, she was passing through an unfortunate phase ; she was growing stouter, and the expressive, sorrowful charm, the surprised, wistful expressions which she had formerly had, seemed to have vanished with her first youth, with the result that she became most precious to Swann at the very moment when he found her distinctly less good-looking. He would gaze at her for hours on end, trying to recapture the charm which he had once seen in her and could not find again. And yet the knowledge that, within this new and strange chrysalis, it was still Odette that lurked, still the same volatile temperament, artful and evasive, was enough to keep Swann seeking, with as much passion as ever, to captivate her. Then he would look at photographs of her, taken two years before, and would remember how exquisite she had been. And that would console him, a little, for all the sufferings that he voluntarily endured on her account.

When the Verdurins took her off to Saint-Germain, or to Chatou, or to Meulan, as often as not, if the weather was fine, they would propose to remain there for the night, and not to go home until next day. Mme. Verdurin would endeavour to set at rest the scruples of the pianist, whose aunt had remained in Paris : " She will be only too glad to be rid of you for a day. How on earth could she be anxious, when she knows you're with us ? Anyhow, I'll take you all under my wing ; she can put the blame on me."

If this attempt failed, M. Verdurin would set off across country until he came to a telegraph office or some other kind of messenger, after first finding out which of the ' faithful ' had anyone whom they must warn. But Odette would thank him, and assure him that she had no message for anyone, for she had told Swann, once and for all, that she could not possibly send messages to him, before all those people, without compromising herself. Sometimes she would be absent for several days on end, when the Verdurins took her to see the tombs at Dreux, or to Compiègne, on the painter's advice, to watch the sun setting through the forest—after which they went on to the Château of Pierrefonds.

" To think that she could visit really historic buildings with me, who have spent ten years in the study of architecture, who am constantly bombarded, by people who really count, to take them over Beauvais or Saint-Loup-de-Naud, and refuse to take anyone but her ; and instead of that she trundles off with the lowest, the most brutally degraded of creatures, to go into ecstasies over the petrified excretions of Louis-Philippe and Viollet-le-Duc ! One hardly needs much knowledge of art, I should say, to do that; though, surely, even without any particularly refined sense of smell, one would not deliberately choose to spend a holiday in the latrines, so as to be within range of their fragrant exhalations."

But when she had set off for Dreux or Pierrefonds—alas, without allowing him to appear there, as though by accident, at her side, for, as she said, that would " create a dreadful impression,"—he would plunge into the most intoxicating romance in the lover's library, the railway time-table, from which he learned the ways of joining her there in the afternoon, in the evening, even in the morning. The ways ? More than that, the authority, the right to join her. For, after all, the time-table, and the trains themselves, were not meant for dogs. If the public were carefully informed, by means of printed advertisements, that at eight o'clock in the morning a train started for Pierrefonds which arrived there at ten, that could only be because going to Pierrefonds was a lawful act, for which permission from Odette would be superfluous ; an act, moreover, which might be performed from a motive altogether different from the desire to see Odette, since persons who had never even heard of her performed it daily, and in such numbers as justified the labour and expense of stoking the engines.

So it came to this ; that she could not prevent him from going to Pierrefonds if he chose to do so. Now that was precisely what he found that he did choose to do, and would at that moment be doing were he, like the travelling public, not acquainted with Odette. For a long time past he had wanted to form a more definite impression of Viollet-le-Duc's work as a restorer. And the weather being what it was, he felt an overwhelming desire to spend the day roaming in the forest of Compiègne.

It was, indeed, a piece of bad luck that she had forbidden him access to the one spot that tempted him to-day. To-day ! Why, if he went down there, in defiance of her prohibition, he would be able to see her that very day ! But then, whereas, if she had met, at Pierrefonds, some one who did not matter, she would have hailed him with obvious pleasure : " What, you here ? " and would have invited him to come and see her at the hotel where she was staying with the Verdurins, if, on the other hand, it was himself, Swann, that she encountered there, she would be annoyed, would complain that she was being followed, would love him less in consequence, might even turn away in anger when she caught sight of him " So, then, I am not to be allowed to go away for a day anywhere ! " she would reproach him on her return, whereas in fact it was he himself who was not allowed to go.

He had had the sudden idea, so as to contrive to visit Compiègne and Pierrefonds without letting it be supposed that his object was to meet Odette, of securing an invitation from one of his friends, the Marquis de Forestelle, who had a country house in that neighbourhood. This friend, to whom Swann suggested the plan without disclosing its ulterior purpose, was beside himself with joy; he did not conceal his astonishment at Swann's consenting at last, after fifteen years, to come down and visit his property, and since he did not (he told him) wish to stay there, promised to spend some days, at least, in taking him for walks and excursions in the district. Swann imagined himself down there already with M. de Forestelle. Even before he saw Odette, even if he did not succeed in seeing her there, what a joy it would be to set foot on that soil where, not knowing the exact spot in which, at any moment, she was to be found, he would feel all around him the thrilling possibility of her suddenly appearing : in the courtyard of the Château, now beautiful in his eyes since it was on her account that he had gone to visit it ; in all the streets of the town, which struck him as romantic ; down every ride of the forest, roseate with the deep and tender glow of sunset ;—innumerable and alternative hiding-places, to which would fly simultaneously for refuge, in the uncertain ubiquity of his hopes, his happy, vagabond and divided heart. "We mustn't, on any account," he would warn M. de Forestelle, " run across Odette and the Verdurins. I have just heard that they are at Pierrefonds, of all places, to-day. One has plenty of time to see them in Paris ; it would hardly be worth while coming down here if one couldn't go a yard without meeting them." And his host would fail to understand why, once they had reached the place, Swann would change his plans twenty times in an hour, inspect the dining-rooms of all the hotels in Compiègne without being able to make up his mind to settle down in any of them, although he had found no trace anywhere of the Verdurins, seeming to be in search of what he had claimed to be most anxious to avoid, and would in fact avoid, the moment he found it, for if he had come upon the little ' group,' he would have hastened away at once with studied indifference, satisfied that he had seen Odette and she him, especially that she had seen him when he was not, apparently, thinking about her. But no; she would guess at once that it was for her sake that he had come there. And when M. de Forestelle came to fetch him, and it was time to start, he excused himself : " No, I'm afraid not ; I can't go to Pierrefonds to-day. You see, Odette is there." And Swann was happy in spite of everything in feeling that if he, alone among mortals, had not the right to go to Pierrefonds that day, it was because he was in fact, for Odette, some one who differed from all other mortals, her lover ; and because that restriction which for him alone was set upon the universal right to travel freely where one would, was but one of the many forms of that slavery, that love which was so dear to him. Decidedly, it was better not to risk a quarrel with her, to be patient, to wait for her return. He spent his days in poring over a map of the forest of Compiègne, as though it had been that of the 'Pays du Tendre'; he surrounded himself with photographs of the Château of Pierrefonds. When the day dawned on which it was possible that she might return, he opened the time-table again, calculated what train she must have taken, and, should she have postponed her departure, what trains were still left for her to take. He did not leave the house, for fear of missing a telegram, he did not go to bed, in case, having come by the last train, she decided to surprise him with a midnight visit. Yes !

The front-door bell rang. There seemed some delay in opening the door, he wanted to awaken the porter, he leaned out
of the window to shout to Odette, if it was Odette, for in
spite of the orders which he had gone downstairs a dozen
times to deliver in person, they were quite capable of telling
her that he was not at home. It was only a servant coming in.
He noticed the incessant rumble of passing carriages, to which
he had never before paid any attention. He could hear them,
one after another, a long way off, coming nearer, passing his
door without stopping, and bearing away into the distance a
message which was not for him. He waited all night, to no
purpose, for the Verdurins had returned unexpectedly, and
Odette had been in Paris since midday ; it had not occurred
to her to tell him ; not knowing what to do with herself she
had spent the evening alone at a theatre, had long since gone
home to bed, and was peacefully asleep.

As a matter of fact, she had never given him a thought.
And such moments as these, in which she forgot Swann's
very existence, were of more value to Odette, did more to
attach him to her, than all her infidelities. For in this way
Swann was kept in that state of painful agitation which had
once before been effective in making his interest blossom into
love, on the night when he had failed to find Odette at the
Verdurins' and had hunted for her all evening. And he did
not have (as I had, afterwards, at Combray in my childhood)
happy days in which to forget the sufferings that would return
with the night. For his days, Swann must pass them without
Odette ; and as he told himself, now and then, to allow so
pretty a woman to go out by herself in Paris was just as rash
as to leave a case filled with jewels in the middle of the street.
In this mood he would scowl furiously at the passers-by, as
though they were so many pickpockets. But their faces—a

108

collective and formless mass—escaped the grasp of his imagination, and so failed to feed the flame of his jealousy. The effort exhausted Swann's brain, until, passing his hand over his eyes, he cried out : " Heaven help me ! " as people, after lashing themselves into an intellectual frenzy in their endeavours to master the problem of the reality of the external world, or that of the immortality of the soul, afford relief to their weary brains by an unreasoning act of faith. But the thought of his absent mistress was incessantly, indissolubly blended with all the simplest actions of Swann's daily life— when he took his meals, opened his letters, went for a walk or to bed—by the fact of his regret at having to perform those actions without her ; like those initials of Philibert the Fair which, in the church of Brou, because of her grief, her longing for him, Margaret of Austria intertwined everywhere with her own. On some days, instead of staying at home, he would go for luncheon to a restaurant not far off, to which he had been attracted, some time before, by the excellence of its cookery, but to which he now went only for one of those reasons, at once mystical and absurd, which people call ' romantic'; because this restaurant (which, by the way, still exists) bore the same name as the street in which Odette lived : the Lapérouse. Sometimes, when she had been away on a short visit somewhere, several days would elapse before she thought of letting him know that she had returned to Paris. And then she would say quite simply, without taking (as she would once have taken) the precaution of covering herself, at all costs, with a little fragment borrowed from the truth, that she had just, at that very moment, arrived by the morning train. What she said was a falsehood ; at least for Odette it was a falsehood, inconsistent, lacking (what it would have had, if true) the support of her memory of her actual arrival at the

station ; she was even prevented from forming a mental
picture of what she was saying, while she said it, by the con-
tradictory picture, in her mind, of whatever quite different
thing she had indeed been doing at the moment when she
pretended to have been alighting from the train. In Swann's
mind, however, these words, meeting no opposition, settled
and hardened until they assumed the indestructibility of a
truth so indubitable that, if some friend happened to tell him
that he had come by the same train and had not seen Odette,
Swann would have been convinced that it was his friend who
had made a mistake as to the day or hour, since his version
did not agree with the words uttered by Odette. These words
had never appeared to him false except when, before hearing
them, he had suspected that they were going to be. For him
to believe that she was lying, an anticipatory suspicion was
indispensable. It was also, however, sufficient. Given that ;
everything that Odette might say appeared to him suspect.
Did she mention a name ; it was obviously that of one of her
lovers ; once this supposition had taken shape, he would spend
weeks in tormenting himself ; on one occasion he even
approached a firm of 'inquiry agents' to find out the address
and the occupation of the unknown rival who would give
him no peace until he could be proved to have gone abroad,
and who (he ultimately learned) was an uncle of Odette, and
had been dead for twenty years.

Although she would not allow him, as a rule, to meet her
at public gatherings, saying that people would talk, it happened occasionally that, at an evening party to which he and
she had each been invited—at Forcheville's, at the painter's,
or at a charity ball given in one of the Ministries—he found
himself in the same room with her. He could see her, but
dared not remain for fear of annoying her by seeming to be

spying upon the pleasures which she tasted in other company, pleasures which—while he drove home in utter loneliness, and went to bed, as anxiously as I myself was to go to bed, some years later, on the evenings when he came to dine with us at Combray—seemed illimitable to him since he had not been able to see their end. And, once or twice, he derived from such evenings that kind of happiness which one would be inclined (did it not originate in so violent a reaction from an anxiety abruptly terminated) to call peaceful, since it consists in a pacifying of the mind : he had looked in for a moment at a revel in the painter's studio, and was getting ready to go home ; he was leaving behind him Odette, transformed into a brilliant stranger, surrounded by men to whom her glances and her gaiety, which were not for him, seemed to hint at some voluptuous pleasure to be enjoyed there or elsewhere (possibly at the Bal des Incohérents, to which he trembled to think that she might be going on afterwards) which made Swann more jealous than the thought of their actual physical union, since it was more difficult to imagine ; he was opening the door to go, when he heard himself called back in these words (which, by cutting off from the party that possible ending which had so appalled him, made the party itself seem innocent in retrospect, made Odette's return home a thing no longer inconceivable and terrible, but tender and familiar, a thing that kept close to his side, like a part of his own daily life, in his carriage ; a thing that stripped Odette herself of the excess of brilliance and gaiety in her appearance, shewed that it was only a disguise which she had assumed for a moment, for his sake and not in view of any mysterious pleasures, a disguise of which she had already wearied)—in these words, which Odette flung out after him as he was crossing the threshold : "Can't you wait a minute for me ? I'm

just going ; we'll drive back together and you can drop me."
It was true that on one occasion Forcheville had asked to be
driven home at the same time, but when, on reaching Odette's
gate, he had begged to be allowed to come in too, she had
replied, with a finger pointed at Swann : " Ah ! That
depends on this gentleman. You must ask him. Very well,
you may come in, just for a minute, if you insist, but you
mustn't stay long, for, I warn you, he likes to sit and talk
quietly with me, and he's not at all pleased if I have visitors
when he's here. Oh, if you only knew the creature as I know
him ; isn't that so, my love, there's no one that really knows
you, is there, except me ? "

And Swann was, perhaps, even more touched by the
spectacle of her addressing him thus, in front of Forcheville,
not only in these tender words of predilection, but also with
certain criticisms, such as : " I feel sure you haven't written
yet to your friends, about dining with them on Sunday.
You needn't go if you don't want to, but you might at least
be polite," or, " Now, have you left your essay on Vermeer
here, so that you can do a little more to it to-morrow. What
a lazy-bones ! I'm going to make you work, I can tell you,"
which proved that Odette kept herself in touch with his social
engagements and his literary work, that they had indeed a
life in common. And as she spoke she bestowed on him a smile
which he interpreted as meaning that she was entirely his.

And then, while she was making them some orangeade,
suddenly, just as when the reflector of a lamp that is badly
fitted begins by casting all round an object, on the wall beyond
it, huge and fantastic shadows which, in time, contract and
are lost in the shadow of the object itself, all the terrible and
disturbing ideas which he had formed of Odette melted away
and vanished in the charming creature who stood there before

his eyes. He had the sudden suspicion that this hour spent
in Odette's house, in the lamp-light, was, perhaps, after all,
not an artificial hour, invented for his special use (with the
object of concealing that frightening and delicious thing
which was incessantly in his thoughts without his ever being
able to form a satisfactory impression of it, an hour of Odette's
real life, of her life when he was not there, looking on) with
theatrical properties and pasteboard fruits, but was perhaps
a genuine hour of Odette's life ; that, if he himself had not
been there, she would have pulled forward the same armchair for Forcheville, would have poured out for him, not
any unknown brew, but precisely that orangeade which she
was now offering to them both ; that the world inhabited
by Odette was not that other world, fearful and supernatural,
in which he spent his time in placing her—and which existed,
perhaps, only in his imagination, but the real universe, ex-
haling no special atmosphere of gloom, comprising that table
at which he might sit down, presently, and write, and this
drink which he was being permitted, now, to taste ; all the
objects which he contemplated with as much curiosity and
admiration as gratitude, for if, in absorbing his dreams, they
had delivered him from an obsession, they themselves were,
in turn, enriched by the absorption ; they shewed him the
palpable realisation of his fancies, and they interested his
mind ; they took shape and grew solid before his eyes, and at
the same time they soothed his troubled heart. Ah ! had
fate but allowed him to share a single dwelling with Odette,
so that in her house he should be in his own ; if, when asking
his servant what there would be for luncheon, it had been
Odette's bill of fare that he had learned from the reply ; if,
when Odette wished to go for a walk, in the morning, along
the Avenue du Bois-de-Boulogne, his duty as a good husband

had obliged him, though he had no desire to go out, to accompany her, carrying her cloak when she was too warm; and in the evening, after dinner, if she wished to stay at home, and not to dress, if he had been forced to stay beside her, to do what she asked ; then how completely would all the trivial details of Swann's life, which seemed to him now so gloomy, simply because they would, at the same time, have formed part of the life of Odette, have taken on—like that lamp, that orangeade, that armchair, which had absorbed so much of his dreams, which materialised so much of his longing,—a sort of superabundant sweetness and a mysterious solidity.

And yet he was inclined to suspect that the state for which he so much longed was a calm, a peace, which would not have created an atmosphere favourable to his love. When Odette ceased to be for him a creature always absent, regretted, imagined ; when the feeling that he had for her was no longer the same mysterious disturbance that was wrought in him by the phrase from the sonata, but constant affection and grati-tude, when those normal relations were established between them which would put an end to his melancholy madness ; then, no doubt, the actions of Odette's daily life would appear to him as being of but little intrinsic interest—as he had several times, already, felt that they might be, on the day, for instance, when he had read, through its envelope, her letter to Forcheville. Examining his complaint with as much scientific detachment as if he had inoculated himself with it in order to study its effects, he told himself that, when he was cured of it, what Odette might or might not do would be indifferent to him. But in his morbid state, to tell the truth, he feared death itself no more than such a recovery, which would, in fact, amount to the death of all that he then was.

After these quiet evenings, Swann's suspicions would be

temporarily lulled ; he would bless the name of Odette, and next day, in the morning, would order the most attractive jewels to be sent to her, because her kindnesses to him overnight had excited either his gratitude, or the desire to see them repeated, or a paroxysm of love for her which had need of some such outlet.

But at other times, grief would again take hold of him ; he would imagine that Odette was Forcheville's mistress, and that, when they had both sat watching him from the depths of the Verdurins' landau, in the Bois, on the evening before the party at Chatou to which he had not been invited, while he implored her in vain, with that look of despair on his face which even his coachman had noticed, to come home with him, and then turned away, solitary, crushed,—she must have employed, to draw Forcheville's attention to him, while she murmured : " Do look at him, storming ! " the same glance, brilliant, malicious, sidelong, cunning, as on the evening when Forcheville had driven Saniette from the Verdurins',

At such times Swann detested her. " But I've been a fool, too," he would argue. " I'm paying for other men's pleasures with my money. All the same, she'ld better take care, and not pull the string too often, for I might very well stop giving her anything at all. At any rate, we'ld better knock off supplementary favours for the time being. To think that, only yesterday, when she said she would like to go to Bayreuth for theseason, I was such an ass as to offer to take one of those jolly little places the King of Bavaria has there, for the two of us. However she didn't seem particularly keen ; she hasn't said yes or no yet. Let's hope that she'll refuse. Good God ! Think of listening to Wagner for a fortnight on end with her, who takes about as much interest in music as a fish does in little apples ; it will be fun ! " And his hatred, like his love, needing to manifest itself in action, he amused himself with urging his evil imaginings further and further, because, thanks to the perfidies with which he charged Odette, he detested her still more, and would be able, if it turned out—as he tried to convince himself—that she was indeed guilty of them, to take the opportunity of punishing her, emptying upon her the overflowing vials of his wrath. In this way, he went so far as to suppose that he was going to receive a letter from her, in which she would ask him for money to take the house at Bayreuth, but with the warning that he was not to come there himself, as she had promised Forcheville and the Verdurins to invite them. Oh, how he would have loved it, had it been conceivable that she would have that audacity. What joy he would have in refusing, in drawing up that vindictive reply, the terms of which he amused himself by selecting and declaiming aloud, as though he had actually received her letter.

The very next day, her letter came. She wrote that the Verdurins and their friends had expressed a desire to be present at these performances of Wagner, and that, if he would be so good as to send her the money, she would be able at last, after going so often to their house, to have the pleasure of entertaining the Verdurins in hers. Of him she said not a word ; it was to be taken for granted that their presence at Bayreuth would be a bar to his.

Then that annihilating answer, every word of which he had carefully rehearsed overnight, without venturing to hope that it could ever be used, he had the satisfaction of having it conveyed to her. Alas ! he felt only too certain that with the money which she had, or could easily procure, she would be able, all the same, to take a house at Bayreuth, since she wished to do so, she who was incapable of distinguishing between Bach and Clapisson. Let her take it, then ; she would have to live in it more frugally, that was all. No means (as there would have been if he had replied by sending her several thousand-franc notes) of organising, each evening, in her hired castle, those exquisite little suppers, after which she might perhaps be seized by the whim (which, it was possible, had never yet seized her) of falling into the arms of Forcheville. At any rate, this loathsome expedition, it would not be Swann who had to pay for it. Ah ! if he could only manage to prevent it, if she could sprain her ankle before starting, if the driver of the carriage which was to take her to the station would consent (no matter how great the bribe) to smuggle her to some place where she could be kept for a time in seclusion, that perfidious woman, her eyes tinselled with a smile of complicity for Forcheville, which was what Odette had become for Swann in the last forty-eight hours.

But she was never that for very long ; after a few days the shining, crafty eyes lost their brightness and their duplicity, that picture of an execrable Odette saying to Forcheville : " Look at him storming ! " began to grow pale and to dissolve. Then gradually reappeared and rose before him, softly radiant, the face of the other Odette, of that Odette who also turned with a smile to Forcheville, but with a smile in which there was nothing but affection for Swann, when she said : " You mustn't stay long, for this gentleman doesn't much like my having visitors when he's here. Oh ! if you only knew the creature as I know him ! " that same smile with which she used to thank Swann for some instance of his courtesy which she prized so highly, for some advice for which she had asked him in one of those grave crises in her life, when she could turn to him alone.

Then, to this other Odette, he would ask himself what could have induced him to write that outrageous letter, of which, probably, until then, she had never supposed him capable, a letter which must have lowered him from the high, from the supreme place which, by his generosity, by his loyalty, he had won for himself in her esteem. He would become less dear to her, since it was for those qualities, which she found neither in Forcheville nor in any other, that she loved him. It was for them that Odette so often shewed him a reciprocal kindness, which counted for less than nothing in his moments of jealousy, because it was not a sign of reciprocal desire, was indeed a proof rather of affection than of love, but the importance of which he began once more to feel in proportion as the spontaneous relaxation of his suspicions, often accelerated by the distraction brought to him by reading about art or by the conversation of a friend, rendered his passion less exacting of reciprocities.

Now that, after this swing of the pendulum, Odette had naturally returned to the place from which Swann's jealousy had for the moment driven her, in the angle in which he found her charming, he pictured her to himself as full of tenderness, with a look of consent in her eyes, and so beautiful that he could not refrain from moving his lips towards her, as though she had actually been in the room for him to kiss ; and he preserved a sense of gratitude to her for that bewitching, kindly glance, as strong as though she had really looked thus at him, and it had not been merely his imagination that had portrayed it in order to satisfy his desire.

What distress he must have caused her ! Certainly he found adequate reasons for his resentment, but they would not have been sufficient to make him feel that resentment, if he had not so passionately loved her. Had he not nourished grievances, just as serious, against other women, to whom he would, none the less, render willing service to-day, feeling no anger towards them because he no longer loved them ? If the day ever came when he would find himself in the same state of indifference with regard to Odette, he would then understand that it was his jealousy alone which had led him to find something atrocious, unpardonable, in this desire (after all, so natural a desire, springing from a childlike ingenuousness and also from a certain delicacy in her nature) to be able, in her turn, when an occasion offered, to repay the Verdurins for their hospitality, and to play the hostess in a house of her own.

He returned to the other point of view—opposite to that of his love and of his jealousy, to which he resorted at times by a sort of mental equity, and in order to make allowance for different eventualities—from which he tried to form a fresh judgment of Odette, based on the supposition that he had never been in love with her, that she was to him just a woman like other women, that her life had not been (whenever he himself was not present) different, a texture woven in secret apart from him, and warped against him.

Wherefore believe that she would enjoy down there with Forcheville or with other men intoxicating pleasures which she had never known with him, and which his jealousy alone had fabricated in all their elements ? At Bayreuth, as in Paris, if it should happen that Forcheville thought of him at all, it would only be as of some one who counted for a great deal in the life of Odette, some one for whom he was obliged to make way, when they met in her house. If Forcheville and she scored a triumph by being down there together in spite of him, it was he who had engineered that triumph by striving in vain to prevent her from going there, whereas if he had approved of her plan, which for that matter was quite defensible, she would have had the appearance of being there by his counsel, she would have felt herself sent there, housed there by him, and for the pleasure which she derived from entertaining those people who had so often entertained her, it was to him that she would have had to acknowledge her indebtedness.

And if—instead of letting her go off thus, at cross-purposes with him, without having seen him again—he were to send her this money, if he were to encourage her to take this journey, and to go out of his way to make it comfortable and pleasant for her, she would come running to him, happy, grateful, and he would have the joy—the sight of her face—which he had not known for nearly a week, a joy which none other could replace. For the moment that Swann was able to form a picture of her without revulsion, that he could see once again the friendliness in her smile, and that the desire to tear her away from every rival was no longer imposed by his jealousy upon his love, that love once again became, more than anything, a taste for the sensations which Odette's person gave him, for the pleasure which he found in admiring, as one might a spectacle, or in questioning, as one might a pheno-menon, the birth of one of her glances, the formation of one of her smiles, the utterance of an intonation of her voice. And this pleasure, different from every other, had in the end created in him a need of her, which she alone, by her presence or by her letters, could assuage, almost as disinterested, almost as artistic, as perverse as another need which characterised this new period in Swann's life, when the sereness, the depression of the preceding years had been followed by a sort of spiritual superabundance, without his knowing to what he owed this unlooked-for enrichment of his life, any more than

a person in delicate health who from a certain moment grows
stronger, puts on flesh, and seems for a time to be on the road
to a complete recovery :—this other need, which, too, developed in him independently of the visible, material world,
was the need to listen to music and to learn to know it.

And so, by the chemical process of his malady, after he had
created jealousy out of his love, he began again to generate
tenderness, pity for Odette. She had become once more the
old Odette, charming and kind. He was full of remorse for
having treated her harshly. He wished her to come to him,
and, before she came, he wished to have already procured for
her some pleasure, so as to watch her gratitude taking shape
in her face and moulding her smile.

So, too, Odette, certain of seeing him come to her in a few
days, as tender and submissive as before, and plead with her
for a reconciliation, became inured, was no longer afraid of
displeasing him, or even of making him angry, and refused
him, whenever it suited her, the favours by which he set
most store.

Perhaps she did not realise how sincere he had been with
her during their quarrel, when he had told her that he would
not send her any money, but would do what he could to hurt
her. Perhaps she did not realise, either, how sincere he still
was, if not with her, at any rate with himself, on other
occasions when, for the sake of their future relations, to shew
Odette that he was capable of doing without her, that a
rupture was still possible between them, he decided to wait
some time before going to see her again.

Sometimes several days had elapsed, during which she had
caused him no fresh anxiety ; and as, from the next few
visits which he would pay her, he knew that he was likely to
derive not any great pleasure, but, more probably, some annoy-

ance which would put an end to the state of calm in which he found himself, he wrote to her that he was very busy, and would not be able to see her on any of the days that he had suggested. Meanwhile, a letter from her, crossing his, asked him to postpone one of those very meetings. He asked himself, why ; his suspicions, his grief, again took hold of him. He could no longer abide, in the new state of agitation into which he found himself plunged, by the arrangements which he had made in his preceding state of comparative calm ; he would run to find her, and would insist upon seeing her on each of the following days. And even if she had not written first, if she merely acknowledged his letter, it was enough to make him unable to rest without seeing her. For, upsetting all Swann's calculations, Odette's acceptance had entirely changed his attitude. Like everyone who possesses something precious, so as to know what would happen if he ceased for a moment to possess it, he had detached the precious object from his mind, leaving, as he thought, everything else in the same state as when it was there. But the absence of one part from a whole is not only that, it is not simply a partial omission, it is a disturbance of all the other parts, a new state which it was impossible to foresee from the old.

But at other times—when Odette was on the point of going away for a holiday—it was after some trifling quarrel for which he had chosen the pretext, that he decided not to write to her and not to see until her return, giving the appearance (and expecting the reward) of a serious rupture, which she would perhaps regard as final, to a separation, the greater part of which was inevitable, since she was going away, which, in fact, he was merely allowing to start a little sooner than it must. At once he could imagine Odette, puzzled, anxious, distressed at having received neither visit nor letter from him,

and this picture of her, by calming his jealousy, made it easy
for him to break himself of the habit of seeing her. At odd
moments, no doubt, in the furthest recesses of his brain, where
his determination had thrust it away, and thanks to the length
of the interval, the three weeks' separation to which he had
agreed, it was with pleasure that he would consider the idea
that he would see Odette again on her return ; but it was also
with so little impatience that he began to ask himself whether
he would not readily consent to the doubling of the period of
so easy an abstinence. It had lasted, so far, but three days, a
much shorter time than he had often, before, passed without
seeing Odette, and without having, as on this occasion he had,
premeditated a separation. And yet, there and then, some tiny
trace of contrariety in his mind, or of weakness in his body,—
by inciting him to regard the present as an exceptional
moment, one not to be governed by the rules, one in which
prudence itself would allow him to take advantage of the
soothing effects of a pleasure and to give his will (until the
time should come when its efforts might serve any purpose)
a holiday—suspended the action of his will, which ceased to
exert its inhibitive control ; or, without that even, the thought
of some information for which he had forgotten to ask Odette,
such as if she had decided in what colour she would have her
carriage repainted, or, with regard to some investment,
whether they were 'ordinary' or 'preference' shares that
she wished him to buy (for it was all very well to shew her
that he could live without seeing her, but if, after that, the
carriage had to be painted over again, if the shares produced no
dividend, a fine lot of good he would have done),—and
suddenly, like a stretched piece of elastic which is let go, or
the air in a pneumatic machine which is ripped open, the idea
of seeing her again, from the remote point in time to which it

had been attached, sprang back into the field of the present and of immediate possibilities.

It sprang back thus without meeting any further resistance, so irresistible, in fact, that Swann had been far less unhappy in watching the end gradually approaching, day by day, of the fortnight which he must spend apart from Odette, than he was when kept waiting for ten minutes while his coachman brought round the carriage which was to take him to her, minutes which he passed in transports of impatience and joy, in which he recaptured a thousand times over, to lavish on it all the wealth of his affection, that idea of his meeting with Odette, which, by so abrupt a repercussion, at a moment when he supposed it so remote, was once more present and on the very surface of his consciousness. The fact was that this idea no longer found, as an obstacle in its course, the desire to contrive without further delay to resist its coming, which had ceased to have any place in Swann's mind since, having proved to himself—or so, at least, he believed—that he was so easily capable of resisting it, he no longer saw any inconvenience in postponing a plan of separation which he was now certain of being able to put into operation whenever he would. Furthermore, this idea of seeing her again came back to him adorned with a novelty, a seductiveness, armed with a virulence, all of which long habit had enfeebled, but which had acquired new vigour during this privation, not of three days but of a fortnight, (for a period of abstinence may be calculated, by anticipation, as having lasted already until the final date assigned to it) and had converted what had been, until then, a pleasure in store, which could easily be sacrificed, into an unlooked-for happiness which he was powerless to resist. Finally, the idea returned to him with its beauty enhanced by his own ignorance of what Odette might have thought, might, perhaps, have done on finding that he shewed no sign of life, with the result that what he was going now to meet was the entrancing revelation of an Odette almost unknown.

But she, just as she had supposed that his refusal to send her money was only a feint, saw nothing but a pretext in the question which he came, now, to ask her, about the repainting of her carriage, or the purchase of stock. For she could not reconstruct the several phases of these crises through which he passed, and in the general idea which she formed of them she made no attempt to understand their mechanism, looking only to what she knew beforehand, their necessary, never-failing and always identical termination. An imperfect idea (though possibly all the more profound in consequence), if one were to judge it from the point of view of Swann, who would doubtless have considered that Odette failed to understand him, just as a morphinomaniac or a consumptive, each persuaded that he has been thrown back, one by some outside event, at the moment when he was just going to shake himself free from his inveterate habit, the other by an accidental indisposition at the moment when he was just going to be finally cured, feels himself to be misunderstood by the doctor who does not attach the same importance to these pretended contingencies, mere disguises, according to him, assumed, so as to be perceptible by his patients, by the vice of one and the morbid state of the other, which in reality have never ceased to weigh heavily and incurably upon them while they were nursing their dreams of normality and health. And, as a matter of fact, Swann's love had reached that stage at which the physician and (in the case of certain affections) the boldest of surgeons ask themselves whether to deprive a patient of his vice or to rid him of his malady is still reasonable, or indeed possible.

Certainly, of the extent of this love Swann had no direct knowledge. When he sought to measure it, it happened sometimes that he found it diminished, shrunken almost to nothing; for instance, the very moderate liking, amounting almost to dislike, which, in the days before he was in love with Odette, he had felt for her expressive features, her faded complexion, returned on certain days. " Really, I am making distinct headway," he would tell himself on the morrow, " when I come to think it over carefully, I find that I got hardly any pleasure, last night, out of being in bed with her ; it's an odd thing, but I actually thought her ugly." And certainly he was sincere, but his love extended a long way beyond the province of physical desire. Odette's person, indeed, no longer held any great place in it. When his eyes fell upon the photograph of Odette on his table, or when she came to see him, he had difficulty in identifying her face, either in the flesh or on the pasteboard, with the painful and continuous anxiety which dwelt in his mind. He would say to himself, almost with astonishment, " It is she ! " as when suddenly some one shews us in a detached, externalised form one of our own maladies, and we find in it no resemblance to what we are suffering. "She ? "—he tried to ask himself what that meant ; for it is something like love, like death (rather than like those vague conceptions of maladies), a thing which one repeatedly calls in question, in order to make oneself probe further into it, in the fear that the question will find no answer, that the substance will escape our grasp—the mystery of personality. And this malady, which was Swann's love, had so far multiplied, was so closely interwoven with all his habits, with all his actions, with his thoughts, his health, his sleep, his life, even with what he hoped for after his death, was so entirely one with him that it would have been im-

possible to wrest it away without almost entirely destroying
him ; as surgeons say, his case was past operation.

By this love Swann had been so far detached from all other
interests that when by chance he reappeared in the world of
fashion, reminding himself that his social relations, like a
beautifully wrought setting (although she would not have been
able to form any very exact estimate of its worth), might, still,
add a little to his own value in Odette's eyes (as indeed they
might have done had they not been cheapened by his love
itself, which for Odette depreciated everything that it touched
by seeming to denounce such things as less precious than itself),
he would feel there, simultaneously with his distress at being
in places and among people that she did not know, the same
detached sense of pleasure as he would have derived from a
novel or a painting in which were depicted the amusements
of a leisured class ; just as, at home, he used to enjoy the
thought of the smooth efficiency of his household, the
smartness of his own wardrobe and of his servants' liveries,
the soundness of his investments, with the same relish as when
he read in Saint-Simon, who was one of his favourite authors,
of the machinery of daily life at Versailles, what Mme. de
Maintenon ate and drank, or the shrewd avarice and great
pomp of Lulli. And in the small extent to which this detachment was not absolute, the reason for this new pleasure which
Swann was tasting was that he could emigrate for a moment
into those few and distant parts of himself which had remained
almost foreign to his love and to his pain. In this respect the
personality, with which my great-aunt endowed him, of
' young Swann', as distinct from the more individual personality of Charles Swann, was that in which he now most
delighted. Once when, because it was the birthday of the
Princesse de Parme (and because she could often be of use,

indirectly, to Odette, by letting her have seats for galas and
jubilees and all that sort of thing), he had decided to send her
a basket of fruit, and was not quite sure where or how to order
it, he had entrusted the task to a cousin of his mother who,
delighted to be doing a commission for him, had written to
him, laying stress on the fact that she had not chosen all the
fruit at the same place, but the grapes from Crapote, whose
speciality they were, the strawberries from Jauret, the
pears from Chevet, who always had the best, and so on,
" every fruit visited and examined, one by one, by myself."
And in the sequel, by the cordiality with which the Princess
thanked him, he had been able to judge of the flavour of the
strawberries and of the ripeness of the pears. But, most of all,
that " every fruit visited and examined, one by one, by
myself " had brought balm to his sufferings by carrying his
mind off to a region which he rarely visited, although it was
his by right, as the heir of a rich and respectable middle-class
family in which had been handed down from generation to
generation the knowledge of the 'right places' and the art of
ordering things from shops.

Of a truth, he had too long forgotten that he was 'young
Swann' not to feel, when he assumed that part again for a
moment, a keener pleasure than he was capable of feeling at
other times—when, indeed, he was grown sick of pleasure ;
and if the friendliness of the middle-class people, for whom he
had never been anything else than 'young Swann', was less
animated than that of the aristocrats (though more flattering,
for all that, since in the middle-class mind friendship is
inseparable from respect), no letter from a Royal Personage,
offering him some princely entertainment, could ever be so
attractive to Swann as the letter which asked him to be a
witness, or merely to be present at a wedding in the family

of some old friends of his parents; some of whom had ' kept
up ' with him, like my grandfather, who, the year before
these events, had invited him to my mother's wedding, while
others barely knew him by sight, but were, they thought,
in duty bound to shew civility to the son, to the worthy suc-
cessor of the late M. Swann.

But, by virtue of his intimacy, already time-honoured, with
so many of them, the people of fashion, in a certain sense, were
also a part of his house, his service, and his family. He felt,
when his mind dwelt upon his brilliant connections, the same
external support, the same solid comfort as when he looked at
the fine estate, the fine silver, the fine table-linen which had
come down to him from his forebears. And the thought that,
if he were seized by a sudden illness and confined to the house,
the people whom his valet would instinctively run to find
would be the Duc de Chartres, the Prince de Reuss, the Duc
de Luxembourg and the Baron de Charlus, brought him the
same consolation as our old Françoise derived from the
knowledge that she would, one day, be buried in her own fine
cloths, marked with her name, not darned at all (or so exquisitely darned that it merely enhanced one's idea of the skill
and patience of the seamstress), a shroud from the constant
image of which in her mind's eye she drew a certain satisfactory sense, if not actually of wealth and prosperity, at any
rate of self-esteem. But most of all,—since in every one of
his actions and thoughts which had reference to Odette,
Swann was constantly subdued and swayed by the unconfessed feeling that he was, perhaps not less dear, but at least
less welcome to her than anyone, even the most wearisome
of the Verdurins' ' faithful,'—when he betook himself to a
world in which he was the paramount example of taste, a
man whom no pains were spared to attract, whom people

were genuinely sorry not to see, he began once again to believe in the existence of a happier life, almost to feel an appetite for it, as an invalid may feel who has been in bed for months and on a strict diet, when he picks up a newspaper and reads the account of an official banquet or the advertisement of a cruise round Sicily.

If he was obliged to make excuses to his fashionable friends for not paying them visits, it was precisely for the visits that he did pay her that he sought to excuse himself to Odette. He still paid them (asking himself at the end of each month whether, seeing that he had perhaps exhausted her patience, and had certainly gone rather often to see her, it would be enough if he sent her four thousand francs), and for each visit he found a pretext, a present that he had to bring her, some information which she required, M. de Charlus, whom he had met actually going to her house, and who had insisted upon Swann's accompanying him. And, failing any excuse, he would beg M. de Charlus to go to her at once, and to tell her, as though spontaneously, in the course of conversation, that he had just remembered something that he had to say to Swann, and would she please send a message to Swann's house asking him to come to her then and there ; but as a rule Swann waited at home in vain, and M. de Charlus informed him, later in the evening, that his device had not proved successful. With the result that, if she was now frequently away from Paris, even when she was there he scarcely saw her ; that she who, when she was in love with him, used to say, " I am always free " and " What can it matter to me, what other people think ? " now, whenever he wanted to see her, appealed to the proprieties or pleaded some engagement. When he spoke of going to a charity entertainment, or a private view, or a first-night at which she was to be present, she would expostulate that he wished to advertise their relations in public, that he was treating her like a woman off the streets. Things came to such a pitch that, in an effort to save himself from being altogether forbidden to meet her anywhere, Swann, remembering that she knew and was deeply attached to my great-uncle Adolphe, whose friend he himself also had been, went one day to see him in his little flat in the Rue de Belle-chasse, to ask him to use his influence with Odette. As it happened, she invariably adopted, when she spoke to Swann about my uncle, a poetical tone, saying : " Ah, he ! He is not in the least like you ; it is an exquisite thing, a great, a beautiful thing, his friendship for me. He's not the sort of man who would have so little consideration for me as to let himself be seen with me everywhere in public." This was embarrassing for Swann, who did not know quite to what rhetorical pitch he should screw himself up in speaking of Odette to my uncle. He began by alluding to her excellence, *a priori*, the axiom of her seraphic super-humanity, the revelation of her inexpressible virtues, no conception of which could possibly be formed. " I should like to speak to you about her," he went on, " you, who know what a woman supreme above all women, what an adorable being, what an angel Odette is. But you know, also, what life is in Paris. Everyone doesn't see Odette in the light in which you and I have been privileged to see her. And so there are people who think that I am behaving rather foolishly ; she won't even allow me to meet her out of doors, at the theatre. Now you, in whom she has such enormous confidence, couldn't you say a few words for me to her, just to assure her that she ex-aggerates the harm which my bowing to her in the street might do her ? "

My uncle advised Swann not to see Odette for some days,

after which she would love him all the more ; he advised
Odette to let Swann meet her everywhere, and as often as he
pleased. A few days later Odette told Swann that she had
just had a rude awakening ; she had discovered that my uncle
was the same as other men ; he had tried to take her by
assault. She calmed Swann, who, at first, was for rushing out
to challenge my uncle to a duel, but he refused to shake hands
with him when they met again. He regretted this rupture
all the more because he had hoped, if he had met my uncle
Adolphe again sometimes and had contrived to talk things
over with him in strict confidence, to be able to get him to
throw a light on certain rumours with regard to the life that
Odette had led, in the old days, at Nice. For my uncle
Adolphe used to spend the winter there, and Swann thought
that it might indeed have been there, perhaps, that he had
first known Odette. The few words which some one had let
fall, in his hearing, about a man who, it appeared, had been
Odette's lover, had left Swann dumbfoundered. But the very
things which he would, before knowing them, have regarded
as the most terrible to learn and the most impossible to
believe, were, once he knew them, incorporated for all time
in the general mass of his sorrow ; he admitted them, he could
no longer have understood their not existing. Only, each one
of them in its passage traced an indelible line, altering the
picture that he had formed of his mistress. At one time indeed
he felt that he could understand that this moral ' lightness,'
of which he would never have suspected Odette, was perfectly well known, and that at Baden or Nice, when she had
gone, in the past, to spend several months in one or the other
place, she had enjoyed a sort of amorous notoriety. He
attempted, in order to question them, to get into touch again
with certain men of that stamp ; but these were aware that

he knew Odette, and, besides, he was afraid of putting the thought of her into their heads, of setting them once more upon her track. But he, to whom, up till then, nothing could have seemed so tedious as was all that pertained to the cosmopolitan life of Baden or of Nice, now that he learned that Odette had, perhaps, led a 'gay' life once in those pleasure-cities, although he could never find out whether it had been solely to satisfy a want of money which, thanks to himself, she no longer felt, or from some capricious instinct which might, at any moment, revive in her, he would lean, in impotent anguish, blinded and dizzy, over the bottomless abyss into which had passed, in which had been engulfed those years of his own, early in MacMahon's *Septennat*, in which one spent the winter on the Promenade des Anglais, the summer beneath the limes of Baden, and would find in those years a sad but splendid profundity, such as a poet might have lent to them ; and he would have devoted to the reconstruction of all the insignificant details that made up the daily round on the Côte d'Azur in those days, if it could have helped him to understand something that still baffled him in the smile or in the eyes of Odette, more enthusiasm than does the aesthete who ransacks the extant documents of fifteenth century Florence, so as to try to penetrate further into the soul of the Primavera, the fair Vanna or the Venus of Botticelli. He would sit, often, without saying a word to her, only gazing at her and dreaming ; and she would comment : " You do look sad ! " It was not very long since, from the idea that she was an excellent creature, comparable to the best women that he had known, he had passed to that of her being 'kept' ; and yet already, by an inverse process, he had returned from the Odette de Crécy, perhaps too well known to the holiday-makers, to the 'ladies' men' of Nice and

Baden, to this face, the expression on which was often so gentle, to this nature so eminently human. He would ask himself : " What does it mean, after all, to say that everyone at Nice knows who Odette de Crécy is ? Reputations of that sort, even when they're true, are always based upon other people's ideas"; he would reflect that this legend—even if it were authentic—was something external to Odette, was not inherent in her like a mischievous and ineradicable personality ; that the creature who might have been led astray was a woman with frank eyes, a heart full of pity for the sufferings of others, a docile body which he had pressed tightly in his arms and explored with his fingers, a woman of whom he might one day come into absolute possession if he succeeded in making himself indispensable to her. There she was, often tired, her face left blank for the nonce by that eager, feverish preoccupation with the unknown things which made Swann suffer ; she would push back her hair with both hands ; her forehead, her whole face would seem to grow larger ; then, suddenly, some ordinary human thought, some worthy sentiment such as are to be found in all creatures when, in a moment of rest or meditation, they are free to express themselves, would flash out from her eyes like a ray of gold. And immediately the whole of her face would light up like a grey landscape, swathed in clouds which, suddenly, are swept away and the dull scene transfigured, at the moment of the sun's setting. The life which occupied Odette at such times, even the future which she seemed to be dreamily regarding, Swann could have shared with her. No evil disturbance seemed to have left any effect on them. Rare as they became, those moments did not occur in vain. By the process of memory, Swann joined the fragments together, abolished the intervals between them, cast, as in molten gold, the image of

an Odette compact of kindness and tranquillity, for whom he
was to make, later on (as we shall see in the second part of this
story) sacrifices which the other Odette would never have
won from him. But how rare those moments were, and how
seldom he now saw her ! Even in regard to their evening
meetings, she would never tell him until the last minute
whether she would be able to see him, for, reckoning on his
being always free, she wished first to be certain that no one
else would offer to come to her. She would plead that she
was obliged to wait for an answer which was of the very
greatest importance, and if, even after she had made Swann
come to her house, any of her friends asked her, half-way
through the evening, to join them at some theatre, or at
supper afterwards, she would jump for joy and dress herself
with all speed. As her toilet progressed, every movement that
she made brought Swann nearer to the moment when he
would have to part from her, when she would fly off with
irresistible force ; and when at length she was ready, and,
plunging into her mirror a last glance strained and brightened
by her anxiety to look well, smeared a little salve on her lips,
fixed a stray lock of hair over her brow, and called for her
cloak of sky-blue silk with golden tassels, Swann would be
looking so wretched that she would be unable to restrain a
gesture of impatience as she flung at him : " So that is how
you thank me for keeping you here till the last minute ! And
I thought I was being so nice to you. Well, I shall know
better another time ! " Sometimes, at the risk of annoying
her, he made up his mind that he would find out where she
had gone, and even dreamed of a defensive alliance with
Forcheville, who might perhaps have been able to tell him.
But anyhow, when he knew with whom she was spending the
evening, it was very seldom that he could not discover, among

all his innumerable acquaintance, some one who knew—if only indirectly—the man with whom she had gone out, and could easily obtain this or that piece of information about him. And while he was writing to one of his friends, asking him to try to get a little light thrown upon some point or other, he would feel a sense of relief on ceasing to vex himself with questions to which there was no answer and transferring to some one else the strain of interrogation. It is true that Swann was little the wiser for such information as he did receive. To know a thing does not enable us, always, to prevent its happening, but after all the things that we know we do hold, if not in our hands, at any rate in our minds, where we can dispose of them as we choose, which gives us the illusion of a sort of power to control them. He was quite happy whenever M. de Charlus was with Odette. He knew that between M. de Charlus and her nothing untoward could ever happen, that when M. de Charlus went anywhere with her, it was out of friendship for himself, and that he would make no difficulty about telling him everything that she had done. Sometimes she had declared so emphatically to Swann that it was impossible for him to see her on a particular evening, she seemed to be looking forward so keenly to some outing, that Swann attached a very real importance to the fact that M. de Charlus was free to accompany her. Next day, without daring to put many questions to M. de Charlus, he would force him, by appearing not quite to understand his first answers, to give him more, after each of which he would feel himself increasingly relieved, for he very soon learned that Odette had spent her evening in the most innocent of dissipations.

" But what do you mean, my dear Mémé, I don't quite understand   You didn't go straight from her house to the Musée Grévin? Surely you went somewhere else first? No? That is very odd! You don't know how amusing you are, my dear Mémé. But what an odd idea of hers to go on to the Chat Noir afterwards; it was her idea, I suppose? No? Yours? That's strange. After all, it wasn't a bad idea; she must have known dozens of people there? No? She never spoke to a soul? How extraordinary! Then you sat there like that, just you and she, all by yourselves? I can picture you, sitting there! You are a worthy fellow, my dear Mémé; I'm exceedingly fond of you."

Swann was now quite at ease. To him, who had so often happened, when talking to friends who knew nothing of his love, friends to whom he hardly listened, to hear certain detached sentences (as, for instance, "I saw Mme. de Crécy yesterday; she was with a man I didn't know."), sentences which dropped into his heart and passed at once into a solid state, grew hard as stalagmites, and seared and tore him as they lay there irremovable,—how charming, by way of contrast, were the words: "She didn't know a soul; she never spoke to a soul." How freely they coursed through him, how fluid they were, how vaporous, how easy to breathe! And yet, a moment later, he was telling himself that Odette must find him very dull if those were the pleasures that she preferred to his company. And their very insignificance, though it reassured him, pained him as if her enjoyment of them had been an act of treachery.

Even when he could not discover where she had gone, it would have sufficed to alleviate the anguish that he then felt, for which Odette's presence, the charm of her company, was the sole specific (a specific which in the long run served, like many other remedies, to aggravate the disease, but at least brought temporary relief to his sufferings), it would have sufficed, had Odette only permitted him to remain in her house while she was out, to wait there until that hour of her return, into whose stillness and peace would flow, to be mingled and lost there, all memory of those intervening hours which some sorcery, some cursed spell had made him imagine as, somehow, different from the rest. But she would not ; he must return home ; he forced himself, on the way, to form various plans, ceased to think of Odette ; he even reached the stage, while he undressed, of turning over all sorts of happy ideas in his mind ; it was with a light heart, buoyed with the anticipation of going to see some favourite work of art on the morrow, that he jumped into bed and turned out the light ; but no sooner had he made himself ready to sleep, relaxing a self-control of which he was not even conscious, so habitual had it become, than an icy shudder convulsed his body and he burst into sobs. He did not wish to know why, but dried his eyes, saying with a smile : " This is delightful ; I'm becoming neurasthenic." After which he could not save himself from utter exhaustion at the thought that, next day, he must begin afresh his attempt to find out what Odette had been doing, must use all his influence to contrive to see her. This compulsion to an activity without respite, without variety, without result, was so cruel a scourge that one day, noticing a swelling over his stomach, he felt an actual joy in the idea that he had, perhaps, a tumour which would prove fatal, that he need not concern himself with anything further, that it was his malady which was going to govern his life, to make a plaything of him, until the not-distant end. If indeed, at this period, it often happened that, though without admitting it even to himself, he longed for death, it was in order to escape not so much from the keenness of his sufferings as from the monotony of his struggle.

And yet he would have wished to live until the time came when he no longer loved her, when she would have no reason for lying to him, when at length he might learn from her whether, on the day when he had gone to see her in the afternoon, she had or had not been in the arms of Forcheville. Often for several days on end the suspicion that she was in love with some one else would distract his mind from the question of Forcheville, making it almost immaterial to him, like those new developments of a continuous state of ill-health which seem for a little time to have delivered us from their predecessors. There were even days when he was not tormented by any suspicion. He fancied that he was cured. But next morning, when he awoke, he felt in the same place the same pain, a sensation which, the day before, he had, as it were, diluted in the torrent of different impressions. But it had not stirred from its place. Indeed, it was the sharpness of this pain that had awakened him.

Since Odette never gave him any information as to those vastly important matters which took up so much of her time every day (albeit he had lived long enough in the world to know that such matters are never anything else than pleasures) he could not sustain for any length of time the effort to imagine them ; his brain would become a void ; then he would pass a finger over his tired eyelids, in the same way as he might have wiped his eyeglass, and would cease altogether to think. There emerged, however, from this unexplored tract, certain occupations which reappeared from time to time, vaguely connected by Odette with some obligation towards distant relatives or old friends who, inasmuch as they were the only people whom she was in the habit of mentioning as preventing her from seeing him, seemed to Swann to compose the necessary, unalterable setting of her life. Because of the tone in which she referred, from time to time, to " the day when I go with my friend to the Hippodrome," if, when he felt unwell and had thought, " Perhaps Odette would be kind and come to see me," he remembered, suddenly, that it was one of those very days, he would correct himself with an " Oh, no ! It's not worth while asking her to come ; I should have thought of it before, this is the day when she goes with her friend to the Hippodrome. We must confine ourselves to what is possible ; no use wasting our time in proposing things that can't be accepted and are declined in advance." And this duty that was incumbent upon Odette, of going to the Hippodrome, to which Swann thus gave way, seemed to him to be not merely ineluctable in itself ; but the mark of necessity which stamped it seemed to make plausible and legitimate everything that was even remotely connected with it. If, when Odette, in the street, had acknowledged the salute of a passer-by, which had aroused Swann's jealousy, she replied to his questions by associating the stranger with any of the two or three paramount duties of which she had often spoken to him ; if, for instance, she said : " That's a gentleman who was in my friend's box the other day ; the one I go to the Hippodrome with," that explanation would set Swann's suspicions at rest ; it was, after all, inevitable that this friend should have other guests than Odette in her box at the Hippodrome, but he had never sought to form or succeeded in forming any coherent impression of them. Oh ! how he would have loved to know her, that friend who went to the Hippodrome, how he would have loved her to invite him there with Odette. How readily he would have sacrificed all his acquaintance for no matter what person who was in the habit of seeing Odette, were she but a manicurist or a girl out of a shop. He would have taken more trouble, incurred more expense for them than for queens. Would they not have supplied him, out of what was contained in their knowledge of the life of Odette, with the one potent anodyne for his pain ? With what joy would he have hastened to spend his days with one or other of those humble folk with whom Odette kept up friendly relations, either with some ulterior motive or from genuine simplicity of nature. How willingly would he have fixed his abode for ever in the attics of some sordid but enviable house, where Odette went but never took him, and where, if he had lived with the little retired dress-maker, whose lover he would readily have pretended to be, he would have been visited by Odette almost daily. In those regions, that were almost slums, what a modest existence, abject, if you please, but delightful, nourished by tran-quillity and happiness, he would have consented to lead indefinitely.

It sometimes happened, again, that, when, after meeting Swann, she saw some man approaching whom he did not know, he could distinguish upon Odette's face that look of sorrow which she had worn on the day when he had come to her while Forcheville was there. But this was rare ; for, on the days when, in spite of all that she had to do, and of her dread of what people would think, she did actually manage to see Swann, the predominant quality in her attitude, now, was self-assurance ; a striking contrast, perhaps an unconscious revenge for, perhaps a natural reaction from the timorous emotion which, in the early days of their friendship, she had felt in his presence, and even in his absence, when she began a letter to him with the words : " My dear, my hand trembles so that I can scarcely write." (So, at least, she pre-tended, and a little of that emotion must have been sincere, or she would not have been anxious to enlarge and emphasise it.) So Swann had been pleasing to her then. Our hands do not tremble except for ourselves, or for those whom we love. When they have ceased to control our happiness how peaceful, how easy, how bold do we become in their presence ! In speaking to him, in writing to him now, she no longer employed those words by which she had sought to give herself the illusion that he belonged to her, creating opportunities for saying " my " and " mine " when she referred to him : " You are all that I have in the world ; it is the perfume of our friendship, I shall keep it," nor spoke to him of the future, of death itself, as of a single adventure which they would have to share. In those early days, whatever he might say to her, she would answer admiringly : " You know, you will never be like other people ! "—she would gaze at his long, slightly bald head, of which people who knew only of his successes used to think : " He's not regularly good-looking, if you like, but he is smart ; that tuft, that eyeglass, that smile ! " and, with more curiosity perhaps to know him as he really was than desire to become his mistress, she would sigh :

" I do wish I could find out what there is in that head of yours ! "

But now, whatever he might say, she would answer, in a tone sometimes of irritation, sometimes indulgent : " Ah ! so you never will be like other people ! "

She would gaze at his head, which was hardly aged at all by his recent anxieties (though people now thought of it, by the same mental process which enables one to discover the meaning of a piece of symphonic music of which one has read the programme, or the ' likenesses ' in a child whose family one has known : " He's not positively ugly, if you like, but he is really rather absurd ; that eyeglass, that tuft, that smile ! " realising in their imagination, fed by suggestion, the invisible boundary which divides, at a few months' interval, the head of an ardent lover from a cuckold's), and would say :

" Oh, I do wish I could change you ; put some sense into that head of yours."

Always ready to believe in the truth of what he hoped, if it was only Odette's way of behaving to him that left room for doubt, he would fling himself greedily upon her words : " You can if you like," he would tell her.

And he tried to explain to her that to comfort him, to control him, to make him work would be a noble task, to which numbers of other women asked for nothing better than to be allowed to devote themselves, though it is only fair to add that in those other women's hands the noble task would have seemed to Swann nothing more than an indiscreet and intolerable usurpation of his freedom of action. " If she didn't love me, just a little," he told himself, "she would not wish to have me altered. To alter me, she will have to see me more often." And so he was able to trace, in these faults which she found in him, a proof at least of her interest, perhaps even of her love ; and, in fact, she gave him so little, now, of the last, that he was obliged to regard as proofs of her interest in him the various things which, every now and then, she forbade him to do. One day she announced that she did not care for his coachman, who, she thought, was perhaps setting Swann against her, and, anyhow, did not shew that promptness and deference to Swann's orders which she would have liked to see. She felt that he wanted to hear her say : " Don't have him again when you come to me," just as he might have wanted her to kiss him. So, being in a good temper, she said it ; and he was deeply moved. That evening, when talking to M. de Charlus, with whom he had the satisfaction of being able to speak of her openly (for the most trivial remarks that he uttered now, even to people who had never heard of her, had always some sort of reference to Odette), he said to him :

" I believe, all the same, that she loves me ; she is so nice to me now, and she certainly takes an interest in what I do."

And if, when he was starting off for her house, getting into his carriage with a friend whom he was to drop somewhere on the way, his friend said : "Hullo ! that isn't Loredan on the box ? " with what melancholy joy would Swann answer him :

"Oh ! Good heavens, no ! I can tell you, I daren't take Loredan when I go to the Rue La Pérouse ; Odette doesn't like me to have Loredan, she thinks he doesn't suit me. What on earth is one to do ? Women, you know, women. My dear fellow, she would be furious. Oh, lord, yes ; I've only to take Rémi there ; I should never hear the last of it ! "

These new manners, indifferent, listless, irritable, which Odette now adopted with Swann, undoubtedly made him suffer ; but he did not realise how much he suffered ; since it had been with a regular progression, day after day, that Odette had chilled towards him, it was only by directly contrasting what she was to-day with what she had been at first that he could have measured the extent of the change that had taken place. Now this change was his deep, his secret wound, which pained him day and night, and whenever he felt that his thoughts were straying too near it, he would quickly turn them into another channel for fear of being made to suffer too keenly. He might say to himself in a vague way: " There was a time when Odette loved me more," but he never formed any definite picture of that time. Just as he had in his study a cupboard at which he contrived never to look, which he turned aside to avoid passing whenever he entered or left the room, because in one of its drawers he had locked away the chrysanthemum which she had given him on one of those first evenings when he had taken her home in his carriage, and the letters in which she said : " Why did you not forget your heart also ? I should never have let you have that back," and " At whatever hour of the day or night you may need me, just send me a word, and dispose of me as you please," so there was a place in his heart to which he would never allow his thoughts to trespass too near, forcing them, if need be, to evade it by a long course of reasoning so that they should not have to pass within reach of it ; the place in which lingered his memories of happy days.

But his so meticulous prudence was defeated one evening when he had gone out to a party.

It was at the Marquise de Saint-Euverte's, on the last, for that season, of the evenings on which she invited people to listen to the musicians who would serve, later on, for her charity concerts. Swann, who had intended to go to each of the previous evenings in turn, but had never been able to make up his mind, received, while he was dressing for this party, a visit from the Baron de Charlus, who came with an offer to go with him to the Marquise's, if his company could be of any use in helping Swann not to feel quite so bored when he got there, to be a little less unhappy. But Swann had thanked him with :

" You can't conceive how glad I should be of your company. But the greatest pleasure that you can give me will be if you will go instead to see Odette. You know what a splendid influence you have over her. I don't suppose she'll be going anywhere this evening, unless she goes to see her old dressmaker, and I'm sure she would be delighted if you went with her there. In any case, you'll find her at home before then. Try to keep her amused, and also to give her a little sound advice. If you could arrange something for to-morrow which would please her, something that we could all three do together. Try to put out a feeler, too, for the summer ; see if there's anything she wants to do, a cruise that we might all three take ; anything you can think of. I don't count upon seeing her to-night, myself ; still if she would like me to come, or if you find a loophole, you've only to send me a line at Mme. de Saint-Euverte's up till midnight ; after that I shall be here. Ever so many thanks for all you are doing for me—you know what I feel about you ! "

His friend promised to go and do as Swann wished as soon as he had deposited him at the door of the Saint-Euverte house, where he arrived soothed by the thought that M. de Charlus would be spending the evening in the Rue La Pérouse, but in a state of melancholy indifference to everything that did not involve Odette, and in particular to the details of fashionable life, a state which invested them with the charm that is to be found in anything which, being no longer an object of our desire, appears to us in its own guise. On alighting from his carriage, in the foreground of that fictitious summary of their domestic existence which hostesses are pleased to offer to their guests on ceremonial occasions, and in which they shew a great regard for accuracy of costume and setting, Swann was amused to discover the heirs and successors of Balzac's ' tigers '—now ' grooms '—who normally followed their mistress when she walked abroad, but now, hatted and booted, were posted out of doors, in front of the house on the

gravelled drive, or outside the stables, as gardeners might
be drawn up for inspection at the ends of their several flower-
beds. The peculiar tendency which he had always had to
look for analogies between living people and the portraits in
galleries reasserted itself here, but in a more positive and more
general form ; it was society as a whole, now that he was
detached from it, which presented itself to him in a series of
pictures. In the cloak-room, into which, in the old days,
when he was still a man of fashion, he would have gone in his
overcoat, to emerge from it in evening dress, but without
any impression of what had occurred there, his mind having
been, during the minute or two that he had spent in it, either
still at the party which he had just left, or already at the party
into which he was just about to be ushered, he now noticed,
for the first time, roused by the unexpected arrival of so
belated a guest, the scattered pack of splendid effortless
animals, the enormous footmen who were drowsing here
and there upon benches and chests, until, pointing their noble
greyhound profiles, they towered upon their feet and gathered
in a circle round about him.

One of them, of a particularly ferocious aspect, and not
unlike the headsman in certain Renaissance pictures which
represent executions, tortures, and the like, advanced upon
him with an implacable air to take his ' things.' But the
harshness of his steely glare was compensated by the softness
of his cotton gloves, so effectively that, as he approached
Swann, he seemed to be exhibiting at once an utter contempt
for his person and the most tender regard for his hat. He
took it with a care to which the precision of his movements
imparted something that was almost over-fastidious, and with
a delicacy that was rendered almost touching by the evidence
of his splendid strength. Then he passed it to one of his

satellites, a novice and timid, who was expressing the panic that overpowered him by casting furious glances in every direction, and displayed all the dumb agitation of a wild animal in the first hours of its captivity.

A few feet away, a strapping great lad in livery stood musing, motionless, statuesque, useless, like that purely decorative warrior whom one sees in the most tumultuous of Mantegna's paintings, lost in dreams, leaning upon his shield, while all around him are fighting and bloodshed and death ; detached from the group of his companions who were thronging about Swann, he seemed as determined to remain unconcerned in the scene, which he followed vaguely with his cruel, greenish eyes, as if it had been the Massacre of the Innocents or the Martyrdom of Saint James. He seemed precisely to have sprung from that vanished race—if, indeed, it ever existed, save in the reredos of San Zeno and the frescoes of the Eremitani, where Swann had come in contact with it, and where it still dreams—fruit of the impregnation of a classical statue by some one of the Master's Paduan models, or of Albert Durer's Saxons. And the locks of his reddish hair, crinkled by nature, but glued to his head by brilliantine, were treated broadly as they are in that Greek sculpture which the Mantuan painter never ceased to study, and which, if in its creator's purpose it represents but man, manages at least to extract from man's simple outlines such a variety of richness, borrowed, as it were, from the whole of animated nature, that a head of hair, by the glossy undulation and beak-like points of its curls, or in the overlaying of the florid triple diadem of its brushed tresses, can suggest at once a bunch of seaweed, a brood of fledgling doves, a bed of hyacinths and a serpent's writhing back. Others again, no less colossal, were disposed upon the steps of a monumental staircase which, by

their decorative presence and marmorean immobility, was
made worthy to be named, like that god-crowned ascent in
the Palace of the Doges, the 'Staircase of the Giants,' and
on which Swann now set foot, saddened by the thought that
Odette had never climbed it. Ah, with what joy would he,
on the other hand, have raced up the dark, evil-smelling,
breakneck flights to the little dressmaker's, in whose attic he
would so gladly have paid the price of a weekly stage-box at
the Opera for the right to spend the evening there when
Odette came, and other days too, for the privilege of talking
about her, of living among people whom she was in the habit
of seeing when he was not there, and who, on that account,
seemed to keep secret among themselves some part of the
life of his mistress more real, more inaccessible and more
mysterious than anything that he knew. Whereas upon that
pestilential, enviable staircase to the old dressmaker's, since
there was no other, no service stair in the building, one saw
in the evening outside every door an empty, unwashed milk-
can set out, in readiness for the morning round, upon the
door-mat ; on the despicable, enormous staircase which
Swann was at that moment climbing, on either side of him,
at different levels, before each anfractuosity made in its walls
by the window of the porter's lodge or the entrance to a set
of rooms, representing the departments of indoor service
which they controlled, and doing homage for them to the
guests, a gate-keeper, a major-domo, a steward (worthy men
who spent the rest of the week in semi-independence in their
own domains, dined there by themselves like small shop-
keepers, and might to-morrow lapse to the plebeian service
of some successful doctor or industrial magnate), scrupulous
in carrying out to the letter all the instructions that had been
heaped upon them before they were allowed to don the

brilliant livery which they wore only at long intervals, and in which they did not feel altogether at their ease, stood each in the arcade of his doorway, their splendid pomp tempered by a democratic good-fellowship, like saints in their niches, and a gigantic usher, dressed Swiss Guard fashion, like the beadle in a church, struck the pavement with his staff as each fresh arrival passed him. Coming to the top of the staircase, up which he had been followed by a servant with a pallid countenance and a small pigtail clubbed at the back of his head, like one of Goya's sacristans or a tabellion in an old play, Swann passed by an office in which the lackeys, seated like notaries before their massive registers, rose solemnly to their feet and inscribed his name. He next crossed a little hall which—just as certain rooms are arranged by their owners to serve as the setting for a single work of art (from which they take their name), and, in their studied bareness, contain nothing else besides—displayed to him as he entered it, like some priceless effigy by Benvenuto Cellini of an armed watchman, a young footman, his body slightly bent forward, rearing above his crimson gorget an even more crimson face, from which seemed to burst forth torrents of fire, timidity and zeal, who, as he pierced the Aubusson tapestries that screened the door of the room in which the music was being given with his impetuous, vigilant, desperate gaze, appeared, with a soldierly impassibility or a supernatural faith—an allegory of alarums, incarnation of alertness, commemoration of a riot—to be looking out, angel or sentinel, from the tower of dungeon or cathedral, for the approach of the enemy or for the hour of Judgment. Swann had now only to enter the concert-room, the doors of which were thrown open to him by an usher loaded with chains, who bowed low before him as though tendering to him the keys of a conquered city.

But he thought of the house in which at that very moment he might have been, if Odette had but permitted, and the remembered glimpse of an empty milk-can upon a door-mat wrung his heart.

He speedily recovered his sense of the general ugliness of the human male when, on the other side of the tapestry curtain, the spectacle of the servants gave place to that of the guests. But even this ugliness of faces, which of course were mostly familiar to him, seemed something new and uncanny, now that their features,—instead of being to him symbols of practical utility in the identification of this or that man, who until then had represented merely so many pleasures to be sought-after, boredoms to be avoided, or courtesies to be acknowledged—were at rest, measurable by aesthetic co-ordinates alone, in the autonomy of their curves and angles. And in these men, in the thick of whom Swann now found himself packed, there was nothing (even to the monocle which many of them wore, and which, previously, would, at the most, have enabled Swann to say that so-and-so wore a monocle) which, no longer restricted to the general connotation of a habit, the same in all of them, did not now strike him with a sense of individuality in each. Perhaps because he did not regard General de Froberville and the Marquis de Bréauté, who were talking together just inside the door, as anything more than two figures in a picture, whereas they were the old and useful friends who had put him up for the Jockey Club and had supported him in duels, the General's monocle, stuck like a shell-splinter in his common, scarred, victorious, overbearing face, in the middle of a forehead which it left half-blinded, like the single-eyed flashing front of the Cyclops, appeared to Swann as a monstrous wound which it might have been glorious to receive but which it was certainly not decent to expose, while that which M. de Bréauté wore, as a festive badge, with his pearl-grey gloves, his crush hat and white tie, substituting it for the familiar pair of glasses (as Swann himself did) when he went out to places, bore, glued to its other side, like a specimen prepared on a slide for the microscope, an infinitesimal gaze that swarmed with friendly feeling and never ceased to twinkle at the loftiness of ceilings, the delightfulness of parties, the interestingness of programmes and the excellence of refreshments.

"Hallo! you here! why, it's ages since I've seen you," the General greeted Swann and, noticing the look of strain on his face and concluding that it was perhaps a serious illness that had kept him away, went on, "You're looking well, old man!" while M. de Bréauté turned with, "My dear fellow, what on earth are you doing here?" to a 'society novelist' who had just fitted into the angle of eyebrow and cheek his own monocle, the sole instrument that he used in his psychological investigations and remorseless analyses of character, and who now replied, with an air of mystery and importance, rolling the 'r' :—"I am observing!"

The Marquis de Forestelle's monocle was minute and rimless, and, by enforcing an incessant and painful contraction of the eye over which it was incrusted like a superfluous cartilage, the presence of which there was inexplicable and its substance unimaginable, it gave to his face a melancholy refinement, and led women to suppose him capable of suffering terribly when in love. But that of M. de Saint-Candé, girdled, like Saturn, with an enormous ring, was the centre of gravity of a face which composed itself afresh every moment in relation to the glass, while his thrusting red nose and swollen sarcastic lips endeavoured by their grimaces to rise to the level of the steady flame of wit that sparkled in the polished disk, and saw itself preferred to the most ravishing eyes in the world by the smart, depraved young women whom it set dreaming of artificial charms and a refinement of sensual bliss ; and then, behind him, M. de Palancy, who with his huge carp's head and goggling eyes moved slowly up and down the stream of festive gatherings, unlocking his great mandibles at every moment as though in search of his orientation, had the air of carrying about upon his person only an accidental and perhaps purely symbolical fragment of the glass wall of his aquarium, a part intended to suggest the whole which recalled to Swann, a fervent admirer of Giotto's Vices and Virtues at Padua, that Injustice by whose side a leafy bough evokes the idea of the forests that enshroud his secret lair.

Swann had gone forward into the room, under pressure from Mme. de Saint-Euverte and in order to listen to an aria from *Orfeo* which was being rendered on the flute, and had taken up a position in a corner from which, unfortunately, his horizon was bounded by two ladies of ' uncertain ' age, seated side by side, the Marquise de Cambremer and the Vicomtesse de Franquetot, who, because they were cousins, used to spend their time at parties in wandering through the rooms, each clutching her bag and followed by her daughter, hunting for one another like people at a railway station, and could never be at rest until they had reserved, by marking them with their fans or handkerchiefs, two adjacent chairs ; Mme. de Cambremer, since she knew scarcely anyone, being all the more glad of a companion, while Mme. de Franquetot, who, on the contrary, was extremely popular, thought it effective and original to shew all her fine friends that she preferred to their company that of an obscure country cousin with whom she had childish memories in common. Filled with

ironical melancholy, Swann watched them as they listened to
the pianoforte intermezzo (Liszt's 'Saint Francis preaching
to the birds') which came after the flute, and followed the
virtuoso in his dizzy flight ; Mme. de Franquetot anxiously,
her eyes starting from her head, as though the keys over which
his fingers skipped with such agility were a series of trapezes,
from any one of which he might come crashing, a hundred
feet, to the ground, stealing now and then a glance of astonishment and unbelief at her companion, as who should say :
" It isn't possible, I would never have believed that a human
being could do all that!"; Mme. de Cambremer, as a woman
who had received a sound musical education, beating time
with her head—transformed for the nonce into the pendulum
of a metronome, the sweep and rapidity of whose movements
from one shoulder to the other (performed with that look of
wild abandonment in her eye which a sufferer shews who is
no longer able to analyse his pain, nor anxious to master it,
and says merely " I can't help it ") so increased that at every
moment her diamond earrings caught in the trimming of her
bodice, and she was obliged to put straight the bunch of black
grapes which she had in her hair, though without any interruption of her constantly accelerated motion. On the
other side (and a little way in front) of Mme. de Franquetot,
was the Marquise de Gallardon, absorbed in her favourite
meditation, namely upon her own kinship with the Guermantes family, from which she derived both publicly and in
private a good deal of glory not unmingled with shame, the
most brilliant ornaments of that house remaining somewhat
aloof from her, perhaps because she was just a tiresome old
woman, or because she was a scandalous old woman, or
because she came of an inferior branch of the family, or very
possibly for no reason at all. When she found herself seated

next to some one whom she did not know, as she was at this moment next to Mme. de Franquetot, she suffered acutely from the feeling that her own consciousness of her Guermantes connection could not be made externally manifest in visible characters, like those which, in the mosaics in Byzantine churches, placed one beneath another, inscribe in a vertical column by the side of some Sacred Personage the words which he is supposed to be uttering. At this moment she was pondering the fact that she had never received an invitation, or even a call, from her young cousin the Princesse des Laumes, during the six years that had already elapsed since the latter's marriage. The thought filled her with anger—and with pride ; for, by virtue of having told everyone who expressed surprise at never seeing her at Mme. des Laumes's, that it was because of the risk of meeting the Princesse Mathilde there—a degradation which her own family, the truest and bluest of Legitimists, would never have forgiven her, she had come gradually to believe that this actually was the reason for her not visiting her young cousin. She remembered, it is true, that she had several times inquired of Mme. des Laumes how they might contrive to meet, but she remembered it only in a confused way, and besides did more than neutralise this slightly humiliating reminiscence by murmuring, " After all, it isn't for me to take the first step ; I am at least twenty years older than she is." And fortified by these unspoken words she flung her shoulders proudly back until they seemed to part company with her bust, while her head, which lay almost horizontally upon them, made one think of the ' stuck-on ' head of a pheasant which is brought to the table regally adorned with its feathers. Not that she in the least degree resembled a pheasant, having been endowed by nature with a short and

squat and masculine figure ; but successive mortifications
had given her a backward tilt, such as one may observe in
trees which have taken root on the very edge of a precipice
and are forced to grow backwards to preserve their balance.
Since she was obliged, in order to console herself for not being
quite on a level with the rest of the Guermantes, to repeat to
herself incessantly that it was owing to the uncompromising
rigidity of her principles and pride that she saw so little of
them, the constant iteration had gradually remoulded her
body, and had given her a sort of 'bearing' which was
accepted by the plebeian as a sign of breeding, and even
kindled, at times, a momentary spark in the jaded eyes of
old gentlemen in clubs. Had anyone subjected Mme. de
Gallardon's conversation to that form of analysis which by
noting the relative frequency of its several terms would
furnish him with the key to a ciphered message, he would
at once have remarked that no expression, not even the
commonest forms of speech, occurred in it nearly so often
as "at my cousins the Guermantes'," "at my aunt Guermantes's," "Elzéar de Guermantes's health," "my cousin
Guermantes's box." If anyone spoke to her of a distinguished
personage, she would reply that, although she was not
personally acquainted with him, she had seen him hundreds
of times at her aunt Guermantes's, but she would utter this
reply in so icy a tone, with such a hollow sound, that it was
at once quite clear that if she did not know the celebrity
personally that was because of all the obstinate, ineradicable
principles against which her arching shoulders were stretched
back to rest, as on one of those ladders on which gymnastic
instructors make us 'extend' so as to develop the expansion
of our chests.

At this moment the Princesse des Laumes, who had not

been expected to appear at Mme. de Saint-Euverte's that evening, did in fact arrive. To shew that she did not wish any special attention, in a house to which she had come by an act of condescension, to be paid to her superior rank, she had entered the room with her arms pressed close to her sides, even when there was no crowd to be squeezed through, no one attempting to get past her; staying purposely at the back, with the air of being in her proper place, like a king who stands in the waiting procession at the doors of a theatre where the management have not been warned of his coming; and strictly limiting her field of vision—so as not to seem to be advertising her presence and claiming the consideration that was her due—to the study of a pattern in the carpet or of her own skirt, she stood there on the spot which had struck her as the most modest (and from which, as she very well knew, a cry of rapture from Mme. de Saint-Euverte would extricate her as soon as her presence there was noticed), next to Mme. de Cambremer, whom, however, she did not know. She observed the dumb-show by which her neighbour was expressing her passion for music, but she refrained from copying it. This was not to say that, for once that she had consented to spend a few minutes in Mme. de Saint-Euverte's house, the Princesse des Laumes would not have wished (so that the act of politeness to her hostess which she had performed by coming might, so to speak, ' count double ') to shew herself as friendly and obliging as possible. But she had a natural horror of what she called ' exaggerating,' and always made a point of letting people see that she ' simply must not ' indulge in any display of emotion that was not in keeping with the tone of the circle in which she moved, although such displays never failed to make an impression upon her, by virtue of that spirit of imitation, akin to timidity, which is

developed in the most self-confident persons, by contact with
an unfamiliar environment, even though it be inferior to their
own. She began to ask herself whether these gesticulations
might not, perhaps, be a necessary concomitant of the piece
of music that was being played, a piece which, it might be,
was in a different category from all the music that she had
ever heard before ; and whether to abstain from them was not
a sign of her own inability to understand the music, and of
discourtesy towards the lady of the house ; with the result
that, in order to express by a compromise both of her con-
tradictory inclinations in turn, at one moment she would
merely straighten her shoulder-straps or feel in her golden
hair for the little balls of coral or of pink enamel, frosted with
tiny diamonds, which formed its simple but effective ornament, studying, with a cold interest, her impassioned
neighbour, while at another she would beat time for a few
bars with her fan, but, so as not to forfeit her independence,
she would beat a different time from the pianist's. When he
had finished the Liszt Intermezzo and had begun a Prelude
by Chopin, Mme. de Cambremer turned to Mme. de
Franquetot with a tender smile, full of intimate reminiscence,
as well as of satisfaction (that of a competent judge) with the
performance. She had been taught in her girlhood to fondle
and cherish those long-necked, sinuous creatures, the phrases
of Chopin, so free, so flexible, so tactile, which begin by seeking their ultimate resting-place somewhere beyond and far
wide of the direction in which they started, the point which
one might have expected them to reach, phrases which divert
themselves in those fantastic bypaths only to return more
deliberately—with a more premeditated reaction, with more
precision, as on a crystal bowl which, if you strike it, will ring and
throb until you cry aloud in anguish—to clutch at one's heart.

Brought up in a provincial household with few friends or visitors, hardly ever invited to a ball, she had fuddled her mind, in the solitude of her old manor-house, over setting the pace, now crawling-slow, now passionate, whirling, breathless, for all those imaginary waltzing couples, gathering them like flowers, leaving the ball-room for a moment to listen, where the wind sighed among the pine-trees, on the shore of the lake, and seeing him of a sudden advancing towards her, more different from anything one had ever dreamed of than earthly lovers are, a slender young man, whose voice was resonant and strange and false, in white gloves. But nowadays the old-fashioned beauty of this music seemed to have become a trifle stale. Having forfeited, some years back, the esteem of ' really musical ' people, it had lost its distinction and its charm, and even those whose taste was frankly bad had ceased to find in it more than a moderate pleasure to which they hardly liked to confess. Mme. de Cambremer cast a furtive glance behind her. She knew that her young daughter-in-law (full of respect for her new and noble family, except in such matters as related to the intellect, upon which, having ' got as far ' as Harmony and the Greek alphabet, she was specially enlightened) despised Chopin, and felt quite ill when she heard him played. But finding herself free from the scrutiny of this Wagnerian, who was sitting, at some distance, in a group of her own contemporaries, Mme. de Cambremer let herself drift upon a stream of exquisite memories and sensations. The Princesse des Laumes was touched also. Though without any natural gift for music, she had received, some fifteen years earlier, the instruction which a music-mistress of the Faubourg Saint-Germain, a woman of genius who had been, towards the end of her life, reduced to penury, had started, at seventy, to give to the daughters and grand-

daughters of her old pupils. This lady was now dead. But
her method, an echo of her charming touch, came to life
now and then in the fingers of her pupils, even of those who
had been in other respects quite mediocre, had given up music,
and hardly ever opened a piano. And so Mme. des Laumes
could let her head sway to and fro, fully aware of the cause,
with a perfect appreciation of the manner in which the pianist
was rendering this Prelude, since she knew it by heart. The
closing notes of the phrase that he had begun sounded already
on her lips. And she murmured " How charming it is ! "
with a stress on the opening consonants of the adjective, a
token of her refinement by which she felt her lips so romantic-
ally compressed, like the petals of a beautiful, budding flower,
that she instinctively brought her eyes into harmony, illuminating them for a moment with a vague and sentimental
gaze. Meanwhile Mme. de Gallardon had arrived at the
point of saying to herself how annoying it was that she had
so few opportunities of meeting the Princesse des Laumes,
for she meant to teach her a lesson by not acknowledging
her bow. She did not know that her cousin was in the
room. A movement of Mme. Franquetot's head disclosed
the Princess. At once Mme. de Gallardon dashed towards
her, upsetting all her neighbours ; although determined
to preserve a distant and glacial manner which should remind
everyone present that she had no desire to remain on friendly
terms with a person in whose house one might find oneself, any day, cheek by jowl with the Princesse Mathilde,
and to whom it was not her duty to make advances since she
was not 'of her generation', she felt bound to modify this air
of dignity and reserve by some non-committal remark which
would justify her overture and would force the Princess to
engage in conversation ; and so, when she reached her

cousin, Mme. de Gallardon, with a stern countenance and one hand thrust out as though she were trying to 'force' a card, began with : " How is your husband ? " in the same anxious tone that she would have used if the Prince had been seriously ill. The Princess, breaking into a laugh which was one of her characteristics, and was intended at once to shew the rest of an assembly that she was making fun of some one and also to enhance her own beauty by concentrating her features around her animated lips and sparkling eyes, answered : " Why, he's never been better in his life ! " And she went on laughing.

Mme. de Gallardon then drew herself up and, chilling her expression still further, perhaps because she was still uneasy about the Prince's health, said to her cousin :

" Oriane," (at once Mme. des Laumes looked with amused astonishment towards an invisible third, whom she seemed to call to witness that she had never authorised Mme. de Gallardon to use her Christian name) " I should be so pleased if you would look in, just for a minute, to-morrow evening, to hear a quintet, with the clarinet, by Mozart. I should like to have your opinion of it."

She seemed not so much to be issuing an invitation as to be asking a favour, and to want the Princess's opinion of the Mozart quintet just as though it had been a dish invented by a new cook, whose talent it was most important that an epicure should come to judge.

" But I know that quintet quite well. I can tell you now— that I adore it."

" You know, my husband isn't at all well ; it's his liver. He would like so much to see you," Mme. de Gallardon resumed, making it now a corporal work of charity for the Princess to appear at her party.

The Princess never liked to tell people that she would not go to their houses. Every day she would write to express her regret at having been kept away—by the sudden arrival of her husband's mother, by an invitation from his brother, by the Opera, by some excursion to the country—from some party to which she had never for a moment dreamed of going. In this way she gave many people the satisfaction of feeling that she was on intimate terms with them, that she would gladly have come to their houses, and that she had been prevented from doing so only by some princely occurrence which they were flattered to find competing with their own humble entertainment. And then, as she belonged to that witty 'Guermantes set'—in which there survived something of the alert mentality, stripped of all commonplace phrases and conventional sentiments, which dated from Mérimée, and found its final expression in the plays of Meilhac and Halévy —she adapted its formula so as to suit even her social engagements, transposed it into the courtesy which was always struggling to be positive and precise, to approximate itself to the plain truth. She would never develop at any length to a hostess the expression of her anxiety to be present at her party ; she found it more pleasant to disclose to her all the various little incidents on which it would depend whether it was or was not possible for her to come.

" Listen, and I'll explain ; " she began to Mme. Gallardon. " To-morrow evening I must go to a friend of mine, who has been pestering me to fix a day for ages. If she takes us to the theatre afterwards, then I can't possibly come to you, much as I should love to ; but if we just stay in the house, I know there won't be anyone else there, so I can slip away."

" Tell me, have you seen your friend M. Swann ? "

" No ! my precious Charles ! I never knew he was here. Where is he ? I must catch his eye."

" It's a funny thing that he should come to old Saint-Euverte's," Mme. de Gallardon went on. " Oh, I know he's very clever," meaning by that ' very cunning ', " but that makes no difference ; fancy a Jew here, and she the sister and sister-in-law of two Archbishops."

" I am ashamed to confess that I am not in the least shocked," said the Princesse des Laumes.

" I know he's a converted Jew, and all that, and his parents and grandparents before him. But they do say that the converted ones are worse about their religion than the practising ones, that it's all just a pretence ; is that true, d'you think ? "

" I can throw no light at all on the matter."

The pianist, who was ' down ' to play two pieces by Chopin, after finishing the Prelude had at once attacked a Polonaise. But once Mme. de Gallardon had informed her cousin that Swann was in the room, Chopin himself might have risen from the grave and played all his works in turn without Mme. des Laumes's paying him the slightest attention. She belonged to that one of the two divisions of the human race in which the untiring curiosity which the other half feels about the people whom it does not know is replaced by an unfailing interest in the people whom it does. As with many women of the Faubourg Saint-Germain, the presence, in any room in which she might find herself, of another member of her set, even although she had nothing in particular to say to him, would occupy her mind to the exclusion of every other consideration. From that moment, in the hope that Swann would catch sight of her, the Princess could do nothing but (like a tame white mouse when a lump of sugar is put down before its nose and then taken away) turn her face, in which were crowded a thousand signs of intimate connivance, none of them with the least relevance to the sentiment underlying Chopin's music, in the direction where Swann was, and, if he moved, divert accordingly the course of her magnetic smile.

"Oriane, don't be angry with me," resumed Mme. de Gallardon, who could never restrain herself from sacrificing her highest social ambitions, and the hope that she might one day emerge into a light that would dazzle the world, to the immediate and secret satisfaction of saying something disagreeable, "people do say about your M. Swann that he's the sort of man one can't have in the house ; is that true ? "

"Why, you, of all people, ought to know that it's true," replied the Princesse des Laumes, " for you must have asked him a hundred times, and he's never been to your house once."

And leaving her cousin mortified afresh, she broke out again into a laugh which scandalised everyone who was trying to listen to the music, but attracted the attention of Mme. de Saint-Euverte, who had stayed, out of politeness, near the piano, and caught sight of the Princess now for the first time. Mme. de Saint-Euverte was all the more delighted to see Mme. des Laumes, as she imagined her to be still at Guermantes, looking after her father-in-law, who was ill.

" My dear Princess, you here ? "

" Yes, I tucked myself away in a corner, and I've been hearing such lovely things."

" What, you've been in the room quite a time ? "

" Oh, yes, quite a long time, which seemed very short ; it was only long because I couldn't see you."

Mme. de Saint-Euverte offered her own chair to the Princess, who declined it with :

" Oh, please, no ! Why should you ? It doesn't matter in the least where I sit." And deliberately picking out, so as the better to display the simplicity of a really great lady, a low seat without a back : " There now, that hassock, that's all I want. It will make me keep my back straight. Oh! Good heavens, I'm making a noise again ; they'll be telling you to have me ' chucked out '."

Meanwhile, the pianist having doubled his speed, the emotion of the music-lovers was reaching its climax, a servant was handing refreshments about on a salver, and was making the spoons rattle, and, as on every other 'party-night', Mme. de Saint-Euverte was making signs to him, which he never saw, to leave the room. A recent bride, who had been told that a young woman ought never to appear bored, was smiling vigorously, trying to catch her hostess's eye so as to flash a token of her gratitude for the other's having ' thought of her ' in connection with so delightful an entertainment. And yet, although she remained more calm than Mme. de Franquetot, it was not without some uneasiness that she followed the flying fingers ; what alarmed her being not the pianist's fate but the piano's, on which a lighted candle, jumping at each *fortissimo*, threatened, if not to set its shade on fire, at least to spill wax upon the ebony. At last she could contain herself no longer, and, running up the two steps of the platform on which the piano stood, flung herself on the candle to adjust its sconce. But scarcely had her hand come within reach of it when, on a final chord, the piece finished, and the pianist rose to his feet. Nevertheless the bold initiative shewn by this young woman and the moment of blushing confusion between her and the pianist which resulted from it, produced an impression that was favourable on the whole.

" Did you see what that girl did just now, Princess ? "

asked General de Froberville, who had come up to Mme. des
Laumes as her hostess left her for a moment. " Odd, wasn't
it ? Is she one of the performers ? "

" No, she's a little Mme. de Cambremer," replied the
Princess carelessly, and then, with more animation : " I am
only repeating what I heard just now, myself ; I haven't the
faintest notion who said it, it was some one behind me who
said that they were neighbours of Mme. de Saint-Euverte
in the country, but I don't believe anyone knows them, really.
They must be ' country cousins ' ! By the way, I don't know
whether you're particularly ' well-up ' in the brilliant society
which we see before us, because I've no idea who all these
astonishing people can be. What do you suppose they do
with themselves when they're not at Mme. de Saint-Euverte's
parties ? She must have ordered them in with the musicians
and the chairs and the food. ' Universal providers ', you know.
You must admit, they're rather splendid, General. But can
she really have the courage to hire the same ' supers ' every
week ? It isn't possible ! "

" Oh, but Cambremer is quite a good name ; old, too,"
protested the General.

" I see no objection to its being old," the Princess answered
dryly, " but whatever else it is it's not euphonious," she went
on, isolating the word euphonious as though between inverted
commas, a little affectation to which the Guermantes set were
addicted.

" You think not, eh ! She's a regular little peach, though,"
said the General, whose eyes never strayed from Mme. de
Cambremer. " Don't you agree with me, Princess ? "

" She thrusts herself forward too much ; I think, in so
young a woman, that's not very nice—for I don't suppose
she's my generation," replied Mme. des Laumes (the last

word being common, it appeared, to Gallardon and Guermantes). And then, seeing that M. de Froberville was still
gazing at Mme. de Cambremer, she added, half out of malice
towards the lady, half wishing to oblige the General : " Not
very nice . . . for her husband ! I am sorry that I do not
know her, since she seems to attract you so much ; I might
have introduced you to her," said the Princess, who, if she
had known the young woman, would most probably have
done nothing of the sort. " And now I must say good
night, because one of my friends is having a birthday party,
and I must go and wish her many happy returns," she
explained, modestly and with truth, reducing the fashionable
gathering to which she was going to the simple proportions
of a ceremony which would be boring in the extreme, but
at which she was obliged to be present, and there would be
something touching about her appearance. " Besides, I must
pick up Basin. While I've been here, he's gone to see those
friends of his—you know them too, I'm sure,—who are
called after a bridge—oh, yes, the Iénas."

" It was a battle before it was a bridge, Princess ; it was
a victory ! " said the General. " I mean to say, to an old
soldier like me," he went on, wiping his monocle and re-
placing it, as though he were laying a fresh dressing on the
raw wound underneath, while the Princess instinctively
looked away, " that Empire nobility, well, of course, it's not
the same thing, but, after all, taking it as it is, it's very fine
of its kind ; they were people who really did fight like
heroes."

" But I have the deepest respect for heroes," the Princess
assented, though with a faint trace of irony. " If I don't go
with Basin to see this Princesse d'Iéna, it isn't for that, at all ;
it's simply because I don't know them. Basin knows them ;

he worships them. Oh, no, it's not what you think ; he's
not in love with her. I've nothing to set my face against !
Besides, what good has it ever done when I have set my face
against them ? " she queried sadly, for the whole world knew
that, ever since the day upon which the Prince des Laumes
had married his fascinating cousin, he had been consistently
unfaithful to her. " Anyhow, it isn't that at all. They're
people he has known for ever so long, they do him very well,
and that suits me down to the ground. But I must tell you
what he's told me about their house ; it's quite enough. Can
you imagine it, all their furniture is ' Empire ' ! "

" But, my dear Princess, that's only natural ; it belonged
to their grandparents."

" I don't say it didn't, but that doesn't make it any less
ugly. I quite understand that people can't always have nice
things, but at least they needn't have things that are merely
grotesque. What do you say ? I can think of nothing more
devastating, more utterly smug than that hideous style—
cabinets covered all over with swans' heads, like bath-taps ! "

" But I believe, all the same, that they've got some lovely
things ; why, they must have that famous mosaic table on
which the Treaty of . . ."

" Oh, I don't deny, they may have things that are interesting enough from the historic point of view. But things
like that can't, ever, be beautiful . . . because they're simply
horrible ! I've got things like that myself, that came to
Basin from the Montesquious. Only, they're up in the attics
at Guermantes, where nobody ever sees them. But, after
all, that's not the point, I would fly to see them, with Basin ;
I would even go to see them among all their sphinxes and
brasses, if I knew them, but—I don't know them ! D'you
know, I was always taught, when I was a little girl, that it

was not polite to call on people one didn't know." She assumed a tone of childish gravity. " And so I am just doing what I was taught to do. Can't you see those good people, with a totally strange woman bursting into their house ? Why, I might get a most hostile reception."

And she coquettishly enhanced the charm of the smile which the idea had brought to her lips, by giving to her blue eyes, which were fixed on the General, a gentle, dreamy expression.

" My dear Princess, you know that they'ld be simply wild with joy."

" No, why ? " she inquired, with the utmost vivacity, either so as to seem unaware that it would be because she was one of the first ladies in France, or so as to have the pleasure of hearing the General tell her so. " Why ? How can you tell ? Perhaps they would think it the most unpleasant thing that could possibly happen. I know nothing about them, but if they're anything like me, I find it quite boring enough to see the people I do know ; I'm sure if I had to see people I didn't know as well, even if they had 'fought like heroes', I should go stark mad. Besides, except when it's an old friend like you, whom one knows quite apart from that, I'm not sure that ' heroism ' takes one very far in society. It's often quite boring enough to have to give a dinner-party, but if one had to offer one's arm to Spartacus, to let him take one down . . . ! Really, no ; it would never be Vercingetorix I should send for, to make a fourteenth. I feel sure, I should keep him for really big 'crushes'. And as I never give any . . ."

" Ah ! Princess, it's easy to see you're not a Guermantes for nothing. You have your share of it, all right, the ' wit of the Guermantes ' ! "

" But people always talk about the wit of *the* Guermantes ;
I never could make out why. Do you really know any *others*
who have it ? " she rallied him, with a rippling flow of
laughter, her features concentrated, yoked to the service of
her animation, her eyes sparkling, blazing with a radiant sunshine of gaiety which could be kindled only by such speeches
—even if the Princess had to make them herself—as were
in praise of her wit or of her beauty. " Look, there's Swann
talking to your Cambremer woman ; over there, beside old
Saint-Euverte, don't you see him ? Ask him to introduce
you. But hurry up, he seems to be just going ! "

" Did you notice how dreadfully ill he's looking ? " asked
the General.

" My precious Charles ? Ah, he's coming at last ; I was
beginning to think he didn't want to see me ! "

Swann was extremely fond of the Princesse des Laumes,
and the sight of her recalled to him Guermantes, a property
close to Combray, and all that country which he so dearly
loved and had ceased to visit, so as not to be separated from
Odette. Slipping into the manner, half-artistic, half-amor-
ous—with which he could always manage to amuse the
Princess—a manner which came to him quite naturally whenever he dipped for a moment into the old social atmosphere,
and wishing also to express in words, for his own satisfaction,
the longing that he felt for the country :

" Ah ! " he exclaimed, or rather intoned, in such a way as
to be audible at once to Mme. de Saint-Euverte, to whom he
spoke, and to Mme. des Laumes, for whom he was speaking,
" Behold our charming Princess ! See, she has come up on
purpose from Guermantes to hear Saint Francis preach to
the birds, and has only just had time, like a dear little tit-
mouse, to go and pick a few little hips and haws and put them

in her hair ; there are even some drops of dew upon them still, a little of the hoar-frost which must be making the Duchess, down there, shiver. It is very pretty indeed, my dear Princess."

"What ! The Princess came up on purpose from Guermantes ? But that's too wonderful ! I never knew ; I'm quite bewildered," Mme. de Saint-Euverte protested with quaint simplicity, being but little accustomed to Swann's way of speaking. And then, examining the Princess's head-dress, "Why, you're quite right ; it is copied from . . . what shall I say, not chestnuts, no,—oh, it's a delightful idea, but how can the Princess have known what was going to be on my programme? The musicians didn't tell me, even."

Swann, who was accustomed, when he was with a woman whom he had kept up the habit of addressing in terms of gallantry, to pay her delicate compliments which most other people would not and need not understand, did not con-descend to explain to Mme. de Saint-Euverte that he had been speaking metaphorically. As for the Princess, she was in fits of laughter, both because Swann's wit was highly ap-preciated by her set, and because she could never hear a com-pliment addressed to herself without finding it exquisitely subtle and irresistibly amusing.

"Indeed ! I'm delighted, Charles, if my little hips and haws meet with your approval. But tell me, why did you bow to that Cambremer person, are you also her neighbour in the country ? "

Mme. de Saint-Euverte, seeing that the Princess seemed quite happy talking to Swann, had drifted away.

"But you are, yourself, Princess ! "

"I ! Why, they must have 'countries' everywhere, those creatures ! Don't I wish I had ! "

"No, not the Cambremers ; her own people. She was a Legrandin, and used to come to Combray. I don't know whether you are aware that you are Comtesse de Combray, and that the Chapter owes you a due."

"I don't know what the Chapter owes me, but I do know that I'm 'touched' for a hundred francs, every year, by the Curé, which is a due that I could very well do without. But surely these Cambremers have rather a startling name. It ends just in time, but it ends badly !" she said with a laugh.

"It begins no better." Swann took the point.

"Yes ; that double abbreviation !"

"Some one very angry and very proper who didn't dare to finish the first word."

"But since he couldn't stop himself beginning the second, he'ld have done better to finish the first and be done with it. We are indulging in the most refined form of humour, my dear Charles, in the very best of taste—but how tiresome it is that I never see you now," she went on in a coaxing tone, "I do so love talking to you. Just imagine, I could not make that idiot Froberville see that there was anything funny about the name Cambremer. Do agree that life is a dreadful business. It's only when I see you that I stop feeling bored."

Which was probably not true. But Swann and the Princess had the same way of looking at the little things of life— the effect, if not the cause of which was a close analogy between their modes of expression and even of pronunciation. This similarity was not striking because no two things could have been more unlike than their voices. But if one took the trouble to imagine Swann's utterances divested of the sonority that enwrapped them, of the moustache from under which they emerged, one found that they were the same phrases, the same inflexions, that they had the 'tone' of the

Guermantes set. On important matters, Swann and the Princess had not an idea in common. But since Swann had become so melancholy, and was always in that trembling condition which precedes a flood of tears, he had the same need to speak about his grief that a murderer has to tell some one about his crime. And when he heard the Princess say that life was a dreadful business, he felt as much comforted as if she had spoken to him of Odette.

"Yes, life is a dreadful business! We must meet more often, my dear friend. What is so nice about you is that you are not cheerful. We could spend a most pleasant evening together."

"I'm sure we could ; why not come down to Guermantes ? My mother-in-law would be wild with joy. It's supposed to be very ugly down there, but I must say, I find the neighbourhood not at all unattractive ; I have a horror of 'picturesque spots'."

"I know it well, it's delightful!" replied Swann. "It's almost too beautiful, too much alive for me just at present ; it's a country to be happy in. It's perhaps because I have lived there, but things there speak to me so. As soon as a breath of wind gets up, and the cornfields begin to stir, I feel that some one is going to appear suddenly, that I am going to hear some news ; and those little houses by the water's edge . . . I should be quite wretched ! "

"Oh ! my dearest Charles, do take care ; there's that appalling Rampillon woman ; she's seen me ; hide me somewhere, do tell me again, quickly, what it was that happened to her ; I get so mixed up ; she's just married off her daughter, or her lover, (I never can remember)— perhaps both—to each other ! Oh, no, I remember now, she's been dropped by her Prince . . . Pretend to be talking, so that the poor old Berenice shan't come and invite me to dinner. Anyhow, I'm going. Listen, my dearest Charles, now that I have seen you, once in a blue moon, won't you let me carry you off and take you to the Princesse de Parme's, who would be so pleased to see you (you know), and Basin too, for that matter ; he's meeting me there. If one didn't get news of you, sometimes, from Mémé . . . Remember, I never see you at all now ! "

Swann declined. Having told M. de Charlus that, on leaving Mme. de Saint-Euverte's, he would go straight home, he did not care to run the risk, by going on now to the Princesse de Parme's, of missing a message which he had, all the time, been hoping to see brought in to him by one of the footmen, during the party, and which he was perhaps going to find left with his own porter, at home.

" Poor Swann," said Mme. des Laumes that night to her husband ; " he is always charming, but he does look so dreadfully unhappy. You will see for yourself, for he has promised to dine with us one of these days. I do feel that it's really absurd that a man of his intelligence should let himself be made to suffer by a creature of that kind, who isn't even interesting, for they tell me, she's an absolute idiot ! " she concluded with the wisdom invariably shewn by people who, not being in love themselves, feel that a clever man ought to be unhappy only about such persons as are worth his while ; which is rather like being astonished that anyone should condescend to die of cholera at the bidding of so insignificant a creature as the comma bacillus.

Swann now wished to go home, but, just as he was making his escape, General de Froberville caught him and asked for an introduction to Mme. de Cambremer, and he was obliged to go back into the room to look for her.

" I say, Swann, I'ld rather be married to that little woman than killed by savages, what do you say ? "

The words 'killed by savages' pierced Swann's aching heart ; and at once he felt the need of continuing the conversation. " Ah ! " he began, " some fine lives have been lost in that way . . . There was, you remember, that explorer whose remains Dumont d'Urville brought back, La Pérouse . . ." (and he was at once happy again, as though he had named Odette). " He was a fine character, and interests me very much, does La Pérouse," he ended sadly.

" Oh, yes, of course, La Pérouse," said the General. " It's quite a well-known name. There's a street called that."

" Do you know anyone in the Rue La Pérouse ? " asked Swann excitedly.

" Only Mme. de Chanlivault, the sister of that good fellow Chaussepierre. She gave a most amusing theatre-party the other evening. That's a house that will be really smart some day, you'll see ! "

" Oh, so she lives in the Rue La Pérouse. It's attractive ; I like that street ; it's so sombre."

" Indeed it isn't. You can't have been in it for a long time ; it's not at all sombre now ; they're beginning to build all round there."

When Swann did finally introduce M. de Froberville to the young Mme. de Cambremer, since it was the first time that she had heard the General's name, she hastily outlined upon her lips the smile of joy and surprise with which she would have greeted him if she had never, in the whole of her life, heard anything else ; for, as she did not yet know all the friends of her new family, whenever anyone was presented to her, she assumed that he must be one of them, and thinking that she would shew her tact by appearing to have heard

'such a lot about him' since her marriage, she would hold
out her hand with an air of hesitation which was meant as a
proof at once of the inculcated reserve which she had to over-
come and of the spontaneous friendliness which successfully
overcame it. And so her parents-in-law, whom she still regarded as the most eminent pair in France, declared that she
was an angel ; all the more that they preferred to appear,
in marrying her to their son, to have yielded to the attraction
rather of her natural charm than of her considerable fortune.

" It's easy to see that you're a musician heart and soul,
Madame," said the General, alluding to the incident of the
candle.

Meanwhile the concert had begun again, and Swann saw
that he could not now go before the end of the new number.
He suffered greatly from being shut up among all these people
whose stupidity and absurdities wounded him all the more
cruelly since, being ignorant of his love, incapable, had they
known of it, of taking any interest, or of doing more than
smile at it as at some childish joke, or deplore it as an act of
insanity, they made it appear to him in the aspect of a sub-
jective state which existed for himself alone, whose reality
there was nothing external to confirm ; he suffered over-
whelmingly, to the point at which even the sound of the
instruments made him want to cry, from having to prolong
his exile in this place to which Odette would never come, in
which no one, nothing was aware of her existence, from
which she was entirely absent.

But suddenly it was as though she had entered, and this
apparition tore him with such anguish that his hand rose impulsively to his heart. What had happened was that the
violin had risen to a series of high notes, on which it rested
as though expecting something, an expectancy which it pro-

longed without ceasing to hold on to the notes, in the exaltation with which it already saw the expected object approaching, and with a desperate effort to continue until its
arrival, to welcome it before itself expired, to keep the way
open for a moment longer, with all its remaining strength,
that the stranger might enter in, as one holds a door open that
would otherwise automatically close. And before Swann had
had time to understand what was happening, to think : " It
is the little phrase from Vinteuil's sonata. I mustn't listen ! ",
all his memories of the days when Odette had been in love
with him, which he had succeeded, up till that evening, in
keeping invisible in the depths of his being, deceived by this
sudden reflection of a season of love, whose sun, they supposed, had dawned again, had awakened from their slumber,
had taken wing and risen to sing maddeningly in his ears,
without pity for his present desolation, the forgotten strains
of happiness.

In place of the abstract expressions " the time when I was
happy ", " the time when I was loved ", which he had often
used until then, and without much suffering, for his intelligence had not embodied in them anything of the past save
fictitious extracts which preserved none of the reality, he now
recovered everything that had fixed unalterably the peculiar,
volatile essence of that lost happiness ; he could see it all ;
the snowy, curled petals of the chrysanthemum which she had
tossed after him into his carriage, which he had kept pressed
to his lips—the address ' Maison Dorée ', embossed on the
note-paper on which he had read " My hand trembles so as
I write to you ", the frowning contraction of her eyebrows
when she said pleadingly : " You won't let it be very long
before you send for me ? " ; he could smell the heated iron of
the barber whom he used to have in to singe his hair while

Loredan went to fetch the little working girl ; could feel the
torrents of rain which fell so often that spring, the ice-cold
homeward drive in his victoria, by moonlight ; all the network of mental habits, of seasonable impressions, of sensory
reactions, which had extended over a series of weeks its uniform meshes, by which his body now found itself inextricably
held. At that time he had been satisfying a sensual curiosity to
know what were the pleasures of those people who lived for
love alone. He had supposed that he could stop there, that
he would not be obliged to learn their sorrows also ; how
small a thing the actual charm of Odette was now in com-
parison with that formidable terror which extended it like
a cloudy halo all around her, that enormous anguish of not
knowing at every hour of the day and night what she had
been doing, of not possessing her wholly, at all times and in all
places ! Alas, he recalled the accents in which she had
exclaimed : "But I can see you at any time ; I am always
free ! "——she, who was never free now ; the interest, the
curiosity that she had shewn in his life, her passionate desire
that he should do her the favour—of which it was he who,
then, had felt suspicious, as of a possibly tedious waste of his
time and disturbance of his arrangements—of granting her
access to his study ; how she had been obliged to beg that he
would let her take him to the Verdurins' ; and, when he did
allow her to come to him once a month, how she had first,
before he would let himself be swayed, had to repeat what a
joy it would be to her, that custom of their seeing each other
daily, for which she had longed at a time when to him it had
seemed only a tiresome distraction, for which, since that time,
she had conceived a distaste and had definitely broken herself
of it, while it had become for him so insatiable, so dolorous a
need. Little had he suspected how truly he spoke when, on

their third meeting, as she repeated : " But why don't you let me come to you oftener ? " he had told her, laughing, and in a vein of gallantry, that it was for fear of forming a hopeless passion. Now, alas, it still happened at times that she wrote to him from a restaurant or hotel, on paper which bore a printed address, but printed in letters of fire that seared his heart. " Written from the Hôtel Vouillemont. What on earth can she have gone there for ? With whom ? What happened there ? " He remembered the gas-jets that were being extinguished along the Boulevard des Italiens when he had met her, when all hope was gone, among the errant shades upon that night which had seemed to him almost supernatural and which now (that night of a period when he had not even to ask himself whether he would be annoying her by looking for her and by finding her, so certain was he that she knew no greater happiness than to see him and to let him take her home) belonged indeed to a mysterious world to which one never may return again once its doors are closed. And Swann could distinguish, standing, motionless, before that scene of happiness in which it lived again, a wretched figure which filled him with such pity, because he did not at first recognise who it was, that he must lower his head, lest anyone should observe that his eyes were filled with tears. It was himself.

When he had realised this, his pity ceased ; he was jealous, now, of that other self whom she had loved, he was jealous of those men of whom he had so often said, without much suffering : " Perhaps she's in love with them," now that he had exchanged the vague idea of loving, in which there is no love, for the petals of the chrysanthemum and the ' letter-heading ' of the Maison d'Or ; for they were full of love. And then, his anguish becoming too keen, he passed his hand over his forehead, let the monocle drop from his eye, and wiped its glass. And doubtless, if he had caught sight of himself at that moment, he would have added to the collection of the monocles which he had already identified, this one which he removed, like an importunate, worrying thought, from his head, while from its misty surface, with his handkerchief, he sought to obliterate his cares.

There are in the music of the violin—if one does not see the instrument itself, and so cannot relate what one hears to its form, which modifies the fullness of the sound—accents which are so closely akin to those of certain contralto voices, that one has the illusion that a singer has taken her place amid the orchestra. One raises one's eyes ; one sees only the wooden case, magical as a Chinese box ; but, at moments, one is still tricked by the deceiving appeal of the Siren ; at times, too, one believes that one is listening to a captive spirit, struggling in the darkness of its masterful box, a box quivering with enchantment, like a devil immersed in a stoup of holy water ; sometimes, again, it is in the air, at large, like a pure and supernatural creature that reveals to the ear, as it passes, its invisible message.

As though the musicians were not nearly so much playing the little phrase as performing the rites on which it insisted before it would consent to appear, as proceeding to utter the incantations necessary to procure, and to prolong for a few moments, the miracle of its apparition, Swann, who was no more able now to see it than if it had belonged to a world of ultra-violet light, who experienced something like the refreshing sense of a metamorphosis in the momentary blindness with which he had been struck as he approached it, Swann felt that it was present, like a protective goddess, a confidant of his love, who, so as to be able to come to him through the crowd, and to draw him aside to speak to him, had disguised herself in this sweeping cloak of sound. And as she passed him, light, soothing, as softly murmured as the perfume of a flower, telling him what she had to say, every word of which he closely scanned, sorry to see them fly away so fast, he made involuntarily with his lips the motion of kissing, as it went by him, the harmonious, fleeting form.

He felt that he was no longer in exile and alone since she, who addressed herself to him, spoke to him in a whisper of Odette. For he had no longer, as of old, the impression that Odette and he were not known to the little phrase. Had it not often been the witness of their joys ? True that, as often, it had warned him of their frailty. And indeed, whereas, in that distant time, he had divined an element of suffering in its smile, in its limpid and disillusioned intonation, to-night he found there rather the charm of a resignation that was almost gay. Of those sorrows, of which the little phrase had spoken to him then, which he had seen it—without his being touched by them himself—carry past him, smiling, on its sinuous and rapid course, of those sorrows which were now become his own, without his having any hope of being, ever, delivered from them, it seemed to say to him, as once it had said of his happiness : " What does all that matter ; it is all nothing." And Swann's thoughts were borne for the first time on a wave of pity and tenderness towards that Vinteuil, towards that unknown, exalted brother who also must have suffered so greatly ; what could his life have been ? From the depths of what well of sorrow could he have drawn that god-like strength, that unlimited power of creation ?

When it was the little phrase that spoke to him of the vanity of his sufferings, Swann found a sweetness in that very wisdom which, but a little while back, had seemed to him intolerable when he thought that he could read it on the faces of indifferent strangers, who would regard his love as a digression that was without importance. 'Twas because the little phrase, unlike them, whatever opinion it might hold on the short duration of these states of the soul, saw in them something not, as everyone else saw, less serious than the events of everyday life, but, on the contrary, so far superior to everyday life as to be alone worthy of the trouble of expressing it. Those graces of an intimate sorrow, 'twas them that the phrase endeavoured to imitate, to create anew ; and even their essence, for all that it consists in being incommunicable and in appearing trivial to everyone save him who has experience of them, the little phrase had captured, had rendered visible. So much so that it made their value be confessed, their divine sweetness be tasted by all those same onlookers—provided only that they were in any sense musical —who, the next moment, would ignore, would disown them in real life, in every individual love that came into being beneath their eyes. Doubtless the form in which it had codified those graces could not be analysed into any logical elements. But ever since, more than a year before, discovering to him many of the riches of his own soul, the love of music had been born, and for a time at least had dwelt in him, Swann had regarded musical *motifs* as actual ideas, of another world, of another order, ideas veiled in shadows, unknown, impenetrable by the human mind, which none the less were perfectly distinct one from another, unequal among themselves in value and in significance. When, after that first evening at the Verdurins', he had had the little phrase played over to him again, and had sought to disentangle from his confused impressions how it was that, like a perfume or a caress, it swept over and enveloped him, he had observed that it was to the closeness of the intervals between the five notes which composed it and to the constant repetition of two of them that was due that impression of a frigid, a contracted sweetness ; but in reality he knew that he was basing this conclusion not upon the phrase itself, but merely upon certain equivalents, substituted (for his mind's convenience) for the mysterious entity of which he had become aware, before ever he knew the Verdurins, at that earlier party, when for the first time he had heard the sonata played. He knew that his memory of the piano falsified still further the perspective in which he saw the music, that the field open to the musician is not a miserable stave of seven notes, but an immeasurable keyboard (still, almost all of it, unknown), on which, here and there only, separated by the gross darkness of its unexplored tracts, some few among the millions of keys, keys of tenderness, of passion, of courage, of serenity, which compose it, each one differing from all the rest as one universe differs from another, have been discovered by certain great artists who do us the service, when they awaken in us the emotion corresponding to the theme which they have found, of shewing us what richness, what variety lies hidden, unknown to us, in that great black impenetrable night, discouraging exploration, of our soul, which we have been content to regard as valueless and waste and void. Vinteuil had been one of those musicians. In his little phrase, albeit it presented to the mind's eye a clouded surface, there was contained, one felt, a matter so consistent, so explicit, to which the phrase gave so new, so original a force, that those who had once heard it preserved the memory of it in the treasure-chamber of their minds. Swann would repair to it as to a conception of love and happiness, of which at once he knew as well in what respects it was peculiar as he would know of the *Princesse de Clèves*, or of *René*, should either of those titles occur to him. Even when he was not thinking of the little phrase, it existed, latent, in his mind, in the same way as certain other conceptions without material equivalent, such as our notions of light, of sound, of perspective, of bodily desire, the rich possessions wherewith our inner temple is diversified and adorned. Perhaps we shall lose them, perhaps they will be obliterated, if we return to nothing in the dust. But so long as we are alive, we can no more bring ourselves to a state in which we shall not have known them than we can with regard to any material object, than we can, for example, doubt the luminosity of a lamp that has just been lighted, in view of the changed aspect of everything in the room, from which has vanished even the memory of the darkness. In that way Vinteuil's phrase, like some theme, say, in *Tristan*, which represents to us also a certain acquisition of sentiment, had espoused our mortal state, had endued a vesture of humanity that was affecting enough. Its destiny was linked, for the future, with that of the human soul, of which it was one of the special, the most distinctive ornaments. Perhaps it is not-being that is the true state, and all our dream of life is without existence ; but, if so, we feel that it must be that these phrases of music, these conceptions which exist in relation to our dream, are nothing either. We shall perish, but we have for our hostages these divine captives who shall follow and share our fate. And death in their company is something less bitter, less inglorious, perhaps even less certain.

So Swann was not mistaken in believing that the phrase of the sonata did, really, exist. Human as it was from this point of view, it belonged, none the less, to an order of supernatural creatures whom we have never seen, but whom, in spite of that, we recognise and acclaim with rapture when some explorer of the unseen contrives to coax one forth, to bring it down from that divine world to which he has access to shine for a brief moment in the firmament of ours. This was what Vinteuil had done for the little phrase. Swann felt that the composer had been content (with the musical instruments at his disposal) to draw aside its veil, to make it visible, following and respecting its outlines with a hand so loving, so prudent, so delicate and so sure, that the sound altered at every moment, blunting itself to indicate a shadow, springing back into life when it must follow the curve of some more bold projection. And one proof that Swann was not mistaken when he believed in the real existence of this phrase, was that anyone with an ear at all delicate for music would at once have detected the imposture had Vinteuil, endowed with less power to see and to render its forms, sought to dissemble (by adding a line, here and there, of his own invention) the dimness of his vision or the feebleness of his hand.

The phrase had disappeared. Swann knew that it would come again at the end of the last movement, after a long passage which Mme. Verdurin's pianist always 'skipped'. There were in this passage some admirable ideas which Swann had not distinguished on first hearing the sonata, and which he now perceived, as if they had, in the cloak-room of his memory, divested themselves of their uniform disguise of novelty. Swann listened to all the scattered themes which entered into the composition of the phrase, as its premisses enter into the inevitable conclusion of a syllogism ; he was assisting at the mystery of its birth. " Audacity," he exclaimed to himself, "as inspired, perhaps, as a Lavoisier's or an Ampère's, the audacity of a Vinteuil making experiment, discovering the secret laws that govern an unknown force, driving across a region unexplored towards the one possible goal

the invisible team in which he has placed his trust and which
he never may discern!" How charming the dialogue which
Swann now heard between piano and violin, at the beginning
of the last passage. The suppression of human speech, so far
from letting fancy reign there uncontrolled (as one might
have thought), had eliminated it altogether. Never was
spoken language of such inflexible necessity, never had it
known questions so pertinent, such obvious replies. At first
the piano complained alone, like a bird deserted by its mate ;
the violin heard and answered it, as from a neighbouring tree.
It was as at the first beginning of the world, as if there were
not yet but these twain upon the earth, or rather in this world
closed against all the rest, so fashioned by the logic of its
creator that in it there should never be any but themselves ;
the world of this sonata. Was it a bird, was it the soul, not
yet made perfect, of the little phrase, was it a fairy, invisibly
somewhere lamenting, whose plaint the piano heard and
tenderly repeated ? Its cries were so sudden that the violinist
must snatch up his bow and race to catch them as they came.
Marvellous bird ! The violinist seemed to wish to charm, to
tame, to woo, to win it. Already it had passed into his soul,
already the little phrase which it evoked shook like a medium's
the body of the violinist, ' possessed ' indeed. Swann knew
that the phrase was going to speak to him once again. And
his personality was now so divided that the strain of waiting
for the imminent moment when he would find himself face
to face, once more, with the phrase, convulsed him in one
of those sobs which a fine line of poetry or a piece of alarming
news will wring from us, not when we are alone, but when we
repeat one or the other to a friend, in whom we see ourselves
reflected, like a third person, whose probable emotion softens
him. It reappeared, but this time to remain poised in the air,

and to sport there for a moment only, as though immobile, and shortly to expire. And so Swann lost nothing of the precious time for which it lingered. It was still there, like an iridescent bubble that floats for a while unbroken. As a rainbow, when its brightness fades, seems to subside, then soars again and, before it is extinguished, is glorified with greater splendour than it has ever shewn ; so to the two colours which the phrase had hitherto allowed to appear it added others now, chords shot with every hue in the prism, and made them sing. Swann dared not move, and would have liked to compel all the other people in the room to remain still also, as if the slightest movement might embarrass the magic presence, supernatural, delicious, frail, that would so easily vanish. But no one, as it happened, dreamed of speaking. The ineffable utterance of one solitary man, absent, perhaps dead (Swann did not know whether Vinteuil were still alive), breathed out above the rites of those two hierophants, sufficed to arrest the attention of three hundred minds, and made of that stage on which a soul was thus called into being one of the noblest altars on which a supernatural ceremony could be performed. It followed that, when the phrase at last was finished, and only its fragmentary echoes floated among the subsequent themes which had already taken its place, if Swann at first was annoyed to see the Comtesse de Monteriender, famed for her imbecilities, lean over towards him to confide in him her impressions, before even the sonata had come to an end ; he could not refrain from smiling, and perhaps also found an underlying sense, which she was incapable of perceiving, in the words that she used. Dazzled by the virtuosity of the performers, the Comtesse exclaimed to Swann : " It's astonishing ! I have never seen anything to beat it . . . " But a scrupulous regard for accuracy making her correct her first assertion, she added the reservation . "anything to beat it . . . since the table-turning ! "

From that evening, Swann understood that the feeling which Odette had once had for him would never revive, that his hopes of happiness would not be realised now. And the days on which, by a lucky chance, she had once more shewn herself kind and loving to him, or if she had paid him any attention, he recorded those apparent and misleading signs of a slight movement on her part towards him with the same tender and sceptical solicitude, the desperate joy that people reveal who, when they are nursing a friend in the last days of an incurable malady, relate, as significant facts of infinite value : " Yesterday he went through his accounts himself, and actually corrected a mistake that we had made in adding them up ; he ate an egg to-day and seemed quite to enjoy it, if he digests it properly we shall try him with a cutlet to-morrow,"—although they themselves know that these things are meaningless on the eve of an inevitable death. No doubt Swann was assured that if he had now been living at a distance from Odette he would gradually have lost all interest in her, so that he would have been glad to learn that she was leaving Paris for ever ; he would have had the courage to remain there ; but he had not the courage to go.

He had often thought of going. Now that he was once again at work upon his essay on Vermeer, he wanted to return, for a few days at least, to The Hague, to Dresden, to Brunswick. He was certain that a 'Toilet of Diana' which had been acquired by the Mauritshuis at the Goldschmidt sale as a Nicholas Maes was in reality a Vermeer. And he would have liked to be able to examine the picture on the spot, so as to strengthen his conviction. But to leave Paris while Odette was there, and even when she was not there—for in strange places where our sensations have not been numbed by habit, we refresh, we revive an old pain—was for him so cruel a project that he felt himself to be capable of entertaining it incessantly in his mind only because he knew himself to be resolute in his determination never to put it into effect. But it would happen that, while he was asleep, the intention to travel would reawaken in him (without his remembering that this particular tour was impossible) and would be realised. One night he dreamed that he was going away for a year ; leaning from the window of the train towards a young man on the platform who wept as he bade him farewell, he was seeking to persuade this young man to come away also. The train began to move ; he awoke in alarm, and remembered that he was not going away, that he would see Odette that evening, and next day and almost every day. And then, being still deeply moved by his dream, he would thank heaven for those special circumstances which made him independent, thanks to which he could remain in Odette's vicinity, and could even succeed in making her allow him to see her sometimes ; and, counting over the list of his advantages : his social position—his fortune, from which she stood too often in need of assistance not to shrink from the prospect of a definite rupture (having even, so people said, an ulterior plan of getting him to marry her)—his friendship with M. de Charlus, which, it must be confessed, had never won him any very great favour from Odette, but which gave him the pleasant feeling that she was always hearing complimentary things said about him by this common friend for whom she had so great an esteem—and even his own intelligence, the whole of which he employed in weaving, every day, a fresh plot which would make his presence, if not agreeable, at any rate necessary to Odette—he thought of what might have happened to him if all these advantages had been lacking, he thought that, if he had been, like so many other men, poor and humble, without resources, forced to undertake any task that might be offered to him, or tied down by parents or by a wife, he might have been obliged to part from Odette, that that dream, the terror of which was still so recent, might well have been true ; and he said to himself : " People don't know when they are happy. They're never so unhappy as they think they are." But he reflected that this existence had lasted already for several years, that all that he could now hope for was that it should last for ever, that he would sacrifice his work, his pleasures, his friends, in fact the whole of his life to the daily expectation of a meeting which, when it occurred, would bring him no happiness ; and he asked himself whether he was not mistaken, whether the circumstances that had favoured their relations and had prevented a final rupture had not done a disservice to his career, whether the outcome to be desired was not that as to which he rejoiced that it happened only in dreams—his own departure ; and he said to himself that people did not know when they were unhappy, that they were never so happy as they supposed.

Sometimes he hoped that she would die, painlessly, in some accident, she who was out of doors, in the streets, crossing busy thoroughfares, from morning to night. And as she always returned safe and sound, he marvelled at the strength, at the suppleness of the human body, which was able continually to hold in check, to outwit all the perils that environed it (which to Swann seemed innumerable, since his own secret desire had strewn them in her path), and so allowed its occupant, the soul, to abandon itself, day after day, and almost with impunity, to its career of mendacity, to the pursuit of pleasure. And Swann felt a very cordial sympathy with that

Mahomet II whose portrait by Bellini he admired, who, on finding that he had fallen madly in love with one of his wives, stabbed her, in order, as his Venetian biographer artlessly relates, to recover his spiritual freedom. Then he would be ashamed of thinking thus only of himself, and his own sufferings would seem to deserve no pity now that he himself was disposing so cheaply of Odette's very life.

Since he was unable to separate himself from her without a subsequent return, if at least he had seen her continuously and without separations his grief would ultimately have been assuaged, and his love would, perhaps, have died. And from the moment when she did not wish to leave Paris for ever he had hoped that she would never go. As he knew that her one prolonged absence, every year, was in August and September, he had abundant opportunity, several months in advance, to dissociate from it the grim picture of her absence throughout Eternity which was lodged in him by anticipation, and which, consisting of days closely akin to the days through which he was then passing, floated in a cold transparency in his mind, which it saddened and depressed, though without causing him any intolerable pain. But that conception of the future, that flowing stream, colourless and unconfined, a single word from Odette sufficed to penetrate through all Swann's defences, and like a block of ice immobilised it, congealed its fluidity, made it freeze altogether ; and Swann felt himself suddenly filled with an enormous and unbreakable mass which pressed on the inner walls of his consciousness until he was fain to burst asunder ; for Odette had said casually, watching him with a malicious smile : " Forcheville is going for a fine trip at Whitsuntide. He's going to Egypt ! " and Swann had at once understood that this meant : " I am going to Egypt at Whitsuntide with Forcheville."

And, in fact, if, a few days later, Swann began : " About that trip that you told me you were going to take with Forcheville," she would answer carelessly : " Yes, my dear boy, we're starting on the 19th ; we'll send you a ' view ' of the Pyramids." Then he was determined to know whether she was Forcheville's mistress, to ask her point-blank, to insist upon her telling him. He knew that there were some perjuries which, being so superstitious, she would not commit, and besides, the fear, which had hitherto restrained his curiosity, of making Odette angry if he questioned her, of making himself odious, had ceased to exist now that he had lost all hope of ever being loved by her.

One day he received an anonymous letter which told him that Odette had been the mistress of countless men (several of whom it named, among them Forcheville, M. de Bréauté and the painter) and women, and that she frequented houses of ill-fame. He was tormented by the discovery that there was to be numbered among his friends a creature capable of sending him such a letter (for certain details betrayed in the writer a familiarity with his private life). He wondered who it could be. But he had never had any suspicion with regard to the unknown actions of other people, those which had no visible connection with what they said. And when he wanted to know whether it was rather beneath the apparent character of M. de Charlus, or of M. des Laumes, or of M. d'Orsan that he must place the untravelled region in which this ignoble action might have had its birth ; as none of these men had ever, in conversation with Swann, suggested that he approved of anonymous letters, and as everything that they had ever said to him implied that they strongly disapproved, he saw no further reason for associating this infamy with the character of any one of them more than with the rest. M. de Charlus

was somewhat inclined to eccentricity, but he was fundamentally good and kind ; M. des Laumes was a trifle dry,
but wholesome and straight. As for M. d'Orsan, Swann had
never met anyone who, even in the most depressing circumstances, would come to him with a more heartfelt utterance,
would act more properly or with more discretion. So much
so that he was unable to understand the rather indelicate part
commonly attributed to M. d'Orsan in his relations with a
certain wealthy woman, and that whenever he thought of
him he was obliged to set that evil reputation on one side, as
irreconcilable with so many unmistakable proofs of his
genuine sincerity and refinement. For a moment Swann felt
that his mind was becoming clouded, and he thought of something else so as to recover a little light ; until he had the
courage to return to those other reflections. But then, after
not having been able to suspect anyone, he was forced to
suspect everyone that he knew. After all, M. de Charlus
might be most fond of him, might be most good-natured ;
but he was a neuropath ; to-morrow, perhaps, he would
burst into tears on hearing that Swann was ill ; and to-day,
from jealousy, or in anger, or carried away by some sudden
idea, he might have wished to do him a deliberate injury.
Really, that kind of màn was the worst of all. The Prince
des Laumes was, certainly, far less devoted to Swann than was
M. de Charlus. But for that very reason he had not the same
susceptibility with regard to him ; and besides, his was a
nature which, though, no doubt, it was cold, was as incapable
of a base as of a magnanimous action. Swann regretted that
he had formed no attachments in his life except to such people.
Then he reflected that what prevents men from doing harm
to their neighbours is fellow-feeling, that he could not, in
the last resort, answer for any but men whose natures were

SWANN'S WAY

analogous to his own, as was, so far as the heart went, that
of M. de Charlus. The mere thought of causing Swann so
much distress would have been revolting to him. But with
a man who was insensible, of another order of humanity, as
was the Prince des Laumes, how was one to foresee the
actions to which he might be led by the promptings of a
different nature? To have a good heart was everything, and
M. de Charlus had one. But M. d'Orsan was not lacking in
that either, and his relations with Swann—cordial, but scarcely
intimate, arising from the pleasure which, as they held the same
views about everything, they found in talking together—were
more quiescent than the enthusiastic affection of M. de
Charlus, who was apt to be led into passionate activity,
good or evil. If there was anyone by whom Swann felt
that he had always been understood, and (with delicacy)
loved, it was M. d'Orsan. Yes, but the life he led ; it could
hardly be called honourable. Swann regretted that he had
never taken any notice of those rumours, that he himself
had admitted, jestingly, that he had never felt so keen a
sense of sympathy, or of respect, as when he was in thoroughly
'detrimental' society. "It is not for nothing," he now
assured himself, " that when people pass judgment upon their
neighbour, their finding is based upon his actions. It is those
alone that are significant, and not at all what we say or what
we think. Charlus and des Laumes may have this or that
fault, but they are men of honour. Orsan, perhaps, has not
the same faults, but he is not a man of honour. He may have
acted dishonourably once again." Then he suspected Rémi,
who, it was true, could only have inspired the letter, but
he now felt himself, for a moment, to be on the right track.
To begin with, Loredan had his own reasons for wishing
harm to Odette. And then, how were we not to suppose that

our servants, living in a situation inferior to our own, adding to our fortunes and to our frailties imaginary riches and vices for which they at once envied and despised us, should not find themselves led by fate to act in a manner abhorrent to people of our own class ? He also suspected my grandfather. On every occasion when Swann had asked him to do him any service, had he not invariably declined ? Besides, with his ideas of middle-class respectability, he might have thought that he was acting for Swann's good. He suspected, in turn, Bergotte, the painter, the Verdurins ; paused for a moment to admire once again the wisdom of people in society, who refused to mix in the artistic circles in which such things were possible, were, perhaps, even openly avowed, as excellent jokes ; but then he recalled the marks of honesty that were to be observed in those Bohemians, and contrasted them with the life of expedients, often bordering on fraudulence, to which the want of money, the craving for luxury, the corrupting influence of their pleasures often drove members of the aristocracy. In a word, this anonymous letter proved that he himself knew a human being capable of the most infamous conduct, but he could see no reason why that infamy should lurk in the depths—which no strange eye might explore—of the warm heart rather than the cold, the artist's rather than the business-man's, the noble's rather than the flunkey's. What criterion ought one to adopt, in order to judge one's fellows ? After all, there was not a single one of the people whom he knew who might not, in certain circumstances, prove capable of a shameful action. Must he then cease to see them all ? His mind grew clouded ; he passed his hands two or three times across his brow, wiped his glasses with his handkerchief, and remembering that, after all, men who were as good as himself frequented the society of M. de Charlus, the Prince des Laumes and the rest, he persuaded himself that this meant, if not that they were incapable of shameful actions, at least that it was a necessity in human life, to which everyone must submit, to frequent the society of people who were, perhaps, not incapable of such actions. And he continued to shake hands with all the friends whom he had suspected, with the purely formal reservation that each one of them had, possibly, been seeking to drive him to despair. As for the actual contents of the letter, they did not disturb him ; for in not one of the charges which it formulated against Odette could he see the least vestige of fact. Like many other men, Swann had a naturally lazy mind, and was slow in invention. He knew quite well as a general truth, that human life is full of contrasts, but in the case of any one human being he imagined all that part of his or her life with which he was not familiar as being identical with the part with which he was. He imagined what was kept secret from him in the light of what was revealed. At such times as he spent with Odette, if their conversation turned upon an indelicate act committed, or an indelicate sentiment expressed by some third person, she would ruthlessly condemn the culprit by virtue of the same moral principles which Swann had always heard expressed by his own parents, and to which he himself had remained loyal ; and then, she would arrange her flowers, would sip her tea, would shew an interest in his work. So Swann extended those habits to fill the rest of her life, he reconstructed those actions when he wished to form a picture of the moments in which he and she were apart. If anyone had portrayed her to him as she was, or rather as she had been for so long with himself, but had substituted some other man, he would have been distressed, for such a portrait would have struck him as lifelike. But to suppose that she went to bad houses, that she abandoned herself to orgies with other women, that she led the crapulous existence of the most abject, the most contemptible of mortals—would be an insane wandering of the mind, for the realisation of which, thank heaven, the chrysanthemums that he could imagine, the daily cups of tea, the virtuous indignation left neither time nor place. Only, now and again, he gave Odette to understand that people maliciously kept him informed of everything that she did ; and making opportune use of some detail—insignificant but true—which he had accidentally learned, as though it were the sole fragment which he would allow, in spite of himself, to pass his lips, out of the numberless other fragments of that complete reconstruction of her daily life which he carried secretly in his mind, he led her to suppose that he was perfectly informed upon matters, which, in reality, he neither knew nor suspected, for if he often adjured Odette never to swerve from or make alteration of the truth, that was only, whether he realised it or no, in order that Odette should tell him everything that she did. No doubt, as he used to assure Odette, he loved sincerity, but only as he might love a pander who could keep him in touch with the daily life of his mistress. Moreover, his love of sincerity, not being disinterested, had not improved his character. The truth which he cherished was that which Odette would tell him ; but he himself, in order to extract that truth from her, was not afraid to have recourse to falsehood, that very falsehood which he never ceased to depict to Odette as leading every human creature down to utter degradation. In a word, he lied as much as did Odette, because, while more unhappy than she, he was no less egotistical. And she, when she heard him repeating thus to her the things that she had done, would stare at him with a look of distrust and, at all hazards, of indignation, so as not to appear to be humiliated, and to be blushing for her actions. One day, after the longest period of calm through which he had yet been able to exist without being overtaken by an attack of jealousy, he had accepted an invitation to spend the evening at the theatre with the Princesse des Laumes. Having opened his newspaper to find out what was being played, the sight of the title—*Les Filles de Marbre*, by Théodore Barrière,—struck him so cruel a blow that he recoiled instinctively from it and turned his head away. Illuminated, as though by a row of footlights, in the new surroundings in which it now appeared, that word 'marble', which he had lost the power to distinguish, so often had it passed, in print, beneath his eyes, had suddenly become visible once again, and had at once brought back to his mind the story which Odette had told him, long ago, of a visit which she had paid to the Salon at the Palais d'Industrie with Mme. Verdurin, who had said to her, " Take care, now ! I know how to melt you, all right. You're not made of marble." Odette had assured him that it was only a joke, and he had not attached any importance to it at the time. But he had had more confidence in her then than he had now. And the anonymous letter referred explicitly to relations of that sort. Without daring to lift his eyes to the newspaper, he opened it, turned the page so as not to see again the words, *Filles de Marbre*, and began to read mechanically the news from the provinces. There had been a storm in the Channel, and damage was reported from Dieppe, Cabourg, Beuzeval. . . . Suddenly he recoiled again in horror.

The name of Beuzeval had suggested to him that of another place in the same district, Beuzeville, which carried also, bound to it by a hyphen, a second name, to wit Bréauté, which he had often seen on maps, but without ever previously remarking that it was the same name as that borne by his friend M. de Bréauté, whom the anonymous letter accused of having been Odette's lover. After all, when it came to M. de Bréauté, there was nothing improbable in the charge ; but so far as Mme. Verdurin was concerned, it was a sheer impossibility. From the fact that Odette did occasionally tell a lie, it was not fair to conclude that she never, by any chance, told the truth, and in these bantering conversations with Mme. Verdurin which she herself had repeated to Swann, he could recognise those meaningless and dangerous pleasantries which, in their inexperience of life and ignorance of vice, women often utter (thereby certifying their own innocence), who—as, for instance, Odette,—would be the last people in the world to feel any undue affection for one another. Whereas, on the other hand, the indignation with which she had scattered the suspicions which she had unintentionally brought into being, for a moment, in his mind by her story, fitted in with everything that he knew of the tastes, the temperament of his mistress. But at that moment, by an inspiration of jealousy, analogous to the inspiration which reveals to a poet or a philosopher, who has nothing, so far, but an odd pair of rhymes or a detached observation, the idea or the natural law which will give power, mastery to his work, Swann recalled for the first time a remark which Odette had made to him, at least two years before : " Oh, Mme. Verdurin, she won't hear of anything just now but me. I'm a 'love', if you please, and she kisses me, and wants me to go with her everywhere, and call her by her Christian name." So far from seeing in these expressions any connection with the absurd insinuations, intended to create an atmosphere of vice, which Odette had since repeated to him, he had welcomed them as a proof of Mme. Verdurin's warm-hearted and generous friendship. But now this old memory of her affection for Odette had coalesced suddenly with his more recent memory of her unseemly conversation. He could no longer separate them in his mind, and he saw them blended in reality, the affection imparting a certain seriousness and importance to the pleasantries which, in return, spoiled the affection of its innocence. He went to see Odette. He sat down, keeping at a distance from her. He did not dare to embrace her, not knowing whether in her, in himself, it would be affection or anger that a kiss would provoke. He sat there silent, watching their love expire. Suddenly he made up his mind.

" Odette, my darling," he began, " I know, I am being simply odious, but I must ask you a few questions. You remember what I once thought about you and Mme. Verdurin ? Tell me, was it true ? Have you, with her or anyone else, ever ? "

She shook her head, pursing her lips together ; a sign which people commonly employ to signify that they are not going, because it would bore them to go, when some one has asked, " Are you coming to watch the procession go by ? ", or " Will you be at the review ? ". But this shake of the head, which is thus commonly used to decline participation in an event that has yet to come, imparts for that reason an element of uncertainty to the denial of participation in an event that is past. Furthermore, it suggests reasons of personal convenience, rather than any definite repudiation, any moral impossibility. When he saw Odette thus make him a sign that the insinuation was false, he realised that it was quite possibly true.

" I have told you, I never did ; you know quite well," she added, seeming angry and uncomfortable.

" Yes, I know all that ; but are you quite sure ? Don't say to me, ' You know quite well ' ; say, ' I have never done anything of that sort with any woman '."

She repeated his words like a lesson learned by rote, and as though she hoped, thereby, to be rid of him : " I have never done anything of that sort with any woman."

" Can you swear it to me on your Laghetto medal ? "

Swann knew that Odette would never perjure herself on that.

" Oh, you do make me so miserable," she cried, with a jerk of her body as though to shake herself free of the constraint of his question. " Have you nearly done ? What is the matter with you to-day ? You seem to have made up your mind that I am to be forced to hate you, to curse you ! Look, I was anxious to be friends with you again, for us to have a nice time together, like the old days ; and this is all the thanks I get ! "

However, he would not let her go, but sat there like a surgeon who waits for a spasm to subside that has interrupted his operation but need not make him abandon it.

" You are quite wrong in supposing that I bear you the least ill-will in the world, Odette," he began with a persuasive and deceitful gentleness. " I never speak to you except of what I already know, and I always know a great deal more than I say. But you alone can mollify by your confession what makes me hate you so long as it has been reported to me only by other people. My anger with you is never due to your actions ; I can and do forgive you everything because I love you ; but to your untruthfulness, the ridiculous untruthfulness which makes you persist in denying things which I know to be true. How can you expect that I shall continue to love you, when I see you maintain, when

I hear you swear to me a thing which I know to be false?
Odette, do not prolong this moment which is torturing us
both. If you are willing to end it at once, you shall be free of
it for ever. Tell me, upon your medal, yes or no, whether
you have ever done those things."

" How on earth can I tell ? " she was furious. " Perhaps
I have, ever so long ago, when I didn't know what I was
doing, perhaps two or three times."

Swann had prepared himself for all possibilities. Reality
must, therefore, be something which bears no relation to
possibilities, any more than the stab of a knife in one's body
bears to the gradual movement of the clouds overhead, since
those words " two or three times " carved, as it were, a cross
upon the living tissues of his heart. A strange thing, indeed,
that those words, " two or three times," nothing more than a
few words, words uttered in the air, at a distance, could so
lacerate a man's heart, as if they had actually pierced it,
could sicken a man, like a poison that he had drunk. Instinctively Swann thought of the remark that he had heard at
Mme. de Saint-Euverte's : " I have never seen anything to
beat it since the table-turning." The agony that he now
suffered in no way resembled what he had supposed. Not
only because, in the hours when he most entirely mistrusted
her, he had rarely imagined such a culmination of evil, but
because, even when he did imagine that offence, it remained
vague, uncertain, was not clothed in the particular horror
which had escaped with the words " perhaps two or three
times," was not armed with that specific cruelty, as different
from anything that he had known as a new malady by which
one is attacked for the first time. And yet this Odette, from
whom all this evil sprang, was no less dear to him, was, on the
contrary, more precious, as if, in proportion as his sufferings

increased, there increased at the same time the price of the
sedative, of the antidote which this woman alone possessed.
He wished to pay her more attention, as one attends to a
disease which one discovers, suddenly, to have grown more
serious. He wished that the horrible thing which, she had
told him, she had done " two or three times " might be prevented from occurring again. To ensure that, he must watch
over Odette. People often say that, by pointing out to a
man the faults of his mistress, you succeed only in strengthen-
ing his attachment to her, because he does not believe you ;
yet how much more so if he does ! But, Swann asked himself,
how could he manage to protect her ? He might perhaps be
able to preserve her from the contamination of any one
woman, but there were hundreds of other women ; and he
realised how insane had been his ambition when he had begun
(on the evening when he had failed to find Odette at the
Verdurins') to desire the possession—as if that were ever
possible—of another person. Happily for Swann, beneath the
mass of suffering which had invaded his soul like a conquering
horde of barbarians, there lay a natural foundation, older,
more placid, and silently laborious, like the cells of an injured
organ which at once set to work to repair the damaged tissues,
or the muscles of a paralysed limb which tend to recover their
former movements. These older, these autochthonous in-
dwellers in his soul absorbed all Swann's strength, for a while,
in that obscure task of reparation which gives one an illusory
sense of repose during convalescence, or after an operation.
This time it was not so much—as it ordinarily was—in
Swann's brain that the slackening of tension due to exhaustion
took effect, it was rather in his heart. But all the things in
life that have once existed tend to recur, and, like a dying
animal that is once more stirred by the throes of a convulsion

which was, apparently, ended, upon Swann's heart, spared for
a moment only, the same agony returned of its own accord
to trace the same cross again. He remembered those moonlit
evenings, when, leaning back in the victoria that was taking
him to the Rue La Pérouse, he would cultivate with voluptuous enjoyment the emotions of a man in love, ignorant of the
poisoned fruit that such emotions must inevitably bear. But
all those thoughts lasted for no more than a second, the time
that it took him to raise his hand to his heart, to draw breath
again and to contrive to smile, so as to dissemble his torment.
Already he had begun to put further questions. For his
jealousy, which had taken an amount of trouble, such as no
enemy would have incurred, to strike him this mortal blow,
to make him forcibly acquainted with the most cruel pain
that he had ever known, his jealousy was not satisfied that
he had yet suffered enough, and sought to expose his bosom
to an even deeper wound. Like an evil deity, his jealousy
was inspiring Swann, was thrusting him on towards destruc-
tion. It was not his fault, but Odette's alone, if at first his
punishment was not more severe.

" My darling," he began again, " it's all over now ; was
it with anyone I know ? "

" No, I swear it wasn't ; besides, I think I exaggerated,
I never really went as far as that."

He smiled, and resumed with : " Just as you like. It
doesn't really matter, but it's unfortunate that you can't give
me any name. If I were able to form an idea of the person
that would prevent my ever thinking of her again. I say it
for your own sake, because then I shouldn't bother you any
more about it. It's so soothing to be able to form a clear
picture of things in one's mind. What is really terrible is
what one cannot imagine. But you've been so sweet to me ;

I don't want to tire you. I do thank you, with all my heart, for all the good that you have done me. I've quite finished now. Only one word more : how many times ? "

" Oh, Charles ! can't you see, you're killing me ? It's all ever so long ago. I've never given it a thought. Anyone would say that you were positively trying to put those ideas into my head again. And then you'ld be a lot better off ! " she concluded, with unconscious stupidity but with intentional malice.

" I only wished to know whether it had been since I knew you. It's only natural. Did it happen here, ever ? You can't give me any particular evening, so that I can remind myself what I was doing at the time ? You understand, surely, that it's not possible that you don't remember with whom, Odette, my love."

" But I don't know ; really, I don't. I think it was in the Bois, one evening when you came to meet us on the Island. You had been dining with the Princesse des Laumes," she added, happy to be able to furnish him with an exact detail, which testified to her veracity. " At the next table there was a woman whom I hadn't seen for ever so long. She said to me, ' Come along round behind the rock, there, and look at the moonlight on the water ! ' At first I just yawned, and said, ' No, I'm too tired, and I'm quite happy where I am, thank you.' She swore there'd never been anything like it in the way of moonlight. ' I've heard that tale before,' I said to her ; you see, I knew quite well what she was after." Odette narrated this episode almost as if it were a joke, either because it appeared to her to be quite natural, or because she thought that she was thereby minimising its importance, or else so as not to appear ashamed. But, catching sight of Swann's face, she changed her tone, and :

" You are a fiend ! " she flung at him, " you enjoy tormenting me, making me tell you lies, just so that you'll leave me in peace."

This second blow struck at Swann was even more ex-cruciating than the first. Never had he supposed it to have been so recent an affair, hidden from his eyes that had been too innocent to discern it, not in a past which he had never known, but in evenings which he so well remembered, which he had lived through with Odette, of which he had supposed himself to have such an intimate, such an exhaustive know-ledge, and which now assumed, retrospectively, an aspect of cunning and deceit and cruelty. In the midst of them parted, suddenly, a gaping chasm, that moment on the Island in the Bois de Boulogne. Without being intelligent, Odette had the charm of being natural. She had recounted, she had acted the little scene with so much simplicity that Swann, as he gasped for breath, could vividly see it : Odette yawning, the " rock, there," . . . He could hear her answer—alas, how light-heartedly—" I've heard that tale before ! " He felt that she would tell him nothing more that evening, that no further revelation was to be expected for the present. He was silent for a time, then said to her :

" My poor darling, you must forgive me ; I know, I am hurting you dreadfully, but it's all over now ; I shall never think of it again."

But she saw that his eyes remained fixed upon the things that he did not know, and on that past era of their love, monotonous and soothing in his memory because it was vague, and now rent, as with a sword-wound, by the news of that minute on the Island in the Bois, by moonlight, while he was dining with the Princesse des Laumes. But he had so far acquired the habit of finding life interesting—of marvelling

at the strange discoveries that there were to be made in it—
that even while he was suffering so acutely that he did not
believe it possible to endure such agony for any length of time,
he was saying to himself : " Life is indeed astonishing, and
holds some fine surprises ; it appears that vice is far more
common than one has been led to believe. Here is a woman
in whom I had absolute confidence, who looks so simple,
so honest, who, in any case, even allowing that her morals
are not strict, seemed quite normal and healthy in her tastes
and inclinations. I receive a most improbable accusation,
I question her, and the little that she admits reveals far more
than I could ever have suspected." But he could not confine
himself to these detached observations. He sought to form
an exact estimate of the importance of what she had just told
him, so as to know whether he might conclude that she had
done these things often, and was likely to do them again. He
repeated her words to himself : " I knew quite well what
she was after." " Two or three times." " I've heard that
tale before." But they did not reappear in his memory
unarmed ; each of them held a knife with which it stabbed
him afresh. For a long time, like a sick man who cannot
restrain himself from attempting, every minute, to make the
movement that, he knows, will hurt him, he kept on murmuring to himself : " I'm quite happy where I am, thank
you ", " I've heard that tale before." but the pain was so
intense that he was obliged to stop. He was amazed to find
that actions which he had always, hitherto, judged so lightly,
had dismissed, indeed, with a laugh, should have become as
serious to him as a disease which might easily prove fatal.
He knew any number of women whom he could ask to keep
an eye on Odette, but how was he to expect them to adjust
themselves to his new point of view, and not to remain at

that which for so long had been his own, which had always
guided him in his voluptuous existence ; not to say to him
with a smile : " You jealous monster, wanting to rob other
people of their pleasure !" By what trap-door, suddenly
lowered, had he (who had never found, in the old days, in
his love for Odette, any but the most refined of pleasures) been
precipitated into this new circle of hell from which he could
not see how he was ever to escape. Poor Odette ! He wished
her no harm. She was but half to blame. Had he not been
told that it was her own mother who had sold her, when she
was still little more than a child, at Nice, to a wealthy
Englishman. But what an agonising truth was now contained
for him in those lines of Alfred de Vigny's *Journal d'un
Poète* which he had previously read without emotion :
" When one feels oneself smitten by love for a woman, one
ought to say to oneself, ' What are her surroundings ? What
has been her life ? ' All one's future happiness lies in the
answer." Swann was astonished that such simple phrases,
spelt over in his mind, as, " I've heard that tale before," or
" I knew quite well what she was after," could cause him so
much pain. But he realised that what he had mistaken for
simple phrases were indeed parts of the panoply which held
and could inflict on him the anguish that he had felt while
Odette was telling her story. For it was the same anguish
that he now was feeling afresh. It was no good, his knowing
now,—indeed, it was no good, as time went on, his having
partly forgotten and altogether forgiven the offence—whenever he repeated her words his old anguish refashioned him
as he had been before Odette began to speak : ignorant, trust-
ful ; his merciless jealousy placed him once again, so that he
might be effectively wounded by Odette's admission, in the
position of a man who does not yet know the truth ; and

after several months this old story would still dumbfounder
him, like a sudden revelation. He marvelled at the terrible
recreative power of his memory. It was only by the weaken-
ing of that generative force, whose fecundity diminishes as age
creeps over one, that he could hope for a relaxation of his
torments. But, as soon as the power that any one of Odette's
sentences had to make Swann suffer seemed to be nearly
exhausted, lo and behold another, one of those to which he
had hitherto paid least attention, almost a new sentence, came
to relieve the first, and to strike at him with undiminished
force. The memory of the evening on which he had dined
with the Princesse des Laumes was painful to him, but it was
no more than the centre, the core of his pain. That radiated
vaguely round about it, overflowing into all the preceding
and following days. And on whatever point in it he might
intend his memory to rest, it was the whole of that season,
during which the Verdurins had so often gone to dine upon
the Island in the Bois, that sprang back to hurt him. So
violently, that by slow degrees the curiosity which his
jealousy was ever exciting in him was neutralised by his fear
of the fresh tortures which he would be inflicting upon himself were he to satisfy it. He recognised that all the period of
Odette's life which had elapsed before she first met him, a
period of which he had never sought to form any picture in
his mind, was not the featureless abstraction which he could
vaguely see, but had consisted of so many definite, dated years,
each crowded with concrete incidents. But were he to learn
more of them, he feared lest her past, now colourless, fluid
and supportable, might assume a tangible, an obscene form,
with individual and diabolical features. And he continued to
refrain from seeking a conception of it, not any longer now
from laziness of mind, but from fear of suffering. He hoped

that, some day, he might be able to hear the Island in the Bois, or the Princesse des Laumes mentioned without feeling any twinge of that old rending pain ; meanwhile he thought it imprudent to provoke Odette into furnishing him with fresh sentences, with the names of more places and people and of different events, which, when his malady was still scarcely healed, would make it break out again in another form.

But, often enough, the things that he did not know, that he dreaded, now, to learn, it was Odette herself who, spontaneously and without thought of what she did, revealed them to him ; for the gap which her vices made between her actual life and the comparatively innocent life which Swann had believed, and often still believed his mistress to lead, was far wider than she knew. A vicious person, always affecting the same air of virtue before people whom he is anxious to keep from having any suspicion of his vices, has no register, no gauge at hand from which he may ascertain how far those vices (their continuous growth being imperceptible by himself) have gradually segregated him from the normal ways of life. In the course of their cohabitation, in Odette's mind, with the memory of those of her actions which she concealed from Swann, her other, her innocuous actions were gradually coloured, infected by these, without her being able to detect anything strange in them, without their causing any explosion in the particular region of herself in which she made them live, but when she related them to Swann, he was overwhelmed by the revelation of the duplicity to which they pointed. One day, he was trying—without hurting Odette—to discover from her whether she had ever had any dealings with procuresses. He was, as a matter of fact, convinced that she had not ; the anonymous letter had put the

idea into his mind, but in a purely mechanical way ; it had
been received there with no credulity, but it had, for all that,
remained there, and Swann, wishing to be rid of the burden—
a dead weight, but none the less disturbing—of this suspicion,
hoped that Odette would now extirpate it for ever.

" Oh dear, no ! Not that they don't simply persecute me
to go to them," her smile revealed a gratified vanity which she
no longer saw that it was impossible should appear legitimate
to Swann. " There was one of them waited more than two
hours for me yesterday, said she would give me any money
I asked. It seems, there's an Ambassador who said to her,
' I'll kill myself if you don't bring her to me '—meaning me !
They told her I'd gone out, but she waited and waited, and
in the end I had to go myself and speak to her, before she'ld
go away. I do wish you could have seen the way I tackled
her ; my maid was in the next room, listening, and told me
I shouted fit to bring the house down :—' But when you
hear me say that I don't want to ! The idea of such a thing,
I don't like it at all ! I should hope I'm still free to do as
I please and when I please and where I please ! If I needed
the money, I could understand . . . ' The porter has orders
not to let her in again ; he will tell her that I am out of town.
Oh, I do wish I could have had you hidden somewhere in
the room while I was talking to her. I know, you'ld have
been pleased, my dear. There's some good in your little
Odette, you see, after all, though people do say such dreadful
things about her."

Besides, her very admissions—when she made any—of
faults which she supposed him to have discovered, rather
served Swann as a starting-point for fresh doubts than they
put an end to the old. For her admissions never exactly
coincided with his doubts. In vain might Odette expurgate

her confession of all its essential part, there would remain in
the accessories something which Swann had never yet
imagined, which crushed him anew, and was to enable him
to alter the terms of the problem of his jealousy. And these
admissions he could never forget. His spirit carried them
along, cast them aside, then cradled them again in its bosom,
like corpses in a river. And they poisoned it.

She spoke to him once of a visit that Forcheville had paid
her on the day of the Paris-Murcie Fête. "What ! you knew
him as long ago as that ? Oh, yes, of course you did," he
corrected himself, so as not to shew that he had been ignorant
of the fact. And suddenly he began to tremble at the thought
that, on the day of the Paris-Murcie Fête, when he had
received that letter which he had so carefully preserved, she
had been having luncheon, perhaps, with Forcheville at the
Maison d'Or. She swore that she had not. "Still, the
Maison d'Or reminds me of something or other which, I
knew at the time, wasn't true," he pursued, hoping to
frighten her. "Yes, that I hadn't been there at all that evening when I told you I had just come from there, and you
had been looking for me at Prévost's," she replied (judging
by his manner that he knew) with a firmness that was based
not so much upon cynicism as upon timidity, a fear of crossing
Swann, which her own self-respect made her anxious to
conceal, and a desire to shew him that she could be perfectly
frank if she chose. And so she struck him with all the sharpness and force of a headsman wielding his axe, and yet could
not be charged with cruelty, since she was quite unconscious
of hurting him ; she even began to laugh, though this may
perhaps, it is true, have been chiefly to keep him from thinking that she was ashamed, at all, or confused. "It's quite
true, I hadn't been to the Maison Dorée. I was coming

away from Forcheville's. I had, really, been to Prévost's—
that wasn't a story—and he met me there and asked me to
come in and look at his prints. But some one else came to
see him. I told you that I was coming from the Maison d'Or
because I was afraid you might be angry with me. It was
rather nice of me, really, don't you see ? I admit, I did
wrong, but at least I'm telling you all about it now, a'n't I ?
What have I to gain by not telling you, straight, that I lunched
with him on the day of the Paris-Murcie Fête, if it were
true ? Especially as at that time we didn't know one another
quite so well as we do now, did we, dear ? "

He smiled back at her with the sudden, craven weakness of
the utterly spiritless creature which these crushing words
had made of him. And so, even in the months of which he
had never dared to think again, because they had been too
happy, in those months when she had loved him, she was
already lying to him ! Besides that moment (that first evening
on which they had " done a cattleya ") when she had told
him that she was coming from the Maison Dorée, how many
others must there have been, each of them covering a falsehood of which Swann had had no suspicion. He recalled how
she had said to him once : " I need only tell Mme. Verdurin
that my dress wasn't ready, or that my cab came late. There
is always some excuse." From himself too, probably, many
times when she had glibly uttered such words as explain a
delay or justify an alteration of the hour fixed for a meeting,
those moments must have hidden, without his having the
least inkling of it at the time, an engagement that she had
had with some other man, some man to whom she had said :
" I need only tell Swann that my dress wasn't ready, or that
my cab came late. There is always some excuse." And
beneath all his most pleasant memories, beneath the simplest

words that Odette had ever spoken to him in those old days,
words which he had believed as though they were the words
of a Gospel, beneath her daily actions which she had recounted
to him, beneath the most ordinary places, her dressmaker's
flat, the Avenue du Bois, the Hippodrome, he could feel
(dissembled there, by virtue of that temporal superfluity
which, after the most detailed account of how a day has been
spent, always leaves something over, that may serve as a
hiding place for certain unconfessed actions), he could feel
the insinuation of a possible undercurrent of falsehood which
debased for him all that had remained most precious, his
happiest evenings, the Rue La Pérouse itself, which Odette
must constantly have been leaving at other hours than those
of which she told him ; extending the power of the dark
horror that had gripped him when he had heard her admission
with regard to the Maison Dorée, and, like the obscene creatures in the 'Desolation of Nineveh', shattering, stone by stone,
the whole edifice of his past. . . . If, now, he turned aside
whenever his memory repeated the cruel name of the Maison
Dorée, it was because that name recalled to him, no longer,
as, such a little time since, at Mme. de Saint-Euverte's party,
the good fortune which he long had lost, but a misfortune of
which he was now first aware. Then it befell the Maison
Dorée, as it had befallen the Island in the Bois, that gradually
its name ceased to trouble him. For what we suppose to be
our love, our jealousy are, neither of them, single, continuous
and individual passions. They are composed of an infinity of
successive loves, of different jealousies, each of which is
ephemeral, although by their uninterrupted multitude they
give us the impression of continuity, the illusion of unity.
The life of Swann's love, the fidelity of his jealousy, were
formed out of death, of infidelity, of innumerable desires,

innumerable doubts, all of which had Odette for their object.
If he had remained for any length of time without seeing her,
those that died would not have been replaced by others.
But the presence of Odette continued to sow in Swann's heart
alternate seeds of love and suspicion.

On certain evenings she would suddenly resume towards
him a kindness of which she would warn him sternly that he
must take immediate advantage, under penalty of not seeing
it repeated for years to come ; he must instantly accompany
her home, to "do a cattleya", and the desire which she pretended to have for him was so sudden, so inexplicable, so
imperious, the kisses which she lavished on him were so
demonstrative and so unfamiliar, that this brutal and un-
natural fondness made Swann just as unhappy as any lie or
unkind action. One evening when he had thus, in obedience
to her command, gone home with her, and while she was
interspersing her kisses with passionate words, in strange
contrast to her habitual coldness, he thought suddenly that
he heard a sound ; he rose, searched everywhere and found
nobody, but he had not the courage to return to his place by
her side ; whereupon she, in a towering rage, broke a vase,
with " I never can do anything right with you, you impossible person ! " And he was left uncertain whether she
had not actually had some man concealed in the room, whose
jealousy she had wished to wound, or else to inflame his
senses.

Sometimes he repaired to 'gay' houses, hoping to learn
something about Odette, although he dared not mention her
name. " I have a little thing here, you're sure to like," the
'manageress' would greet him, and he would stay for an
hour or so, talking dolefully to some poor girl who sat there
astonished that he went no further. One of them, who was

still quite young and attractive, said to him once, "Of course, what I should like would be to find a real friend, then he might be quite certain, I should never go with any other men again." " Indeed, do you think it possible for a woman really to be touched by a man's being in love with her, and never to be unfaithful to him ? " asked Swann anxiously. " Why, surely ! It all depends on their characters ! " Swann could not help making the same remarks to these girls as would have delighted the Princesse des Laumes. To the one who was in search of a friend he said, with a smile : " But how nice of you, you've put on blue eyes, to go with your sash." " And you too, you've got blue cuffs on." " What a charming conversation we are having, for a place of this sort ! I'm not boring you, am I ; or keeping you ? " " No, I've nothing to do, thank you. If you bored me I should say so But I love hearing you talk." " I am highly flattered. . . . Aren't we behaving prettily ? " he asked the ' manageress', who had just looked in. " Why, yes, that's just what I was saying to myself, how sensibly they're behaving ! But that's how it is ! People come to my house now, just to talk. The Prince was telling me, only the other day, that he's far more comfortable here than with his wife. It seems that, nowadays, all the society ladies are like that ; a perfect scandal, I call it. But I'll leave you in peace now, I know when I'm not wanted," she ended discreetly, and left Swann with the girl who had the blue eyes. But presently he rose and said good-bye to her. She had ceased to interest him. She did not know Odette.

The painter having been ill, Dr. Cottard recommended a sea-voyage ; several of the 'faithful' spoke of accompanying him ; the Verdurins could not face the prospect of being left alone in Paris, so first of all hired, and finally purchased a yacht ; thus Odette was constantly going on a cruise. Whenever she had been away for any length of time, Swann would feel that he was beginning to detach himself from her, but, as though this moral distance were proportionate to the physical distance between them, whenever he heard that Odette had returned to Paris, he could not rest without seeing her. Once, when they had gone away, as everyone thought, for a month only, either they succumbed to a series of temptations, or else M. Verdurin had cunningly arranged everything beforehand, to please his wife, and disclosed his plans to the 'faithful' only as time went on ; anyhow, from Algiers they flitted to Tunis ; then to Italy, Greece, Constantinople, Asia Minor. They had been absent for nearly a year, and Swann felt perfectly at ease and almost happy. Albeit M. Verdurin had endeavoured to persuade the pianist and Dr. Cottard that their respective aunt and patients had no need of them, and that, in any event, it was most rash to allow Mme. Cottard to return to Paris, where, Mme. Verdurin assured him, a revolution had just broken out, he was obliged to grant them their liberty at Constantinople. And the painter came home with them. One day, shortly after the return of these four travellers, Swann, seeing an omnibus approach him, labelled 'Luxembourg', and having some business there, had jumped on to it and had found himself sitting opposite Mme. Cottard, who was paying a round of visits to people whose 'day' it was, in full review order, with a plume in her hat, a silk dress, a muff, an umbrella (which would do for a parasol if the rain kept off), a card-case, and a pair of white gloves fresh from the cleaners. Wearing these badges of rank, she would, in fine weather, go on foot from one house to another in the same neighbourhood, but when she had to proceed to another district, would make use

of a transfer-ticket on the omnibus. For the first minute or
two, until the natural courtesy of the woman broke through
the starched surface of the doctor's-wife, not being certain,
either, whether she ought to mention the Verdurins before
Swann, she produced, quite naturally, in her slow and awkward, but not unattractive voice, which, every now and then,
was completely drowned by the rattling of the omnibus,
topics selected from those which she had picked up and would
repeat in each of the score of houses up the stairs of which
she clambered in the course of an afternoon.

"I needn't ask you, M. Swann, whether a man so much
in the movement as yourself has been to the Mirlitons, to see
the portrait by Machard that the whole of Paris is running
after. Well, and what do you think of it ? Whose camp are
you in, those who bless or those who curse ? It's the same
in every house in Paris now, no one will speak of anything
else but Machard's portrait ; you aren't smart, you aren't
really cultured, you aren't up-to-date unless you give an
opinion on Machard's portrait."

Swann having replied that he had not seen this portrait,
Mme. Cottard was afraid that she might have hurt his
feelings by obliging him to confess the omission.

"Oh, that's quite all right ! At least you have the courage
to be quite frank about it. You don't consider yourself dis-
graced because you haven't seen Machard's portrait. I do
think that so nice of you. Well now, I have seen it ; opinion
is divided, you know, there are some people who find it
rather laboured, like whipped cream, they say ; but I think
it's just ideal. Of course, she's not a bit like the blue and
yellow ladies that our friend Biche paints. That's quite
clear. But I must tell you, perfectly frankly (you'll think me
dreadfully old-fashioned, but I always say just what I think),

that I don't understand his work. I can quite see the good
points there are in his portrait of my husband ; oh, dear me,
yes ; and it's certainly less odd than most of what he does,
but even then he had to give the poor man a blue moustache !
But Machard ! Just listen to this now, the husband of my
friend, I am on my way to see at this very moment (which
has given me the very great pleasure of your company), has
promised her that, if he is elected to the Academy (he is one
of the Doctor's colleagues), he will get Machard to paint her
portrait. So she's got something to look forward to ! I have
another friend who insists that she'ld rather have Leloir.
I'm only a wretched Philistine, and I've no doubt Leloir has
perhaps more knowledge of painting even than Machard.
But I do think that the most important thing about a portrait,
especially when it's going to cost ten thousand francs, is that
it should be like, and a pleasant likeness, if you know what
I mean."

Having exhausted this topic, to which she had been inspired
by the loftiness of her plume, the monogram on her card-case,
the little number inked inside each of her gloves by the
cleaner, and the difficulty of speaking to Swann about the
Verdurins, Mme. Cottard, seeing that they had still a long
way to go before they would reach the corner of the Rue
Bonaparte, where the conductor was to set her down,
listened to the promptings of her heart, which counselled
other words than these.

" Your ears must have been burning," she ventured,
" while we were on the yacht with Mme. Verdurin. We
were talking about you all the time."

Swann was genuinely astonished, for he supposed that his
name was never uttered in the Verdurins' presence.

" You see," Mme. Cottard went on, " Mme. de Crécy

was there ; need I say more ? When Odette is anywhere
it's never long before she begins talking about you. And you
know quite well, it isn't nasty things she says. What ! you
don't believe me ! " she went on, noticing that Swann looked
sceptical. And, carried away by the sincerity of her conviction, without putting any evil meaning into the word,
which she used purely in the sense in which one employs it to
speak of the affection that unites a pair of friends ; " Why,
she *adores* you ! No, indeed ; I'm sure it would never do
to say anything against you when she was about ; one would
soon be taught one's place ! Whatever we might be doing,
if we were looking at a picture, for instance, she would say,
' If only we had him here, he's the man who could tell us
whether it's genuine or not. There's no one like him for
that.' And all day long she would be saying, ' What can he
be doing just now ? I do hope, he's doing a little work ! It's
too dreadful that a fellow with such gifts as he has should
be so lazy.' (Forgive me, won't you.) ' I can see him this very
moment ; he's thinking of us, he's wondering where we are.'
Indeed, she used an expression which I thought very pretty
at the time. M. Verdurin asked her, ' How in the world can
you see what he's doing, when he's a thousand miles away ? '
And Odette answered, ' Nothing is impossible to the eye of
a friend.'

"No, I assure you, I'm not saying it just to flatter you ;
you have a true friend in her, such as one doesn't often find.
I can tell you, besides, in case you don't know it, that you're
the only one. Mme. Verdurin told me as much herself on
our last day with them (one talks more freely, don't you know,
before a parting), ' I don't say that Odette isn't fond of us,
but anything that we may say to her counts for very little
beside what Swann might say.' Oh, mercy, there's the con-

ductor stopping for me ; here have I been chatting away to you, and would have gone right past the Rue Bonaparte, and never noticed. . . Will you be so very kind as to tell me whether my plume is straight ? "

And Mme. Cottard withdrew from her muff, to offer it to Swann, a white-gloved hand from which there floated, with a transfer-ticket, an atmosphere of fashionable life that pervaded the omnibus, blended with the harsher fragrance of newly cleaned kid. And Swann felt himself overflowing with gratitude to her, as well as to Mme. Verdurin (and almost to Odette, for the feeling that he now entertained for her was no longer tinged with pain, was scarcely even to be described, now, as love), while from the platform of the omnibus he followed her with loving eyes, as she gallantly threaded her way along the Rue Bonaparte, her plume erect, her skirt held up in one hand, while in the other she clasped her umbrella and her card-case, so that its monogram could be seen, her muff dancing in the air before her as she went.

To compete with and so to stimulate the moribund feelings that Swann had for Odette, Mme. Cottard, a wiser physician, in this case, than ever her husband would have been, had grafted among them others more normal, feelings of gratitude, of friendship, which in Swann's mind were to make Odette seem again more human (more like other women, since other women could inspire the same feelings in him), were to hasten her final transformation back into that Odette, loved with an undisturbed affection, who had taken him home one evening after a revel at the painter's, to drink orangeade with Forcheville, that Odette with whom Swann had calculated that he might live in happiness.

In former times, having often thought with terror that a day must come when he would cease to be in love with Odette, he had determined to keep a sharp look-out, and as soon as he felt that love was beginning to escape him, to cling tightly to it and to hold it back. But now, to the faintness of his love there corresponded a simultaneous faintness in his desire to remain her lover. For a man cannot change, that is to say become another person, while he continues to obey the dictates of the self which he has ceased to be. Occasionally the name, if it caught his eye in a newspaper, of one of the men whom he supposed to have been Odette's lovers, re-awakened his jealousy. But it was very slight, and, inasmuch as it proved to him that he had not completely emerged from that period in which he had so keenly suffered—though in it he had also known a way of feeling so intensely happy—and that the accidents of his course might still enable him to catch an occasional glimpse, stealthily and at a distance, of its beauties, this jealousy gave him, if anything, an agreeable thrill, as to the sad Parisian, when he has left Venice behind him and must return to France, a last mosquito proves that Italy and summer are still not too remote. But, as a rule, with this particular period of his life from which he was emerging, when he made an effort, if not to remain in it, at least to obtain, while still he might, an uninterrupted view of it, he discovered that already it was too late ; he would have looked back to distinguish, as it might be a landscape that was about to disappear, that love from which he had departed ; but it is so difficult to enter into a state of complete duality and to present to oneself the lifelike spectacle of a feeling which one has ceased to possess, that very soon, the clouds gathering in his brain, he could see nothing, he would abandon the attempt, would take the glasses from his nose and wipe them ; and he told himself that he would do better to rest for a little, that there would be time enough later on, and settled back into

his corner with as little curiosity, with as much torpor as the
drowsy traveller who pulls his cap down over his eyes so as
to get some sleep in the railway-carriage that is drawing him,
he feels, faster and faster, out of the country in which he has
lived for so long, and which he vowed that he would not allow
to slip away from him without looking out to bid it a last
farewell. Indeed, like the same traveller, if he does not awake
until he has crossed the frontier and is again in France, when
Swann happened to alight, close at hand, upon something
which proved that Forcheville had been Odette's lover, he
discovered that it caused him no pain, that love was now
utterly remote, and he regretted that he had had no warning
of the moment in which he had emerged from it for ever.
And just as, before kissing Odette for the first time, he had
sought to imprint upon his memory the face that for so long
had been familiar, before it was altered by the additional
memory of their kiss, so he could have wished—in thought at
least—to have been in a position to bid farewell, while she
still existed, to that Odette who had inspired love in him and
jealousy, to that Odette who had caused him so to suffer, and
whom now he would never see again. He was mistaken. He
was destined to see her once again, a few weeks later. It was
while he was asleep, in the twilight of a dream. He was
walking with Mme. Verdurin, Dr. Cottard, a young man
in a fez whom he failed to identify, the painter, Odette,
Napoleon III and my grandfather, along a path which
followed the line of the coast, and overhung the sea, now at a
great height, now by a few feet only, so that they were continually going up and down ; those of the party who had
reached the downward slope were no longer visible to those
who were still climbing ; what little daylight yet remained
was failing, and it seemed as though a black night was imme-

diately to fall on them. Now and then the waves dashed
against the cliff, and Swann could feel on his cheek a shower
of freezing spray. Odette told him to wipe this off, but he
could not, and felt confused and helpless in her company, as
well as because he was in his nightshirt. He hoped that, in
the darkness, this might pass unnoticed ; Mme. Verdurin,
however, fixed her astonished gaze upon him for an endless
moment, in which he saw her face change its shape, her nose
grow longer, while beneath it there sprouted a heavy
moustache. He turned away to examine Odette ; her cheeks
were pale, with little fiery spots, her features drawn and
ringed with shadows ; but she looked back at him with eyes
welling with affection, ready to detach themselves like tears
and to fall upon his face, and he felt that he loved her so much
that he would have liked to carry her off with him at once.
Suddenly Odette turned her wrist, glanced at a tiny watch,
and said : " I must go." She took leave of everyone, in the
same formal manner, without taking Swann aside, without
telling him where they were to meet that evening, or next
day. He dared not ask, he would have liked to follow her,
he was obliged, without turning back in her direction, to
answer with a smile some question by Mme. Verdurin ; but
his heart was frantically beating, he felt that he now hated
Odette, he would gladly have crushed those eyes which, a
moment ago, he had loved so dearly, have torn the blood into
those lifeless cheeks. He continued to climb with Mme.
Verdurin, that is to say that each step took him farther from
Odette, who was going downhill, and in the other direction.
A second passed and it was many hours since she had left
him. The painter remarked to Swann that Napoleon III had
eclipsed himself immediately after Odette. " They had
obviously arranged it between them," he added ; " they must

have agreed to meet at the foot of the cliff, but they wouldn't say good-bye together ; it might have looked odd. She is his mistress." The strange young man burst into tears. Swann endeavoured to console him. " After all, she is quite right," he said to the young man, drying his eyes for him and taking off the fez to make him feel more at ease. " I've advised her to do that, myself, a dozen times. Why be so distressed ? He was obviously the man to understand her." So Swann reasoned with himself, for the young man whom he had failed, at first, to identify, was himself also ; like certain novelists, he had distributed his own personality between two characters, him who was the ' first person ' in the dream, and another whom he saw before him, capped with a fez.

As for Napoleon III, it was to Forcheville that some vague association of ideas, then a certain modification of the Baron's usual physiognomy, and lastly the broad ribbon of the Legion of Honour across his breast, had made Swann give that name ; but actually, and in everything that the person who appeared in his dream represented and recalled to him, it was indeed Forcheville. For, from an incomplete and changing set of images, Swann in his sleep drew false deductions, enjoying, at the same time, such creative power that he was able to reproduce himself by a simple act of division, like certain lower organisms ; with the warmth that he felt in his own palm he modelled the hollow of a strange hand which he thought that he was clasping, and out of feelings and impressions of which he was not yet conscious, he brought about sudden vicissitudes which, by a chain of logical sequences, would produce, at definite points in his dream, the person required to receive his love or to startle him awake. In an instant night grew black about him ; an alarum rang, the inhabitants ran past him, escaping from their blazing houses ; he could hear the thunder of the surging waves, and also of his own heart, which, with equal violence, was anxiously beating in his breast. Suddenly the speed of these palpitations redoubled, he felt a pain, a nausea that were inexplicable ; a peasant, dreadfully burned, flung at him as he passed : " Come and ask Charlus where Odette spent the night with her friend. He used to go about with her, and she tells him everything. It was they that started the fire." It was his valet, come to awaken him, and saying :—

" Sir, it is eight o'clock, and the barber is here. I have told him to call again in an hour."

But these words, as they dived down through the waves of sleep in which Swann was submerged, did not reach his consciousness without undergoing that refraction which turns a ray of light, at the bottom of a bowl of water, into another sun ; just as, a moment earlier, the sound of the door-bell, swelling in the depths of his abyss of sleep into the clangour of an alarum, had engendered the episode of the fire. Meanwhile the scenery of his dream-stage scattered in dust, he opened his eyes, heard for the last time the boom of a wave in the sea, grown very distant. He touched his cheek. It was dry. And yet he could feel the sting of the cold spray, and the taste of salt on his lips. He rose, and dressed himself. He had made the barber come early because he had written, the day before, to my grandfather, to say that he was going, that after-noon, to Combray, having learned that Mme. de Cambremer —Mlle. Legrandin that had been—was spending a few days there. The association in his memory of her young and charming face with a place in the country which he had not visited for so long, offered him a combined attraction which had made him decide at last to leave Paris for a while. As the different changes and chances that bring us into the company of certain other people in this life do not coincide with the periods in which we are in love with those people, but, overlapping them, may occur before love has begun, and may be repeated after love is ended, the earliest appearances, in our life, of a creature who is destined to afford us pleasure later on, assume retrospectively in our eyes a certain value as an indication, a warning, a presage. It was in this fashion that Swann had often carried back his mind to the image of Odette, encountered in the theatre, on that first evening when he had no thought of ever seeing her again—and that he now recalled the party at Mme. de Saint-Euverte's, at which he had introduced General de Froberville to Mme. de Cambremer. So manifold are our interests in life that it is not uncommon that, on a single occasion, the foundations of a happiness which does not yet exist are laid down simultaneously with aggravations of a grief from which we are still suffering. And, no doubt, that might have occurred to Swann elsewhere than at Mme. de Saint-Euverte's. Who, indeed, can say whether, in the event of his having gone, that evening, somewhere else, other happinesses, other griefs would not have come to him, which, later, would have appeared to have been inevitable ? But what did seem to him to have been inevitable was what had indeed taken place, and he was not far short of seeing something providential in the fact that he had at last decided to go to Mme. de Saint-Euverte's that evening, because his mind, anxious to admire the richness of invention that life shews, and incapable of facing a difficult problem for any length of time, such as to discover what, actually, had been most to be wished for, came to the conclusion that the sufferings through which he had passed that evening, and the pleasures, at that time unsuspected, which were already being brought to birth,—the exact balance between which was too difficult to establish—were linked by a sort of concatenation of necessity.

But while, an hour after his awakening, he was giving instructions to the barber, so that his stiffly brushed hair should not become disarranged on the journey, he thought once again of his dream ; he saw once again, as he had felt them close beside him, Odette's pallid complexion, her too thin cheeks, her drawn features, her tired eyes, all the things which—in the course of those successive bursts of affection which had made of his enduring love for Odette a long oblivion of the first impression that he had formed of her—he had ceased to observe after the first few days of their intimacy, days to which, doubtless, while he slept, his memory had returned to seek the exact sensation of those things. And with that old, intermittent fatuity, which reappeared in him now that he was no longer unhappy, and lowered, at the same time, the average level of his morality, he cried out in his heart : " To think that I have wasted years of my life, that I have longed for death, that the greatest love that I have ever known has been for a woman who did not please me, who was not in my style ! "

AMONG the rooms which used most commonly to take shape in my mind during my long nights of sleeplessness, there was none that differed more utterly from the rooms at Combray, thickly powdered with the motes of an atmosphere granular, pollenous, edible and instinct with piety, than my room in the Grand Hôtel de la Plage, at Balbec, the walls of which, washed with ripolin, contained, like the polished sides of a basin in which the water glows with a blue, lurking fire, a finer air, pure, azure-tinted, saline. The Bavarian upholsterer who had been entrusted with the furnishing of this hotel had varied his scheme of decoration in different rooms, and in that which I found myself occupying had set against the walls, on three sides of it, a series of low book-cases with glass fronts, in which, according to where they stood, by a law of nature which he had, perhaps, forgotten to take into account, was reflected this or that section of the ever-changing view of the sea, so that the walls were lined with a frieze of sea-scapes, interrupted only by the polished mahogany of the actual shelves. And so effective was this that the whole room had the appearance of one of those model bedrooms which you see nowadays in Housing Exhibitions, decorated with works of art which are calculated by their designer to refresh the eyes of whoever may ultimately have to sleep in the rooms, the subjects being kept in some degree of harmony with the locality and surroundings of the houses for which the rooms are planned.

And yet nothing could have differed more utterly, either, from the real Balbec than that other Balbec of which I had often dreamed, on stormy days, when the wind was so strong that Françoise, as she took me to the Champs-Elysées, would warn me not to walk too near the side of the street, or I might

have my head knocked off by a falling slate, and would re-
count to me, with many lamentations, the terrible disasters
and shipwrecks that were reported in the newspaper. I longed
for nothing more than to behold a storm at sea, less as a mighty
spectacle than as a momentary revelation of the true life of
nature ; or rather there were for me no mighty spectacles
save those which I knew to be not artificially composed
for my entertainment, but necessary and unalterable,—the
beauty of landscapes or of great works of art. I was not
curious, I did not thirst to know anything save what I believed
to be more genuine than myself, what had for me the supreme
merit of shewing me a fragment of the mind of a great genius,
or of the force or the grace of nature as she appeared when
left entirely to herself, without human interference. Just as
the lovely sound of her voice, reproduced, all by itself, upon
the phonograph, could never console a man for the loss of
his mother, so a mechanical imitation of a storm would have
left me as cold as did the illuminated fountains at the Exhibition. I required also, if the storm was to be absolutely
genuine, that the shore from which I watched it should be a
natural shore, not an embankment recently constructed by a
municipality. Besides, nature, by all the feelings that she
aroused in me, seemed to me the most opposite thing in the
world to the mechanical inventions of mankind. The less
she bore their imprint, the more room she offered for the
expansion of my heart. And, as it happened, I had preserved
the name of Balbec, which Legrandin had cited to us, as that
of a sea-side place in the very midst of " that funereal coast,
famed for the number of its wrecks, swathed, for six months
in the year, in a shroud of fog and flying foam from the waves.

" You feel, there, below your feet still," he had told me,
" far more even than at Finistère (and even though hotels

are now being superimposed upon it, without power, however, to modify that oldest bone in the earth's skeleton) you
feel there that you are actually at the land's end of France, of
Europe, of the Old World. And it is the ultimate encamp-
ment of the fishermen, precisely like the fishermen who have
lived since the world's beginning, facing the everlasting
kingdom of the sea-fogs and shadows of the night." One day
when, at Combray, I had spoken of this coast, this Balbec,
before M. Swann, hoping to learn from him whether it was
the best point to select for seeing the most violent storms, he
had replied : "I should think I did know Balbec ! The
church at Balbec, built in the twelfth and thirteenth centuries, and still half romanesque, is perhaps the most curious
example to be found of our Norman gothic, and so exceptional that one is tempted to describe it as Persian in its
inspiration." And that region, which, until then, had seemed
to me to be nothing else than a part of immemorial nature,
that had remained contemporaneous with the great phenomena of geology—and as remote from human history as the
Ocean itself, or the Great Bear, with its wild race of fishermen for whom, no more than for their whales, had there been
any Middle Ages—it had been a great joy to me to see it
suddenly take its place in the order of the centuries, with a
stored consciousness of the romanesque epoch, and to know
that the gothic trefoil had come to diversify those wild rocks
also, at the appointed hour, like those frail but hardy plants
which, in the Polar regions, when the spring returns, scatter
their stars about the eternal snows. And if gothic art brought
to those places and people a classification which, otherwise,
they lacked, they too conferred one upon it in return. I tried
to form a picture in my mind of how those fishermen had
lived, the timid and unsuspected essay towards social inter-

course which they had attempted there, clustered upon a promontory of the shores of Hell, at the foot of the cliffs of death ; and gothic art seemed to me a more living thing now that, detaching it from the towns in which, until then, I had always imagined it, I could see how, in a particular instance, upon a reef of savage rocks, it had taken root and grown until it flowered in a tapering spire. I was taken to see reproductions of the most famous of the statues at Balbec,— shaggy, blunt-faced Apostles, the Virgin from the porch,— and I could scarcely breathe for joy at the thought that I might myself, one day, see them take a solid form against their eternal background of salt fog. Thereafter, on dear, tempestuous February nights, the wind—breathing into my heart, which it shook no less violently than the chimney of my bedroom, the project of a visit to Balbec—blended in me the desire for gothic architecture with that for a storm upon the sea.

I should have liked to take, the very next day, the good, the generous train at one twenty-two, of which never without a palpitating heart could I read, in the railway company's bills or in advertisements of circular tours, the hour of departure : it seemed to me to cut, at a precise point in every afternoon, a most fascinating groove, a mysterious mark, from which the diverted hours still led one on, of course, towards evening, towards to-morrow morning, but to an evening and morning which one would behold, not in Paris but in one of those towns through which the train passed and among which it allowed one to choose ; for it stopped at Bayeux, at Coutances, at Vitré, at Questambert, at Pontorson, at Balbec, at Lannion, at Lamballe, at Benodet, at Pont-Aven, at Quimperlé, and progressed magnificently surcharged with names which it offered me, so that, among them all,

I did not know which to choose, so impossible was it to sacrifice any. But even without waiting for the train next day, I could, by rising and dressing myself with all speed, leave Paris that very evening, should my parents permit, and arrive at Balbec as dawn spread westward over the raging sea, from whose driven foam I would seek shelter in that church in the Persian manner. But at the approach of the Easter holidays, when my parents had promised to let me spend them, for once, in the North of Italy, lo! in place of those dreams of tempests, by which I had been entirely possessed, not wishing to see anything but waves dashing in from all sides, mounting always higher, upon the wildest of coasts, beside churches as rugged and precipitous as cliffs, in whose towers the sea-birds would be wailing; suddenly, effacing them, taking away all their charm, excluding them because they were its opposite and could only have weakened its effect, was substituted in me the converse dream of the most variegated of springs, not the spring of Combray, still pricking with all the needle-points of the winter's frost, but that which already covered with lilies and anemones the meadows of Fiesole, and gave Florence a dazzling golden background, like those in Fra Angelico's pictures. From that moment, only sunlight, perfumes, colours, seemed to me to have any value; for this alternation of images had effected a change of front in my desire, and—as abrupt as those that occur sometimes in music,—a complete change of tone in my sensibility. Thus it came about that a mere atmospheric variation would be sufficient to provoke in me that modulation, without there being any need for me to await the return of a season. For often we find a day, in one, that has strayed from another season, and makes us live in that other, summons at once into our presence and makes us long for its peculiar pleasures, and interrupts the dreams that we were in process of weaving, by inserting, out of its turn, too early or too late, this leaf, torn from another chapter, in the interpolated calendar of Happiness. But soon it happened that, like those natural phenomena from which our comfort or our health can derive but an accidental and all too modest benefit, until the day when science takes control of them, and, producing them at will, places in our hands the power to order their appearance, withdrawn from the tutelage and independent of the consent of chance ; similarly the production of these dreams of the Atlantic and of Italy ceased to depend entirely upon the changes of the seasons and of the weather. I need only, to make them reappear, pronounce the names : Balbec, Venice, Florence, within whose syllables had gradually accumulated all the longing inspired in me by the places for which they stood. Even in spring, to come in a book upon the name of Balbec sufficed to awaken in me the desire for storms at sea and for the Norman gothic ; even on a stormy day the name of Florence or of Venice would awaken the desire for sunshine, for lilies, for the Palace of the Doges and for Santa Maria del Fiore.

But if their names thus permanently absorbed the image that I had formed of these towns, it was only by transforming that image, by subordinating its reappearance in me to their own special laws ; and in consequence of this they made it more beautiful, but at the same time more different from anything that the towns of Normandy or Tuscany could in reality be, and, by increasing the arbitrary delights of my imagination, aggravated the disenchantment that was in store for me when I set out upon my travels. They magnified the idea that I formed of certain points on the earth's surface, making them more special, and in consequence more real.

I did not then represent to myself towns, landscapes, historic buildings, as pictures more or less attractive, cut out here and there of a substance that was common to them all, but looked on each of them as on an unknown thing, different from all the rest, a thing for which my soul was athirst, by the knowledge of which it would benefit. How much more individual still was the character that they assumed from being designated by names, names that were only for themselves, proper names such as people have. Words present to us little pictures of things, lucid and normal, like the pictures that are hung on the walls of schoolrooms to give children an illustration of what is meant by a carpenter's bench, a bird, an ant-hill; things chosen as typical of everything else of the same sort. But names present to us—of persons and of towns which they accustom us to regard as individual, as unique, like persons—a confused picture, which draws from the names, from the brightness or darkness of their sound, the colour in which it is uniformly painted, like one of those posters, entirely blue or entirely red, in which, on account of the limitations imposed by the process used in their reproduction, or by a whim on the designer's part, are blue or red not only the sky and the sea, but the ships and the church and the people in the streets. The name of Parma, one of the towns that I most longed to visit, after reading the *Chartreuse*, seeming to me compact and glossy, violet-tinted, soft, if anyone were to speak of such or such a house in Parma, in which I should be lodged, he would give me the pleasure of thinking that I was to inhabit a dwelling that was compact and glossy, violet-tinted, soft, and that bore no relation to the houses in any other town in Italy, since I could imagine it only by the aid of that heavy syllable of the name of Parma, in which no breath of air stirred, and of all that I had made it assume of Stendhalian sweetness and the reflected hue of violets. And when I thought of Florence, it was of a town miraculously embalmed, and flower-like, since it was called the City of the Lilies, and its Cathedral, Our Lady of the Flower. As for Balbec, it was one of those names in which, as on an old piece of Norman pottery that still keeps the colour of the earth from which it was fashioned, one sees depicted still the representation of some long-abolished custom, of some feudal right, of the former condition of some place, of an obsolete way of pronouncing the language, which had shaped and wedded its incongruous syllables and which I never doubted that I should find spoken there at once, even by the inn-keeper who would pour me out coffee and milk on my arrival, taking me down to watch the turbulent sea, unchained, before the church ; to whom I lent the aspect, disputatious, solemn and mediaeval, of some character in one of the old romances.

Had my health definitely improved, had my parents allowed me, if not actually to go down to stay at Balbec, at least to take, just once, so as to become acquainted with the architecture and landscapes of Normandy or of Brittany, that one twenty-two train into which I had so often clambered in imagination, I should have preferred to stop, and to alight from it, at the most beautiful of its towns ; but in vain might I compare and contrast them ; how was one to choose, any more than between individual people, who are not inter-changeable, between Bayeux, so lofty in its noble coronet of rusty lace, whose highest point caught the light of the old gold of its second syllable ; Vitré, whose acute accent barred its ancient glass with wooden lozenges ; gentle Lamballe, whose whiteness ranged from egg-shell yellow to a pearly grey ; Coutances, a Norman Cathedral, which its final consonants, rich and yellowing, crowned with a tower of butter ;

Lannion with the rumble and buzz, in the silence of its village street, of the fly on the wheel of the coach ; Questambert, Pontorson, ridiculously silly and simple, white feathers and yellow beaks strewn along the road to those well-watered and poetic spots ; Benodet, a name scarcely moored that seemed to be striving to draw the river down into the tangle of its seaweeds ; Pont-Aven, the snowy, rosy flight of the wing of a lightly poised coif, tremulously reflected in the greenish waters of a canal ; Quimperlé, more firmly attached, this, and since the Middle Ages, among the rivulets with which it babbled, threading their pearls upon a grey background, like the pattern made, through the cobwebs upon a window, by rays of sunlight changed into blunt points of tarnished silver ?

These images were false for another reason also ; namely, that they were necessarily much simplified ; doubtless the object to which my imagination aspired, which my senses took in but incompletely and without any immediate pleasure, I had committed to the safe custody of names ; doubtless because I had accumulated there a store of dreams, those names now magnetised my desires ; but names themselves are not very comprehensive ; the most that I could do was to include in each of them two or three of the principal curiosities of the town, which would lie there side by side, without interval or partition ; in the name of Balbec, as in the magnifying glasses set in those penholders which one buys at sea-side places, I could distinguish waves surging round a church built in the Persian manner. Perhaps, indeed, the enforced simplicity of these images was one of the reasons for the hold that they had over me. When my father had decided, one year, that we should go for the Easter holidays to Florence and Venice, not finding room to introduce into the name of Florence the elements that ordinarily constitute a town, I was

obliged to let a supernatural city emerge from the impregnation by certain vernal scents of what I supposed to be, in its
essentials, the genius of Giotto. All the more—and because
one cannot make a name extend much further in time than
in space—like some of Giotto's paintings themselves which
shew us at two separate moments the same person engaged in
different actions, here lying on his bed, there just about to
mount his horse, the name of Florence was divided into two
compartments. In one, beneath an architectural dais, I gazed
upon a fresco over which was partly drawn a curtain of morning sunlight, dusty, aslant, and gradually spreading ; in the
other (for, since I thought of names not as an inaccessible
ideal but as a real and enveloping substance into which I was
about to plunge, the life not yet lived, the life intact and pure
which I enclosed in them, gave to the most material pleasures,
to the simplest scenes, the same attraction that they have in
the works of the Primitives), I moved swiftly—so as to
arrive, as soon as might be, at the table that was spread for me,
with fruit and a flask of Chianti—across a Ponte Vecchio
heaped with jonquils, narcissi and anemones. That (for all that
I was still in Paris) was what I saw, and not what was actually
round about me. Even from the simplest, the most realistic
point of view, the countries for which we long occupy, at any
given moment, a far larger place in our true life than the
country in which we may happen to be. Doubtless, if, at that
time, I had paid more attention to what was in my mind
when I pronounced the words " going to Florence, to Parma,
to Pisa, to Venice," I should have realised that what I saw
was in no sense a town, but something as different from anything that I knew, something as delicious as might be for a
human race whose whole existence had passed in a series of
late winter afternoons, that inconceivable marvel, a morning

in spring. These images, unreal, fixed, always alike, filling all my nights and days, differentiated this period in my life from those which had gone before it (and might easily have been confused with it by an observer who saw things only from without, that is to say, who saw nothing), as in an opera a fresh melody introduces a novel atmosphere which one could never have suspected if one had done no more than read the libretto, still less if one had remained outside the theatre, counting only the minutes as they passed. And besides, even from the point of view of mere quantity, in our life the days are not all equal. To reach the end of a day, natures that are slightly nervous, as mine was, make use, like motor-cars, of different 'speeds.' There are mountainous, uncomfortable days, up which one takes an infinite time to pass, and days downward sloping, through which one can go at full tilt, singing as one goes. During this month—in which I went laboriously over, as over a tune, though never to my satisfaction, these visions of Florence, Venice, Pisa, from which the desire that they excited in me drew and kept something as profoundly personal as if it had been love, love for another person—I never ceased to believe that they corresponded to a reality independent of myself, and they made me conscious of as glorious a hope as could have been cherished by a Christian in the primitive age of faith, on the eve of his entry into Paradise. Moreover, without my paying any heed to the contradiction that there was in my wishing to look at and to touch with my organs of sense what had been elaborated by the spell of my dreams and not perceived by my senses at all—though all the more tempting to them, in consequence, more different from anything that they knew— it was that which recalled to me the reality of these visions, which inflamed my desire all the more by seeming to hint

239

a promise that my desire should be satisfied. And for all that the motive force of my exaltation was a longing for aesthetic enjoyments, the guide-books ministered even more to it than books on aesthetics, and, more again than the guide-books, the railway time-tables. What moved me was the thought that this Florence which I could see, so near and yet inaccessible, in my imagination, if the tract which separated it from me, in myself, was not one that I might cross, could yet be reached by a circuit, by a digression, were I to take the plain, terrestrial path. When I repeated to myself, giving thus a special value to what I was going to see, that Venice was the " School of Giorgione, the home of Titian, the most complete museum of the domestic architecture of the Middle Ages," I felt happy indeed. As I was even more when, on one of my walks, as I stepped out briskly on account of the weather, which, after several days of a precocious spring, had relapsed into winter (like the weather that we had invariably found await-ing us at Combray, in Holy Week),—seeing upon the boule-vards that the chestnut-trees, though plunged in a glacial atmosphere that soaked through them like a stream of water, were none the less beginning, punctual guests, arrayed already for the party, and admitting no discouragement, to shape and chisel and curve in its frozen lumps the irrepressible verdure whose steady growth the abortive power of the cold might hinder but could not succeed in restraining—I reflected that already the Ponte Vecchio was heaped high with an abundance of hyacinths and anemones, and that the spring sunshine was already tinging the waves of the Grand Canal with so dusky an azure, with emeralds so splendid that when they washed and were broken against the foot of one of Titian's paintings they could vie with it in the richness of their colouring. I could no longer contain my joy when my father, in the intervals of tapping the barometer and complaining of the cold, began to look out which were the best trains, and when I understood that by making one's way, after luncheon, into the coal-grimed laboratory, the wizard's cell that undertook to contrive a complete transmutation of its surroundings, one could awaken, next morning, in the city of marble and gold, in which " the building of the wall was of jasper and the foundation of the wall an emerald." So that it and the City of the Lilies were not just artificial scenes which I could set up at my pleasure in front of my imagination, but did actually exist at a certain distance from Paris which must inevitably be traversed if I wished to see them, at their appointed place on the earth's surface, and at no other ; in a word they were entirely real. They became even more real to me when my father, by saying : " Well, you can stay in Venice from the 20th to the 29th, and reach Florence on Easter morning," made them both emerge, no longer only from the abstraction of Space, but from that imaginary Time in which we place not one, merely, but several of our travels at once, which do not greatly tax us since they are but possibilities,—that Time which reconstructs itself so effectively that one can spend it again in one town after one has already spent it in another— and consecrated to them some of those actual, calendar days which are certificates of the genuineness of what one does on them, for those unique days are consumed by being used, they do not return, one cannot live them again here when one has lived them elsewhere ; I felt that it was towards the week that would begin with the Monday on which the laundress was to bring back the white waistcoat that I had stained with ink, that they were hastening to busy themselves with the duty of emerging from that ideal Time in which they did not, as yet, exist, those two Queen Cities of which I was soon to be able, by the most absorbing kind of geometry, to inscribe the domes and towers on a page of my own life. But I was still on the way, only, to the supreme pinnacle of happiness ; I reached it finally (for not until then did the revelation burst upon me that on the clattering streets, reddened by the light reflected from Giorgione's frescoes, it was not, as I had, despite so many promptings, continued to imagine, the men " majestic and terrible as the sea, bearing armour that gleamed with bronze beneath the folds of their blood-red cloaks," who would be walking in Venice next week, on the Easter vigil ; but that I myself might be the minute personage whom, in an enlarged photograph of St. Mark's that had been lent to me, the operator had portrayed, in a bowler hat, in front of the portico), when I heard my father say : " It must be pretty cold, still, on the Grand Canal ; whatever you do, don't forget to pack your winter greatcoat and your thick suit." At these words I was raised to a sort of ecstasy ; a thing that I had until then deemed impossible, I felt myself to be penetrating indeed between those " rocks of amethyst, like a reef in the Indian Ocean " ; by a supreme muscular effort, a long way in excess of my real strength, stripping myself, as of a shell that served no purpose, of the air in my own room which surrounded me, I replaced it by an equal quantity of Venetian air, that marine atmosphere, indescribable and peculiar as the atmosphere of the dreams which my imagination had secreted in the name of Venice ; I could feel at work within me a miraculous disincarnation ; it was at once accompanied by that vague desire to vomit which one feels when one has a very sore throat ; and they had to put me to bed with a fever so persistent that the Doctor not only assured my parents that a visit, that spring, to Florence and Venice was absolutely out of the question, but warned them that, even when I should have completely recovered, I must, for at least a year, give up all idea of travelling, and be kept from anything that was liable to excite me.

And, alas, he forbade also, most categorically, my being allowed to go to the theatre, to hear Berma ; the sublime artist, whose genius Bergotte had proclaimed, might, by introducing me to something else that was, perhaps, as important and as beautiful, have consoled me for not having been to Florence and Venice, for not going to Balbec. My parents had to be content with sending me, every day, to the Champs-Elysées, in the custody of a person who would see that I did not tire myself ; this person was none other than Françoise, who had entered our service after the death of my aunt Léonie. Going to the Champs-Elysées I found unendurable. If only Bergotte had described the place in one of his books, I should, no doubt, have longed to see and to know it, like so many things else of which a simulacrum had first found its way into my imagination. That kept things warm, made them live, gave them personality, and I sought then to find their counterpart in reality, but in this public garden there was nothing that attached itself to my dreams.

* *

One day, as I was weary of our usual place, beside the wooden horses, Françoise had taken me for an excursion— across the frontier guarded at regular intervals by the little bastions of the barley-sugar women—into those neighbouring but foreign regions, where the faces of the passers-by were strange, where the goat-carriage went past ; then she had gone away to lay down her things on a chair that stood with its back to a shrubbery of laurels ; while I waited for her I was pacing the broad lawn, of meagre close-cropped grass already faded by the sun, dominated, at its far end, by a statue rising from a fountain, in front of which a little girl with reddish hair was playing with a shuttlecock ; when, from the path, another little girl, who was putting on her cloak and covering up her battledore, called out sharply : " Good-bye, Gilberte, I'm going home now ; don't forget, we're coming to you this evening, after dinner." The name Gilberte passed close by me, evoking all the more forcibly her whom it labelled in that it did not merely refer to her, as one speaks of a man in his absence, but was directly addressed to her ; it passed thus close by me, in action, so to speak, with a force that increased with the curve of its trajectory and as it drew near to its target ;—carrying in its wake, I could feel, the knowledge, the impression of her to whom it was addressed that belonged not to me but to the friend who called to her, everything that, while she uttered the words, she more or less vividly reviewed, possessed in her memory, of their daily intimacy, of the visits that they paid to each other, of that unknown existence which was all the more inaccessible, all the more painful to me from being, conversely, so familiar, so tractable to this happy girl who let her message brush past me without my being able to penetrate its surface, who flung it on the air with a light-hearted cry : letting float in the atmosphere the delicious attar which that message had dis-tilled, by touching them with precision, from certain invisible points in Mlle. Swann's life, from the evening to come, as it would be, after dinner, at her home,—forming, on its celestial passage through the midst of the children and their nursemaids, a little cloud, exquisitely coloured, like the cloud that, curling over one of Poussin's gardens, reflects minutely, like a cloud in the opera, teeming with chariots and horses, some apparition of the life of the gods ; casting, finally, on that ragged grass, at the spot on which she stood (at once a scrap of withered lawn and a moment in the afternoon of the fair player, who continued to beat up and catch her shuttle-cock until a governess, with a blue feather in her hat, had called her away) a marvellous little band of light, of the colour of heliotrope, spread over the lawn like a carpet on which I could not tire of treading to and fro with lingering feet, nostalgic and profane, while Françoise shouted : " Come on, button up your coat, look, and let's get away!" and I remarked for the first time how common her speech was, and that she had, alas, no blue feather in her hat.

Only, would *she* come again to the Champs-Elysées ? Next day she was not there ; but I saw her on the following days ; I spent all my time revolving round the spot where she was at play with her friends, to such effect that once, when, they found, they were not enough to make up a prisoner's base, she sent one of them to ask me if I cared to complete their side, and from that day I played with her whenever she came. But this did not happen every day ; there were days when she had been prevented from coming by her lessons, by her catechism, by a luncheon-party, by the whole of that life, separated from my own, which twice only, condensed into the name of Gilberte, I had felt pass so painfully close to me, in the hawthorn lane near Combray and on the grass of the Champs-Elysées. On such days she would have told us beforehand that we should not see her ; if it were because of her lessons, she would say : " It is too tiresome, I shan't be able to come to-morrow ; you will all be enjoying yourselves here without me," with an air of regret which to some extent consoled me ; if, on the other hand, she had been invited to a party, and I, not knowing this, asked her whether she was coming to play with us, she would reply : " Indeed I hope not ! Indeed I hope Mamma will let me go to my friend's." But on these days I did at least know that I should not see her, whereas on others, without any warning, her mother would take her for a drive, or some such thing, and next day she would say : " Oh, yes ! I went out with Mamma," as though it had been the most natural thing in the world, and not the greatest possible misfortune for some one else There were also the days of bad weather on which her governess, afraid, on her own account, of the rain, would not bring Gilberte to the Champs-Elysées.

And so, if the heavens were doubtful, from early morning I would not cease to interrogate them, observing all the omens. If I saw the lady opposite, just inside her window, putting on her hat, I would say to myself : " That lady is going out ; it must, therefore, be weather in which one can go out. Why should not Gilberte do the same as that lady ? " But the day grew dark. My mother said that it might clear again, that one burst of sunshine would be enough, but that more probably it would rain ; and if it rained, of what use would it be to go to the Champs-Elysées ? And so, from breakfast-time, my anxious eyes never left the uncertain, clouded sky. It remained dark. Outside the window, the balcony was grey. Suddenly, on its sullen stone, I did not indeed see a less negative colour, but I felt as it were an effort towards a less negative colour, the pulsation of a hesitating ray that struggled to discharge its light. A moment later the balcony was as pale and luminous as a standing water at dawn, and a thousand shadows from the iron-work of its balustrade had come to rest on it. A breath of wind dispersed them ; the stone grew dark again, but, like tamed creatures, they returned ; they began, imperceptibly, to grow lighter, and by one of those continuous crescendos, such as, in music, at the

end of an overture, carry a single note to the extreme
fortissimo, making it pass rapidly through all the intermediate
stages, I saw it attain to that fixed, unalterable gold of fine
days, on which the sharply cut shadows of the wrought iron
of the balustrade were outlined in black like a capricious
vegetation, with a fineness in the delineation of their smallest
details which seemed to indicate a deliberate application, an
artist's satisfaction, and with so much relief, so velvety a
bloom in the restfulness of their sombre and happy mass that
in truth those large and leafy shadows which lay reflected
on that lake of sunshine seemed aware that they were pledges
of happiness and peace of mind.

Brief, fading ivy, climbing, fugitive flora, the most colourless, the most depressing, to many minds, of all that creep on
walls or decorate windows ; to me the dearest of them all,
from the day when it appeared upon our balcony, like the
very shadow of the presence of Gilberte, who was perhaps
already in the Champs-Elysées, and as soon as I arrived there
would greet me with : " Let's begin at once. You are on my
side." Frail, swept away by a breath, but at the same time
in harmony, not with the season, with the hour ; promise of
that immediate pleasure which the day will deny or fulfil, and
thereby of the one paramount immediate pleasure, the pleasure
of loving and of being loved ; more soft, more warm upon the
stone than even moss is ; alive, a ray of sunshine sufficing for
its birth, and for the birth of joy, even in the heart of winter.

And on those days when all other vegetation had disappeared, when the fine jerkins of green leather which
covered the trunks of the old trees were hidden beneath the
snow ; after the snow had ceased to fall, but when the sky
was still too much overcast for me to hope that Gilberte would
venture out, then suddenly—inspiring my mother to say :

" Look, it's quite fine now ; I think you might perhaps try going to the Champs-Elysées after all."—on the mantle of snow that swathed the balcony, the sun had appeared and was stitching seams of gold, with embroidered patches of dark shadow. That day we found no one there, or else a solitary girl, on the point of departure, who assured me that Gilberte was not coming. The chairs, deserted by the imposing but uninspiring company of governesses, stood empty. Only, near the grass, was sitting a lady of uncertain age who came in all weathers, dressed always in an identical style, splendid and sombre, to make whose acquaintance I would have, at that period, sacrificed, had it lain in my power, all the greatest opportunities in my life to come. For Gilberte went up every day to speak to her ; she used to ask Gilberte for news of her " dearest mother " and it struck me that, if I had known her, I should have been for Gilberte some one wholly different, some one who knew people in her parents' world. While her grandchildren played together at a little distance, she would sit and read the *Débats*, which she called " My old *Débats* ! " as, with an aristocratic familiarity, she would say, speaking of the police-sergeant or the woman who let the chairs, " My old friend the police-sergeant," or " The chair-keeper and I, who are old friends."

Françoise found it too cold to stand about, so we walked to the Pont de la Concorde to see the Seine frozen over, on to which everyone, even children, walked fearlessly, as though upon an enormous whale, stranded, defenceless, and about to be cut up. We returned to the Champs-Elysées ; I was growing sick with misery between the motionless wooden horses and the white lawn, caught in a net of black paths from which the snow had been cleared, while the statue that surmounted it held in its hand a long pendent icicle which seemed to explain its gesture. The old lady herself, having folded up her *Débats,* asked a passing nursemaid the time, thanking her with " How very good of you ! " then begged the road-sweeper to tell her grandchildren to come, as she felt cold, adding " A thousand thanks. I am sorry to give you so much trouble ! " Suddenly the sky was rent in two : between the punch-and-judy and the horses, against the opening horizon, I had just seen, like a miraculous sign, Mademoiselle's blue feather. And now Gilberte was running at full speed towards me, sparkling and rosy beneath a cap trimmed with fur, enlivened by the cold, by being late, by her anxiety for a game ; shortly before she reached me, she slipped on a piece of ice and, either to regain her balance, or because it appeared to her graceful, or else pretending that she was on skates, it was with outstretched arms that she smilingly advanced, as though to embrace me. " Bravo ! bravo ! that's splendid ; ' topping,' I should say, like you— ' sporting,' I suppose I ought to say, only I'm a hundred-and-one, a woman of the old school," exclaimed the lady, uttering, on behalf of the voiceless Champs-Elysées, their thanks to Gilberte for having come, without letting herself be frightened away by the weather. " You are like me, faithful at all costs to our old Champs-Elysées ; we are two brave souls ! You wouldn't believe me, I dare say, if I told you that I love them, even like this. This snow (I know, you'll laugh at me), it makes me think of ermine ! " And the old lady began to laugh herself.

The first of these days—to which the snow, a symbol of the powers that were able to deprive me of the sight of Gilberte, imparted the sadness of a day of separation, almost the aspect of a day of departure, because it changed the outward form and almost forbade the use of the customary scene of our only

encounters, now altered, covered, as it were, in dust-sheets—
that day, none the less, marked a stage in the progress of my
love, for it was, in a sense, the first sorrow that she was to
share with me. There were only our two selves of our little
company, and to be thus alone with her was not merely like
a beginning of intimacy, but also on her part—as though she
had come there solely to please me, and in such weather—it
seemed to me as touching as if, on one of those days on which
she had been invited to a party, she had given it up in order
to come to me in the Champs-Elysées ; I acquired more
confidence in the vitality, in the future of a friendship which
could remain so much alive amid the torpor, the solitude, the
decay of our surroundings ; and while she dropped pellets
of snow down my neck, I smiled lovingly at what seemed to
me at once a predilection that she shewed for me in thus
tolerating me as her travelling companion in this new, this
wintry land, and a sort of loyalty to me which she preserved
through evil times. Presently, one after another, like shyly
hopping sparrows, her friends arrived, black against the snow.
We got ready to play and, since this day which had begun so
sadly was destined to end in joy, as I went up, before the game
started, to the friend with the sharp voice whom I had heard,
that first day, calling Gilberte by name, she said to me : " No,
no, I'm sure you'ld much rather be in Gilberte's camp ;
besides, look, she's signalling to you." She was in fact
summoning me to cross the snowy lawn to her camp, to
' take the field,' which the sun, by casting over it a rosy gleam,
the metallic lustre of old and worn brocades, had turned into a
Field of the Cloth of Gold.

This day, which I had begun with so many misgivings,
was, as it happened, one of the few on which I was not unduly
wretched.

For, although I no longer thought, now, of anything save not to let a single day pass without seeing Gilberte (so much so that once, when my grandmother had not come home by dinner-time, I could not resist the instinctive reflection that, if she had been run over in the street and killed, I should not for some time be allowed to play in the Champs-Elysées ; when one is in love one has no love left for anyone.) yet those moments which I spent in her company, for which I had waited with so much impatience all night and morning, for which I had quivered with excitement, to which I would have sacrificed everything else in the world, were by no means happy moments ; well did I know it, for they were the only moments in my life on which I concentrated a scrupulous, undistracted attention, and yet I could not discover in them one atom of pleasure. All the time that I was away from Gilberte, I wanted to see her, because, having incessantly sought to form a mental picture of her, I was unable, in the end, to do so, and did not know exactly to what my love corresponded. Besides, she had never yet told me that she loved me. Far from it, she had often boasted that she knew other little boys whom she preferred to myself, that I was a good companion, with whom she was always willing to play, although I was too absent-minded, not attentive enough to the game. Moreover, she had often shewn signs of apparent coldness towards me, which might have shaken my faith that I was for her a creature different from the rest, had that faith been founded upon a love that Gilberte had felt for me, and not, as was the case, upon the love that I felt for her, which strengthened its resistance to the assaults of doubt by making it depend entirely upon the manner in which I was obliged, by an internal compulsion, to think of Gilberte. But my feelings with regard to her I had never yet ventured to express to her in words. Of course, on every page of my exercise-books, I wrote out, in endless repetition, her name and address, but at the sight of those vague lines which I might trace, without her having to think, on that account, of me, I felt discouraged, because they spoke to me, not of Gilberte, who would never so much as see them, but of my own desire, which they seemed to shew me in its true colours, as something purely personal, unreal, tedious and ineffective. The most important thing was that we should see each other, Gilberte and I, and should have an opportunity of making a mutual confession of our love which, until then, would not officially (so to speak) have begun. Doubtless the various reasons which made me so impatient to see her would have appeared less urgent to a grown man. As life goes on, we acquire such adroitness in the culture of our pleasures, that we content ourselves with that which we derive from thinking of a woman, as I was thinking of Gilberte, without troubling ourselves to ascertain whether the image corresponds to the reality,—and with the pleasure of loving her, without needing to be sure, also, that she loves us ; or again that we renounce the pleasure of confessing our passion for her, so as to preserve and enhance the passion that she has for us, like those Japanese gardeners who, to obtain one perfect blossom, will sacrifice the rest. But at the period when I was in love with Gilberte, I still believed that Love did really exist, apart from ourselves ; that, allowing us, at the most, to surmount the obstacles in our way, it offered us its blessings in an order in which we were not free to make the least alteration ; it seemed to me that if I had, on my own initiative, substituted for the sweetness of a confession a pretence of indifference, I should not only have been depriving myself of one of the joys of which I had most often dreamed, I should have been fabricating, of my own free will, a love that was artificial and without value, that bore no relation to the truth, whose mysterious and fore-ordained ways I should thus have been declining to follow.

But when I arrived at the Champs-Elysées,—and, as at first sight it appeared, was in a position to confront my love, so as to make it undergo the necessary modifications, with its living and independent cause—as soon as I was in the presence of that Gilberte Swann on the sight of whom I had counted to revive the images that my tired memory had lost and could not find again, of that Gilberte Swann with whom I had been playing the day before, and whom I had just been prompted to greet, and then to recognise, by a blind instinct like that which, when we are walking, sets one foot before the other, without giving us time to think what we are doing, then at once it became as though she and the little girl who had inspired my dreams had been two different people. If, for instance, I had retained in my memory overnight two fiery eyes above plump and rosy cheeks, Gilberte's face would now offer me (and with emphasis) something that I distinctly had not remembered, a certain sharpening and prolongation of the nose which, instantaneously associating itself with certain others of her features, assumed the importance of those characteristics which, in natural history, are used to define a species, and transformed her into a little girl of the kind that have sharpened profiles. While I was making myself ready to take advantage of this long expected moment, and to surrender myself to the impression of Gilberte which I had prepared beforehand but could no longer find in my head, to an extent which would enable me, during the long hours which I must spend alone, to be certain that it was indeed herself whom I had in mind, that it was indeed my love for her that I was gradually making grow, as a book grows

when one is writing it, she threw me a ball ; and, like the
idealist philosopher whose body takes account of the external
world in the reality of which his intellect declines to believe,
the same self which had made me salute her before I had
identified her now urged me to catch the ball that she tossed
to me (as though she had been a companion, with whom I had
come to play, and not a sister-soul with whom my soul had
come to be united), made me, out of politeness, until the time
came when she had to go, address a thousand polite and trivial
remarks to her, and so prevented me both from keeping a
silence in which I might at last have laid my hand upon the
indispensable, escaped idea, and from uttering the words
which might have made that definite progress in the course of
our love on which I was always obliged to count only for the
following afternoon. There was, however, an occasional
development. One day, we had gone with Gilberte to the
stall of our own special vendor, who was always particularly
nice to us, since it was to her that M. Swann used to send for
his gingerbread, of which, for reasons of health, (he suffered
from a racial eczema, and from the constipation of the
prophets) he consumed a great quantity,—Gilberte pointed
out to me with a laugh two little boys who were like the little
artist and the little naturalist in the children's story-books.
For one of them would not have a red stick of rock because
he preferred the purple, while the other, with tears in his
eyes, refused a plum which his nurse was buying for him,
because, as he finally explained in passionate tones :
" I want the other plum ; it's got a worm in it ! " I purchased two ha'penny marbles. With admiring eyes I saw,
luminous and imprisoned in a bowl by themselves, the agate
marbles which seemed precious to me because they were
as fair and smiling as little girls, and because they cost five-

pence each. Gilberte, who was given a great deal more pocket money than I ever had, asked me which I thought the prettiest. They were as transparent, as liquid-seeming as life itself. I would not have had her sacrifice a single one of them. I should have liked her to be able to buy them, to liberate them all. Still, I pointed out one that had the same colour as her eyes. Gilberte took it, turned it about until it shone with a ray of gold, fondled it, paid its ransom, but at once handed me her captive, saying: "Take it; it is for you, I give it to you, keep it to remind yourself of me."

Another time, being still obsessed by the desire to hear Berma in classic drama, I had asked her whether she had not a copy of a pamphlet in which Bergotte spoke of Racine, and which was now out of print. She had told me to let her know the exact title of it, and that evening I had sent her a little telegram, writing on its envelope the name, Gilberte Swann, which I had so often traced in my exercise-books. Next day she brought me in a parcel tied with pink bows and sealed with white wax, the pamphlet, a copy of which she had managed to find. "You see, it is what you asked me for," she said, taking from her muff the telegram that I had sent her. But in the address on the pneumatic message—which, only yesterday, was nothing, was merely a 'little blue' that I had written, and, after a messenger had delivered it to Gilberte's porter and a servant had taken it to her in her room, had become a thing without value or distinction, one of the 'little blues' that she had received in the course of the day— I had difficulty in recognising the futile, straggling lines of my own handwriting beneath the circles stamped on it at the post-office, the inscriptions added in pencil by a postman, signs of effectual realisation, seals of the external world, violet bands symbolical of life itself, which for the first time came to espouse, to maintain, to raise, to rejoice my dream.

And there was another day on which she said to me : " You know, you may call me ' Gilberte ' ; in any case, I'm going to call you by your first name. It's too silly not to." Yet she continued for a while to address me by the more formal '*vous*', and, when I drew her attention to this, smiled, and composing, constructing a phrase like those that are put into the grammar-books of foreign languages with no other object than to teach us to make use of a new word, ended it with my Christian name. And when I recalled, later, what I had felt at the time, I could distinguish the impression of having been held, for a moment, in her mouth, myself, naked, without, any longer, any of the social qualifications which belonged equally to her other companions and, when she used my surname, to my parents, accessories of which her lips—by the effort that she made, a little after her father's manner, to articulate the words to which she wished to give a special value—had the air of stripping, of divesting me, as one peels the skin from a fruit of which one is going to put only the pulp into one's mouth, while her glance, adapting itself to the same new degree of intimacy as her speech, fell on me also more directly, not without testifying to the consciousness, the pleasure, even the gratitude that it felt, accompanying itself with a smile.

But at that actual moment, I was not able to appreciate the worth of these new pleasures. They were given, not by the little girl whom I loved, to me who loved her, but by the other, her with whom I used to play, to my other self, who possessed neither the memory of the true Gilberte, nor the fixed heart which alone could have known the value of a happiness for which it alone had longed. Even after I had returned home

I did not taste them, since, every day, the necessity which made me hope that on the morrow I should arrive at the clear, calm, happy contemplation of Gilberte, that she would at last confess her love for me, explaining to me the reasons by which she had been obliged, hitherto, to conceal it, that same necessity forced me to regard the past as of no account, to look ahead of me only, to consider the little advantages that she had given me not in themselves and as if they were self-sufficient, but like fresh rungs of the ladder on which I might set my feet, which were going to allow me to advance a step further and finally to attain the happiness which I had not yet encountered.

If, at times, she shewed me these marks of her affection, she troubled me also by seeming not to be pleased to see me, and this happened often on the very days on which I had most counted for the realisation of my hopes. I was sure that Gilberte was coming to the Champs-Elysées, and I felt an elation which seemed merely the anticipation of a great happiness when—going into the drawing-room in the morning to kiss Mamma, who was already dressed to go out, the coils of her black hair elaborately built up, and her beautiful hands, plump and white, fragrant still with soap—I had been apprised, by seeing a column of dust standing by itself in the air above the piano, and by hearing a barrel-organ playing, beneath the window, *En revenant de la revue*, that the winter had received, until nightfall, an unexpected, radiant visit from a day of spring. While we sat at luncheon, by opening her window, the lady opposite had sent packing, in the twinkling of an eye, from beside my chair—to sweep in a single stride over the whole width of our dining-room—a sunbeam which had lain down there for its midday rest and returned to continue it there a moment later. At school, during the one o'clock

lesson, the sun made me sick with impatience and boredom
as it let fall a golden stream that crept to the edge of my desk,
like an invitation to the feast at which I could not myself
arrive before three o'clock, until the moment when Françoise
came to fetch me at the school-gate, and we made our way
towards the Champs-Elysées through streets decorated with
sunlight, dense with people, over which the balconies,
detached by the sun and made vaporous, seemed to float in
front of the houses like clouds of gold. Alas ! in the Champs-
Elysées I found no Gilberte ; she had not yet arrived.
Motionless, on the lawn nurtured by the invisible sun which,
here and there, kindled to a flame the point of a blade of grass,
while the pigeons that had alighted upon it had the appearance
of ancient sculptures which the gardener's pick had heaved to
the surface of a hallowed soil, I stood with my eyes fixed on
the horizon, expecting at every moment to see appear the
form of Gilberte following that of her governess, behind the
statue that seemed to be holding out the child, which it had
in its arms, and which glistened in the stream of light, to
receive benediction from the sun. The old lady who read
the *Débats* was sitting on her chair, in her invariable place,
and had just accosted a park-keeper, with a friendly wave of
her hand towards him as she exclaimed " What a lovely day ! "
And when the chair-woman came up to collect her penny,
with an infinity of smirks and affectations she folded the ticket
away inside her glove, as though it had been a posy of flowers,
for which she had sought, in gratitude to the donor, the most
becoming place upon her person. When she had found it, she
performed a circular movement with her neck, straightened
her boa, and fastened upon the collector, as she shewed her
the end of yellow paper that stuck out over her bare wrist,
the bewitching smile with which a woman says to a young

man, pointing to her bosom : " You see, I'm wearing your roses ! "

I dragged Françoise, on the way towards Gilberte, as far as the Arc de Triomphe ; we did not meet her, and I was returning towards the lawn convinced, now, that she was not coming, when, in front of the wooden horses, the little girl with the sharp voice flung herself upon me : " Quick, quick, Gilberte's been here a quarter of an hour. She's just going. We've been waiting for you, to make up a prisoner's base."

While I had been going up the Avenue des Champs-Elysées, Gilberte had arrived by the Rue Boissy-d'Anglas, Mademoiselle having taken advantage of the fine weather to go on some errand of her own ; and M. Swann was coming to fetch his daughter. And so it was my fault ; I ought not to have strayed from the lawn ; for one never knew for certain from what direction Gilberte would appear, whether she would be early or late, and this perpetual tension succeeded in making more impressive not only the Champs-Elysées in their entirety, and the whole span of the afternoon, like a vast expanse of space and time, on every point and at every moment of which it was possible that the form of Gilberte might appear, but also that form itself, since behind its appearance I felt that there lay concealed the reason for which it had shot its arrow into my heart at four o'clock instead of at half-past two; crowned with a smart hat, for paying calls, instead of the plain cap, for games; in front of the Ambassadeurs and not between the two puppet-shows ; I divined one of those occupations in which I might not follow Gilberte, occupations that forced her to go out or to stay at home, I was in contact with the mystery of her unknown life. It was this mystery, too, which troubled me when, running at the sharp-voiced girl's bidding, so as to begin our game without more delay, I saw Gilberte, so quick and informal with us, make a ceremonious bow to the old lady with the *Débats* (who acknowledged it with "What a lovely sun! You'ld think there was a fire burning.") speaking to her with a shy smile, with an air of constraint which called to my mind the other little girl that Gilberte must be when at home with her parents, or with friends of her parents, paying visits, in all the rest, that escaped me, of her existence. But of that existence no one gave me so strong an impression as did M. Swann, who came a little later to fetch his daughter. That was because he and Mme. Swann—inasmuch as their daughter lived with them, as her lessons, her games, her friendships depended upon them—contained for me, like Gilberte, perhaps even more than Gilberte, as befitted subjects that had an all-powerful control over her in whom it must have had its source, an undefined, an inaccessible quality of melancholy charm. Everything that concerned them was on my part the object of so constant a preoccupation that the days on which, as on this day, M. Swann (whom I had seen so often, long ago, without his having aroused my curiosity, when he was still on good terms with my parents) came for Gilberte to the Champs-Elysées, once the pulsations to which my heart had been excited by the appearance of his grey hat and hooded cape had subsided, the sight of him still impressed me as might that of an historic personage, upon whom one had just been studying a series of books, and the smallest details of whose life one learned with enthusiasm. His relations with the Comte de Paris, which, when I heard them discussed at Combray, seemed to me unimportant, became now in my eyes something marvellous, as if no one else had ever known the House of Orleans ; they set him in vivid detachment against the vulgar background of pedestrians of different

classes who encumbered that particular path in the Champs-
Elysées, in the midst of whom I admired his condescending
to figure without claiming any special deference, which as
it happened none of them dreamed of paying him, so profound
was the incognito in which he was wrapped.

He responded politely to the salutations of Gilberte's companions, even to mine, for all that he was no longer on good
terms with my family, but without appearing to know who
I was. (This reminded me that he had constantly seen me in
the country ; a memory which I had retained, but kept out
of sight, because, since I had seen Gilberte again, Swann had
become to me pre-eminently her father, and no longer the
Combray Swann ; as the ideas which, nowadays, I made his
name connote were different from the ideas in the system of
which it was formerly comprised, which I utilised not at all
now when I had occasion to think of him, he had become
a new, another person ; still I attached him by an artificial
thread, secondary and transversal, to our former guest ; and
as nothing had any longer any value for me save in the extent
to which my love might profit by it, it was with a spasm of
shame and of regret at not being able to erase them from my
memory that I recaptured the years in which, in the eyes of
this same Swann who was at this moment before me in the
Champs-Elysées, and to whom, fortunately, Gilberte had
perhaps not mentioned my name, I had so often, in the
evenings, made myself ridiculous by sending to ask Mamma to
come upstairs to my room to say good-night to me, while she
was drinking coffee with him and my father and my grandparents at the table in the garden.) He told Gilberte that she
might play one game ; he could wait for a quarter of an hour ;
and, sitting down, just like anyone else, on an iron chair, paid
for his ticket with that hand which Philippe VII had so often

held in his own, while we began our game upon the lawn, scattering the pigeons, whose beautiful, iridescent bodies (shaped like hearts and, surely, the lilacs of the feathered kingdom) took refuge as in so many sanctuaries, one on the great basin of stone, on which its beak, as it disappeared below the rim, conferred the part, assigned the purpose of offering to the bird in abundance the fruit or grain at which it appeared to be pecking, another on the head of the statue, which it seemed to crown with one of those enamelled objects whose polychrome varies in certain classical works the monotony of the stone, and with an attribute which, when the goddess bears it, entitles her to a particular epithet and makes of her, as a different Christian name makes of a mortal, a fresh divinity.

On one of these sunny days which had not realised my hopes, I had not the courage to conceal my disappointment from Gilberte.

" I had ever so many things to ask you," I said to her ; " I thought that to-day was going to mean so much in our friendship. And no sooner have you come than you go away ! Try to come early to-morrow, so that I can talk to you."

Her face lighted up and she jumped for joy as she answered: " To-morrow, you may make up your mind, my dear friend, I shan't come ! First of all I've a big luncheon-party ; then in the afternoon I am going to a friend's house to see King Theodosius arrive from her windows ; won't that be splendid ?—and then, next day, I'm going to *Michel Strogoff*, and after that it will soon be Christmas, and the New Year holidays ! Perhaps they'll take me south, to the Riviera ; won't that be nice ? Though I should miss the Christmas-tree here ; anyhow, if I do stay in Paris, I shan't be coming here, because I shall be out paying calls with Mamma. Good-bye—there's Papa calling me."

I returned home with Françoise through streets that were still gay with sunshine, as on the evening of a holiday when the merriment is over. I could scarcely drag my legs along.

" I'm not surprised ; " said Françoise, " it's not the right weather for the time of year ; it's much too warm. Oh dear, oh dear, to think of all the poor sick people there must be everywhere ; you would think that up there, too, everything's got out of order."

I repeated to myself, stifling my sobs, the words in which Gilberte had given utterance to her joy at the prospect of not coming back, for a long time, to the Champs-Elysées. But already the charm with which, by the mere act of thinking, my mind was filled as soon as it thought of her, the privileged position, unique even if it were painful, in which I was inevitably placed in relation to Gilberte by the contraction of a scar in my mind, had begun to add to that very mark of her indifference something romantic, and in the midst of my tears my lips would shape themselves in a smile which was indeed the timid outline of a kiss. And when the time came for the postman I said to myself, that evening as on every other : " I am going to have a letter from Gilberte, she is going to tell me, at last, that she has never ceased to love me, and to explain to me the mysterious reason by which she has been forced to conceal her love from me until now, to put on the appearance of being able to be happy without seeing me ; the reason for which she has assumed the form of the other Gilberte, who is simply a companion."

Every evening I would beguile myself into imagining this letter, believing that I was actually reading it, reciting each of its sentences in turn. Suddenly I would stop, in alarm. I had realised that, if I was to receive a letter from Gilberte, it could not, in any case, be this letter, since it was I myself who had just composed it. And from that moment I would strive to keep my thoughts clear of the words which I should have liked her to write to me, from fear lest, by first selecting them myself, I should be excluding just those identical words, —the dearest, the most desired—from the field of possible events. Even if, by an almost impossible coincidence, it had been precisely the letter of my invention that Gilberte had addressed to me of her own accord, recognising my own work in it I should not have had the impression that I was receiving something that had not originated in myself, something real, something new, a happiness external to my mind, independent of my will, a gift indeed from love.

While I waited I read over again a page which, although it had not been written to me by Gilberte, came to me, none the less, from her, that page by Bergotte upon the beauty of the old myths from which Racine drew his inspiration, which (with the agate marble) I always kept within reach. I was touched by my friend's kindness in having procured the book for me ; and as everyone is obliged to find some reason for his passion, so much so that he is glad to find in the creature whom he loves qualities which (he has learned by reading or in conversation) are worthy to excite a man's love, that he assimilates them by imitation and makes out of them fresh reasons for his love, even although these qualities be diametrically opposed to those for which his love would have sought, so long as it was spontaneous—as Swann, before my day, had sought to establish the aesthetic basis of Odette's beauty—I, who had at first loved Gilberte, in Combray days, on account of all the unknown element in her life into which

I would fain have plunged headlong, have undergone rein-
carnation, discarding my own separate existence as a thing
that no longer mattered, I thought now, as of an inestimable
advantage, that of this, my own, my too familiar, my contemptible existence Gilberte might one day become the
humble servant, the kindly, the comforting collaborator, who
in the evenings, helping me in my work, would collate for me
the texts of rare pamphlets. As for Bergotte, that infinitely
wise, almost divine old man, because of whom I had first,
before I had even seen her, loved Gilberte, now it was for
Gilberte's sake, chiefly, that I loved him. With as much
pleasure as the pages that he had written about Racine,
I studied the wrapper, folded under great seals of white wax
and tied with billows of pink ribbon, in which she had brought
those pages to me. I kissed the agate marble, which was the
better part of my love's heart, the part that was not frivolous
but faithful, and, for all that it was adorned with the mysterious
charm of Gilberte's life, dwelt close beside me, inhabited my
chamber, shared my bed. But the beauty of that stone, and
the beauty also of those pages of Bergotte which I was glad
to associate with the idea of my love for Gilberte, as if, in
the moments when my love seemed no longer to have any
existence, they gave it`a kind of consistency, were, I per-
ceived, anterior to that love, which they in no way resembled ;
their elements had been determined by the writer's talent, or
by geological laws, before ever Gilberte had known me,
nothing in book or stone would have been different if Gilberte
had not loved me, and there was nothing, consequently that
authorised me to read in them a message of happiness. And
while my love, incessantly waiting for the morrow to bring
a confession of Gilberte's love for me, destroyed, unravelled
every evening, the ill-done work of the day, in some shadowed

part of my being was an unknown weaver who would not leave where they lay the severed threads, but collected and rearranged them, without any thought of pleasing me, or of toiling for my advantage, in the different order which she gave to all her handiwork. Without any special interest in my love, not beginning by deciding that I was loved, she placed, side by side, those of Gilberte's actions that had seemed to me inexplicable and her faults which I had excused. Then, one with another, they took on a meaning. It seemed to tell me, this new arrangement, that when I saw Gilberte, instead of coming to me in the Champs-Elysées, going to a party, or on errands with her governess, when I saw her prepared for an absence that would extend over the New Year holidays, I was wrong in thinking, in saying : " It is because she is frivolous," or " easily led." For she would have ceased to be either if she had loved me, and if she had been forced to obey it would have been with the same despair in her heart that I felt on the days when I did not see her. It shewed me further, this new arrangement, that I ought, after all, to know what it was to love, since I loved Gilberte ; it drew my attention to the constant anxiety that I had to ' shew off ' before her, by reason of which I tried to persuade my mother to get for Françoise a waterproof coat and a hat with a blue feather, or, better still, to stop sending with me to the Champs-Elysées an attendant with whom I blushed to be seen (to all of which my mother replied that I was not fair to Françoise, that she was an excellent woman and devoted to us all) and also that sole, exclusive need to see Gilberte, the result of which was that, months in advance, I could think of nothing but how to find out at what date she would be leaving Paris and where she was going, feeling that the most attractive country in the world would be but a place of exile if she were not to be there, and asking only to be allowed to stay for ever in Paris, so long as I might see her in the Champs-Elysées ; and it had little difficulty in making me see that neither my anxiety nor my need could be justified by anything in Gilberte's conduct. She, on the contrary, was genuinely fond of her governess, without troubling herself over what I might choose to think about it. It seemed quite natural to her not to come to the Champs-Elysées if she had to go shopping with Mademoiselle, delightful if she had to go out somewhere with her mother. And even supposing that she would ever have allowed me to spend my holidays in the same place as herself, when it came to choosing that place she considered her parents' wishes, a thousand different amusements of which she had been told, and not at all that it should be the place to which my family were proposing to send me. When she assured me (as sometimes happened) that she liked me less than some other of her friends, less than she had liked me the day before, because by my clumsiness I had made her side lose a game, I would beg her pardon, I would beg her to tell me what I must do in order that she should begin again to like me as much as, or more than the rest ; I hoped to hear her say that that was already my position ; I besought her ; as though she had been able to modify her affection for me as she or I chose, to give me pleasure, merely by the words that she would utter, as my good or bad conduct should deserve. Was I, then, not yet aware that what I felt, myself, for her, depended neither upon her actions nor upon my desires ?

It shewed me finally, the new arrangement planned by my unseen weaver, that, if we find ourselves hoping that the actions of a person who has hitherto caused us anxiety may prove not to have been sincere, they shed in their wake a light which our hopes are powerless to extinguish, a light to which, rather than to our hopes, we must put the question, what will be that person's actions on the morrow.

These new counsels, my love listened and heard them ; they persuaded it that the morrow would not be different from all the days that had gone before ; that Gilberte's feeling for me, too long established now to be capable of alteration, was indifference ; that in my friendship with Gilberte, it was I alone who loved. "That is true," my love responded, "there is nothing more to be made of that friendship. It will not alter now." And so the very next day (unless I were to wait for a public holiday, if there was one approaching, some anniversary, the New Year, perhaps, one of those days which are not like other days, on which time starts afresh, casting aside the heritage of the past, declining its legacy of sorrows) I would appeal to Gilberte to terminate our old and to join me in laying the foundations of a new friendship.

I had always, within reach, a plan of Paris, which, because I could see drawn on it the street in which M. and Mme. Swann lived, seemed to me to contain a secret treasure. And to please myself, as well as by a sort of chivalrous loyalty, in any connection or with no relevance at all, I would repeat the name of that street until my father, not being, like my mother and grandmother, in the secret of my love, would ask : " But why are you always talking about that street ? There's nothing wonderful about it. It is an admirable street to live in because it's only a few minutes' walk from the Bois, but there are a dozen other streets just the same."

I made every effort to introduce the name of Swann into my conversation with my parents ; in my now mind, of course, I never ceased to murmur it ; but I needed also to hear its exquisite sound, and to make myself play that chord, the voiceless rendering of which did not suffice me. Moreover, that name of Swann, with which I had for so long been familiar, was to me now (as happens at times to people suffering from aphasia, in the case of the most ordinary words) the name of something new. It was for ever present in my mind, which could not, however, grow accustomed to it. I analysed it, I spelt it ; its orthography came to me as a surprise. And with its familiarity it had simultaneously lost its innocence. The pleasure that I derived from the sound of it I felt to be so guilty, that it seemed to me as though the others must read my thoughts, and would change the conversation if I endeavoured to guide it in that direction. I fell back upon subjects which still brought me into touch with Gilberte, I eternally repeated the same words, and it was no use my knowing that they were but words—words uttered in her absence, which she could not hear, words without virtue in themselves, repeating what were, indeed, facts, but powerless to modify them—for still it seemed to me that by dint of handling, of stirring in this way everything that had reference to Gilberte, I might perhaps make emerge from it something that would bring me happiness. I told my parents again that Gilberte was very fond of her governess, as if the statement, when repeated for the hundredth time, would at last have the effect of making Gilberte suddenly burst into the room, come to live with us for ever. I had already sung the praises of the old lady who read the *Débats* (I had hinted to my parents that she must at least be an Ambassador's widow, if not actually a Highness) and I continued to descant on her beauty, her splendour, her nobility, until the day on which I mentioned that, by what I had heard Gilberte call her, she appeared to be a Mme. Blatin.

" Oh, now I know whom you mean," cried my mother, while I felt myself grow red all over with shame. " On guard ! on guard !—as your grandfather says. And so it's she that you think so wonderful ? Why, she's perfectly horrible, and always has been. She's the widow of a bailiff. You can't remember, when you were little, all the trouble I used to have to avoid her at your gymnastic lessons, where she was always trying to get hold of me—I didn't know the woman, of course—to tell me that you were ' much too nice-looking for a boy.' She has always had an insane desire to get to know people, and she must be quite insane, as I have always thought, if she really does know Mme. Swann. For even if she does come of very common people, I have never heard anything said against her character. But she must always be forcing herself upon strangers. She is, really, a horrible woman, frightfully vulgar, and besides, she is always creating awkward situations."

As for Swann, in my attempts to resemble him, I spent the whole time, when I was at table, in drawing my finger along my nose and in rubbing my eyes. My father would exclaim : " The child's a perfect idiot, he's becoming quite impossible." More than all else I should have liked to be as bald as Swann. He appeared to me to be a creature so extra- ordinary that I found it impossible to believe that people whom I knew and often saw knew him also, and that in the course of the day anyone might run against him. And once my mother, while she was telling us, as she did every evening at dinner, where she had been and what she had done that afternoon, merely by the words : " By the way, guess whom I saw at the Trois Quartiers—at the umbrella counter— Swann ! " caused to burst open in the midst of her narrative (an arid desert to me) a mystic blossom. What a melancholy satisfaction to learn that, that very afternoon, threading through the crowd his supernatural form, Swann had gone to buy an umbrella. Among the events of the day, great and small, but all equally unimportant, that one alone aroused in me those peculiar vibrations by which my love for Gilberte was invariably stirred. My father complained that I took no interest in anything, because I did not listen while he was speaking of the political developments that might follow the visit of King Theodosius, at that moment in France as the nation's guest and (it was hinted) ally. And yet how intensely interested I was to know whether Swann had been wearing his hooded cape!

" Did you speak to him ? " I asked.

" Why, of course I did," answered my mother, who always seemed afraid lest, were she to admit that we were not on the warmest of terms with Swann, people would seek to reconcile us more than she cared for, in view of the existence of Mme. Swann, whom she did not wish to know. " It was he who came up and spoke to me. I hadn't seen him."

" Then you haven't quarrelled ? "

" Quarrelled ? What on earth made you think that we had quarrelled ? " she briskly parried, as though I had cast doubt on the fiction of her friendly relations with Swann, and was planning an attempt to ' bring them together.'

" He might be cross with you for never asking him here."

" One isn't obliged to ask everyone to one's house, you know ; has he ever asked me to his ? I don't know his wife."

" But he used often to come, at Combray."

" I should think he did ! He used to come at Combray, and now, in Paris, he has something better to do, and so have I. But I can promise you, we didn't look in the least like people who had quarrelled. We were kept waiting there for some time, while they brought him his parcel. He asked after

you ; he told me you had been playing with his daughter—. "
my mother went on, amazing me with the portentous revelation of my own existence in Swann's mind ; far more than
that, of my existence in so complete, so material a form that
when I stood before him, trembling with love, in the Champs-
Elysées, he had known my name, and who my mother was,
and had been able to blend with my quality as his daughter's
playmate certain facts with regard to my grandparents and
their connections, the place in which we lived, certain details
of our past life, all of which I myself perhaps did not know.
But my mother did not seem to have noticed anything
particularly attractive in that counter at the Trois Quartiers
where she had represented to Swann, at the moment in which
he caught sight of her, a definite person with whom he had
sufficient memories in common to impel him to come up
to her and to speak.

Nor did either she or my father seem to find any occasion
now to mention Swann's family, the grandparents of Gilberte,
nor to use the title of stockbroker, topics as which nothing
else gave me so keen a pleasure. My imagination had isolated
and consecrated in the social Paris a certain family, just as it
had set apart in the structural Paris a certain house, on whose
porch it had fashioned sculptures and made its windows
precious. But these ornaments I alone had eyes to see. Just
as my father and mother looked upon the house in which
Swann lived as one that closely resembled the other houses
built at the same period in the neighbourhood of the Bois, so
Swann's family seemed to them to be in the same category
as many other families of stockbrokers. Their judgment was
more or less favourable according to the extent to which the
family in question shared in merits that were common to the
rest of the universe, and there was about it nothing that they

could call unique. What, on the other hand, they did appreciate in the Swanns they found in equal, if not in greater measure elsewhere. And so, after admitting that the house was in a good position, they would go on to speak of some other house that was in a better, but had nothing to do with Gilberte, or of financiers on a larger scale than her grandfather had been ; and if they had appeared, for a moment, to be of my opinion, that was a mistake which was very soon corrected. For in order to distinguish in all Gilberte's surroundings, an indefinable quality analogous, in the scale of emotions, to what in the scale of colours is called infra-red, a supplementary sense of perception was required, with which love, for the time being, had endowed me ; and this my parents lacked.

On the days when Gilberte had warned me that she would not be coming to the Champs-Elysées, I would try to arrange my walks so that I should be brought into some kind of contact with her. Sometimes I would lead Françoise on a pilgrimage to the house in which the Swanns lived, making her repeat to me unendingly all that she had learned from the governess with regard to Mme. Swann. " It seems, she puts great faith in medals. She would never think of starting on a journey if she had heard an owl hoot, or the death-watch in the wall, or if she had seen a cat at midnight, or if the furniture had creaked. Oh yes ! she's a most religious lady, she is ! " I was so madly in love with Gilberte that if, on our way, I caught sight of their old butler taking the dog out, my emotion would bring me to a standstill, I would fasten on his white whiskers eyes that melted with passion. And Françoise would rouse me with : " What's wrong with you now, child ? " and we would continue on our way until we reached their gate, where a porter, different from every other porter in the world, and saturated, even to the braid on his livery, with the same melancholy charm that I had felt to be latent in the name of Gilberte, looked at me as though he knew that I was one of those whose natural unworthiness would for ever prevent them from penetrating into the mysteries of the life inside, which it was his duty to guard, and over which the ground-floor windows appeared conscious of being protectingly closed, with far less resemblance, between the nobly sweeping arches of their muslin curtains, to any other windows in the world than to Gilberte's glancing eyes. On other days we would go along the boulevards, and I would post myself at the corner of the Rue Duphot ; I had heard that Swann was often to be seen passing there, on his way to the dentist's ; and my imagination so far differentiated Gilberte's father from the rest of humanity, his presence in the midst of a crowd of real people introduced among them so miraculous an element, that even before we reached the Madeleine I would be trembling with emotion at the thought that I was approaching a street from which that supernatural apparition might at any moment burst upon me unawares.

But most often of all, on days when I was not to see Gilberte, as I had heard that Mme. Swann walked almost every day along the Allée des Acacias, round the big lake, and in the Allée de la Reine Marguerite, I would guide Françoise in the direction of the Bois de Boulogne. It was to me like one of those zoological gardens in which one sees assembled together a variety of flora, and contrasted effects in landscape ; where from a hill one passes to a grotto, a meadow, rocks, a stream, a trench, another hill, a marsh, but knows that they are there only to enable the hippopotamus, zebra, crocodile, rabbit, bear and heron to disport themselves in a natural or a picturesque setting ; this, the Bois, equally complex, uniting a multitude of little worlds, distinct and separate—placing a stage set with red trees, American oaks, like an experimental forest in Virginia, next to a fir-wood by the edge of the lake, or to a forest grove from which would suddenly emerge, in her lissom covering of furs, with the large, appealing eyes of a dumb animal, a hastening walker—was the Garden of Woman ; and like the myrtle-alley in the Aeneid, planted for their delight with trees of one kind only, the Allée des Acacias was thronged by the famous Beauties of the day. As, from a long way off, the sight of the jutting crag from which it dives into the pool thrills with joy the children who know that they are going to behold the seal, long before I reached the acacia-alley, their fragrance, scattered abroad, would make me feel that I was approaching the incomparable presence of a vegetable personality, strong and tender ; then, as I drew near, the sight of their topmost branches, their lightly tossing foliage, in its easy grace, its coquettish outline, its delicate fabric, over which hundreds of flowers were laid, like winged and throbbing colonies of precious insects ; and finally their name itself, feminine, indolent and seductive, made my heart beat, but with a social longing, like those waltzes which remind us only of the names of the fair dancers, called aloud as they entered the ball-room. I had been told that I should see in the alley certain women of fashion, who, in spite of their not all having husbands, were constantly mentioned in conjunction with Mme. Swann, but most often by their professional names ;—their new names, when they had any, being but a sort of incognito, a veil which those who would speak of them were careful to draw aside, so as to make themselves understood. Thinking that Beauty—in the order of feminine elegance—was governed by occult laws into the knowledge of which they had been initiated,

and that they had the power to realise it, I accepted before
seeing them, like the truth of a coming revelation, the appearance of their clothes, of their carriages and horses, of a
thousand details among which I placed my faith as in an
inner soul which gave the cohesion of a work of art to that
ephemeral and changing pageant. But it was Mme. Swann
whom I wished to see, and I waited for her to go past, as
deeply moved as though she were Gilberte, whose parents,
saturated, like everything in her environment, with her own
special charm, excited in me as keen a passion as she did
herself, indeed a still more painful disturbance, (since their
point of contact with her was that intimate, that internal part
of her life which was hidden from me), and furthermore, for
I very soon learned, as we shall see in due course, that they
did not like my playing with her, that feeling of veneration
which we always have for those who hold, and exercise
without restraint, the power to do us an injury.

I assigned the first place, in the order of aesthetic merit and
of social grandeur, to simplicity, when I saw Mme. Swann
on foot, in a 'polonaise' of plain cloth, a little toque on her
head trimmed with a pheasant's wing, a bunch of violets in
her bosom, hastening along the Allée des Acacias as if it had
been merely the shortest way back to her own house, and
acknowledging with a rapid glance the courtesy of the gentle-
men in carriages, who, recognising her figure at a distance,
were raising their hats to her and saying to one another that
there was never anyone so well turned out as she. But instead
of simplicity it was to ostentation that I must assign the first
place if, after I had compelled Françoise, who could hold out
no longer, and complained that her legs were 'giving'
beneath her, to stroll up and down with me for another hour,
I saw at length, emerging from the Porte Dauphine, figuring

for me a royal dignity, the passage of a sovereign, an impression such as no real Queen has ever since been able to give
me, because my notion of their power has been less vague, and
more founded upon experience—borne along by the flight of
a pair of fiery horses, slender and shapely as one sees them in
the drawings of Constantin Guys, carrying on its box an
enormous coachman, furred like a cossack, and by his side
a diminutive groom, like Toby, "the late Beaudenord's
tiger," I saw—or rather I felt its outlines engraved upon my
heart by a clean and killing stab—a matchless victoria, built
rather high, and hinting, through the extreme modernity of
its appointments, at the forms of an earlier day, deep down in
which lay negligently back Mme. Swann, her hair, now
quite pale with one grey lock, girt with a narrow band of
flowers, usually violets, from which floated down long veils,
a lilac parasol in her hand, on her lips an ambiguous smile in
which I read only the benign condescension of Majesty,
though it was pre-eminently the enticing smile of the
courtesan, which she graciously bestowed upon the men who
bowed to her. That smile was, in reality, saying to one :
" Oh yes, I do remember, quite well ; it was wonderful ! "
to another : " How I should have loved to ! We were unfortunate ! ", to a third : " Yes, if you like ! I must just
keep in the line for a minute, then as soon as I can I will break
away." When strangers passed she still allowed to linger about
her lips a lazy smile, as though she expected or remembered
some friend, which made them say : " What a lovely
woman ! ". And for certain men only she had a sour,
strained, shy, cold smile which meant : " Yes, you old goat,
I know that you've got a tongue like a viper, that you can't
keep quiet for a moment. But do you suppose that I care
what you say ? " Coquelin passed, talking, in a group of

listening friends, and with a sweeping wave of his hand bade a theatrical good day to the people in the carriages. But I thought only of Mme. Swann, and pretended to have not yet seen her, for I knew that, when she reached the pigeon-shooting ground, she would tell her coachman to ' break away ' and to stop the carriage, so that she might come back on foot. And on days when I felt that I had the courage to pass close by her I would drag Françoise off in that direction ; until the moment came when I saw Mme. Swann, letting trail behind her the long train of her lilac skirt, dressed, as the populace imagine queens to be dressed, in rich attire such as no other woman might wear, lowering her eyes now and then to study the handle of her parasol, paying scant attention to the passers-by, as though the important thing for her, her one object in being there was to take exercise, without think-ing that she was seen, and that every head was turned towards her. Sometimes, however, when she had looked back to call her dog to her, she would cast, almost imperceptibly, a sweep-ing glance round about.

Those even who did not know her were warned by some-thing exceptional, something beyond the normal in her—or perhaps by a telepathic suggestion such as would move an ignorant audience to a frenzy of applause when Berma was 'sublime'—that she must be some one well-known. They would ask one another, " Who is she ? ", or sometimes would interrogate a passing stranger, or would make a mental note of how she was dressed so as to fix her identity, later, in the mind of a friend better informed than themselves, who would at once enlighten them. Another pair, half-stopping in their walk, would exchange :

" You know who that is ? Mme. Swann ! That conveys nothing to you ? Odette de Crécy, then ? "

"Odette de Crécy ! Why, I thought as much. Those great, sad eyes . . . But I say, you know, she can't be as young as she was once, eh ? I remember, I had her on the day that MacMahon went."

" I shouldn't remind her of it, if I were you. She is now Mme. Swann, the wife of a gentleman in the Jockey Club, a friend of the Prince of Wales. Apart from that, though, she is wonderful still."

"Oh, but you ought to have known her then ; Gad, she was lovely ! She lived in a very odd little house with a lot of Chinese stuff. I remember, we were bothered all the time by the news-boys, shouting outside ; in the end she made me get up and go."

Without listening to these memories, I could feel all about her the indistinct murmur of fame. My heart leaped with impatience when I thought that a few seconds must still elapse before all these people, among whom I was dismayed not to find a certain mulatto banker who (or so I felt) had a contempt for me, were to see the unknown youth, to whom they had not, so far, been paying the slightest attention, salute (without knowing her, it was true, but I thought that I had sufficient authority since my parents knew her husband and I was her daughter's playmate) this woman whose reputation for beauty, for misconduct, and for elegance was universal. But I was now close to Mme. Swann ; I pulled off my hat with so lavish, so prolonged a gesture that she could not repress a smile. People laughed. As for her, she had never seen me with Gilberte, she did not know my name, but I was for her—like one of the keepers in the Bois, like the boatman, or the ducks on the lake, to which she threw scraps of bread—one of the minor personages, familiar, name-less, as devoid of individual character as a stage-hand in a theatre, of her daily walks abroad.

On certain days when I had missed her in the Allée des Acacias I would be so fortunate as to meet her in the Allée de la Reine Marguerite, where women went who wished to be alone, or to appear to be wishing to be alone ; she would not be alone for long, being soon overtaken by some man or other, often in a grey ' tile ' hat, whom I did not know, and who would talk to her for some time, while their two carriages crawled behind.

* * *

That sense of the complexity of the Bois de Boulogne which made it an artificial place and, in the zoological or mythological sense of the word, a Garden, I captured again, this year, as I crossed it on my way to Trianon, on one of those mornings, early in November, when in Paris, if we stay indoors, being so near and yet prevented from witnessing the transformation scene of autumn, which is drawing so rapidly to a close without our assistance, we feel a regret for the fallen leaves that becomes a fever, and may even keep us awake at night. Into my closed room they had been drifting already for a month, summoned there by my desire to see them, slipping between my thoughts and the object, whatever it might be, upon which I was trying to concentrate them, whirling in front of me like those brown spots that sometimes, whatever we may be looking at, will seem to be dancing or swimming before our eyes. And on that morning, not hearing the splash of the rain as on the previous days, seeing the smile of fine weather at the corners of my drawn curtains, as from the corners of closed lips may escape the secret of their happiness, I had felt that I could actually see those yellow leaves, with the light shining through them, in their supreme beauty; and being no more able to restrain myself from going to look at the trees than, in my childhood's days, when the wind howled in the chimney, I had been able to resist the longing to visit the sea, I had risen and left the house to go to Trianon, passing through the Bois de Boulogne. It was the hour and the season in which the Bois seems, perhaps, most multiform, not only because it is then most divided, but because it is divided in a different way. Even in the unwooded parts, where the horizon is large, here and there against the background of a dark and distant mass of trees, now leafless or still keeping their summer foliage unchanged, a double row of orange-red chestnuts seemed, as in a picture just begun, to be the only thing painted, so far, by an artist who had not yet laid any colour on the rest, and to be offering their cloister, in full daylight, for the casual exercise of the human figures that would be added to the picture later on.

Farther off, at a place where the trees were still all green, one alone, small, stunted, lopped, but stubborn in its resistance, was tossing in the breeze an ugly mane of red. Elsewhere, again, might be seen the first awakening of this May-time of the leaves, and those of an ampelopsis, a smiling miracle, like a red hawthorn flowering in winter, had that very morning all 'come out', so to speak, in blossom. And the Bois had the temporary, unfinished, artificial look of a nursery garden or a park in which, either for some botanic purpose or in preparation for a festival, there have been embedded among the trees of commoner growth, which have not yet been uprooted and transplanted elsewhere, a few rare specimens, with fantastic foliage, which seem to be clearing all round themselves an empty space, making room, giving air, diffusing light. Thus it was the time of year at which the Bois de Boulogne displays more separate characteristics, assembles more distinct elements in a composite whole than

at any other. It was also the time of day. In places where
the trees still kept their leaves, they seemed to have undergone
an alteration of their substance from the point at which they
were touched by the sun's light, still, at this hour in the morning, almost horizontal, as it would be again, a few hours later,
at the moment when, just as dusk began, it would flame up
like a lamp, project afar over the leaves a warm and artificial glow, and set ablaze the few topmost boughs of a tree
that would itself remain unchanged, a sombre incombustible
candelabrum beneath its flaming crest. At one spot the
light grew solid as a brick wall, and like a piece of yellow
Persian masonry, patterned in blue, daubed coarsely upon the
sky the leaves of the chestnuts ; at another, it cut them off
from the sky towards which they stretched out their curling,
golden fingers. Half-way up the trunk of a tree draped with
wild vine, the light had grafted and brought to blossom, too
dazzling to be clearly distinguished, an enormous posy, of
red flowers apparently, perhaps of a new variety of carnation.
The different parts of the Bois, so easily confounded in summer in the density and monotony of their universal green, were
now clearly divided. A patch of brightness indicated the
approach to almost every one of them, or else a splendid mass
of foliage stood out before it like an oriflamme. I could make
out, as on a coloured map, Armenonville, the Pré Catalan,
Madrid, the Race Course and the shore of the lake. Here and
there would appear some meaningless erection, a sham grotto,
a mill, for which the trees made room by drawing away from
it, or which was borne upon the soft green platform of a
grassy lawn. I could feel that the Bois was not really a wood,
that it existed for a purpose alien to the life of its trees ; my
sense of exaltation was due not only to admiration of the
autumn tints but to a bodily desire. Ample source of a joy

which the heart feels at first without being conscious of its cause, without understanding that it results from no external impulse! Thus I gazed at the trees with an unsatisfied longing which went beyond them and, without my knowledge, directed itself towards that masterpiece of beautiful strolling women which the trees enframed for a few hours every day. I walked towards the Allée des Acacias. I passed through forest groves in which the morning light, breaking them into new sections, lopped and trimmed the trees, united different trunks in marriage, made nosegays of their branches. It would skilfully draw towards it a pair of trees ; making deft use of the sharp chisel of light and shade, it would cut away from each of them half of its trunk and branches, and, weaving together the two halves that remained, would make of them either a single pillar of shade, defined by the surrounding light, or a single luminous phantom whose artificial, quivering contour was encompassed in a network of inky shadows. When a ray of sunshine gilded the highest branches, they seemed, soaked and still dripping with a sparkling moisture, to have emerged alone from the liquid, emerald-green atmosphere in which the whole grove was plunged as though beneath the sea. For the trees continued to live by their own vitality, and when they had no longer any leaves, that vitality gleamed more brightly still from the nap of green velvet that carpeted their trunks, or in the white enamel of the globes of mistletoe that were scattered all the way up to the topmost branches of the poplars, rounded as are the sun and moon in Michael Angelo's ' Creation '. But, forced for so many years now, by a sort of grafting process, to share the life of feminine humanity, they called to my mind the figure of the dryad, the fair worldling, swiftly walking, brightly coloured, whom they sheltered with their branches as she passed beneath them,

and obliged to acknowledge, as they themselves acknowledged, the power of the season ; they recalled to me the
happy days when I was young and had faith, when I would
hasten eagerly to the spots where masterpieces of female
elegance would be incarnate for a few moments beneath the
unconscious, accommodating boughs. But the beauty for
which the firs and acacias of the Bois de Boulogne made me
long, more disquieting in that respect than the chestnuts and
lilacs of Trianon which I was going to see, was not fixed
somewhere outside myself in the relics of an historical period,
in works of art, in a little temple of love at whose door was
piled an oblation of autumn leaves ribbed with gold. I reached
the shore of the lake ; I walked on as far as the pigeon-
shooting ground. The idea of perfection which I had within
me I had bestowed, in that other time, upon the height of a
victoria, upon the raking thinness of those horses, frenzied and
light as wasps upon the wing, with bloodshot eyes like the
cruel steeds of Diomed, which now, smitten by a desire to
see again what I had once loved, as ardent as the desire that
had driven me, many years before, along the same paths,
I wished to see renewed before my eyes at the moment when
Mme. Swann's enormous coachman, supervised by a groom
no bigger than his fist, and as infantile as Saint George in
the picture, endeavoured to curb the ardour of the flying,
steel-tipped pinions with which they thundered along the
ground. Alas ! there was nothing now but motor-cars driven
each by a moustached mechanic, with a tall footman towering
by his side. I wished to hold before my bodily eyes, that I
might know whether they were indeed as charming as they
appeared to the eyes of memory, little hats, so low-crowned as
to seem no more than garlands about the brows of women.
All the hats now were immense, covered with fruits and

flowers and all manner of birds. In place of the lovely gowns in which Mme. Swann walked like a Queen, appeared Greco-Saxon tunics, with Tanagra folds, or sometimes, in the Directoire style, 'Liberty chiffons' sprinkled with flowers like sheets of wallpaper. On the heads of the gentle-men who might have been eligible to stroll with Mme. Swann in the Allée de la Reine Marguerite, I found not the grey 'tile' hats of old, nor any other kind. They walked the Bois bare-headed. And seeing all these new elements of the spectacle, I had no longer the faith which, applied to them, would have given them consistency, unity, life ; they passed in a scattered sequence before me, at random, without reality, containing in themselves no beauty that my eyes might have endeavoured, as in the old days, to extract from them and to compose in a picture. They were just women, in whose elegance I had no belief, and whose clothes seemed to me unimportant. But when a belief vanishes, there sur-vives it—more and more ardently, so as to cloak the absence of the power, now lost to us, of imparting reality to new phenomena—an idolatrous attachment to the old things which our belief in them did once animate, as if it was in that belief and not in ourselves that the divine spark resided, and as if our present incredulity had a contingent cause—the death of the gods.

"Oh, horrible !" I exclaimed to myself. "Does anyone really imagine that these motor-cars are as smart as the old carriage-and-pair ? I dare say, I am too old now—but I was not intended for a world in which women shackle themselves in garments that are not even made of cloth. To what purpose shall I walk among these trees if there is nothing left now of the assembly that used to meet beneath the delicate tracery of reddening leaves, if vulgarity and fatuity have supplanted the exquisite thing that once their branches framed. Oh, horrible ! My consolation is to think of the women whom I have known, in the past, now that there is no standard left of elegance. But how can the people who watch these dreadful creatures hobble by, beneath hats on which have been heaped the spoils of aviary or garden-bed,—how can they imagine the charm that there was in the sight of Mme. Swann, crowned with a close-fitting lilac bonnet, or with a tiny hat from which rose stiffly above her head a single iris?" Could I ever have made them understand the emotion that I used to feel on winter mornings, when I met Mme. Swann on foot, in an otter-skin coat, with a woollen cap from which stuck out two blade-like partridge-feathers, but enveloped also in the deliberate, artificial warmth of her own house, which was suggested by nothing more than the bunch of violets crushed into her bosom, whose flowering, vivid and blue against the grey sky, the freezing air, the naked boughs, had the same charming effect of using the season and the weather merely as a setting, and of living actually in a human atmosphere, in the atmosphere of this woman, as had in the vases and beaupots of her drawing-room, beside the blazing fire, in front of the silk-covered sofa, the flowers that looked out through closed windows at the falling snow ? But it would not have sufficed me that the costumes alone should still have been the same as in those distant years. Because of the solidarity that binds together the different parts of a general impression, parts that our memory keeps in a balanced whole, of which we are not permitted to subtract or to decline any fraction, I should have liked to be able to pass the rest of the day with one of those women, over a cup of tea, in a little house with dark-painted walls (as Mme. Swann's were still in the year after that in which the first part of this story ends) against which would glow the orange flame, the red combustion, the pink and white flickering of her chrysanthemums in the twilight of a November evening, in moments similar to those in which (as we shall see) I had not managed to discover the pleasures for which I longed. But now, albeit they had led to nothing, those moments struck me as having been charming enough in themselves. I sought to find them again as I remembered them. Alas ! there was nothing now but flats decorated in the Louis XVI style, all white paint, with hortensias in blue enamel. Moreover, people did not return to Paris, now, until much later. Mme. Swann would have written to me, from a country house, that she would not be in town before February, had I asked her to reconstruct for me the elements of that memory which I felt to belong to a distant era, to a date in time towards which it was forbidden me to ascend again the fatal slope, the elements of that longing which had become, itself, as inaccessible as the pleasure that it had once vainly pursued. And I should have required also that they were the same women, those whose costume interested me because, at a time when I still had faith, my imagination had individualised them and had provided each of them with a legend. Alas ! in the acacia-avenue—the myrtle-alley—I did see some of them again, grown old, no more now than grim spectres of what once they had been, wandering to and fro, in desperate search of heaven knew what, through the Virgilian groves. They had long fled, and still I stood vainly questioning the deserted paths. The sun's face was hidden. Nature began again to reign over the Bois, from which had vanished all trace of the idea that it was the Elysian Garden of Woman ; above the gimcrack windmill the real sky was grey ; the wind wrinkled the surface of the Grand Lac in little wavelets, like a real lake ; large birds passed swiftly over the Bois, as over a real wood, and with shrill cries perched, one after another, on the great oaks which, beneath their Druidical crown, and with Dodonaic majesty, seemed to proclaim the unpeopled vacancy of this estranged forest, and helped me to understand how paradoxical it is to seek in reality for the pictures that are stored in one's memory, which must inevitably lose the charm that comes to them from memory itself and from their not being apprehended by the senses. The reality that I had known no longer existed. It sufficed that Mme. Swann did not appear, in the same attire and at the same moment, for the whole avenue to be altered. The places that we have known belong now only to the little world of space on which we map them for our own convenience. None of them was ever more than a thin slice, held between the contiguous impressions that composed our life at that time ; remembrance of a particular form is but regret for a particular moment ; and houses, roads, avenues are as fugitive, alas, as the years.

THE END

PRINTED PHOTOLITHO IN GREAT BRITAIN
BY EBENEZER BAYLIS AND SON, LTD.
THE TRINITY PRESS, WORCESTER, AND LONDON